The Last Time
They Met

The Last Time They Met

Anita Shreve

Thorndike Press • Chivers Press
Waterville, Maine USA   Bath, England

This Large Print edition is published by Thorndike Press, USA and by Chivers Press, England.

Published in 2001 in the U.S. by arrangement with Little, Brown & Co., Inc.

Published in 2001 in the U.K. by arrangement with Little, Brown & Company Ltd.

U.S. Hardcover 0-7862-3310-9 (Basic Series Edition)
U.S. Softcover 0-7862-3311-7
U.K. Hardcover 0-7540-1660-9 (Windsor Large Print)
U.K. Softcover 0-7540-9074-4 (Paragon Large Print)

Copyright © 2001 by Anita Shreve

The author is grateful for permission to reprint excerpts from *Long Day's Journey into Night* by Eugene O'Neill.
Copyright © 1956 by Carlotta Monterey O'Neill. Reprinted by permission of Yale University Press.

The characters and events in this book are fictitious. Any similarity to real persons, living or dead, is coincidental and not intended by the author.

The text of this Large Print edition is unabridged.
Other aspects of the book may vary from the original edition.

Set in 16 pt. Plantin by Al Chase.

Printed in the United States on permanent paper.

British Library Cataloguing-in-Publication Data available

Library of Congress Cataloging-in-Publication Data
Shreve, Anita.
    The last time they met : a novel / Anita Shreve.
      p. cm.
    ISBN 0-7862-3310-9 (lg. print : hc : alk. paper)
    ISBN 0-7862-3311-7 (lg. print : sc : alk. paper)
    1. Married people — Fiction.   2. Women poets — Fiction.
  3. Forgiveness — Fiction.   4. Adultery — Fiction.   5. Poets
— Fiction.   6. Large type books.   I. Title.
PS3569.H7385 L37 2001b
813′.54—dc21   2001027267

for Janet

Part One

Fifty-two

She had come from the plane and was even now forgetting the ride from the airport. As she stepped from the car, she emerged to an audience of a doorman in uniform and another man in a dark coat moving through the revolving door of the hotel. The man in the dark coat hesitated, taking a moment to open an umbrella that immediately, in one fluid motion, blew itself inside out. He looked abashed and then purposefully amused — for now she was his audience — as he tossed the useless appendage into a bin and moved on.

She wished the doorman wouldn't take her suitcase, and if it hadn't been for the ornate gold leaf of the canopy and the perfectly polished brass of the entryway, she might have told him it wasn't necessary. She hadn't expected the tall columns that rose to a ceiling she couldn't see clearly without squinting, or the rose carpet through those

9

columns that was long enough for a coronation. The doorman wordlessly gave her suitcase — inadequate in this grandeur — to a
bellman, as if handing off a secret. She
moved past empty groupings of costly furniture to the reception desk.

Linda, who had once minded the commonness of her name, gave her credit card
when asked, wrote her signature on a piece
of paper, and accepted a pair of keys, one
plastic, the other reassuringly real, the
metal key for the minibar, for a drink if it
came to that. She followed directions to a
bank of elevators, noting on a mahogany
table a bouquet of hydrangeas and daylilies
as tall as a ten-year-old boy. Despite the elegance of the hotel, the music in the elevator
was cloying and banal, and she wondered
how it was this detail had been overlooked.
She followed signs and arrows along a wide,
hushed corridor built during an era when
space was not a luxury.

The white paneled door of her room was
heavy and opened with a soft click. There
was a mirrored entryway that seemed to
double as a bar, a sitting room with heavily
draped windows and French doors veiled
with sheers that led to a bedroom larger
than her living room at home. The weight of
unwanted obligation was, for the moment,

10

replaced with wary acceptance of being pampered. But then she looked at the ivory linen pillows on the massive bed and thought of the waste that it was only herself who would sleep there — she who might have been satisfied with a narrow bed in a narrow room, who no longer thought of beds as places where love or sex was offered or received.

She sat for a moment in her wet raincoat, waiting for the bellman to bring her suitcase to her. She closed her eyes and tried to relax, an activity for which she had no talent. She had never been to a yoga class, never meditated, unable to escape the notion that such strategies constituted a surrender, an admission that she could no longer bear to touch the skin of reality, her old lover. As if she would turn her back against a baffled husband, when once she had been so greedy.

She answered the door to a young bellman, overtipping the man to compensate for her pathetically small suitcase. She was aware of scrutiny on his part, impartial scrutiny simply because she was a woman and not entirely old. She crossed to the windows and drew back the drapes, and even the dim light of a rainy day was a shock to the gloom of the room. There were blurred

11

buildings, the gleam of wet streets, glimpses of gray lake between skyscrapers. Two nights in one hotel room. Perhaps by Sunday morning she would know the number, would not have to ask at the front desk, as she so often had to do. Her confusion, she was convinced (as the desk clerks clearly were not), a product simply of physics: she had too much to think about and too little time in which to think it. She had long ago accepted her need for extravagant amounts of time for contemplation (more, she had observed, than others seemed to need or want). And for years she had let herself believe that this was a product of her profession, her art, when it was much the other way around. The spirit sought and found the work, and discontent began when it could not.

And, of course, it was a con, this art. Which was why she couldn't help but approach a podium, any podium, with a mantle of slight chagrin that she could never quite manage to hide, her shoulders hunched inside her jacket or blouse, her eyes not meeting those in the audience, as if the men and women in front of her might challenge her, accuse her of fraud — which, in the end, only she appeared to understand she was guilty of. There was nothing easier nor more agonizing than writing the long narrative verses that her publisher put in print — easy in that they were simply daydreams written in ink; agonizing the moment she returned to consciousness (the telephone rang, the heat kicked on in the basement) and looked at the words on the blue-lined page and saw, for the first time, the dishonest images, the manipulation and the conniving wordplay, all of which, when it had been a good day, worked well for her. She wrote poetry, she had been told, that was *accessible,* a fabulous and slippery word that could be used in the service of both scathing criticism and excessive praise, neither of which she thought she deserved. Her greatest wish was to write anonymously, though she no longer mentioned this to her publishers, for they seemed slightly wounded at these mentions, at the apparent ingratitude for the long — and tedious? — investment they had made in her that was finally, after all these years, beginning to pay off. Some of her collections were selling now (and one of them was selling very well indeed) for reasons no one had predicted and no one seemed to understand, the unexpected sales attributable to that vague and unsettling phenomenon called "word of mouth."

She covered the chintz bedspread with her belongings: the olive suitcase (slim and soft for the new stingy overheads); the detachable computer briefcase (the detaching a necessity for the security checks); and her microfiber purse with its eight compartments for her cell phone, notebook, pen, driver's license, credit cards, hand cream, lipstick, and sunglasses. She used the bathroom with her coat still on and then searched for her contact lens case so that she could remove the miraculous plastic irritants from her eyes, the lenses soiled with airplane air and smoke from a concourse bar, a four-hour layover in Dallas ending in capitulation to a plate of nachos and a Diet Coke. And seeping around the edges, she began to feel the relief that hotel rooms always provided: a place where no one could get to her.

She sat again on the enormous bed, two pillows propped behind her. Across from her was a gilded mirror that took in the entire bed, and she could not look into such a mirror without thinking of various speakable and unspeakable acts that had almost certainly been performed in front of that mirror. (She thought of men as being particularly susceptible to mirrors in hotel rooms.) Her speculation led inevitably to consideration of substances that had spilled or fallen onto that very bedspread (how many times? thousands of times?) and the room was immediately filled with stories: a married man who loved his wife but could make love to her but once a month because he was addicted to fantasizing about her in front of hotel mirrors on his frequent business trips, her body the sole object of his sexual imaginings; a man cajoling a colleague into performing one of the speakable acts upon him, enjoying the image of her subservient head bobbing in the mirror over the dresser and then, when he had collapsed into a sitting position, confessing, in a moment that would ultimately cost him his job, that he had herpes (why were her thoughts about men today so hostile?); a woman who was not beautiful, but was dancing naked in front of the mirror, as she would never do at home, might never do again (there, that was better). She took her glasses off so that she could not see across the room. She leaned against the headboard and closed her eyes.

She had nothing to say. She had said it all. She had written all the poems she would ever write. Though something large and subterranean had fueled her images, she was a minor poet only. She was, possibly, an overachiever. She would coast tonight, segue early into the Q&A, let the audience dictate the tenor of the event. Mercifully, it would be short. She appreciated literary festivals for precisely that reason: she would be but one of many novelists and poets (more novelists than poets), most of whom were better known than she. She knew she ought to examine the program before she went to the cocktail party on the theory that it sometimes helped to find an acquaintance early on so that one was not left stranded, looking both unpopular and easy prey; but if she glanced at the program, it would pull her too early into the evening, and she resisted this invasion. How protective she had recently grown of herself, as if there were something tender and vulnerable in need of defense.

From the street, twelve floors below, there was a clanging of a large machine. In the corridor there were voices, those of a man and a woman, clearly upset.

It was pure self-indulgence, the writing. She could still remember (an antidote to the chagrin?) the exquisite pleasure, the texture, so early on, of her first penciled letters on their stout lines, the practiced slant of the blue-inked cursive on her first copybook (the lavish *F* of Frugality, the elegant *E* of

Envy). She collected them now, old copybooks, small repositories of beautiful handwriting. It was art, found art, of that she was convinced. She had framed some of the individual pages, had lined the walls of her study at home with the prints. She supposed the copybooks (mere schoolwork of anonymous women, long dead) were virtually worthless — she had hardly ever paid more than five or ten dollars for one in a secondhand book store — but they pleased her nevertheless. She was convinced that for her the writing was all about the act of writing itself, even though her own penmanship had deteriorated to an appalling level, nearly code.

She stood up from the bed and put her glasses on. She peered into the mirror. Tonight she would wear long earrings of pink Lucite. She would put her lenses back in and use a lipstick that didn't clash with the Lucite, and that would be that. Seen from a certain angle, she might simply disappear.

The party was in a room reserved for such occasions. Presumably, the view outside attracted, though the city now was gray and darkening yet. Lights twinkled at random, and it was impossible not to think: In this room or that, women will be undressing and

17

men, with ties undone, will be pouring drinks. Though one did not know, and there were other, more grotesque, scenarios to contemplate.

The window shuddered with a gust of wind. For a moment, the lights dimmed, causing a stoppage in the conversation of equal duration, a pause in which she could not help but think of panic in a blackened hotel, of hands groping. Some dreadful music, cousin to the malevolently bland tunes in the hotel elevator, seeped between the talk. She saw no recognizable face, which was disconcerting. There were perhaps twenty-five people in the suite when she arrived, most already drinking, and most, it would appear, already bonded into clusters. Along one wall, a table had been laid with hors d'oeuvres of a conventional sort. She set her purse under a chair by the door and walked to the bar. She asked for a glass of wine, guessing that the chardonnay would not live up to the rose coronation carpet or the bouquets as big as boys, and in this she was not wrong.

A woman said her name, and Linda turned to an outstretched hand belonging to a slight woman in a woolen suit, its cloth the color of irises. It was pleasant to see a woman not dressed in black, as everyone

18

seemed to be these days, but if she mentioned it, this might be taken as insult for being provincial. Linda shook the proffered hand, her own wet and cold from her wineglass.

— *I'm Susan Sefton, one of the organizers of the festival. I am such a fan. I wanted to thank you for coming.*

— *Oh. Thank you,* Linda said. *I'm looking forward to it,* she lied.

The woman had feral teeth but lovely green eyes. Did she do this for a living?

— *In about half an hour, we'll all be heading down to the front of the hotel, where we'll be taken by bus to a restaurant called Le Matin. It's a bistro. Do you like French?*

The answer couldn't matter, though Linda nodded yes. The idea of being carted out to dinner put her in mind of senior citizens, an image not dispelled in the next instant when she was informed that dinner would be early because of the various reading schedules.

— *And then each author will be taken to his or her event. There are four separate venues.* A vinyl binder with colored tabs was consulted. — *You're in Red Wing Hall, and you're reading at nine-thirty.*

Which would ensure a smallish crowd, Linda thought but didn't say. Most people with tickets to a festival — authors included — would be ready to go home by nine-thirty.

— *Do you know Robert Seizek?*

The name was vaguely familiar, though Linda could not then have named a title or even a genre. She made a motion with her head that might be construed as a nod.

— *You and he will be sharing a stage.*

Linda heard the demotion implicit in the fraction, a sense of being only half an entertainment.

— *It was in the program.* The woman seemed defensive, perhaps in response to a look of disappointment. *Didn't you get your packet?*

Linda had, but could hardly admit that now, it being inescapably rude not to have glanced at it.

— *I'll see you get one.* The feral teeth were gone, the smile having faded. Linda would be but one of many wayward writers Susan Sefton was in charge of, most too disorganized or self-absorbed to do what was expected. She looked pointedly at Linda's breast.

— *You have to wear a badge to all events. It's in the packet.* A rule against which writers surely would rebel, Linda thought, looking around at a room filled with white badges encased in plastic and pinned onto lapels and bodices. *Have you met Robert yet? Let me introduce you,* Susan Sefton added, not waiting for an answer to her question.

The woman in the iris-colored suit interrupted a conversation among three men, none of whom seemed to need or want interruption. The talk was of computers (Linda might have guessed this) and tech stocks one might have bought if only one had known. Seizek had a large head — leonine one would have to say — and an even larger body that spoke of appetites, one of which was much in evidence in his nearly lethal breath and in the way he swayed slightly, as if attached to a different gyroscope than the rest of them. Perhaps she would be solo on the stage after all. One of the two remaining authors had an Australian accent that was pleasant to listen to, and Linda deduced (as if tuning into a radio broadcast that had already begun) that he was a novelist about whom it had been said just the Sunday previous in a prominent book review that his prose was "luminous and engaging," his insights "brilliant and incisive." (A novel about an Australian scientist? She tried to remember. No, an engineer.) And it was impossible, despite the overused and thus devalued words of praise, not to regard the man with more interest than she had just seconds earlier, a fact she despised about herself. One bowed to power conferred. And she saw, as she had not before, that the other two men were turned slightly in the direction of the newly anointed, as though their bodies had been drawn off course by a powerful magnet.

— *And you, Ms. Fallon, would you say that your understanding of love came more from love itself or from reading about love?* Seizek spoke thickly, suggesting that she might at any minute be sprayed with sibilants.

Another conversation she had only bits of. The third writer looked at her not at all, as if she were invisible. It would not be fair to say that he was gay. How odd, she thought, that men would talk of love, had been talking of love before she had even joined them, a topic it was supposed was of interest only to women.

She answered without hesitation. *Experience. No one has ever accurately described a marriage.*

— *A novel can't, can it?* This from the Australian, in broad antipodean accent. *A marriage doesn't lend itself to art. Certainly not to satisfying structure or to dialogue worth reading.*

— *You write of love,* the man who could

not be called gay said to Linda, rendering her suddenly visible; and she could not help but be pleased that someone knew her work.

— *I do,* she said, not embarrassed to state her claim in this arena. — *I believe it to be the central drama of our lives.* Immediately, she qualified her bold pronouncement. *For most of us, that is.*

— *Not death?* asked Seizek, a drunk looking for debate.

— *I count it as part of the entire story. All love is doomed, seen in the light of death.*

— *I take it you don't believe that love survives the grave,* the Australian offered.

And she did not, though she had tried to. After Vincent.

— *Why central?* asked the third man, who had a name after all: William Wingate.

— *It contains all theatrical possibilities. Passion, jealousy, betrayal, risk. And is nearly universal. It's something extraordinary that happens to ordinary people.*

— *Not fashionable to write about love, though, is it.* This from Seizek, who spoke dismissively.

— *No. But in my experience, fashion doesn't have a great deal to do with validity.*

— *No, of course not,* Seizek said quickly, not wanting to be thought invalid.

Linda drifted to the edges of the talk, assaulted by a sudden hunger. She hadn't had a proper meal (if one didn't count the small trapezoidal carton of nachos) since breakfast in her hotel room in a city seven hundred miles away. She asked the men if they wanted anything from the buffet table, she was just going to get a cracker, she was starved, she hadn't eaten since breakfast. No, no, the men did not want, but of course she must get herself. The salsa was decent, they said, and they wouldn't be eating for another hour anyway. And, by the way, did anyone know the restaurant? And she reflected, as she turned away from them, that just a year ago, or maybe two, one of the men would have peeled away, followed her to the buffet table, would have viewed the occasion as opportunity. Such were the ironies of age, she thought. When the attention had been ubiquitous, she had minded.

Small bowls of colored food left the guest to guess at their identity: the green might be guacamole, the red was doubtless the decent salsa, and the pink possibly a shrimp or crab dip. But she was stumped as to the grayish-beige, not a good color for food under the best of circumstances. She reached for a small paper plate — the management had not provided for large appetites — and heard the hush before she understood it, a mild hush as if someone had lowered the volume a notch or two. From the corner, she heard a whispered name. It couldn't be, she thought, even as she understood it could. She turned to see the cause of the reverential quiet.

He stood in the doorway, as if momentarily blinded by the unfamiliar. As if having been injured, he was having to relearn certain obvious cues to reality: pods of men and women with drinks in hand, a room attempting to be something it was not, faces that might or might not be familiar. His hair was silver now, the shock of that, badly cut, atrociously cut really, too long at the sides and at the back. How he would be hating this, she thought, already taking his side. His face was ravaged in the folds, but you could not say he was unhandsome. The navy eyes were soft and blinking, as if he had come out of a darkened room. A scar, the old scar that seemed as much a part of him as his mouth, ran the length of his left cheek. He was greeted as a man might who had long been in a coma; as a king who had for years been in exile.

She turned around, unwilling to be the first person he saw in the room.

There were other greetings now, a balloon of quiet but intense attention. Could this be his first public appearance since the accident, since he had taken himself into seclusion, retired from the world? It could, it could. She stood immobile, plate in hand, breathing in a tight, controlled manner. She raised a hand slowly to her hair, tucked a stray strand behind her ear. She rubbed her temple softly with her finger. She picked up a cracker and tried to butter it with a crumbly cheese, but the cracker broke, disintegrating between her fingers. She examined a fruit bowl of strawberries and grapes, the latter gone brown at the edges.

Someone said, too unctuously, *Let me get you a drink.* Another crowed, *I am so pleased.* Still others murmured: *You cannot know,* and *I am such.*

It was nothing, she told herself as she reached for a glass of water. Years had passed, and all of life was different now.

She could feel him moving toward her. How awful that after all this time, she and he would have to greet each other in front of strangers.

He said her name, her very common name.

— *Hello, Thomas,* she said, turning, his name as common as her own, but his having the weight of history.

He had on an ivory shirt and a navy

blazer, the cut long out of style. He had grown thicker through the middle, as might have been anticipated, but still, one thought, looking at him, A tall man, a lanky man. His hair fell forward onto his forehead, and he brushed it away in a gesture that swam up through the years.

He moved across the space between them and kissed her face beside her mouth. Too late, she reached to touch his arm, but he had retreated, leaving her hand to dangle in the air.

Age had diminished him. She watched him take her in, she who would be seen to have been diminished by age as well. Would he be thinking, Her hair gone dry, her face not old?

— *This is very strange,* he said.

— *They are wondering about us already.*

— *It's comforting to think we might provide a story.*

His hands did not seem part of him; they were pale, soft writer's hands, hints of ink forever in the creases of the middle finger of the right hand. *I've followed your career,* he said.

— *What there's been of it.*

— *You've done well.*

— *Only recently.*

The others moved away from them like

boosters falling from a rocket. There was conferred status in his knowing her, not unlike the Australian writer with the good review. A drink appeared for Thomas, who took it and said thank you, disappointing the bearer, who hoped for conversation.

— *I haven't done this sort of thing in years*, he began and stopped.

— *When are you reading?*

— *Tonight.*

— *And me as well.*

— *Are we in competition?*

— *I certainly hope not.*

It was rumored that after many barren years, Thomas was writing again and that the work was extraordinarily good. He had in the past, inexplicably, been passed over for the prizes, though it was understood, by common agreement, that he was, at his best, the best of them.

— *You got here today?* she asked.

— *Just.*

— *You've come from . . . ?*

— *Hull.*

She nodded.

— *And you?* he asked.

— *I'm finishing a tour.*

He tilted his head and half smiled, as if to say, Condolences.

A man hovered near Thomas's elbow,

waiting for admission. *Tell me something,* Thomas said, ignoring the man beside him and leaning forward so that only she could hear. *Did you become a poet because of me?*

She remembered that Thomas's questions were often startling and insulting, though one forgave him always. *It's how we met,* she said, reminding him.

He took a longish sip of his drink. *So it was.*

— *It was out of character for me. That class.*

— *In character, I think. The rest was fraud.*

— *The rest?*

— *The pretending to be fast.*

Fast. She hadn't heard the word used that way in decades.

— *You're more in character now,* he said.

— *How could you possibly know?* she asked, challenging him.

He heard the bite in her voice. *Your body and your gestures give you the appearance of having grown into your character, what I perceive to be your character.*

— *It's only middle age,* she said, at once devaluing both of them.

— *Lovely on you.*

She turned away from the compliment. The man beside Thomas would not go away. Behind him there were others who wanted introductions to the reclusive poet.

She excused herself and moved through all the admirers and the sycophants, who were, of course, not interested in her. This was nothing, she told herself again as she reached the door. Years had passed, and all of life was different now.

She descended in the elevator, which seemed to take an age to reach her floor. She shut the door to her room, her temporary refuge. The festival packet lay under her coat, tossed there as one might have abandoned a newspaper, already read. She sat on the bed and scanned the list of festival participants, and there it was, his name, the print suddenly bolder than the typeface of the other names. In the flap opposite, tucked behind a white plastic badge with her name on it, was a newspaper clipping announcing the festival. The photograph with which the editors had illustrated the piece was of Thomas, a decade younger. He had his face turned to the side, not showing the scar, evasive. Yet, even so, there was something cocky in his expression — a different Thomas than she'd once known, a different Thomas than she'd seen just moments ago.

She stood up from the bed, replacing mild panic with momentum. Their meeting after so many years seemed a large occurrence, though she knew that all the important events of her life had already happened. She considered the possibility of simply remaining in her hotel room and not attending the dinner. Surely, she had no serious obligation to the festival beyond that of appearing at the appropriate time for her reading, something she could do by taxi. Susan Sefton might worry, but Linda could leave a message at the restaurant: she wasn't feeling well; she needed to rest after the long flight. All of which seemed suddenly true: she *wasn't* feeling well; she *did* need to rest. Though it was the shock of seeing Thomas after all these years that was making her slightly ill. That and an attendant guilt, a nearly intolerable guilt now that she had known order in her life, responsibility, had imagined from the other side how inexcusable her actions had been. Years ago, the guilt had been masked by a shamefully insupportable pain — and by lust and love. Love might have made her generous or selfless, but she had not been either.

She walked into the bathroom and leaned into the mirror. Her eyeliner had smudged into a small, humiliating circle below her left eye. It was one thing to resort to artifice, she thought, quite another to be bad at it. Her hair had given up its texture in the humidity and looked insubstantial. She bent and tousled it with her fingers, but when she righted herself, it fell into its former limp shape. The light in the bathroom was unflattering. She refused to catalogue the damage.

Had she become a poet because of Thomas? It was a valid, if impertinent, question. Or had they been drawn together because of a common way of seeing? Thomas's poems were short and blunt, riddled with brilliant juxtapositions, so that one felt, upon finishing a collection, buffeted about. As though one had taken a road with many twists and turns; as though a passenger had jerked the wheel of a car, risking injury. Whereas her work was slow and dreamlike, more elegiac, nearly another form entirely.

She wandered into the bedroom, a woman who had momentarily forgotten where she was, and saw the telephone, lifeline to her children. She read the instructions for making a long-distance call. There would be outrageous surcharges, but she couldn't care about that now. She sat at the edge of the bed and dialed Maria's number and was disappointed when Maria was not at the other end. Linda opened her mouth to leave a message — people who called and did not leave messages annoyed her — but though she dearly wanted to say something to her daughter and, more important, wanted to hear her daughter's voice, she could not find the words. *A man you've never heard me speak about is scratching at the surface.* Illogically, or perhaps not, Linda thought of ovum and sperm and of a single cell poking through a delicate membrane. She replaced the receiver, feeling unusually mute and frustrated. She lay back and closed her eyes.

She pictured her daughter and her son, one sturdy, the other not, and, oddly, it was the boy who was the more fragile. When she thought of Maria, she thought of vivid coloring and clarity (Maria, like her father, spoke her mind and seldom thought the consequences would be disastrous), whereas when she thought of Marcus, she thought of color leached, once there, now gone, though he was only twenty-two. He, poor boy, had inherited Linda's pale, Irish looks, while Vincent's more robust Italian blood had given Maria her sable eyebrows and the blue-black hair that turned heads. And though Vincent had sometimes had shadows on his face, particularly under his eyes (and had those shadows been early signs of disease they might have read if only they had known?), Maria's skin was pink and smooth, now that the mercifully brief ravages of adolescence had subsided. Linda wondered again, as she had often wondered, if it was her own response to her children's coloring that had determined their personalities; if she had not, in fact, mirrored her children back to them, announcing that Maria would always be direct, while something subterranean would form beneath Marcus's skin. (How Marcus all these years must have thought himself misnamed — Marcus Bertollini confounding everyone's expectations of him, he who looked so much more a Phillip or an Edward.) She did not regard these thoughts about her children as disloyal; she loved them in equal measure. They had never competed, having learned at an early age that no competition could ever be won.

The numerals on the clock brightened as the room darkened. Poets and novelists would be convening now in front of the hotel, like schoolchildren embarking on a field trip. I will go down, she decided suddenly. I will not be afraid of this.

At the horizon, the clouds had parted, the

35

pink light a promise of a better day tomorrow. Linda registered everything: the way a woman, stepping up to the bus, could not put her weight on her right knee and had to grasp the railing; the pretentiously scuffed leather portfolio of a poet with fashionable black-framed glasses; the way they all stood in raincoats, nudging and nudged slightly forward, hands in pockets, until they'd formed a thickened cluster. But she willed her antennae not to locate Thomas, who must have been behind her or absent altogether. So that when she was seated at the back of the bus and watched him board, she felt both surprise and embarrassment, the embarrassment for his sudden emasculation, his having to ride a bus as schoolchildren did. He was, in his trench coat, too bulky for his seat, his arms tucked in front of him, his shoulders bulging above his torso. Robert Seizek, more drunk than she had seen any man in years — his face looking as though it would spout water if pinched — needed to be helped up the steps. The authors who had to read that night seemed preoccupied, excessively self-conscious about appearing relaxed.

They drove through graying streets, deserted at this hour, more businesslike than charming. Linda tried not to look at

Thomas, which was difficult to do. He seemed disheveled, so unlike Vincent, who'd always appeared impeccable, compact and neat, like his body. She'd loved the way the cloth of her husband's shirts had fit tightly against his shoulders, the way he'd trimmed his beard, always a perfect sculpture. He'd worn Italian leather belts and custom trousers, and in Vincent this had not been vanity, but rather habit ingrained by immigrant parents anxious to have their child succeed in the new world. What might have been foppish in another was, in Vincent, routine and even elegant; Vincent, who did not believe in treading upon the innocent wishes of one's parents; Vincent, who was often baffled by the generalized insolence of his children's friends.

The bus stopped, and Linda was determined to hang back. She would simply find an empty seat in the restaurant and introduce herself to a stranger. But when she emerged from the bus, she saw that Thomas was hovering near the door, waiting for her.

He contrived, by small movements, to seat them apart from the others. It was a small bistro that was, possibly, authentically French. The festival participants had been put into a narrow room with two long tables and benches at the sides. Linda and

Thomas sat at the end nearest the door, and this, too, seemed the gesture of the man she remembered, a man who had always favored easy exits. She noted that the paper tablecloth, stained already with half-moons of red wine, did not quite reach. Thomas was doodling with his pen. The acoustics of the room were terrible, and she felt as though she were drowning in a sea of voices, unintelligible words. It forced them to lean together, conspiratorially, to speak.

— *It's something of a resurgence, isn't it? This interest in poetry?*

— *But not a renaissance,* she answered after a moment.

— *I'm told there are ten of us here. Out of a roster of sixty. That must be something of a record.*

— *They're better about this abroad.*

— *Have you done that? Gone to festivals abroad?*

— *Occasionally.*

— *So you've been on the circuit for a while.*

— *Hardly.* She resented the barb. She moved away from the conspiratorial bubble.

He leaned in closer and glanced up from his doodling. *You try to do too much in your verse. You should tell your stories as stories. Your audience would like that.*

— *My audience?*

— Your verse is popular. You must know your audience.

She was silent, stung by the implied criticism.

— I believe at heart you are a novelist, he said.

She turned her face away. The gall of him, she thought. She considered standing up to leave, but such a theatrical gesture would show her to be vulnerable, might remind him of other theatrical gestures.

— I've hurt you. To his credit, he looked repentant.

— Of course not, she lied.

— You don't need me or anyone else to tell you your own worth.

— No, I don't, in fact.

— You're a wonderful writer in any form.

And he would believe the compliment. Indeed, would not even think of it as a compliment, which implied something better than the truth.

The food arrived on plates so large that adjustments had to be made all along the table. Linda tried to imagine the appliance that could manage the oversized dishes; and to what end, she wondered, since they only dwarfed the food: Indonesian chicken for herself and salmon with its grill marks for Thomas. Returning pink-eyed from the bar,

Robert Seizek bumped the table, jostling water glasses and wine. Linda saw the furtive and bolder glances in her direction from the others. What prior claim did Linda Fallon have on Thomas Janes?

Thomas took a bite and wiped his lips, uninterested in his food, and in this she saw that he had not changed as well: in half an hour, he would not be able to remember what he had eaten.

— *Are you still a Catholic?* he asked, peering at the V of skin above her ivory blouse. It was a sort of uniform, the silk-like blouses, the narrow skirts. She had three of each in slippery folds inside her suitcase. *You don't wear the cross.*

— *I stopped years ago,* she said, not adding, *When my husband, who knew its meaning, asked me to take it off.* She lifted her glass and drank, too late realizing that the wine would stain her teeth. *One is always a Catholic. Even when one has lapsed.*

— *There was so much harm then.* He looked inward, possibly reminded of Catholic sins. *Are you religious now?*

— *Only on airplanes,* she said quickly, and he laughed. He tried to eat another bite.

— *I am, a bit,* he confessed, startling her, and he seemed almost bashful in the confession. *My mother's minister stayed with me for*

40

days after Billie died, though I hardly knew his presence. Very good in the clinches. Well, they are, aren't they? We often play tennis together now, and I sometimes go to services. So as not to hurt his feelings, I think.

Her breath was tight and seared her chest. This mention of private disaster had come too soon. She heard the phrase again: *After Billie died. . . .*

He went on. *I suppose I feel I ought to show some gratitude. Though they must know that in the end it doesn't help. In the end, nothing helps. Drugs, possibly.*

— *Yes.*

He leaned forward. *Does this happen to you? I think of what we did, and I cannot believe we were ever so cruel.*

She couldn't answer him. He had paid more dearly than any man deserved. And she? What payment had she made? She had had love, and her children were alive. Against all the odds, she had been rewarded. What justice was in that?

She put her fork down, unable even to pretend to eat. There had never been a rehearsal for such a conversation. She folded her fingers under her chin. She could not go forward, for she didn't know how much he could bear. She would take her cues from Thomas, not ask any questions.

41

The massive plates were replaced with smaller ones. The waiter filled their glasses.

— *Do you still have the letters?* he asked.

— *I lost them,* she said, relieved to have moved to safer conversational ground. *They spilled out of a carton. I watched from a second-story window of a house my husband and I were moving into. He had been carrying it, the carton. I held my breath when he picked it up. They would have hurt him, even though . . .*

(*Even though I hadn't seen you in years,* she had been about to say.)

— *No man likes to think there was another who mattered,* Thomas said reasonably.

— *And then, weeks later, when I thought to look for them, they were gone. Nowhere to be found. I tried to ask obliquely, but he seemed not to know what I was talking about. It's a mystery. To this day, I don't know what happened to them.*

— *He destroyed them,* Thomas said simply.

Linda could not imagine that outcome, that act of subterfuge. Vincent had lacked the desire, and therefore the skill, for duplicity. Whereas she and Thomas had been acrobats.

Arms were laid upon the backs of chairs. Food was devoured or ignored. Mirrors against the walls doubled the diners, showing faces where faces had been hidden.

A cohort of small men in soiled aprons threaded themselves around the narrow table like dancers. A lack of windows, reminders of the rain, made the room seem intimate. Those who had no gift for conversation suffered.

— *When did you marry?* Thomas asked lightly.

Discussion of the past invited pain, she thought, though it was foolish to imagine they could continue any conversation without mentioning the worst between them.

— *Nineteen seventy-six,* she said.

— *Twenty-four years ago.*

She nodded, and there was a moment when she knew what he was thinking: of herself preparing for a wedding. Of herself in the throes of the strongest physical love for another.

— *And you have children?* he asked. *I think I might have read that.*

— *I have a daughter who is twenty-three, a son who is twenty-two.*

And there, it was done: the mention of her children.

She watched Thomas struggle to compose his features. How bottomless the grief that could show itself in fresh tears years later.

— *What are their names?*

43

— *Maria and Marcus.*

— *Maria and Marcus . . . ?*

— *Bertollini.*

— *Your husband's name.*

— *Vincent,* she said, not adding that he had died.

— *It's so I can imagine it.*

She nodded.

— *You dress beautifully now.* Thomas kept his eyes on her face as he said this, though she knew that he had already assessed her.

— *Thank you,* she said simply.

— *Billie would have been twelve this spring,* Thomas said.

The name, spoken aloud, was too sad, too harsh. She could see, in the tightness of his mouth, the cost of this.

— *The boat was waterlogged and rotten. The head smelled. You could hear Rich fucking in the forward cabin . . .*

For a moment, he could not go on.

— *We were on our way to Maine,* he said, the tremor in his voice momentarily under better control. *Rich and his girlfriend were on the boat. And Jean, my wife.* He glanced up at Linda. *And our daughter, Billie.*

— *Thomas, stop,* she said quietly. *You don't have to do this. I read about the accident when it happened.* Indeed, she could re-member only too well the way she'd been

44

turning the pages of the *Boston Globe* as she did every morning (Vincent with the *Times* at the other end of the table; her hand was sticky with jelly, she remembered), and the way the words THOMAS JANES and *DAUGHTER* and *DROWNED* had been, with what seemed like impossible and screaming capitals, all contained within the same headline. The way Vincent had instantly put down his paper, saying: *Linda, what's the matter?*

A waiter, balancing plates, created an artificial pause.

— *It wasn't Jean's fault, though I blamed her.*

Linda watched Thomas's fingers tighten on the stem of his glass. She could not dictate how he would tell this story.

— *God, how I blamed her. I would have killed her on the boat if I'd had the strength or courage for it.*

Linda pressed her folded hands against her mouth. How we struggle to hold in what we would say, she thought.

She looked around the room, at all the faces — avid and intensely curious — turned in their direction. This was awful. They could not do this here.

— *Thomas,* she said, standing. *Come with me.*

★ ★ ★

They moved along a quay that jutted into the lake. The drizzle made a net around her hair, her face. Thomas walked with his shoulders slightly stooped, his hands tucked into the long pockets of his trench coat. He had knotted the belt loosely, one of the ties longer than the other. His shoes had not been polished in some time. It wasn't poverty that made him so unkempt, she knew; it was merely lack of care. Another's care or his own.

— *You live in Hull still,* she said.

— *Yes.*

— *And how is Rich?*

— *He's fine. He's married now, with two boys. He married a doctor, as it happened. The boys are great.*

She could not imagine how Thomas managed to play with other people's children, or even to talk to them. Would the ache be constant? Would there be an hour, five hours together, when one simply — and blessedly — forgot?

— *I see your aunt occasionally,* Thomas said. *She always tries to pretend she doesn't know me.*

— *Can you blame her?*

— *No, of course not. I hardly blame anyone now except myself. I suppose this is progress.*

The wind was raw against the open neck of her blouse. She clutched the lapels of her raincoat. *I won't ask about your wife,* she said. *Though I would like to.*

— *You mean Jean?*

She nodded, knowing they couldn't speak yet of Regina. Possibly not ever.

— *Oh, I can talk about Jean.* He seemed to have recovered from his tremulousness in the restaurant. Linda imagined that grief might show itself in a random pattern: some moments would be unbearable; others would be merely bits and pieces of a bad story. *I don't blame her,* he added. *I said that. She was a good woman. Well, still is, I suppose.*

— *You don't see her?*

— *Oh, God, no. I don't think either one of us could bear it. After a year or so, she moved inland, to Indianapolis, where she was originally from. It's safer there, I imagine. No possibility of ocean. I assume she's still alone. Yes, I know she is. She writes occasionally to Rich.*

And why did Thomas continue to torture himself with ocean? she might have asked.

They had walked to what appeared to be an industrial park. She remembered a Christmas Day, years ago, when she and Thomas had strolled empty streets in Boston, the only persons in a deserted universe. But then she had a troubling thought:

47

though she could remember the day — the sense of endless time available to them, the promise of possibility around every corner, the clarity of the air — she could not feel it. And she found that she minded this inability to feel the past. It was disturbing, really, to be so removed from the texture of one's life.

Her skirt moved as they walked. She was ruining her shoes. Beside her, she could feel Thomas's heat, even in the inhospitable chill. There was, about her shoulders, a contraction of self-consciousness. His physical presence was familiar to her, and yet foreign as well. All his cells were different now, overturned three times.

— *Do you teach?* he asked.

— *I do.* She named the college. *Part-time. My husband died two years ago and left insurance money.*

— *I didn't know. I'm sorry.* He who would know better than any man how useless sorry was. *Was it a long illness?*

— *No. It was very sudden.*

Beside her, Thomas seemed to lope rather than to walk.

— *I started touring more aggressively after he died,* she said. *I found I didn't think about Vincent as much in hotel rooms.*

They had reached a bench. He gestured for her to sit. She had her hands in the pockets of her coat and gathered them forward into her lap. The weekend lay before her, more defined than it had been just hours earlier. A year from now, she knew, she might be thinking, That was the weekend that I. . . . It was momentous after all, their having met after years apart. Momentous simply in this exchange of history, in the verification of one's past. Thoughts of something larger were impossible; they ran against the grain these days, against the tide.

— *Was your marriage good?* he asked.

No one ever asked her these sorts of questions anymore. There was, undeniably, a kind of exhilaration in having to answer them.

— *I think it was a wonderful marriage.* She knew nothing of Thomas's second marriage, to the woman named Jean, only of its unspeakable demise and aftermath. *We had a lot of joy together. I remember thinking that when Vincent died: 'We had a lot of joy.' And very little unhappiness.*

— *I'm glad.*

— *But no one gets through life unscathed,* she said. And she wondered: was that true? Did anyone, at fifty-two, have an unscathed life? *Vincent never seemed to suffer, and I found that contagious. Life was more normal, less fraught than it had been.*

Had been with you, she might have added.

— *Reason enough to love anyone, I should think.*

— *We had just come back from what was to be our summerhouse in Maine. We'd gone up for the day to meet with the contractor. It was to have been a magnificent house — well, magnificent to us. After years of saving for it, it was finally a reality. Our only regret was that we hadn't done it when the children were younger, though already we were thinking of grandchildren.* She paused, as if for breath, when really, it was the tamping down of anger that had momentarily stopped her. *I went out to the bank and left him in the house. When I came back he was on the floor, surrounded by oranges.*

— *A heart attack?*

— *A massive stroke.* She paused. *Nothing about his health had ever suggested the possibility. He was only fifty.*

Thomas put a hand on hers, which had escaped from her pocket in the telling of the tale. His was cold, his palm roughened to a papery texture, despite the writer's fingers. He touched her awkwardly, the gesture of a man not used to consoling others.

— *It's such a surprise to see you,* she said. *I*

50

didn't know. I hadn't read the program.

— *Would you have come if you had known?*

The question was a tunnel with a dozen furtive compartments. — *Curiosity might have made me bold.*

Thomas released her hand and took out a pack of cigarettes. In a series of gestures both ancient and familiar to Linda, he lit a cigarette, picked a piece of tobacco off his lip, and blew a thin stream of blue smoke that hung in the damp air, a bit of calligraphy dissipating. There would be, of course, no point in mentioning his health. Thomas would almost certainly say he'd lived too long already.

— *Would it surprise you to learn that I came here because of you?* he asked.

Something more than surprise kept her silent.

— *Yes, it surprised me, too,* he said. *But there it is. I saw your name and thought . . . Well, I don't know what I thought.*

Behind them, a ferry or tugboat blew its whistle.

— *I am hungry, actually,* Thomas said.

— *You have a reading in half an hour.*

— *Payment exacted for all this fun.*

Linda looked at him and laughed.

Thomas stood, the gentle man, and took her arm. *I think this means we owe ourselves a dinner afterwards.*

— *At least that,* Linda said in kind.

They took a taxi to the theater. At the door they parted — with customary good wishes on Linda's part, the obligatory grimace on Thomas's — and truly, he seemed to blanch slightly when Susan Sefton accosted him and impressed upon him the fact of the performance in ten minutes' time.

It was a steeply inclined room that might once have been a lecture hall, with seats that fanned out from a podium like spokes from a wheel. Linda took off her wet raincoat and let it crumple behind her back, the cloth giving off the scent of something vaguely synthetic. Alone now, anonymous, with two strangers seating themselves beside her, she allowed herself to think about Thomas's assertion that he had come to the festival because of her. It wouldn't be entirely true — there would have been a sense of reemerging into a world he'd left behind — but the part that might be true alarmed her. She didn't, couldn't, want such a costly overture.

The trickle into the theater was modest, producing a pockmarked gallery that could be, Linda knew, dispiriting when viewed from a stage. She ached for Thomas to have

52

a good audience. There were students with backpacks, a few couples on what appeared to be dates, some women like herself sitting in small, cheerful groups. The would-be poets came in singly, supplicants seeking words of inspiration or, at the very least, an agent. But then a side door, forgotten or locked until now, swung open to admit a steady stream of people; and Linda watched as row after row filled and spilled into the next, the gallery's complexion clearing. Linda felt, oddly, a mother's pride (or a wife's, she supposed, though she'd had little practice; Vincent had been terrified at just the thought of public speaking). The respectable audience became a flood, the doors held open by bodies that could go no further into the theater. Thomas's years in self-proclaimed and necessary exile had whetted appetites. History was being made, albeit history of a parochial and limited sort.

Beside her, a younger couple speculated about the famous silence.

— *His daughter was killed on a boat.*

— *Oh, God. Can you imagine?*

— *Washed overboard. She was only five. Or six, maybe.*

— *Jesus.*

— *They say he had a breakdown after.*

— *I might have read that.*

The lights dimmed, and an academic introduction was made. An exile, though not its cause, was alluded to. The introduction did not do justice to Thomas, though it suggested a singular achievement that one might honor even if there hadn't been any work in years. The spotlight made unflattering shadows on the academic's face. She herself would soon be standing there.

When Thomas emerged from the wings, a hush, like cloud, settled upon the audience. Thomas moved with old authority, careful not to look up at the several hundred faces. When he reached the podium, he took a glass of water, and she saw (and hoped that others did not) that his hand trembled in its epic progress from the table to the mouth. Behind her, someone said, *Wow, he's really aged,* the words (such power) reducing even the best of them to something less.

Thomas fumbled badly at the beginning, causing an empathetic flush to run along the sides of her neck and lodge behind her ears. He seemed unprepared. In the growing silence, he flicked pages with his forefinger, the paper having the snap and crackle of onionskin. Linda could hear from the audience murmurs of surprise, the slight whine of disappointment. And still the riffling continued. And then, when she thought she could bear it no longer, when she'd bent her head and put her fingers to her eyes, Thomas began to read.

The voice was deep and sonorous, untouched by the years that had ravaged his face. It might have been the voice of a proclamation, the basso profundo of an opera singer. It seemed the audience held its breath, lest breathing cause the people there to miss a word. She strained to comprehend the startling phrases, then was left to tumble down a slide of images that were oddly pleasurable even though their terrible meaning could not be misunderstood: *"Water's silk,"* he read, and *"Bed of sand." "The mother bent, a trampled stem."* The hair on the back of Linda's neck stood up, and chills stippled her arms. She held herself and forgot the audience. One could hardly believe in this marriage of confused and servile grief. She knew, as she had not ever known before — as she was certain those around her had not known before — that she was in the presence of greatness.

He read from *The Magdalene Poems.* A series of poems about a girl who did not become a woman. An elegy for a life not lived.

Thomas stopped and took another epic drink of water. There was the sound of a hundred listeners putting hands to chests and saying, *Oh.* The applause that followed was — one had to say it — thunderous. Thomas looked up and seemed surprised by all the commotion. He did not smile, either to himself or at the audience, and for this Linda was inexplicably relieved: Thomas would not easily be seduced.

The questions that followed the reading were routine (one about his culpability, appalling). He answered dutifully; and mercifully, he was not glib. Linda wasn't certain she could have borne to hear him glib. He seemed exhausted, and a sheen lay on his forehead, white now with true stage fright.

The questions stopped — it wasn't clear by whose mysterious signal — and the applause that followed could be felt in the armrests. Some even stood, as at the theater. Unskilled and unpracticed at accepting praise, Thomas left the stage.

She might have met him backstage and embraced him in mutual exuberance. And perhaps he would be expecting her, would be disappointed by her absence. But then she saw him in the lobby, surrounded by adoring fans, the torturous words inside his head put aside, and she thought: I will not compete for his attention.

Needing air, she walked out into the

night. People stood in gatherings, more exhilarated than subdued. She didn't intend to eavesdrop, but couldn't help but hear the words "shattering" and "brilliant," though one woman seemed incensed that a poet would turn a daughter's death to advantage. "Opportunistic," Linda heard, and "rape of other people's lives." A man responded dismissively. "Dana, it's called art," he said, and Linda knew at once the two were married.

She walked around the block, the experience in the theater seeming to require it. The drizzle turned to serious rain and soaked her hair and shoulders before she could return. She entered a side theater and listened to a Rwandan woman catalogue atrocities. Linda sat benumbed, exhausted of feeling, until it was time for her own reading.

She was taken backstage, snake-infested with coils of electrical cables. Her eyes, not adjusting quickly enough to the darkness, made her stupid and overly cautious, and she knew she was being seen as middle-aged by the younger organizer. Seizek appeared beside her, his breath announcing him before his bulk. He put a proprietary hand on her back, letting it slide to the bottom of her spine — for balance or to assert some male advantage, she wasn't sure. They were led, blinking, onto the stage, which was, indeed, harshly overlit. They sat to either side of the podium. Seizek, ignoring manners and even his own introduction, staggered to the podium first. Nearly too drunk to stand, he produced a flawless reading, a fact more remarkable than his prose, which seemed watered down, as if the author had diluted paragraphs for the sake of length, made careless by a deadline.

The applause was respectable. Some left the theater when Seizek had finished (bored by Seizek's reading? not fans of poetry? not interested in Linda Fallon?), further reducing the audience to a desperate case of acne. She strove to overcome, by act of will, her seeming unpopularity (more likely the wished-for anonymity) as she walked to the podium; and by the time she had adjusted the microphone, she had largely succeeded, even though she couldn't help but notice that Thomas wasn't there. She spoke the words of her verse, words she had some reason to be proud of, words that, though they could no longer be fresh to her, had been crafted with care. But as she read, her mind began to drift, and she thought of Thomas's suggestion that she turn her images into prose. And she found that even as she said the phrases, her second brain was composing sentences, so that when a stray word jolted her from her reverie, she felt panicky, as if she'd lost her place.

The applause was that of an audience made good-humored by promise of release to beds and dinners. There were questions then, one oddly similar to the dyspeptic complaint of the woman who thought it opportunistic to use another's life for purposes of art (why this should so rankle, Linda couldn't imagine, since it was not *her* life in question). The line in the lobby to buy Linda's books was no deeper than twenty, and she was, actually, grateful for the twenty. She contrived to linger longer than she might have, wondering if Thomas would appear after all for the dinner they'd felt was owed to them; but she did not stay long enough to feel foolish if he did eventually arrive. When she left the theater, she walked out into the night and was stopped by a streak of white along the roof of the sky, the low clouds having caught the light of the city.

Water's silk, she thought. *Trampled stem.*

There was comfort in thinking the worst had happened. She was twenty-seven, washed high upon a tide line and left to wither in the sun or be swept away by another wave. She had been beached in Cambridge, where she walked the streets incessantly, her body all legs and arms inside her skirts and blouses, a miniskirt no more remarkable in that season and in that year than a dashiki or a pair of bell-bottoms. What was remarkable was her hair: wild and unruly and unstylish, though no particular style was called for then. It had taken on, in Africa, more color than before, so that it now ran a spectrum from mahogany to whitened pine. From the walking, or from lack of ceremony with food, she had grown lean and wiry as well. Life now was walking in the rain or in the sunshine with a freedom she had never known and did not want. Each morning, she slipped on her sandals and fingered her gold cross, preparing for days filled with guilt and recrimination, and having no wish to erase the event that had bequeathed this legacy. Sometimes, hollowed out, she leaned against a wall and put her head to the cool stones and gasped for breath, struck anew by the magnitude of the loss, the pain as sharp as if it had happened just the day before.

She did not know the city as it was supposed to be known. She did not live as expected. What was expected were lengthy walks among the sycamores, not forgetting that this was hallowed ground. What was expected were conversations that lasted long into the night, watched over by the ghosts of pale scholars and exasperating pedants. In flagrant violation of entitlement, she returned to cheerless rooms in which there was a bed she could scarcely bear to look at. For her, Cambridge was remembering that sordid kissing behind an office door had once been elevated to the status of a sacrament (she who had now been excommunicated); or it was the bitter thrill of a sunset that turned the bricks and stones of the city, and even the faces on the streets (those entitled scholars), a rosy-salmon color that seemed the very hue of love itself. Cambridge was sitting in a bathtub in a rented apartment and making experimental slits along the wrists, slits immediately regretted for the fuss they caused in Emergency. (And mortifying that she should be just one of so many who'd had to resort.) Her skirts hung from her hipbones like wash on the line, and in September, when the weather turned colder, she wore knee-high boots that ought to have been stupendously painful to walk in and weren't.

She was living then on Fairfield Street, in a set of rooms that had a bathtub on a platform in the kitchen (majestic locus for sacrificial rites). She had matching china and expensive crystal from another lethal ritual and the subsequent marriage that had corroded from the inside out, like a shiny car with rust beneath the paint job. (Though she had, in the end, crashed that car head-on.) These she had placed on a shelf in a cupboard in the kitchen, where they gathered dust, mute testament to expectation. She ate, when she ate at all, on a Melamine plate she'd bought at Lechmere's, a plate that held no associations, a dish no lover or husband had ever touched. In the mornings, when school started up again, Linda stood by the door and drank an Instant Breakfast, pleased that so much could be taken care of in so little time. She went out in her miniskirts and boots (staggering now to think of wearing such clothing in front of seventeen-year-old boys), and got into her car and merged into traffic going north to a high school in a suburban town. Within the privacy that only the interior of a car can provide, she cried over her persistent and seemingly inexhaustible loss and often had to fix her face in the rearview mirror before she went into the classroom.

On the holidays, she went to Hull as if threading a minefield — fearful at the entry, mute with gratitude when the fraught journey had been negotiated. And occasionally she was not successful. Against all better judgment, she would sometimes drive by Thomas's family home, trying to imagine which car was his (the VW? the Fiat? the Volvo?); for he, like her, was necessarily drawn back for the holidays. But as much as she feared or hoped for it, they never met by accident, not even at the diner or the gas station. (To think of how she would tremble just to turn the corner into the parking lot of the diner, hardly able to breathe for wondering.)

To ward off men, who seemed ever-present, even on that mostly female faculty, she created the fiction that she was married (and for the convenience of the lie, to a law student who was hardly ever home). This was a life she could well imagine and could recreate in detail at a moment's notice: the phantom (once real enough) husband returning home after a grueling stint in moot court; a blow-out party at the weekend, during which her husband had become deathly ill from bourbon and cider; a gift needed for a professor's wedding. Cambridge was leaving these lies behind and arriving home to quiet rooms, where there was time and space to remember, the space and time seemingly as necessary as the Valium she kept on hand in the medicine cabinet (the Valium an unexpected boon in the aftermath of Emergency).

She was a decent teacher, and sometimes others said so (*I'm told your classes are; You are my favorite*), but it seemed a shriveled life all the same. She supposed there were events that impinged upon her consciousness. Later she would recall that she had been a Marxist for a month and that there had been a man, political and insistent, to whom she had made love in a basement room and with whom she'd developed a taste for marijuana that hadn't gone away until Maria. And for a time she would own a remarkable set of oil paints in a wooden box, a reminder of an attempt to lose herself on canvas. Oddly, she did not put pen to paper, afraid of conflagration, as if the paper itself were flinty.

But mostly she walked alone, down Massachusetts Avenue and onto Irving Street. Along the Charles and to Porter Square. On Saturdays, she walked to Somerville or to the Fenway. She had no destination, the walking destination itself, and sometimes, when it was very bad, she counted rhythmically, the closest she ever came to chanting a mantra. What impressed her most was the endurance of the suffering: it seemed unlikely that one should mind another's loss so much. It was shameful to go on at length, she knew, even in the privacy of one's mind, about personal disasters when so many truly were abused. (More shameful still that news of Entebbe or rioting ghettos put suffering in perspective for only moments at a time, the self needing to return to self; and sometimes news of battles, both foreign and domestic, made the suffering worse: one longed, after all, for someone with whom to share these bulletins from hell.)

On a day in September — there had been months of walking — Linda entered a café in which wooden tables had been set perpendicular to a counter with a glass encasement of sweets. She ordered coffee and a peanut-butter cookie, lunch having along the way been missed, and brought them to her table, where she had laid out grids for lesson plans. It eased the tedium of the job to work in a café, and for a time she lost herself in the explicated themes of *Ethan Frome* and *The Glass Menagerie*. Outside, the sun had warmed the brick but not the people who practiced hunching into their jackets in anticipation of winter. A commotion in a corner claimed her attention, willing to be claimed. A woman with two poodles had set them improbably in booster seats on chairs and was feeding them bits of expensive macaroons from the glass case. She spoke to them as a mother might to toddlers, wiping snouts with a lacy handkerchief and gently scolding one for being greedy.

Linda watched the scene, incredulous.

— *She'll keep their ashes in the cookie jar,* a voice behind her said.

Linda turned to see a man with vivid features and eyebrows as thick as pelts. A wry expression lay easily on his face. A cosmic laugh — unfettered, releasing months of grim remorse — bubbled up inside her and broke the surface. A sheaf of papers fell off the table, and she tried to catch them. She put a hand to her chest, helpless.

There were introductions, the cosmic laugh petering out in small bursts she could not control. The laughing itself was contagious, and the man chuckled from time to time. She put a hand to her mouth, and the girl behind the counter said, *What's so funny?* One of them moved to the other's table (later they would argue who), and Vincent said, apropos the cosmic laugh, *You needed that.*

He had wide brown eyes and smooth skin tanned from some exercise or trip away. His hair was glossy, like that of an animal with a healthy coat.

Turning, her foot bumped the table pedestal, causing coffee to spill onto his polished shoe. She bent to wipe it off with a paper napkin.

— *Careful,* he said to her. *I'm easily aroused.*

She looked up and smiled. As easily as that. And felt another tide come for her at last.

— *He was good to you?*
— *Very. I can't imagine what would have happened, what I'd have become.*
— *Because of me.*
— *Well. Yes. And me as well.*
— *I used to live in Cambridge,* Thomas said. *On Irving Street. Years later, though.*

— *I didn't know that.*

She wondered how often she had walked along that street, which large house he'd lived in. She was leaning against the ferry's bulkhead, watching the northern city slip away. Wind whipped her hair, which stung her face, and she turned her head to free it. She wore, as she did almost every day that didn't require something more inspired, a white shirt and a pair of jeans. And today the raincoat, buttoned against the breezes. Thomas still had on his navy blazer, as if he'd slept in it. He had called before she was even awake, afraid, he'd said, that she'd go off for the day and he wouldn't be able to find her. Would she like to take a ferry ride to an island in the lake? Yes, she said, she thought she would. She boldly asked him why he hadn't come to her reading.

— *It was unnerving seeing you sitting there at mine. It's always harder when someone you know is in the audience. I thought to spare you that.*

And in this, he was, of course, correct.

— *Your work,* she said on the ferry. *I don't know when I've ever heard . . .*

Thomas wore an expression she herself had sometimes felt: pleasure imperfectly masked by modesty.

— *Your work will be taught in classrooms in*

a decade, she added. *Maybe less. I'm sure of it.*

She turned away, letting him have the pleasure without her scrutiny.

— *Why do you call them "The Magdalene Poems?"* she asked after a time.

He hesitated. *You must know why.*

Of course she knew and wished she hadn't asked. For the asking invited confidences and memories she didn't want. *You spell it Magdalene,* she said. *With the* e.

— *That's the way it's spelled in the Bible. But often it's spelled Magdalen without the* e. *There are many versions of the name: Magdala, Madeleine, Mary Magdala. Did you know that Proust's madeleines were named after her?*

— *You've been working on the poems a long time.*

— *I had to let them go. After Africa.*

There was an awkward silence between them.

— *They transcend any subject,* she said quickly. *Good poetry always does.*

— *It's a myth, her being a fallen woman. They thought that only because the first mention of her follows immediately the mention of a fallen woman.*

— *In the Bible, you mean.*

— *Yes. It hardly matters. It's the myth we care about.*

— *And they were lovers?*

— *Jesus and Mary Magdalene?* "She administered to Him of her substance," the Bible says. I'd like to think they were. But the farthest most scholars are willing to go is to say that she let Him be who He was as a man. Seems code to me for sex.

— *And why not?* she mused.

— *All we really know of her is that she was simply a woman not identified as being either a wife or a mother — interesting in itself. And, actually, she's touted now as being her own person. A woman important enough for Jesus to consider a sort of disciple. Important enough to be the first to carry the message of the Resurrection. That's the feminist interpretation, anyway.*

— *What was the reference to the seven devils?*

— *Intriguing to speculate. Luke says, "Mary, called Magdalene, from whom seven demons had gone out." We don't know. Was she afflicted with a malady such as epilepsy? Was it an emotional or spiritual or psychological malaise from which she needed respite? Was she simply mad?*

— *Your poems are exquisite in any event.*

On the port side, Linda saw Robert Seizek grasping the rails as if he were the captain of the ship. Perhaps he was studying the horizon as people do who are about to be seasick. She doubted he would remember his reading the night before, or even that she had been there. On the ferry's benches there were teenagers, underdressed for the outing, small silver rings catching the sun at their navels, despite the chill. Their presence reminded her that it was a Saturday. Each girl wore her hair parted in the middle and pulled tightly against the head into a ponytail. Her own hair dating her because she herself couldn't manage the current, sleeker style. The ponytails flicked in the wind like their namesakes.

— *Whatever happened to Peter?* Thomas asked, lighting a cigarette. The question took her by surprise.

— *I don't know exactly. He went back to London. Once when I was there, I looked in the phone book, but there was no one by that name in the city.*

Thomas nodded, as if the disappearance from one's life of someone to whom one had once been married were commonplace. The sunlight that was reflected from the water was unforgiving, showing every imperfection in his face, never perfect even in his youth. She didn't want to think about her own face and struggled against the urge to put herself in shadow.

— *Have you ever been back?* Thomas meant to Africa.

— No. I would have liked to take my children there. But it was always so expensive, and somehow I never did.

— It's a dangerous country now.

— We thought it was dangerous then.

— It was dangerous then. But it's worse now. I'm told tourists need armed guards.

Inexplicably, it was warmer on the island, and, after they had landed, they had to take off their coats. Thomas removed his blazer, and she found herself studying his hexagonal shoulders in his white shirt. She was conscious of her blouse, of the weight of her breasts, that familiar heaviness. Lately, she'd occasionally had the sensation of milk letting down, and thought it must be hormones run amok.

They walked up a street between wooden cottages, Thomas with his jacket folded over his arm, like a colonial improperly dressed in the heat. It might have been Nairobi or Lamu after all. She wore her coat over her shoulders, not wanting to imitate that masculine gesture.

— Was there a baby? she asked.

— False alarm.

For a moment, the street spun, and Linda struggled to reclaim her bearings.

— What an irony, she whispered.

— What?

72

She wouldn't, couldn't, tell him of the ordeal at the Catholic hospital. Of the hostility of the nuns. Of the kindness of the Belgian doctor who had declared the abortion a necessity. Nor of the undisguised malice of Sister Marie Francis, who had brought the fetus in a jar for Linda to see. She would not be the one to cause Thomas any more pain.

— *You must keep writing,* she said breathlessly after a time. *However difficult.*

For a time, Thomas was silent. *It's a struggle I lose more often than I win.*

— *Does time help?*

— *No.* He seemed to have the conviction of long experience.

They walked up a hill and left the road and sat upon a boulder. For a long moment, she put her head against her knees. When she looked up, her hands were still trembling. She was better dressed for this occasion than Thomas and was reminded that they'd missed, together, the great dressing-down of America. She'd never seen him in a T-shirt, and, not having seen it, could not imagine it. His dress shirt, she saw, was crisp, of excellent quality. She had a sudden longing, instantly disowned, to put her hand to his back. Desire sometimes came to her in the night, unannounced and unwanted — an intrusive presence in her bed.

73

It made her restless and fretful, causing her to realize with renewed finality what she'd lost.

(Vincent and she, lying face-to-face, the surface of their bodies touching at half a dozen places, like electrodes. Maria and Marcus out with friends on a Saturday afternoon; the luxury of time and sunlight on the bed. Vincent saying, his eyes dark and serious, as though he'd had an intimation of mortality, *I hope I die before you do.* Her eyes widening: this from Vincent, who was not a romantic. *I'd have to destroy the bed,* he'd said. *I couldn't bear it.*)

And she, who had once been a romantic, now slept alone in that very bed and couldn't imagine wanting to destroy it.

— *Why did you do it?* Thomas asked.

He was looking resolutely toward the skyline of the northern city. He would have been wanting to ask this question for years. Twenty-five of them, to be precise.

She could not, at first, answer him. They watched together a movie of pleasure boats and tankers going into port.

— *What difference did it make,* she asked. *In the end?*

He looked at her sharply. *We might have worked it out.*

— *How, exactly?*

74

— Maybe with time, we'd have found a way.

— You delude yourself.

— But the way it happened, he said. *You left no possibility.*

Perhaps he felt his daughter's death entitled him to be accusatory, she thought.

— I was drunk, she said. She who did not normally look for excuses.

— Well, yes, he said. *But it was more than that. You meant to hurt.*

— Who? she asked sharply. *Myself? Regina?*

— Regina, certainly.

But she hadn't meant to hurt; she'd meant only to convey what seemed like some great truth, as cosmic in its way as the laughter that would shake her years later. That she should have been so appallingly cruel had always shocked her.

— It was the most selfish moment of my life, Thomas. I can only think I must have wanted it over. All of it.

— Oh, Linda, he said. *Of course, I'm just as guilty as you. More so.*

Her face burned with the memory of that terrible evening. *It's hard to believe that anything could have meant so much,* she said.

She'd been drinking scotch straight up. Against a wall, Peter had stood, not comprehending at first what the fuss was for, but knowing something irretrievable had been said. He'd seemed a minor player then, only a witness to a larger drama. That, too, had been unforgivable on her part. Not to have seen how shamed he'd been. How good he'd been not to make himself the point. Until later that night, in the privacy of their hotel room, when he'd wept for her betrayal, so absolute, so public. And she'd sat mute beside him, feeling only terror that she'd lost her lover.

It was better not to remember.

— *A comedic writer would make of it a farce,* Thomas said. *The confessions in different rooms, and so on.*

— *The comedic writer might not be a Catholic,* she said.

They negotiated a path that ran between low scrub. The cottages were boarded up, waiting for summer owners to return. No cars were allowed on the island, and she wondered how such houses were built. Did walls and tiles and chimneys come across by boat?

— *Islands always remind me of the Isles of Shoals,* Thomas said. *A hellish place.*

It was a moment before she remembered and understood. The realization stopped her on the path.

He turned to see where she had got to. *It doesn't matter. I've been back there any number of times.*

It was a kind of bravery, she thought, the ability to look the worst in the face. Would there be a grave, a marker? How could such a sight be borne?

— *What happened to Regina?* she asked when they had walked on.

— *She's in Auckland now, and has two children.*

— *Auckland, New Zealand?*

— *We write occasionally. She works for a pharmaceutical company.*

The difference in air pressure between the disastrous and the mundane was making Linda light-headed.

— *Her husband owns a sheep farm,* Thomas added.

— *Not permanently scarred, then.*

Thomas began to roll his shirtsleeves. *Well, who would know?*

They stopped at a small white house with bright blue shutters that had been turned into a teahouse for those who had made the journey on foot across the island. Linda, surprised that she and Thomas had walked as far as they had, was perspiring inside her silk-like blouse, its synthetic material seeming considerably less clever a pur-

chase in the unseasonable heat. She untucked the blouse and let it billow over her
jeans. She felt a coolish breeze stir around
her midriff. Her hair was sticky at the back
of her neck, and she freed it with a swipe of
her hand.

— *Hungry?* Thomas asked.

The choices were a table with a cloth
inside the shop or a bare picnic table outside. They took the latter, anchoring nap-
kins with glasses and a ketchup bottle. They
sat side by side, looking out at the water,
which was brilliant apart from shadows cast
by a few scattered benign-looking clouds.
Thomas sat close to her, either deliberately
or having no awareness of private space.
Their arms touched here and there from
elbow to shoulder, a proximity that distracted her. She saw the interior of a car, a
Buick Skylark convertible, white with red
leather interior. She would not have known
the year. The top up, the windows steamed,
a policeman shining a flashlight through the
wet and opaque glass. Did every teenager of
that era have such a memory?

— *I'm supposed to be on a panel,* Thomas
said. *I'm playing hooky from an interview right
now.*

She did not have interviews, apart from a
phoner in the morning.

— *When is your panel?*

Thomas looked at his watch. *At four o'clock.*

— *There's a ferry at two-thirty,* she said. *What's it on, the panel?*

— *"The Phenomenal Ego of the Contemporary Poet."*

She looked at him and laughed.

He turned slightly and raised a foot to the picnic bench, leaning an arm on his knee. Thomas had always had trouble with leverage, had developed back problems, even as a boy. Something to do with the ratio of his height to the width of his bones. His slouch had always given him an appealing lankiness.

A teenage girl came shyly to the table to take their orders. The menu was limited: cheeseburgers, fish burgers, and hot dogs. Linda didn't trust the fish. She ordered a cheeseburger. *I haven't had one of those in years,* she said.

— *Really?* Thomas asked, genuinely surprised. *Did you ever have a lobster again?*

— *Oh sure. You more or less have to in Maine.*

She wanted to move apart from him, simply to dispel the tension. She was aware of physical flaws: her own, which didn't bear thinking about; nicks in the table; a support that was slightly loose; a crust of dried ketchup below the white plastic cap. Boats that had come around the lee side of the island were hitting boisterous waves, the spray explosive, jarring. She noticed that some sort of predatory birds seemed to be reproducing themselves even as she watched, creating a phalanx at a discreet distance, waiting for scraps. Canny birds with long memories.

— *If you want to talk about your daughter,* Linda said, understanding the risk of her invitation, *I'd love to hear about her.*

He sighed. *Actually, it would be a relief. That's one of the problems with not being with the mother of the child. There's no one to bring her alive. There was Rich, but we've exhausted his memories.*

Linda moved away, on the pretense of crossing her legs.

— *But what's to tell?* Thomas seemed defeated before he'd even begun.

She looked at his long back, the shirt disappearing into the crescent of his belt. For a moment, she longed to run her nails along the cloth, up and down his spine. She knew for a certainty that he would groan with pleasure, unable to help himself. Possibly he would bend his head forward, an invitation to scratch the top of his backbone.

Knowledge of another's physical pleasure never went away.

Thomas put his leg down and reached into a back pocket. He pulled out a leather wallet, worn pale at the seams.

— *This is Billie.*

Linda took the picture from him and studied it. Dark curls spilled across a face. Navy irises, as large as marbles, lay cosseted between extravagant and glossy lashes. A pink mouth, neither smiling nor frowning (though the head was tilted warily or fetchingly — it was hard to tell), had perfect shape. The skin was luminous, a pink blush in the plump cheeks. Not credible if seen in a painting, but in this photograph one had to believe in it. How had the picture not burned a hole through the worn leather of its case?

She glanced at Thomas, reassessing him. That Thomas was in the girl could not be denied, even though the father's beauty had been something quite different. Curiosity, bordering on a kind of jealousy, took hold of her as she tried to imagine the mother: Jean, her name was. Thomas's first wife, Regina, a woman she herself had once known, had been large and voluptuous, heavy with her sensuality, but somehow not a threat. Never a threat.

Linda shook her head. That she should be jealous of a woman who had lost everything.

— *That was taken in the backyard of our apartment in Cambridge.* Thomas was seemingly unable to look at the picture himself, though its worn edges spoke of many viewings.

Thomas glanced over at her, then quickly away, as if it were she who now needed the privacy. The cheeseburgers arrived, monumental irrelevance. She handed the photograph back to Thomas.

— *She was very bright,* Thomas said. *Well, all parents say that, don't they. And maybe they're right. Compared to us, I mean.*

Linda's appetite was gone. The cheeseburgers seemed obscene in their lakes of grease, soaking into the paper plates.

— *She could be stubborn. Jesus, could she be stubborn.* Thomas smiled at a memory he did not divulge. *And oddly brave. She wouldn't cry when hurt. Though she could certainly whine when she wanted something.*

— *They all do.*

Thomas ate his cheeseburger, holding his tie as he did so. Well, he'd have to eat, wouldn't he? Linda thought. Otherwise, he'd have starved to death years ago. He glanced at her untouched plate, but said nothing.

— *She was a good little athlete,* Thomas said. *I used to take a plastic lawn chair and sit and watch her T-ball games. Most of the kids would be in the outfield picking dandelions. Some would just sit down.* He laughed.

Linda smiled. *I remember those. Someone would hit a ball to the outfield and all the kids would run to get it.*

— *They say it would have lasted less than a minute. The drowning. A child gulps in water more quickly than an adult. And it was always possible she was knocked unconscious. I've spent years praying for that. That it was a blow and not a drowning. Amazing, isn't it? Hundreds of hours of prayer just to spare her that one minute.*

Not amazing, Linda thought. She'd have done the same.

— *It's awful to think I'm letting go,* he said. *And I am. I don't remember as much as I used to. I don't even remember what I don't remember.*

She touched him then, on the arm. It would have been inhuman not to. *There are just no words, Thomas.*

— *No, there aren't, and isn't that ironic? We who thought we had all the words. Jean, with her camera, has made us irrelevant.*

A motorboat with a young blond woman at the helm sped around the corner. The girl

83

seemed exuberant with her own beauty and the first warm day of the season.

Thomas bent his head slightly forward. *Scratch up near my shoulders,* he said.

On the way to the ferry, Thomas, who was either exceptionally hot or desiring to be cleansed, went into the water. Linda sat on a hillock and watched the way he dove in and stood, staggering with the shock of the cold, shaking his head like a dog, hiking his boxers up to his waist. They hung low on his thighs when he came out and molded his genitals, which had grown longer in the intervening years.

— *It's like electric shock therapy,* Thomas reported as he used his shirt to dry himself.

He shivered on the ferry, despite his jacket. Later they would learn that the lake was polluted. He held his shirt in a ball. She stood near to him to warm him, but the shiver came from deep within and would not be appeased. He seemed oblivious to curious stares, in the boat and at the entrance to the hotel, his hair dried into a comical sculpture by the water and the ferry breezes. He got out at her floor and accompanied her to her room, looking for all the world like a refugee from a disaster (and of course he was, she thought). He stood at the door and finger-combed his hair.

— *I won't ask you in.* She meant it, actually, as a kind of joke, as if they had been on a date. But Thomas, as ever, took her seriously.

— *What's the harm?*

— *What's the harm?* Linda asked, incredulous.

— *Antecedents,* he said. *Does this exist on its own, or because of what went before?*

— *Because of what went before, I should think.*

He studied her. *What large drama, do you suppose, will part us this time?*

— *There doesn't have to be any drama, Thomas. We're too old for drama.*

He turned to leave, then stopped. *Magdalene,* he said.

The name, the old name. Nearly an endearment.

Against her better judgment, she looked for evidence of others before her and found it in a single hair, disturbingly pubic, on the white tile beneath the sink. She was farsighted now and could blur her reflection in the mirror, and sometimes she did that if she was in a hurry. But today, she wanted sight: dispassionate and objective.

She unbuttoned her blouse in the way that a woman who is not being watched will do, unzipped her jeans, and kicked them from her feet. The underwear, unmatched, could stay. She put her hands on her hips and looked into the mirror. She did not like what she saw.

She was what was never possible: a fifty-two-year-old woman with thinning blond hair; no, not even that, not blond, but rather no color, a gray if you will, closer to invisible. Invisible at the roots and spreading out to a dirty gold that did not exist in nature. She examined squarish hips and a thickening waist that just a year ago she'd been convinced was only temporary. She'd read about girls who thought they were too fat when in fact they were frighteningly thin (well, Maria's friend Charlotte had been one); whereas she, Linda, thought she was in general a thin woman when in reality she was overweight. And of course there were her hands, the skin long roughened, announcing her age and then some.

She turned abruptly away from the mirror, a peevish physician annoyed by his patient. She took the terrycloth hotel robe from its hook and meant to put it on, but instead she froze with it in her arms.

Was she mad? What had she been thinking? No one would see her body. So why the lover's examination?

She tried her daughter again, this time on Maria's cell phone. Though Linda had offered to pay for the calls, Maria had refused, her independence, even in the face of impressive student loans, no surprise. Whereas Marcus. Marcus needed to be taken care of, had developed charm to compensate for common sense, a nascent charisma to attract someone who might watch out for him. Such as David, Marcus's lover, who was, at times, excessively protective, monitoring Marcus's eating habits and sleep in a way she herself hadn't done in years. Marcus was brilliant and would never use it; indeed, would make a point of denying this advantage.

Linda lay back on the bed, holding the telephone, hoping her daughter would answer and smiling when she did. *Is this a bad time?* Linda asked.

— *No, I'm finishing lab reports.* Maria was truly happiest when doing two things at once. *How are you?*

— *I'm at a writers' festival,* Linda said. And quickly thought, One needn't tell the truth. The truth being that she'd become unhinged by the unexpected.

The merits of the northern city were discussed.

— *I was just thinking about your father,* Linda added. A partial truth, though it had not been thoughts of Vincent that had unhinged her. And for that she felt a disloyal pang.

— *You're missing him,* Maria said.

Linda could see herself in the mirror over the dresser. She looked better in the softer light of the bedroom — smaller, possibly even desirable in the plush hotel robe. *Will you get any time off this summer?* Linda asked.

— A week. Maybe ten days if I'm lucky.

— Could I talk you into coming up to Maine?

There was a second's hesitation, long enough to forfeit plans already made or hoped for. Linda heard the pause and was annoyed with herself for having asked. She remembered when Maria and Marcus had been children and had begged for rides downtown or had hoped to invite friends to the house. And her own moment's pause while parental agendas had been consulted and discarded. *Of course I can. Of course I will.* When had nature flipped the balance, causing the parent to ask the favor of the child? At twenty? At twenty-two?

— Just for a few days, Linda said immediately, qualifying her request. *I don't expect you to give up your entire vacation.*

— No, I'd love to come. To her credit, Maria sounded enthusiastic. *We'll see about the dates.*

But Linda would release her daughter from this promise; release her to her own young life. *Are you getting any sleep?* the mother asked.

Static stole her daughter's answer. Linda rolled over, dragging the phone off the nightstand. She pulled it up by the cord. One day Maria would be a pediatric cardiologist. Staggering to think of that. Staggering for Linda, who'd been the first in her family ever to go to college.

— *I've met someone,* Maria said, apparently for the second time.

For a moment, Linda was confused, afraid the words had issued from her own mouth.

— *Tell me about him.*

— *He's a resident. His name is Steven.*

An image formed in Linda's mind, doubtless incorrect, doubtless composed of other Stevens, though she couldn't think of any at the moment. *And you like him,* Linda said cautiously.

Another pause on Maria's part, possibly for emphasis. *I do. He's very good-looking.*

— *That counts,* Linda said, never one to dismiss beauty in a man.

— *Maybe I'll bring him to Maine with me.*

And Linda thought, This is serious.

— *What were you remembering about Dad?* Maria asked.

— *About his white shirts. And the way they fit across his shoulders.*

The daughter was silent in the face of a memory too private for a child to share. *Are there people at the festival you know?* she asked instead.

— *I do now,* Linda said, wishing to dispel the sense of being needy.

— *Good,* Maria said, unburdened. *I'd better go. If I don't have these lab reports done by six, the resident will kill me.*

Linda doubted that, though the sacrifice required of someone wishing to be a doctor was staggering. Mistakes were made from lack of sleep. One day Maria, in a fit of tears, had confessed her own.

Linda put the phone down, disconcerted by the mix of truth and lies in a conversation with a child. More lies than truth this time, though it had often been so. One could not prepare a child for the future; such knowledge might be intolerable.

The quiet in the room was absolute. Even the air-conditioning had stopped its hum. It was as though all traffic had suddenly ceased, all radios rendered silent. What time was it? Nearly four? She imagined people lining city streets in homage to the passing of some great hero.

She went out into the sunshine only to retreat from it. In this city, she had been told, there were shops that she should visit (the exchange rate was very good), but when she entered a famous department store, she was saddened by the sight of people buying things to make them happier, or thinner, or impervious to death. She fingered a silk scarf and ran her hand along the shoulder pads of suits, neatly aligned with spaces in between to indicate best quality. She admired a negligee and remembered nights with other negligees, and still the sadness, that cloud, was not swept away. She went up the escalator, up and up, preferring the concrete evidence of floors to the free flight of elevators. She saw a lemon sweater with delicate edging in Children's and tried to think of anyone she knew with a baby, and then reflected that it would have to be a grandchild now. She stood at an entrance to a café, ravenous and impatient to be seated, but when she had been shown to her table, she felt the store to be suddenly airless. She could smell the chemicals in the clothes as she fled, wafting off Men's Shirts in fumes. What had she done? She had raised a family. She would not be remembered. She was deteriorating daily. She could not let her body be seen. She would never sit unclothed upon a beach. Some things could not be gotten back. Most things could not be gotten back. Even her images of Vincent were fading: he was more substantial now in photographs than he was in her memories, like children are after they have grown.

She went outside, supremely conscious of herself as a middle-aged woman in a sensible raincoat despite the heat. Men, as if they had been programmed, did not turn their heads. Whereas Vincent, her admirer, her lover, had pronounced her beautiful even on the morning he had died.

— *You're beautiful,* he'd said.

— *I'm fifty. No one is beautiful at fifty.*

— *You surprise me. Of course you're wrong.*

Amazing how one yearned to be called beautiful, how much the single word could please. She saw a couple, in expensive clothing, arguing as they walked. He had blond hair and a beard and moved inches ahead of his wife, while she gestured angrily and said, *I can't believe you said that.* He kept his hands in his pockets and didn't answer her. He would win the argument, Linda thought, with silence.

She stood before a building of Gothic spires and darkened stones, though she supposed she would never truly be able to regard a Catholic church as just a building. Its authenticity beckoned between the excess of the smart boutiques on either side. (Yet weren't the spires evidence of excess in themselves?) She entered a musty narthex and remembered that as a child she had refused to believe the scent a product simply of mold and dust; instead, she'd been convinced that it was the holy water in the font that had produced that somewhat frightening smell. She was momentarily embarrassed to interrupt a Mass in progress (she who had known Saturday church only for Confession), and she moved quietly to the pews, not genuflecting, not crossing herself, though her body wanted to from habit.

The interior cooled the perspiration at the back of her neck. She let her coat slide from her shoulders and was glad she did not have crinkly and noisy packages. It had not been so long that the words were unfamiliar to her, but still it had been years, and so she listened to the liturgy with small mental exclamations of surprise. And as she did, she had a startling thought: her own poetry mimicked those cadences! How had she not noticed this before? How had someone else, a critic perhaps, not have noticed this as well? The similar rhythms could not be missed. It felt a stunning discovery, like unearthing a letter that explained one's childhood after all.

An older woman in front of her was crying copiously (what grief or sin had caused such tears?), but Linda could not see the features of the other parishioners, ten pews up or more. She said a quick prayer for Marcus, who needed it the most, and when she was finished, she glanced up at the darkened stained glass (so little sunlight between the tall buildings on either side) searching for a likeness of Mary Magdalene. She found John the Baptist and a tableau of the Last Supper, but not the woman she was looking for.

She administered to Him of her substance.

And then, as she had nearly always done in church years ago, she let her mind drift. And with the drifting, she saw images. When she'd been a girl, the images had begun, say, with a mental picture of the cherry tree in the backyard, then would segue to a glass of cherry Coke, and then would find their way to the knee and leg of a boy she had once seen at the diner in a leather jacket ordering a cherry Coke. But that afternoon, she saw faces (Vincent's and Thomas's) and then rumpled bed-clothes (from Vincent and her on the day he had died) and then a small, neat package of laundered linens from Belmont Laundry that had sat upon a chair in her bedroom unopened for months, each image leading to the other as if by a fine thread, the thread invisible, the connections both supple and labyrinthine. The images were sometimes disturbing and at other times pleasing to her, evidence of a life lived, though some memories attested only to foolishness, appalling naïveté.

But then an unbidden and unwanted image sneaked in amongst the others almost before she'd realized it, and instantly she tried to ward it off. She felt it dragging her down, but she could not, for the moment, pull away. She heard a muffled sound — a word? No, more a gasp or a whisper, a man's mouth pressed into the bone of her shoulder, his weight heavy on her thigh. Had he hurt himself, or was this (more likely) yet another utterance in the new language he was teaching her, that strange dialect that had no vocabulary or sentences, but seemed, all the same, full of meaning — full of need and mute pleadings and silent, if extraordinary, gratitude?

Her dress, pale blue, was dry upon her skin and floated like tissue over the hollow of her belly. The sun was on the daybed and on her face. It would be ten or ten-thirty in the morning.

The bristles of his short beard were not soft but instead were prickly like the fur of the thistles that grew in the vacant lot at the end of the block. After the first time, when she, dazed as if by the noonday sun, had examined herself in the mirror, she'd seen that his beard had rubbed the thin skin at the base of her collarbone a shiny pink; and that soreness combined with the other, had been a reminder, all that day and the next, of the fearful thing that had happened to her. But she was not afraid. Not of the man, who seemed if not entirely irrelevant, then not what occupied her mind; and not of the event itself, which she had allowed to happen four times. For something within her welcomed — indeed, was almost glad for — these extraordinary attentions.

She heard another nonword then, also precise in its meaning. He wanted at her chest and was even now fumbling with the buttons of her dress and pushing aside the cloth. He fastened his mouth on her breast, which was new and always changing now. She could not see his face and did not want to — his eyes squeezed shut, the neck wrinkled, the grime caught in the creases. For the thing that they were doing was best done in private, one's own face turned away, the eyes averted.

Her body loosened, and there was a fluttering in her belly. She was moist between her legs, fat there as she was not elsewhere. He hitched himself higher up on her body and struggled for a moment with her skirt. The sucking was like being bled, she thought, and she remembered pictures of leeches covered with bell jars, the glass making perfect circular welts on a woman's back. He pushed a finger inside her, then two, more hurried now, even somewhat frantic. She wondered if it would be like running a finger around the slippery insides of a narrow jar. A fingernail caught on her skin and she flinched, but he seemed not to notice. And now it was not his finger, but the other thing (she had never said the word aloud), and she understood that soon it would be over.

She craned her neck so that she could see through the window at the head of the daybed. A large bird sat motionless on the roof of the house next door. The man finished, as he always did, with a convulsive shudder and a slight hiccup. And when he pulled away, she felt a bit of the wetness trickle out of her, a small spill of fluid upon her thigh. She watched him as he sat at the end of the bed, white and shocky all about his eyes. He zipped his pants and laced up his shoes.

She had no tender word from him, nor did she want one. He said only when he stood, "Don't tell anyone what we did here."

As if she would. As if she would.

In the pew, Linda began to tremble violently from the memory, not retrieved in years, until words — reassuring and comforting — allowed her to be still. It wasn't her doing, she told herself. And it hadn't ruined her life. Life was more than childhood violations, childhood victories. Life was work and loving someone else and having babies; life was Vincent and Marcus and Maria. But as soon as she had the thought, *Maria,* Linda began to tremble again. Seen from the eyes of a mother, the episode was inexcusable and terrifying. All she had to do was imagine Maria on the daybed, and she was filled with fury. Beside her, people filed slowly along the aisle, some glancing in her direction. The Mass was over, and she hadn't noticed.

She took a long breath and slowly let it out. Vincent had been antidote to memory. Now, without him, was she losing that protection? And why that shameful image after so long a time?

She returned to her room, needing food and a cup of tea, but the message light was flashing. Sitting at the edge of the bed, her coat still on, she composed questions and worded probable replies: *How did your panel go? Dinner? Are you sure? Do you think the others would mind?* But when she listened to the message, she heard that it wasn't Thomas who had rung, but rather David, Marcus's lover, asking her to call him as soon as she got in. Proximity to another's grief made her panicky as she misdialed the number twice, saying *Shit* before she got it right. How long had she been gone from the room? One hour? Two hours?

— *Marcus has been arrested for drunk driving.* The lover spoke without preamble.

Linda leaned forward, as if she had not heard correctly. *When?*

— *Early this morning. Around five a.m.*

Instinctively, Linda looked at her watch. They had waited twelve hours to tell her.

— *And there was an accident,* David added.

— *Oh God,* Linda said, incapable of words of more than one syllable. *Was he hurt?*

— *He's banged his knee up pretty bad. He's had an x-ray. They say he bruised some cartilage.*

— *Was anyone else hurt?* Linda asked quickly, already terrified of the reply.

— *No.*

She sighed with relief. And to think that she had just said a prayer for Marcus. *Is he there? Can I talk to him?*

One could not mistake the deliberate pause at the other end. She imagined David

— Marcus's height, but stockier; reddish hair and pale eyes; something soft around the edges though his clothes were beautifully tailored — standing in the kitchen of their Brookline apartment. Or was he with her son in the bedroom?

— *Mrs. Fallon,* David said (David, who seemed incapable of calling her Linda, even after repeated invitations to do so; David, who'd said he couldn't read poetry and hoped she didn't mind), *I think Marcus and I need to handle this together.*

Linda, dismissed, was silent.

— *Of course,* David said immediately, softening the blow, *if the knee thing gets serious, I'll call you right away.*

Linda was surprised she did not feel more resentful than she did.

— *And I think,* David added with another pause, *I think we need to discuss the possibility that Marcus should go into rehab.*

— *Rehab? You mean for being drunk? Is that really necessary?*

— *I'm afraid it is. Marcus has been drinking for days. He missed my concert last night. He passed out and never woke up until I came home. We had a huge fight, and he took off. He called me from the Nashua jail this morning.*

— *Nashua? New Hampshire? What was he doing there?*

101

— I'm not sure he really knows.

Oh Marcus, Linda thought. Oh my poor, poor Marcus. She had seen him drunk at Thanksgiving and again at Christmas, but she hadn't quite realized. Or had she simply refused to see?

— Are you thinking of an intervention? Is that what they call it?

— I don't think that will be necessary, David said thoughtfully, indicating that he had considered it. *At least, I hope not. He just needs a kick in the pants. And he got it in Nashua. He's pretty scared.*

— Do you have any place in mind?

— I'm not sure. I'll have to make some calls. They say Brattleboro is the best.

Linda recoiled at the thought of her son in an institution. She pressed her lips together. If it was as bad as David had said — and of course it was; Marcus had had an accident — what more proof did a mother need?

— I really would like to talk to Marcus, she said again.

— He's sleeping, David said. *They gave him something at the hospital.*

— I see. She took a breath to control her anger. It was unnatural to push a mother away from her cub. Though, to be fair, Marcus was hardly a cub.

— If it's as bad as you say, the past months

must have been difficult for you, Linda said, trying to be generous.

— *I love him.*

The statement, too bald, was like a naked man in the street, something that should be clothed. Vincent's death had freed Marcus. Within a month, he'd told his mother and his sister he was gay. Within the year, he'd found David.

— *I had no idea he was so unhappy.*

— *I don't know how much happiness has to do with it.*

What makes an alcoholic? Linda wondered. Poor mothering? Bad genes? A fatal gene, commonly carried in Irish blood? She'd hardly known her father, but she had known her uncles, alternately morose or exuberant, sometimes brutish. And to think how smug she'd once been, gloating inwardly over the success of her children: Maria at Harvard, now a medical student at Johns Hopkins; and Marcus at Brown, now in graduate school at Boston University. How often had she casually insinuated those prestigious names in conversation? And now there would be this to say: My son is an alcoholic. *My son, Marcus, is an alcoholic.*

Was she an alcoholic as well? All her own drinking put now in a different perspective.

— *The car's totaled,* David said. *They towed it.* Another pause. *He'll lose his license.*

— *Oh, I know he will.* Linda stifled an incipient wail. *We need to get a lawyer.*

And too late, she heard the *we.*

David waited patiently, parent to the parent now. *We have one, Mrs. Fallon. A friend of ours. He's very good.*

On the bed, Linda put a hand to her brow, clammy with the news. *You'll let me know.* Trying to keep hysteria from her voice. *You'll let me know how he is and what you've done. What you've decided.*

She was certain that she heard a sigh. *Of course I will,* David said.

Linda lay back on the bed. Marcus was suffering — with shame and a battered knee. And would suffer worse, in court and certainly in rehabilitation, about which she knew nothing. Was rehab physically painful? Was it excruciatingly dull? She tried to recall all the times she had seen Marcus drinking. There had been beer in his refrigerator at Brown. At the beach, he would sometimes start with gin and tonics at three o'clock. She'd thought then that the drinking had been festive and celebratory, merely summer playfulness. But she had known, hadn't she? She'd *known.* And had forgiven her son even before the word *problem* had had a chance to register, almost as quickly as she'd tried to adjust her expectations when she'd learned that he was gay. And she'd known then, too. Of course she had.

Despair and irritation grew in equal measure. She looked around at the empty room, its luxury fading with this news from home. She stood up from the bed and began to pace, her arms crossed over her chest. She talked to herself, and to Marcus and to Vincent, pale imitations of what was needed. She paced until she had exhausted all her words and thought, I have to leave this room. Or I'll go mad.

The configuration of the hospitality suite seemed different when she entered late into the event; it was nearly time to assemble for dinner. The noise was louder than it had been the night before — more drinking on the last night of the festival? No, it was something else: the festive temperature in the room had been raised a degree or two with a sense of importance that had previously been missing. There was a woman, diminutive and dun-colored, in the center of the largest group. A flashbulb popped, and Linda strained to see, but felt disinclined to join the crowd, a natural diffidence taking precedence over curiosity. She went to the bar and ordered a beer, but then remembered Marcus and changed her mind. She ate instead, cheese and crackers, pickles from a side dish. Her mouth was full of Brie when the Australian, now neglected, appeared at her side and addressed her.

— *You've heard the news.*

— *What news?* She dabbed at her mouth with a napkin.

He looked the healthiest of anyone in the room: fit and tanned — more like someone who wrestled with horses for a living, not with words. It would be fall now in his own country.

The news did indeed take her by surprise: while she and Thomas had been on the ferry, a diminutive, dun-colored woman had won a prestigious prize.

— *Festival lucked out, I'd say,* the Australian offered pleasantly. Linda turned and noticed, as she had not before, the bottles of champagne in buckets on the table.

— *I'm not sure I've ever heard of her.*

— *You're not alone. Plucked from obscurity. She's meant to be very good, I'm told. Well, she would be, wouldn't she? I'd venture there aren't two people in the room who've read her.*

Linda shifted to get a better view. There were more photographers now, asking others to move apart.

— *She uses "fuck" a lot,* the Australian said.

A memory was triggered. Maybe she had read this poet after all. *It's the Age of Fuck,* Linda said, though she herself did not use the word.

— *There are so many flowers already in her room, she's had to ask the bellman to take them down to the front desk.*

Linda felt a touch of envy. She and the Australian smiled, each knowing what the other felt. One could not admit to envy, but one could silently acknowledge it. It would be disingenuous not to.

The Australian's smile faded. Beside her, Linda sensed a bulky presence.

— *Too bad your boy didn't get the prize.* Robert Seizek's lower lip was fat and wet, his sibilants loose and threatening.

— *He's not mine, and he's not a boy,* Linda said of Thomas.

— *Odd thing is,* said the Australian, *there weren't a dozen people at her reading last night. Now they're trying to get her to do a special appearance tonight.*

— *I'm pleased for her,* Linda said, trying to ignore Seizek.

— *She's a librarian in her day job. From Michigan.* The Australian collaborating.

— You're pretty tight with Thomas Janes, Seizek said too loudly, unwilling to be dismissed.

Anger, so successfully tamped just minutes ago, stretched its limbs inside her chest — a caged animal to Seizek's lion. She turned to face him and was daunted (only momentarily) by his excessively large head.

— Thomas Janes has not published any work in years. She spoke in as controlled a voice as she could manage. *And therefore cannot even have come to the attention of any prize judges. Though I'm sure if you were at his reading last night, you'll agree that future publications might win prizes in any number of countries.*

— And if you were at Mr. Janes's panel this afternoon, Seizek said, not missing a beat, *I'm sure you'll agree with me that your boy made a perfect ass of himself.*

Linda glanced at the Australian, who looked away.

She knew that she was behaving like a schoolgirl whose friend had been insulted on the playground. But she couldn't leave now; she was in too deep.

— I for one, Linda said, *would rather have the brilliant words of a man who may or may not have embarrassed himself in public than the watered-down prose of a drunken would-be*

novelist who seems to be itching for a fight I will not give him.

And Seizek said, *sotto voce,* so that only she could hear, thus trumping her in battle etiquette as well, *I didn't know such fire could issue forth from someone whose bland exterior is matched only by the dreariness of her poetry. I suppose there are women who read this stuff? The kind of women who regularly read romance novels, I should have thought. I suppose there might be good money in it? No?*

Linda matched his *sotto voce. Don't fuck with me,* she said, trying the word on a stranger.

Seizek looked startled, even if only for an instant; Linda counted it as a victory, nevertheless. She glanced again at the Australian.

With deliberately slow movements, so as not to appear to be fleeing, Linda turned and made her way to the door.

She liked the word, she thought as she left the room. It sounded good. It *felt* good.

She took out the rest of her anger on the elevator button, which seemed to retaliate by refusing to fetch a car. An elderly couple came and stood beside her. From a room somewhere in the hallway could be heard the sounds of lovemaking: a woman's rhythmic grunts, strenuous and lengthy.

The elderly couple were rigid with embarrassment. Linda felt for them and wished a clever remark would come to her to put the couple at ease, but instead, their embarrassment became infectious. Moving toward the stairs, she thought, What reservoir of guilt has Thomas tapped?

Vincent's apartment in Boston was unlike anything she had ever seen before — unadorned and architectural, like a schoolroom, its centerpiece a draftsman's table that cranked up to different angles with a winch. He had black-and-white photographs on the walls, some of his prodigious family (it would be months before she learned all their names), others of windows that had captured his imagination: austere colonial twelve-over-twelves; vast, complex fanlights set deeply into brick; simple sidelights beside a paneled door. His rooms were clean and masculine, curiously adult and oddly Calvinist in their sunny moral rectitude. Sometimes, when he was gone for brief periods on weekends, she would sit at his draftsman's table with a pad of paper and a pen and write simple paragraphs that functioned as letters to herself, letters that Vincent would never see. He did not know her as troubled, for he had met her laughing; and she discovered that she had no desire to taint the happiness she'd found with him with sordid stories of her recent past. And consequently — and partly as a result of expectation — she rose to his image of herself: sensible and practical (which was largely true), drowsy and easy in bed, and prone to laugh at the foibles of others and of herself. The first night he took her back to his apartment, he made her a meal — spaghetti with red gravy — impressing upon her the fact that he was Italian to her Irish. The sauce was smooth and thick and seemed to have little to do with any tomatoes she had ever seen or eaten. Yet, she, who had been carelessly starving herself, ate ravenously, furthering the impression that she was a woman of appetite, an impression that was not altered in bed when she (who had been starved there as well) responded to her new lover with an almost animal greed. (Was it Vincent's sleek pelt that made her think of seals?) And it was not a lie, this presentation of herself as healthy, for with Vincent she wanted to be and therefore was. And she thought it was probably not so unusual to be a different person with a different man, for all parts were authentically within, waiting to be coaxed out by one person or another, by one set of circumstances or another, and it pleased her to make this discovery. So much so that when, at the end of that first glorious weekend together, she returned to her rooms on Fairfield, she recoiled from the sight of the bathtub on its platform, the single Melamine plate on the dish rack. And immediately she went out and bought more dishes to put in the drainer and a Marimekko spread for her bed, so as not to frighten Vincent away, nor allow herself to be sucked back in. When Vincent first came and stood in the doorway of her apartment and looked around, he fit the surroundings to suit the person he knew (like designing a house, she later thought, only in reverse). And she, too, began to see them differently as well — as unadorned rather than bereft.

Maria had come easily, but Marcus (prophetically) with painful difficulty. By then they were living in a house in Belmont that challenged Vincent at every corner with its banal design and shoddy workmanship. (Vincent, the son of a contractor, was a man who knew improperly mitered trim when he saw it.) Linda wasn't teaching, and Vincent had started an architectural practice of his own, sinking whatever money he made back into the business (as was right, she thought), leaving them little at home; and if they had any stressful times together, it was then, when babies and unpaid bills stole their good tempers. But mostly, she remembered those early years as good ones. Sitting in their small backyard in Belmont (the grill, the swing set, the plastic turtle pool), and watching Vincent plant tomatoes with the children, she would be filled with amazement that, against all the odds, this had been given to her, that she and Vincent had made this family. She could not imagine what would have become of her had she not, for she saw the alternative as only a long, throbbing headache from which there would have been little relief.

One morning, when Marcus was sleeping and Maria was at Montessori, Linda sat down at the kitchen table and wrote not a letter to herself, but a poem, another kind of letter. The poem was about windows and children and panes of glass and small muffled voices, and she found over the next few days that when she wrote and reworked the images and phrases, time passed differently, lurching ahead, so that she was often startled to look up at the clock and realize she was late to pick up Maria or that Marcus had slept too long. Her imagination began to hum, and even when she was not writing, she found herself jotting down metered lines and strange word pairings; and in general she was preoccupied. So much so that Vincent noticed and said so, and she, who for months had written in secret, got out her sheaf of papers and showed them to him. She was shredded with worry while he read them, for they revealed a side of Linda that Vincent was not familiar with and might not want to know (worse still, he might be curious about who had known this Linda, for some of the poems were about Thomas, even when they seemingly weren't). But Vincent didn't ask, and instead said he thought they were very fine; and he seemed genuinely impressed that his wife had secretly harbored this talent he'd known nothing about. All of which was a gift to her, for she wrote with redoubled energy, and not just when the children were away or asleep, but late into the night, pouring words onto paper and reshaping them into small objects one could hold in the mind. And Vincent never said, *Don't write these words about another man* (or even later, about himself), thus freeing her from the most potent censorship there is, the fear of hurting others.

She joined a poetry workshop at night and was stupefied (and secretly heartened) by the dull and overly confessional work of those around her. Emboldened by this, she sent out her first contributions to small literary journals, all of which, in the early months, rejected her work (once misdirecting another's letter to her, so that she was able to quip that they'd started rejecting poems she hadn't even written). To ward off a feeling of failure, she joked that she could wallpaper her bathroom with rejection slips, which she chose to see not as messages to stop, but rather as tickets to the game. Until one afternoon she received a letter from an editor who liked a poem and said he would publish it. He couldn't pay her anything, he added, but he hoped she would give him the honor of being the first to put that particular verse into print. Far from minding the lack of payment, Linda was too thrilled to speak; and when Vincent came home that night, she was still clutching the letter to her breast. Months later, when a poem was accepted by a magazine that did pay, Linda and Vincent celebrated by going out to dinner, Vincent noting that the magazine's check covered the cocktails.

After that, the poems came like water, flooding the bedroom in which she wrote. It was as though she had been pent up, and years of poems had needed to pass through her. Her poetry was printed with some regularity (listing prior publications had a synergistic effect), and when Maria was twelve, her first editor, with whom she now warmly corresponded, wrote to say that he was moving to a publishing house in New York and would she consider allowing him to put out a volume of her verse?

— *You've done it,* Vincent said when she called him at work to tell him.

— *I think I've just begun,* she said.

All this she was remembering as she made her way down the hotel stairs. She opened the door off the stairwell (which reeked of cigarette smoke; chambermaids on their breaks?), not certain of the number of Thomas's room. She thought it was on the seventh floor; had Thomas said 736? But she might be confusing that number with another, earlier, hotel room of her own. She could, she realized, simply go back to her room and call. No, that wouldn't do. She wanted to see Thomas, to speak to him. She knocked at 736, a confident knock, though she braced herself for a baffled, half-dressed businessman appearing to tell a chambermaid that no, he didn't need turn-down service. A tall woman in heels and pearls passed her in the hallway and wouldn't meet her eyes: would Linda seem a woman who had been locked out of her room by an angry husband? Linda rapped again, but still there was no response. Fumbling in her purse, she found a tiny pad of paper and a space pen. These missives, she thought, as she wrote — such old habits, such echoes.

— *My son is an alcoholic,* she wrote. *And what is the antecedent for that?*

Once again, she let herself be herded onto a bus and deposited at a restaurant — this time Japanese, the only food she didn't care for, having never developed a taste for sushi or for vegetables coated with flour and grease. Still, eating out was better than sitting alone in her hotel room and having to resist the temptation to call either Marcus or Thomas, though she was intensely curious as to where each was exactly. Had Marcus gone to Brattleboro already? Had Thomas left for home? She wanted to ask Mary Ndegwa, with whom she ate dinner, if she knew what Thomas had done during his panel to so scandalize an audience she would have said was scandal-proof; but she worried that such a query might bring on a discussion of Thomas's history, which she did not want to address just then. Mary

118

Ndegwa and she, though they had never formally met, had a shared history and passed a nostalgic meal together, Linda enjoying the evocative rhythms of the poet's Kikuyu accent even as they discussed her husband's release from detention, the banning of her own work in Kenya, the horrendous aftermath of the elections of 1997, and the terrible bombing at the American embassy. Kenya was more dangerous as well, Mary Ndegwa told Linda, and though Linda chose to remember the shimmering green tea plantations of the Highlands and the white dhows of Lamu, she could as well recall the great-coated askaris with their pangas and the horrifying cardboard shanty towns of Nairobi. *You must return,* Mary Ndegwa said. *You have been lost for too long.* The African woman laughed suddenly, hiding the gap between her teeth with her hand. Mary Ndegwa, as always, found Americans mysteriously hilarious.

During dinner, Linda noted that Seizek kept his distance, which pleased her inordinately; and the Australian smiled in her direction twice, conspiracy having made them something more than just acquaintances. There was a moment, during the interminably long dinner (which hurt her knees, unused as she was to sitting cross-legged on the floor), when she mused that had she been available for a brief affair, she might have had one with the cowboyish novelist. But brief affairs had never appealed to her (so little investment, despite the momentary reward; and it was the investment that mattered, was it not?), and then she thought about the word *available* and pondered its meaning: Was she truly not available? And if not, to whom or what was she engaged? To the memory of Vincent? To her history with Thomas? To herself as sole proprietor of her own body?

The returning bus made several stops, and only she and an elderly Canadian biographer disembarked at the hotel, Linda slightly (and shamefully) uncomfortable with the association with greater age; and perhaps she emerged from the bus with a slightly jauntier step than was warranted.

He was sitting in a chair facing the entrance when she moved through the revolving door. He stood and they faced each other for an awkward second, a second during which they might easily have embraced. But having missed the moment, now could not. Behind them, the revolving door spun with couples dressed for a Saturday night.

— *I know this is highly inappropriate,* Thomas said. *But would you like a drink?*

— *Yes,* she said simply. *I'd like that very much.*

The mahogany was shiny, without fingerprints. Linda noted white linen cloths stacked high upon a shelf. The bartender was a pro, his movements long practiced, as fluid as a dancer's. He made a sparkling martini that was like a package she did not want to ruin by opening. She'd thought, briefly, about ordering a scotch, for old times' sake, but she knew that she could no longer stomach the smoky drink, and she marveled, as she sat there, at how, years ago, she'd drunk them down like orange juice. (All her own drinking seen now in perspective. . . .) Men, sitting at the bar, appraised her as she entered with Thomas; but then she wondered if their glances were, in fact, directed at her at all: might it not be Thomas who had caught their eye? (The men wouldn't even know they'd looked, she thought, the need to look so ingrained.)

— *You've had a haircut,* she said to him with her own appraisal.

He rubbed the short gray bristles, unused to the feel of his own head.

— *It's cute,* she said. *Even in high school you didn't have a crew cut.*

— *I thought you'd like me more,* he said.

— *You want me to like you more?* Daring to flirt a bit.

— *I do, as a matter of fact.*

Together, as was expected, they clinked glasses.

— *Would you like to talk about your son?*

— *In a while,* she said. *I need a minute. Of nothing.*

Thomas, who would understand needing minutes of nothing, sat beside her on a stool. They exchanged glances in the mirror over the bar.

— *You'd think that after all this time, your aunt would forgive you,* Thomas said. *Isn't that what the Catholic Church teaches? Forgiveness?*

— *She goes to Mass. I don't know that she necessarily forgives.*

Her aunt spent her days in a cramped and darkened room the family had always called the den, sitting on a sofa upholstered in a scratchy plaid fabric. Two windows were draped with lace curtains; the TV was the centerpiece of the room. A bag of crocheting and a missal lay on the maple table beside the sofa. Linda was grateful for the daily excursions to Mass: at least her aunt had to leave the house and walk.

— *I mind because when I see her, I want to*

ask her how you are, and I can't, Thomas said.

Linda was silent.

— *So how are Michael and Tommy and Eileen and all the rest?* Thomas asked, having been denied information about herself. He picked at a small bowl of nuts. He would know her cousins mostly as names with faces attached, though he had played hockey with Michael and had been fond of Jack. But how to reduce six complicated lives, six different lifetimes filled with sorrow and success and shame into six sentences? She thought a minute and then counted off her fingers.

— *Michael lives in Marshfield with a woman who has two boys. They've had a tough time of it financially. Tommy, who didn't go to college, bought Cisco when it was 17, and now he's worth millions. He never married. Eileen is probably the happiest of the lot. Her husband is a lawyer in Andover.* (*That made her happy?* Thomas interjected.) *Vincent and I used to see quite a lot of her and her family,* Linda added. *She has three children, all through school now. Patty is a banker in New York. Never married, which galls my aunt. Erin is in California. She's had problems with drugs. She's spent some time in jail, actually.* Linda paused and watched Thomas's face register his shock; he'd known Erin as only a pretty preteen in a pink dress. *I guess you haven't heard about Jack, then,* she said quietly.

He turned his head to look at her. He who might always expect the worst now. Or perhaps he'd heard a catch in her voice.

— *He died . . .* She stopped, surprised by the threat of fresh tears. *Of leukemia, when he was forty. My aunt's never gotten over it. He was her baby.* Linda picked up a bar napkin in case she needed it. *To think the youngest of us would be the first to go. He left a wife and two babies, twins.*

Thomas shook his head. *I taught Jack to ice-skate,* he said, disbelieving.

— *I remember.* She blinked with other memories. *It was a terrible death. It sometimes makes me glad that Vincent went the way he did. So quick. He might not have known what happened to him.* She stopped, remembering Thomas's prayers for Billie. She wiped her nose and sat up. *So there you have it.*

Thomas nodded slowly.

— *What are the odds that six children would make it to old age?* she wondered aloud. *Probably not very good.*

— *Better than they used to be.*

— *I had dinner with the group,* she said. *But have you eaten?*

— *No. I'm not hungry.*

— What did you do today on your panel? Everyone was all abuzz.

Thomas put a hand over his eyes. *I lost it,* he said, only pretending to be abashed.

— What happened?

— Some woman in the audience took me to task for exploiting Billie's . . . He stopped. *Which was all right, I suppose. But then Robert Seizek, who was on the panel with me, took the woman's point and said so, and I was nearly shaking with the idea that a novelist, a fucking novelist, would say such shit. And, well . . .* He stopped again.

Thomas wore his collar open, his tie loosened. His shirt billowed over his belt, which rode lower than it used to.

— You seem pleased with yourself, she said.

— It was a dull panel.

She laughed.

— I bought one of your books today and reread bits of it in the barber's chair, he said. *I even read the flap copy again.*

— You did? The admission rattled her more than she was prepared to show. When had Thomas had time for this? Her fingers nervously caressed the stem of the glass. Though the vodka was getting to her a bit now, making her stomach warm.

— Do you teach literature or writing? he asked.

— *Mostly workshops.*

Thomas groaned in sympathy. *I tried that. I wasn't any good at it. I couldn't hide my contempt for the work.*

— *That would be a problem.* She turned toward him slightly and crossed her legs. A different tailored blouse tonight, but the same skirt. He would see the uniform for what it was.

— *What's the college like?* he asked. *I've never been there.*

She told him that there was a quadrangle in the shape of a cross, with a chapel at one end and, incongruously, a hotel at the other. There were stone buildings and archways and leaded casement windows, made to look ancient on the Oxford-Cambridge model, but entirely constructed within the last two decades. It was a school unmarked by any idiosyncrasy or ugliness, by any of the *new*, which surely any institution that had truly evolved would possess. It was a universe sprung fully fashioned from the earth without having paid the dues of age. (*Like America,* Thomas said.) And sometimes it seemed a stage set, she told him, although the dramas that were enacted there were real enough: an abnormally high number of professor-student love affairs, alcohol overdoses at frat parties, a near epidemic of razor-cutting (mostly females), the endless machinations of jealous faculty. *I see my job as one of encouragement. It's difficult to teach someone to write.*

— *Do you encourage the poor students?*

— *One has to.*

— *Aren't you just wasting their time? And yours?*

— *It's what I'm there for. I suppose if I had a truly hopeless case, I'd suggest alternatives. If I thought the student could handle it. But I'm a bit of a coward when it comes to criticism. And I'm an easy marker.*

He smiled.

— *I had dinner with Mary Ndegwa,* she said.

— *I've hardly had a chance to see her.*

— *She's very graphic about what she missed.*

— *Well, it's the core of all her poetry.*

— *Her son, Ndegwa, is with the Ministry of Finance.*

Thomas shook his head again — a man who had largely isolated himself and was thus bedazzled by change; a man for whom a child's life stopped at five. *Baby Ndegwa,* he said with something like awe. *I've never been able to write about Kenya. It doesn't seem to belong to me.*

— *We were only visitors.*

In another room, a man began to play a

piano. The bar was rapidly filling. She and Thomas had to speak more loudly to hear each other.

— *Sometimes I think about Peter,* Thomas said. *I often wish I could just call him up and apologize.*

Linda took a sip of her drink. *I can't remember ever making love to him,* she said. *What we did, I mean. I know that it happened, but I can't see it. And I can't understand how I can have been that intimate with someone and have no visceral memory of our time together. I don't know whether I've simply forgotten or I was never paying very close attention.* She paused and shook her head. *What a horrid thing to say. I'd die to think I'd meant so little to someone I was once married to.*

Thomas was silent. Perhaps he was struggling not to ask her if she remembered their own lovemaking.

— *Do you know we only made love four times?* Thomas asked. *In all those years? Four times.*

— *Technically,* she said.

— *Rich was fucking my wife. I saw them through the binoculars. He said he wasn't, but I've never believed him. It's been a thorn between us all these years. If I'm right, I could never forgive him, and he knows that. If I'm wrong, he'll never forgive me for thinking him capable of it. Either way, we're pretty much screwed.*

She waited for Thomas to say more about Rich, but he remained silent. She noticed that Thomas had a new way of holding his mouth; the lips a bit tighter, making him seem more wary. She wondered: was there such a thing as human decency?

— *Thank you for the drink,* she said. *But I have to go back to my room. I'm worried about my son. His lover is going to take him into rehab tonight if Marcus is willing.* She paused. *My son is gay.*

Thomas looked not shocked, but almost weary with the knowledge, as if the weight, the weight, of all these *facts* was almost too much to bear. *Has it been difficult for you?*

— *That? No. Not really.* She slowly slid off the bar stool. *This will be, though.*

There were no messages from anyone. When Linda tried Marcus's number, a voice, David's, said: *You have reached the happy abode of David Shulman and Marcus Bertollini.* Linda cringed for Marcus.

— *That might mean they're on their way to Brattleboro,* she explained to Thomas, who had taken an armchair in the corner of the bedroom. She propped a pillow behind her back and sat with her legs stretched out along the bedspread. She kicked off her shoes, and Thomas took off his jacket. *Whatever became of Donny T.?* she asked suddenly.

— *What made you think of Donny?*

— *I don't know. He was always on the edge.*

— *Of disaster, you mean.*

— *Or of great success.*

— *The success won out. He's some kind of banker and worth millions. Probably billions by now.*

Linda smiled and shook her head slowly. She thought of Donny T. in the backseat of Eddie Garrity's Bonneville, counting dollar bills in the dim light of a single lamp on the pier. Maybe it wasn't the risk that had been the draw all those years ago: maybe it had simply been the money.

— *I want to tell you about Billie,* Thomas said, startling her, until, looking at him, she saw that this had been the nugget of his thoughts all along; and she reflected that his need to tell this story again and again was probably not so very different from that of a woman who had recently given birth and felt it necessary to describe the ordeal in detail to whoever would listen. She herself had done the same.

— *I play it over and over again in my head,* Thomas began. *I always imagine that if I could just reach in and tweak some tiny detail, just one fact, I could easily change everything.* Thomas slid down in his chair and propped his legs on the edge of a hassock. *It was a bogus assignment in the first place. Jean had been hired by the Globe to take pictures of a place where two women had been murdered a hundred and some odd years ago. In eighteen seventy-three. At the Isles of Shoals. Do you know them?*

Linda nodded. *I've never been there, though.*

— *Rich had this idea, since it was summer, that we could combine Jean's assignment with a little vacation. Sail up to the islands and around, maybe head on up to Maine.* Thomas paused. *I hate sailing. It was always Rich's deal.* Thomas shook his head. *He'd brought a woman with him, a woman he'd been seeing, someone I'd met some months before at a party. Her name was Adaline, and she was perfectly nice — in fact she was quite lovely — but in an entirely unintentional way, she was dangerous. Have you ever had that feeling about someone? That he or she was dangerous?*

Linda thought a minute. Only about herself, years ago.

— *I think now that Adaline was a sort of catalyst. For some twisted thing that was playing itself out amongst the three of us — me and Jean*

131

and Rich. Thomas was silent a moment. *Actually, Adaline reminded me of you. She looked just like you did in Africa. I hadn't seen you since then, so in my memory, you were still that person. And what was uncanny was that she wore a cross.* He put his fingers together, remembering. *I couldn't take my eyes off her. And she knew my poetry. And was very flattering about it. And I've never been very good at ignoring flattery.*

— *No one is.*

— *And Jean saw this — how could she not? — and it ate at her, as it would at anyone. I don't think Jean was by nature a particularly jealous person. It was just that, on that boat, you couldn't get away from it; whatever was happening on the boat, you had to live with it. It was in your face, hour after hour after hour.*

— *And Rich saw it too?* Linda asked quietly.

— *I have to assume that he did. Why else did he decide to fuck my wife then, on that trip? Jean and he had known each other for years. I don't think there had been anything between them before that.* Thomas's eyes went inward, searching the past. *No, I'm sure not. I'd have felt it, I think.*

Linda nodded.

— *We were all tense. And Jean and I* . . . He glanced away and back again. *To say we were*

132

having problems sounds banal. And it was, it was banal. But they weren't problems in the way that one can define a problem and then try to solve it and move on. No, it was more that the texture of the marriage had gone wrong.

Thomas sighed.

— *And so what do you do with that? Together you have a beautiful five-year-old girl. You get along well enough. There are no crises to speak of. Do you destroy a marriage because something vague doesn't feel right? And, of course, you don't know for certain that the marriage is irrevocably broken. Part of you is always hoping you can make it right.*

— *Define "right."*

— *See? That's the problem. In a marriage, you're always working towards something, but you're never sure when you've got there. If you've reached it yet. "Is there something more?" you keep asking yourself.*

He slid his tie through his collar and folded it. He laid it on the armrest. *Jean and I weren't sleeping together. Not often, anyway. So there was that to deal with, too, because it was all around us. Sex. In the mornings, you could hear Rich and Adaline fucking in the forward cabin. I've said that.*

The *fucking* so harsh a word, Linda thought. His anger must still be sharp. Bitter.

— I know that Jean thought for years that I'd used her. Right after I met her, there was an uncanny period during which I started writing again after a long dry spell. For years, I've had trouble with writer's block. Jean thought I stayed with her because of that, that she was a sort of muse for me. I was never able to disabuse her of that idea. He ran his hands over his still unfamiliar head. *And it was complicated by the fact that early on — before I knew Jean and I would be married — I'd told her about you. She knew I loved you.* He took a breath. *That was a problem.*

Linda crossed her arms over her chest. Why did this knowledge upset her so?

— How do you take that out of the equation? Thomas asked. *How do you solve a problem like that?*

Linda breathed slowly and evenly. The room was cold, and she rubbed her arms.

— The second day we were there, Jean and Rich went over to the island where the murders had occurred. We were moored just off the island — it had a dreadful name: Smuttynose — and Adaline and I were alone on the boat. Just talking. She'd lost her daughter in a messy divorce, and she was telling me about it. He scratched his head again. *Such irony. To think that I was comforting her, and just hours later it would be me who'd lost a daughter.* He

put his head in his hands for a moment, then looked up. *I happened to see some people over on the island, and I decided it would be Rich and Jean. I thought I'd give them a wave. I picked up the binoculars and saw Rich and Jean embracing. Jean was naked from the waist up.*

Linda gasped. The image was shocking, even in a world of shocking images.

— *I watched for a while, and then I couldn't bear it. I threw the binoculars overboard. Adaline kept saying, "What, Thomas? Thomas, what?" But I couldn't speak. And I don't know why it bothers me so much, even now. After everything else . . .*

He leaned back in the chair.

— *It was your brother,* Linda said. *It was your wife.*

He nodded.

— *It was biblical,* she said.

He nodded again. *What is sex, anyway?* he asked. *Is taking your shirt off in front of your brother-in-law sex? Technically? Where do you draw the line?*

— *There isn't one.*

— *No, of course not.* He took a deep breath. *I was crazed after that. I couldn't think clearly. I was so fucking preoccupied. And then, when they got back . . .* He paused. *There was a storm brewing. A serious storm. I'm not a* sailor, but even I knew it was bad. *There wasn't any time to confront Rich or Jean.* Thomas was shaking his head constantly now as he spoke. *And between the storm and the tension, none of us was paying attention.*

He stood up suddenly, as if gathering courage for the rest. He walked to the window. *We thought Billie was safe with Adaline. Adaline was seasick, and she was lying in the forward cabin with Billie, who was beginning to feel queasy herself. Rich and Jean and I were trying to stabilize the boat and get to shore.* Thomas rubbed his eyes the way only a man would do: vigorously, even viciously. *Adaline left Billie lying on the bed and went through the forward hatch to get some air. Probably to puke, too. I know she thought Billie wouldn't leave the bed.*

Thomas began to pace. He walked to the French doors and through them to the living room. He picked up a small vase and put it down. He walked back to the bedroom. *Jean and I had been trying to get Billie into her life vest. And I suppose we thought we'd done it, or maybe we were interrupted, I can't remember now. But we should have known. Billie didn't want to wear it, and we knew better than anyone just how stubborn she could be. We should have forced her into it and kept our eye on her at all times. Harnessed her, if need be, to the boat.*

Linda closed her eyes. It could be just a moment's inattention. Backing out of the driveway and not noticing your child had moved behind the car. Having a fight with your husband and not seeing that the baby had climbed onto the window ledge. One second. That's all it took.

— *Adaline fell overboard. I went in after her. Rich was trying to keep the boat upright. Jean was frantic. And then . . . And then, it was Rich, I think, who noticed first.* Thomas looked at the ceiling. *Oh, God, this is our punishment, isn't it? These memories. It was an ice pick in the chest. The body knows already, even if the mind won't accept it yet. "Where's Billie?" Rich said.*

Thomas stopped. He looked at Linda. *And that was it,* he said. *That was the end of my life as I'd known it.*

— *Thomas.*

No other words, they who mined and invented words.

— *I was crazed for months. Insane. I'd wake up in the middle of the night screaming. Rich would run into the room — he was staying with me all the time then — and have to pin me to the bed.*

— *Thomas.*

He leaned against the doorjamb, his

hands in his pockets, his shirttails mysteriously come untucked. *It seemed important that I tell you this story.*

She met his eyes, and neither spoke. The earth might have made a revolution for all the time they were silent.

— *I won't make love to you while you're waiting for word of your son,* Thomas said finally. *Though I want to.*

Linda drew her knees up and bent her head to them, so that Thomas couldn't see her face. He didn't move to touch her, as he had said he wouldn't.

The details make it unbearable, she thought.

She pressed her forehead hard against her legs. She knew that any movement in any direction would say everything there was to say. If she rose and walked to the window, each would know that no history could be resurrected, no future be salvaged. And then Thomas would collect his tie and jacket and might ask her when her plane was leaving and might even kiss her on the cheek, though the gesture would be meaningless, without import, without even the wonder of what might have been. For the standing up and walking to the window would obliterate all wonderment, then and forever.

— *I shouldn't have said that,* he said.

— *You can say anything you want.*

— *It's sex and grief,* he explained. *There's some connection I've never understood.*

A need to stay alive, she thought, but didn't offer.

— *I'll go now,* he said from the doorway.

She held her breath. She wouldn't stop him. But she didn't want to watch him leave either.

She heard him cross the floor. She froze, thinking he would touch her. But then she heard the sluicing of his arms into the silky lining of his jacket. She waited until she heard the soft click of the outer door.

She looked up, scarcely believing that he had really gone. She waited, thinking that any minute he'd walk back in, tell her he'd changed his mind or he had more to tell her. But he didn't come back, and the emptiness of the room presented itself to her: an emptiness that might go on forever. A fleeting sense of relief — relief that they had not touched, had not had to decide how to be with each other — gave way to a quiet and dispiriting rage. The rage, perhaps, of being left, vestigial; the rage, certainly, of words left unsaid. For a minute, she teetered between that rising anger and a feeling of bottomless sympathy.

A heavy rain had started outside. More than a heavy rain — sheets of water whipped against her windows. She felt as unstable as the weather. She willed herself to stay on the bed, willed herself to let Thomas walk away. But some great impulse — ruinous and engaging — propelled her to the door.

She found him standing at the elevator. He still held his tie in his hand. He looked drained, slightly dazed, like a man who had just had sex and was returning to his room.

— *Why did you walk away from me that morning in Africa?* she asked.

He was startled by the question, she could see that. In the silence, she heard, through the window at the end of the hallway, car horns and a police siren, the siren with a different tone, more European than American. A room service waiter rolled a noisy cart along the hall and pushed the elevator button, which Linda noticed only now had not been lit. Thomas hadn't summoned the elevator.

— *I had to,* he said finally.

She inhaled a needed breath. *Why? Why did you have to?* Her voice was rising, inappropriate in this hallway. The waiter studied his cart.

— *Regina,* Thomas said distractedly, as if not understanding why the obvious answer wasn't the correct one. *Regina was . . .*

— *Was what?*

— *Linda . . .*

— *Was what?* Her voice too loud now, inappropriate anywhere.

— *Regina was distraught. She was saying she would kill herself. She kept saying I'd be killing two people then. I knew I couldn't leave her alone in Africa.*

— *You left me alone in Africa.*

— *That was your choice.*

— *My choice?* A voice inside her head said, Be careful. That was years ago. But she wasn't certain she could stop the words. Some wounds did not heal, she realized with a small surprise.

— *I had assumed that eventually we'd find a way to be together,* she said. The elevator came, but Thomas did not get on. The waiter gratefully escaped them.

— *Well, you took care of that, didn't you?* Thomas said, unable to suppress a note of sarcasm.

— *You wouldn't have done it yourself?* she asked sharply. *Eventually?*

— *Yes, of course, I would have. I've loved you all my life. I've told you that. But in the event, in the reality of that night, it was unthinkable that I should leave Regina alone. You know that as well as I do.*

141

And, yes, she did know that. The truth would always be exhilarating, she thought.

— *And it was ruined then,* he added. *We'd ruined it. We'd neglected to imagine the chaos.*

— *I'd rack my suffering up against Regina's anytime,* she said.

He seemed taken aback by the contest. She knew that later she would mind this the most: that she'd become common in her anger. That in an instant, she'd reinvented herself as a shrew.

— *Wasn't it worth anything?* she asked. *Wasn't it worth the pain to be together? Tell me you didn't believe we should be together.*

Her questions astounded her as much as she saw they surprised him. And why was she asking them? Did she really regret any choice that had led to her children? Any turn of fate that had produced Maria and Marcus? Would she have wished Vincent unmet, unmarried? Of course not.

— *Apart from Billie, I've hardly thought of anything else for thirty-four years,* Thomas said quietly.

She looked at the patterned carpet. She prayed that Thomas would not cross the hallway and hold her. Reduce them to that. She thought of saying it aloud, forbidding him.

She was sure he would leave her now,

leave her to erase the memory of the last several minutes. Of the weekend altogether, if it came to that. Thomas unmet, unseen, after all these years.

She hadn't the stamina for this anymore.

From somewhere down the hallway, she could hear a telephone ringing. It rang twice, then three times, before she registered what it was. Then, with a mother's instinct, never dormant, she walked quickly along the hallway, listening, until she had come to her room. It was her phone. Shit, she thought. It would be Marcus. She tried the doorknob.

Of course. She had locked herself out.

— *I'll go down and get a key,* Thomas said quickly when he had reached her side.

— *They won't give you one. And, anyway, it will be too late.* The phone continued to ring. It must be important, she thought. She was certain now that it was Marcus. *How could I have been so stupid?* She rattled the doorknob once again.

Thomas stood immobile beside her. The phone was still ringing. She wished it would stop. The argument between them seemed irrelevant now.

— *Actually,* Thomas said. *This is kind of funny.*

She looked up at him. He rubbed a cheek-

143

bone in an effort to suppress a smile. He was right, she thought. It was kind of funny. All the *sturm und drang,* and then the slapstick of a locked door.

— *A farce, after all,* she said.

Behind them, she heard movement. *Excuse me, you need key?* On the maid's trolley were breakfast menus and small Godiva chocolates. Turn-down service. Linda would never turn them away again.

Once inside the door, Linda ran to the phone, praying the ringing would not stop just before she got there. She listened to the voice at the other end. Her free hand spiraled into the air and fluttered awkwardly. Thomas, beside her, held her errant hand.

— *I'm just so relieved to hear your voice,* she said into the phone, half laughing, half crying. She sat heavily on the bed. Thomas sat with her, releasing her hand.

Linda turned and mouthed, *It's OK. It's Marcus.*

— *I'm sorry about David,* Marcus, who sounded remarkably clear-headed, said. *I know he can be an asshole sometimes. I was too groggy to protest. I wanted to talk to you, but he was . . .*

— *Protective.*

— *Yeah.*

— *Where are you?*

— *I'm here. In Brattleboro.* There was a pause. *Mom, are you OK?*

— *I ran to get the phone. I was locked out. It's a long story. I'm glad you let the phone ring so long.*

— *They only let us have one phone call. Like jail. I wasn't sure they'd let me try again.*

— *How are you?*

— *I suppose I should be scared shitless, but, truthfully, all I feel is relief.*

— *Oh, Marcus.*

She put her hand over the mouthpiece. *Marcus is at Brattleboro,* she said to Thomas.

— *Mom? Who are you talking to?*

— *A man, Marcus. A man I used to know. Before your father.*

— *Really? That sounds intriguing.*

She was silent.

— *They only let you talk for five minutes,* Marcus said. *That's what they said. And I can only make two calls a week.*

— *Is David there with you?*

— *No, they made him leave. Almost immediately. I think the theory is that people from home put you in jeopardy. They want them out as soon as possible.*

She, of course, was a person from home.

— *But they do allow visits. They invite you to come. In fact, I think they'll insist that you*

145

come. They have all-day seminars so that you can learn how to handle me when I get out.

She smiled. Marcus's irony might get him through this. Or was the irony part of the problem?

— *You'll have to come with David,* Marcus added tentatively.

— *I like David,* Linda said.

— *No you don't. Sometimes I'm not even sure if I like him. You know how you can love someone but sometimes wonder why you're with him?*

— *Yes. Yes, I do.*

— *I'm going to have to go. There's a man standing next to me, telling me to hang up. I can't call Maria. I've used my one phone call . . .*

— *I'll call her,* Linda said, relieved to have been given a task. — *Don't worry about that.*

— *I love you, Mom.*

The *ease* with which he said it.

— *You're doing the right thing, Marcus. You're doing a wonderful thing.*

— *Mom, just one question. Did you know? Did you know I was a . . . an alcoholic?*

Not telling the truth now would be disastrous. *Yes,* she said.

— *Oh. I just wondered.*

This was not the time to discuss why she had refused to allow herself to think the word, to say the word aloud. *I love you, too, Marcus,* she offered instead.

She held the telephone in her hand for a long minute after he had broken the connection. She tried to picture Marcus at Brattleboro, but all she could see was a prison with a guard standing next to her son. This would be so much harder than either he or she knew.

— *There must be some relief in knowing that he's safe,* Thomas said.

And she nodded with the truth of what he'd said, although she also knew that he might easily have added, with equal sympathy, *None of us is safe.*

For a time, they sat together on the bed, thinking about the phone call, not speaking. It was she, finally, who turned to him. She said his name. Not to keep the wonder alive, but for simple comfort, as two who are lost on a mountain will press their bodies together for warmth. She put a hand on his shirt, and he, his face lit with hope, answered with her name. Not Magdalene this time, but rather Linda, stripping away all artifice so that there was only clarity.

And then, as might have been anticipated, as might have been known, the gesture that she'd made became a sexual one. Animal-

like, Thomas smelled her hair, and she, like-
wise, was jolted by the scent of his skin. So
much to recognize, and yet everything was
different. She could not feel his bones along
his back as she had once been able to, and
she held her breath as his hand traveled
along her belly and touched her breast. For
a moment, the gesture felt illicit, and she
had to remind herself that nothing was illicit
now. And that knowledge was so surprising,
she almost said it aloud, as one will blurt out
a sudden truth. She moved her face to the
side as he kissed her neck and collarbone.
How long would it have been since he had
last made love to a woman? Years ago? Last
week? She didn't want to know.

In silent agreement, they stood and removed their clothing, each avoiding examining the other while they did this, though
together they turned the covers back as a
married couple might. They slid against
each other and along the silky sheets, and
she thought of how, in the early years, they
had not had a bed; and that later the beds,
like their minutes together, had always been
stolen, never their own. And that thought
let in a flood of images that had been lost to
her, small moments obliterated by all that
had come after. She smelled a dank, salt-
scented pier, her slip wet with sea water.

She saw a bedroom in a foreign country, with its roof open to the sky. She saw a boy, standing shyly in a hallway with a box he had wrapped himself. She felt Thomas's breath on her neck and a loosening in her bones. She saw glints upon the water as two teenagers sat on a hill overlooking the Atlantic, aching to possess the light as if it were water or food and could be stored for nourishment.

Thomas was whispering in her ear. She reached up and touched his scar, ran her fingers along the length of it. She wondered what his images were, what he was seeing. Or was it simpler for a man? Would Thomas have a sense of mission, fueled by desire, touching her as he was with his exquisite sense of timing, his perfect pitch?

— *I've always loved you,* he said.

She put her fingers to his lips. She did not want words, she who normally craved them, crawled toward them if need be. But now, she thought, just now everything could be said with the body. There were details, small things such as the softness at his waist or the thinning of his hair, that she would not linger over. Denial was sometimes essential for sex or love. Thomas was trailing his lips along her ribs, and it was lovely, and she was glad that this had not been lost.

★ ★ ★

A voice in the corridor woke her, and she strained to see behind the shades. It was dark still, the middle of the night. She could feel Thomas's breath on her shoulder. She thought immediately that their coming together had been archival and primitive. Indeed, in retrospect, it seemed preordained. And for the first time since Vincent died, Linda was relieved that she was alone in the world, that there had been nothing furtive or illicit about making love with Thomas.

A foot had gone numb, and she tried to extricate it from the tangle of their legs and arms without waking Thomas; but he woke anyway and immediately pulled her closer as if she were about to leave him. *Don't go,* he said.

— *I won't,* she said soothingly.

— *What time is it?*

— *I don't know.*

He kissed her. *Are you . . . ?* He paused, uncharacteristically lost for words.

She smiled. Thomas needing to be reassured, like any man. *I feel wonderful.*

And reassured, he stretched his body along her own. *There are more experiences in life than you'd think for which there are no words,* he said.

— *I know.*

They lay face-to-face, their eyes open.

— *I won't ask you what you were thinking about,* she said.

— *You can ask me anything.*

— *Well, I was thinking about the day we sat on a hill overlooking the water,* she said.

— *That was the first time I ever saw you cry,* he said.

— *It was?*

— *You were crying from the beauty of it, like children do.*

She laughed. *I can't feel that anymore. So much of the immediacy of beauty is gone. Muffled.*

— *Actually, I was thinking about that night on the pier when you jumped in the water in your slip.*

— *My God, I didn't even know you.*

— *I loved it.* He held her with one arm and pulled up the covers with the other. *Listen, I want to sleep with you now. But you have to promise you won't leave me while I'm sleeping.*

— *I promise,* she said. Though he and she both knew that promises could no longer, with any certainty, be made or honored.

The tables were awash with white linen, salmon chargers and heavy silver plate. In the background she could hear the muted hum of a vacuum. There were nearly thirty empty tables, yet still she waited to be seated while a waitress with a humpback consulted a plan. As Linda was led to a table, a man's pager went off with a musical song.

She liked the anonymity of breakfast, the license to watch others. Beside her an elderly woman and a middle-aged daughter were discussing another woman's chemotherapy. Linda fingered the tablecloth and wondered if the linen was washed and starched every day.

Thomas stood at the entrance to the dining room, freshly showered, in a white shirt and gray V-neck sweater. He hadn't seen her yet, and for a moment, she was able to examine him. He seemed taller and trimmer than she'd remembered from the day before, but perhaps that was just his posture. He seemed less unkempt and more relaxed as well. Or happier. Yes, it might be happiness.

— *You're quick,* he said, meaning her showering and dressing. He unsnapped his napkin and placed it over his lap. The humpbacked waitress immediately brought another cup of coffee to the table.

— *I was hungry,* she said.

— *I'm ravenous.*

She smiled. This might be awkward.

What would be expected would be arrangements, tentative promises. *Why don't we plan to meet?* one of them would have to say. *I'd like to see you again,* the other might feel compelled to offer. She wondered if it was possible to live episodically, not planning for the future, not even allowing thoughts of the future to enter into her consciousness. Though such thoughts might be necessary and primeval, the need to plan a vestige from the days of hoarding and storing for the lean months.

— *When does your flight leave?* he asked.

— *I have to head for the airport right after breakfast.*

— *I'll go with you,* he said quickly.

— *When is your flight?*

— *Not until this afternoon. But I won't stay here. I'd rather be at the airport.*

They would go home on different flights. It seemed a waste, all those hours of separate confinement.

They ordered extravagantly, and it was impossible not to see something of a celebration in that extravagance. When the waitress had left, Thomas took Linda's hand, holding it lightly by the fingers. The men in golf shirts at the next table looked like boys compared to Thomas. Underdressed. Ill-mannered.

— *Hull is not so far from Belmont,* Thomas said tentatively.

— *We could meet in Boston for a dinner sometime,* she offered.

— *You could — theoretically — come visit your aunt in Hull.*

She smiled. *Yes. I could theoretically do that.*

— *I'd like to meet your children,* he said.

— *They're both in institutions right now.*

Thomas raised an eyebrow.

— *I mean only that Maria is at Johns Hopkins, interning.*

Thomas nodded. Across the breakfast room, she saw the man who had lost his umbrella at the entrance to the hotel. He was dining alone and reading a newspaper. Beside her, she heard the middle-aged daughter say, *And when does your own therapy start again, Mom?*

— *I love raspberries,* Thomas said, contemplating their rarity in that northern city in April. *Cooked raspberries, especially. Jean used to make these muffins. Oat bran with raspberries and peaches. God, they were good.*

A sensation, not unlike a shiver, quickly passed through Linda. She felt with the shiver the rare sensation that she was exactly where she should be. She was an idea, a memory, one perfect possibility out of an infinite number. And whether she was inventing this notion from need or it was simply a truth floating in the universe, she couldn't say. And wouldn't question. She and Thomas would ride together in the taxi to the airport, a ride she would remember for the rest of her life, which she decided would be long.

They said good-bye at the gate, not making too much of the farewell, for to mark it excessively might suggest finality, which neither of them wanted.

— *I'll call you,* Thomas said, and she did not doubt that he would. He would call her that evening, in fact, already minding a night apart. *To think . . .* he said, and she nodded, her face close to his. She held his hand tightly, as if she were drowning, and her helplessness seemed to move him. He kissed her for such a long time that she was certain that others now were watching them. Thomas stood at the gate as she walked down the ramp, and she could not resist turning to see if he had waited.

She had been assigned to a window, though normally she preferred the aisle. She took her seat, noticing as she stowed her belongings that the man who had lost the umbrella (she would always think of him as The Man with the Umbrella) was seated ahead of her in first class. She wondered briefly where he lived, why his destination was Boston. She imagined him as a leitmotif in her life, passing by at odd moments — in a taxi, or walking just beyond her reach on a busy street. She wondered if he had already been in her life without her noticing: in a hotel in Africa, for example. Or at a diner in Hull. And it was impossible not to imagine that if fate had engineered her life differently, it might have been he who had stood with her at the gate, who had kissed her for so long. None of these mysteries could be known. Guessed at, surely. Believed in, yes. But not known, not absolutely known.

From her briefcase, she took out a book and opened it, though she was too distracted just then to read. In her raincoat, with her white blouse and black skirt underneath, she might have been a lawyer, returning from a deposition; a wife flying home after visiting relatives. Outside her window, the cloud was low to the ground, and she told herself, automatically, that take-offs were safer than landings. A flight attendant shut the door and, shortly afterward, the plane began to move. Linda said a prayer, as she always did, and thought of how Vincent had been cheated of years, of how hard Marcus would have to work to free himself of addiction. She thought of Maria's need to have her own life, and of her aunt sitting with her missal beside her. She thought of Donny T. with his dollars, and of a woman named Jean whom she had never known. Of Regina whom she had wronged, and of Peter, nearly forgotten. She thought of Billie, cheated beyond words. And, finally, of Thomas, her beloved Thomas, wrenched from arrogance with a crushing blow.

What was left but forgiveness? Without it, she was suddenly certain, what there was of her life would be a torture, right down to the death agonies of the nursing home.

A bell dinged, and there was silence. And in the silence, a word formed. Then a sentence. Then a paragraph. She searched for a pen in her purse and began to write in the margin of her book. She wrote down one side and up the other, defacing one book with another. She wrote until her hand hurt, until a flight attendant brought her a small meal. She put her pen down and glanced through the window. It was miraculous, she thought. The plane was emerging from the mist to a universe of blue sky and mountainous cloud.

Part Two

Twenty-six

The mango was alien and fleshy and reminded him of a woman, though he couldn't decide which part. The color running from lizard salmon to grass green, a mottled palette that changed overnight if you left it on the sill. Moody, like Regina. The skin was thick and tough and hard to penetrate; the flesh fibrous and succulent, glistening with juices. The flavor was divine. There was a knack to eating the things he hadn't mastered yet, a way of peeling the skin and removing the stone and cutting the fruit into decorous slices to place on a white china plate; but the best he could manage was to stand over a sink and suck on the flesh. He liked to think about Regina naked in a bathtub, the juices running from the tips of her nipples. The fantasy fading inside a minute: Regina would never eat naked in the tub. Wouldn't allow the mess.

Jesus, it stank in the market. It was the meat, covered with flies, in the dukas by the walls. The scent bloody, a fresh kill, a carcass still oozing. Worse was the smell of the meat cooking, not like any steak or chop he'd ever eaten. He was certain it was horse flesh, though everyone denied it. A woman, barefoot, with a child tied in kitenge cloth to her back, was standing next to him and opening her palm. Not speaking, just waiting with her hand out. He reached into the pocket of his shorts and pulled out a handful of shillings. She mumbled, *Ahsante sana,* and moved on. He brought pockets full of shillings to the market now. It wasn't just the guilt, though there was plenty of that — it was the *hassle* of refusing. Of having to walk on, pretending to be preoccupied, the beggar still following you, muttering, *Tafadhali.* Please, mister. Easier to have a pocketful of money. Giving in to the beggars annoyed Regina no end, made her long-suffering and patient, as if she had to repeat instructions she'd given a hundred times already. It didn't help, she said; it didn't solve the problem.

Solves *my* problem, Thomas thought.

Us and Them. It never went away. He'd been in the country almost a year now, and it was still Us, still Them. And the Us was, as far as he could see, patronizing and clue-less and faintly ridiculous in its collective earnestness. He hadn't met a single American he thought was making a dent — Regina included — though that supposed there was a problem in which one needed to make a dent, that Africa itself was a problem. It was an endless and tiring debate: did Kenya really need or want Americans in their country? Yes, to the former. No, to the latter. Though you really couldn't go around advocating that position. You needed tunnel vision for conviction. Like Regina had. Whereas he, Thomas, lacked vision, tunnel or otherwise. Texture interested him. The physical world. The possibility of rapture in the here and now. Sexual subtext. And words. Always words. He was distrustful of a future he couldn't see. The drop off the earth. The blank screen.

He put the mango in the straw basket. He was supposed to be buying the fruit while Regina bought the meat. Regina was miffed he hadn't done it earlier in the week, for making her do it on her day off. Regina, who saw harrowing cases of amebic dysentery and schistosomiasis, children starving to death right before her eyes. Regina, who had clarity. Already she was talking of returning after her degree.

No, he hadn't done the shopping, he'd told his wife, because he'd spent the week writing. And he'd seen, around her mouth, the effort it had cost her not to say (raised eyebrow, wry smile), *All week?* Her support wearing thin in the face of no income, no success. Worse, all the poems, written in Africa, were relentlessly about Hull. Did it take a decade for experience to seep into words? Would he go home to Hull only to write about Nairobi? No, he didn't think so. Africa resisted comprehension. He couldn't begin to understand the country and therefore couldn't dream about it. And if you couldn't dream about a thing, you couldn't write about it. If he'd been able to write about Africa, he thought, Regina might have forgiven him.

What she wouldn't forgive, he knew, was the pleasure the writing gave him: sensual and tactile, a jolt that ran through him when it worked. Always, he was writing in his head; at parties, he craved to be at a desk. He sometimes thought it was the only honest conduit he had to the world around him, all other endeavors, even his marriage (Jesus, especially his marriage), lost in the excessive caution of failed expectations and injured feelings. But pleasure taxed Re-

gina's notions of work: that one should sacrifice and be in a constant state of mild
suffering. To appease her, Thomas sometimes spoke about the *agony* of writing, of
the *struggle* to overcome writer's block.
Jinxing himself, he was certain, by inviting
its eventual onset.

He wrote in the bedroom of their rented
house in Karen, the house a sprawling
stone-and-stucco villa, made to look British
with parquet floors and leaded-glass casement windows. A canopy of cardinal and
fuchsia bougainvillea clung to the eucalyptus trees overhead, all intertwined into
one great vivid parasite. A cactus garden
had been planted in the back, and it was a
carnival of grotesqueries: long, slithery
green and yellow projectiles with dagger-
like weapons that could kill a man; trees
with pear-like fruit at the end that the birds
plucked before you could get to them; ugly,
bulbous stumps that changed, from time to
time, into lovely heart-red velvety blossoms;
and giant brown euphorbia trees with sup-
plicant arms, hundreds of them, bent
upward to the navy of the equatorial sky.
Along the border of the pebbled drive that
led into town, dozens of jacaranda trees
swayed in the air and met in the center overhead. Each November, they laid down a

thick carpet of lavender petals that Michael, the gardener, would sweep into piles and burn. The scent was like marijuana, only sweeter, and could make Thomas think he was stoned, even when he wasn't. At night, the trees would shed another purple carpet, and returning from the duka early in the morning with a packet of Players (and milk for his cereal if he remembered), Thomas would walk through the fallen blossoms in a state of near bliss.

He woke with the birds and listened to sounds he'd never heard before: the trills of tiny weaver birds; the cat-like wail of peacocks; the screeching of ibises; and the rhythmic moaning of something he couldn't name but that might simply be a dove. Once, he'd seen, through the bedroom window, a tree come shockingly into bloom. Its leaves had been bluish-gray, and on that day it had given birth to an explosion of small yellow puffy balls as big as marbles, thousands upon thousands of them all at once, so that almost instantly a lemon-colored haze had filled the room. It had been one of the small miracles he'd come to expect in Africa. One of God's modest performances.

The performances were everywhere: a Masai warrior wearing only a red loincloth to cover his nakedness, leaning on his spear as he waited for the elevator at the Intercontinental, all the while fiddling with his calculator; a late-model Mercedes parked in front of a mud-and-wattle hut; a chemistry professor at the university who didn't know his own birth date or even how old he was, and was always slightly amused that anyone should care. Even the landscape was contradictory. Waking in the rarefied air of Nairobi under his down sleeping bag (it was fucking freezing at night) and then driving thirty miles west, he would descend into a desert so oppressive and hot that only thorn trees could grow. The thorn trees were the best example of Darwinian selection Thomas had ever seen, self-protective in the extreme.

He added pawpaw and passion fruit to the mango in the straw basket and handed it to a slight Asian man behind a makeshift counter. Thomas wouldn't bargain, though the man might expect it. Regina considered it a point of honor to bargain, part of the Kenyan cultural experience. Not bargaining, she argued, contributed to inflation. Plus, it made Americans look like easy marks. Well, they were, Thomas answered, so why pretend otherwise? And what was wrong with being an easy mark anyway?

Wasn't Jesus an easy mark if it came to that? Though Thomas, not very religious, was hard-pressed to continue this argument.

Kenya was nothing if not a country of contradictions — unnerving and sometimes harrowing. On a Sunday, not long ago, traveling with Regina for her research to the mental hospital at Gil Gil, he'd driven the Ford Escort down the hairpin turns of the escarpment and descended into the floor of the Rift Valley, the butt end of the car shimmying wildly on the corrugated dirt road. Regina had worn a dress he particularly liked: a thin, blouse-like dress of mulberry cotton that fit tightly across her breasts and hips. Regina was voluptuous, a fact she loathed about herself. A fact he had once adored. And might still had she not tainted the adoration with her own physical self-hatred.

She had thick black curly hair that resisted taming and was often wiry around her face. Her eyes were small, and deep vertical concentration lines separated her thick brows. But in the car, with her sunglasses on, she'd looked almost glamorous that day. She had worn lipstick, which she rarely did, an ice-pink frost that had distracted him no end.

The hospital had been a series of cement-

and-tin buildings arranged like an army barracks, men lying or sitting on the tarred courtyard in tattered blue shirts and shorts, their only clothing. Cleanliness seemed next to impossible, and the stench had been nearly unbearable in the heat. The men had reached out to touch Thomas and Regina as they passed, hissing when they did so, as if they'd burned themselves on white skin. In the violent ward, men had hung naked from the barred windows. They were schizophrenic or tubercular, or were inflicted with leprosy or syphilis; and the guide, a Luo man dressed in a pin-striped suit and snowy white shirt (seemingly impossible in that landscape of dust and delusion), had informed Thomas and Regina that they were all officially considered psychotic. Laughing genially, their host had shown them the kitchen, which stank of rotting garbage. A patient, chanting to himself, wiped the floor in a swaying motion with a nearly black rag. The pineapple cutters, allowed the use of knives, were locked in cages while they worked. In the female ward, the women wore green shifts and had their heads shaved once a week. Most were lying on the hot black tarmac, listless or asleep. One woman had pulled her dress up over her head and was naked from the waist down.

When the tour was over, they'd taken tea with their host in delicate bone cups in a room furnished with English antiques — a reserved and formal occasion with many strained silences. Even Regina had been quiet, cowed by the simple excess of the suffering, and baffled by the genteel nonchalance of the administrator. When they'd gotten home, they'd both crawled into bed, too exhausted to speak. Neither one of them had eaten for days afterward.

Thomas glanced around the market for his wife and was guiltily relieved when he couldn't find her. He checked his watch. He would take the fruit out to the car, then walk over to the New Stanley for a quick Tusker. The sun hurt his eyes, and he fumbled for his sunglasses. Another perfect day of blue sky and cartoon cloud. The parking boy he'd hired to watch his car was sitting on the fender of the Escort. The parking boys ran a scam like a protection racket: give them a few shillings and they'd watch your car, a signal to the thieves (other thieves, that is) to stay away. Refuse them the shillings, and they'd stand by your car as a sort of testimonial to its availability.

He flipped the boy a ten-shilling note for another hour. Cheaper than a meter if you thought about it. He bought a newspaper from a vendor outside the market and glanced at the headline. MP TOLD: WEAR TROUSERS TO DEBATE. He would have one drink, stay no longer than fifteen minutes, and then buy a pound of cashews for Regina on his way back. Together, they would go home in the Escort for what was left of the weekend.

He hadn't wanted to believe that Kenya was dangerous and had balked at the idea during the training sessions, which had focused relentlessly on survival, as if Thomas and Regina were soldiers engaged in guerrilla warfare. And of course they were, this particular war born of poverty and not of politics. So great was the difference between the rich and the poor in the country that travelers were occasionally hacked to death with pangas. Great-coated askaris with swords stood guard at the ends of the driveways of the European houses. Tourists were robbed so often in the streets and on buses, the joke about the contribution to the GDP was growing old. Corruption rippled through the government and blossomed at the top. Thomas hadn't believed it then, but now he did. Already he'd been robbed seven times, twice of his car. Once, the entire contents of the house had been stolen, even the curtains and the telephone cord. Regina had been crushed to lose her Maridadi cloth and her Kisii stone sculptures, and he'd been panicky about his poems until he realized he'd memorized every one of them.

Never carry a day pack, they told you at the training sessions. Never stop at a crossing and consult a map (to do so instantly marked you as a tourist). Never wear jewelry or flashy sunglasses. Look as poor as possible. Easy for Thomas, who wore the same pair of khaki shorts and white shirt every day except Tuesdays, the day Mama Kariuki came and did the laundry in the bathtub. And if you do have a wallet or a purse stolen, be careful not to yell, "Stop, thief!" because other Kenyans would chase the suspect, and if they caught him, would try to beat him to death, a horrific attempt at execution before a largely passive audience that Thomas had helplessly observed more than once.

He took a seat at the Thorn Tree, the outdoor café of the New Stanley Hotel, and ordered a Tusker. He opened the newspaper and gave it another glance. MALARIA SWEEPS NORTHERN PROVINCE. KILLER LION MAULS PARTY CHIEF. His eyes glazed over an article about land disputes. He noticed the word *brother* in a piece about a Luo businessman who'd been murdered by his and was reminded of his own brother, Rich, and of the fact that he was coming in a month. They would go on safari together to Ngoro Ngoro and the Serengeti, Thomas promising to take him to the coast, where you could buy the most powerful dope he'd ever smoked. In Malindi, even the women chewed miraa, a twig that was a sort of natural speed. He wouldn't tell Rich about the bhangi or the miraa or about the prostitutes, either, who were cheap and beautiful and dangerous with disease.

A shadow passed across his table. Thomas took it for a cloud, but, glancing up, he saw a man hovering over him, the man smiling, waiting to be noticed.

— *Ah, Mr. Thomas, you have lost yourself.*

Thomas stood. *No, Ndegwa, it is you who have been lost, but now you are found again.*

Ndegwa, his teacher, his age mate, chuckled. Thomas's attempts to mimic the African idiom never failed to amuse Ndegwa, even in the early days, when Thomas had taken a poetry class at the University of Nairobi, the only white student in a roomful of younger Africans and Asians. Privately, Thomas had thought the quality of the work poor, though he'd have been the first to admit to an inability to criticize art produced in another culture. Queried, the

173

other students would doubtless have said his work was self-indulgent, that it lacked political content. Ndegwa, however, had not felt that way. Indeed, he'd seemed almost to favor Thomas, a remarkable feat of literary impartiality, particularly considering Ndegwa's Marxist views.

Thomas shook hands with the massive Kikuyu, Ndegwa's bulk shot forward in a tight-fitting gray suit, his purple-black skin dusty with a patina that wasn't dust at all, but rather color added to the color. He was a big-shouldered and big-bellied man, someone who, indeed, seemed cut more from a political or financial cloth than from that of a literary poet.

— *You know what it is they say about a Tusker?* Ndegwa asked.

Thomas smiled and shook his head.

— *Sit down my friend, and I shall share with you my story of a Tusker.*

Thomas sat, and Ndegwa leaned toward him conspiratorially.

— *The first day you are in my country, you look into your Tusker and you find a worm. You are disgusted, and you give the beer to the street.*

Thomas smiled, knowing that a joke was coming. Ndegwa was heavy-lidded and sensual, his shirt a thick, rough cotton Thomas had seen often in the country.

— *After the first month you are in my country, you look into a Tusker and you find a worm. And you say, "There is a worm in my beer." And you calmly pick it out and put it on the street and then you drink your beer.*

Ndegwa chuckling already, his teeth stained pink. Around them German and American tourists were drinking, the decibel level rising as the hour moved toward noon. Thomas saw a journalist — Norman something — he knew from a London paper.

— *But after a year, my friend, you look into your Tusker and you see the worm, and you say, "There is a worm in my beer." And you take it out and eat it for the protein. And then you drink your beer, and you give nothing to the street.*

Ndegwa laughed loudly at his own joke. Thomas made a show of looking into his beer, which made Ndegwa laugh even more.

— *Time to eat the worm, my friend. You have been in my country how long?*

— *Just over a year.*

— *Is it so much?*

Ndegwa managed elegance, even with his bulk, even on the tiny metal café chair. Kimathi Street was thick with shoppers on the Saturday morning. Ndegwa glanced at the African women while Thomas looked at the white women. Although just then, a cocoa-skinned girl with a gazelle neck and a shaved head passed them, and Thomas couldn't help but examine her. She was dressed in European clothes and red stiletto heels, her throat swathed in gold rings. She looked an exotic slave, though she couldn't have been more than fourteen years old. The Asian man she was with was short and plump, his suit expertly tailored. Child prostitution in Kenya was epidemic.

— *And how are you?* Thomas asked when the girl had passed.

— *Oh, I am just all right. I have no bad luck.* Ndegwa shrugged, the smile fading, taxing belief in his pronouncement. Ndegwa was a brilliant teacher, able to excise the fat from Thomas's lines of poetry with quick swipes of his pen, even as Thomas watched. *Though my government is telling me I cannot write any more poems.*

Thomas took a quick sip of beer, thought about the worm. *Why?*

Ndegwa rubbed his eyes. *They are telling me that my poems mock our government and our leaders.*

Which, of course, they did.

— *And so I have been warned.*

Thomas lightly jolted from complacency. Ndegwa was a better teacher than a writer, though his work was haunting and rhythmic and seeped into the bones the way music did. And even though the words themselves were often not memorable, the distinct cadences of Ndegwa's verse drummed themselves inside the head.

— *You're not serious,* Thomas said.

— *I am afraid I am very serious.*

Thomas was disoriented by Ndegwa's calm demeanor. *What if you stopped writing for a while?* Thomas asked.

Ndegwa sighed, picked his teeth with his tongue. *If you were told you could no longer publish your poems because your words revealed unpleasant truths about your government that the government did not want its people to know, would you stop?*

A decision Thomas would never be forced to make. And one he'd never had to consider. Unpleasant words about his own country were practically a national pastime.

Ndegwa turned his massive body sideways to the table and gazed out at the crowd. The poet had a Bantu profile. Oddly, he wore a woman's watch.

— *In my country, they give you a warning so that you can settle your affairs. And then they arrest you. The warning is a prelude to the arrest.*

Ndegwa coolly drank his beer. Following a detainment, Thomas wondered, what happened? Imprisonment? Death? Surely not.

— *You know this?* Thomas asked.

— *I am knowing this.*

— *But what about your wife and baby?*

— *They are gone to my homeland.*

— *Jesus.*

— *Jesus is not helping me too much.*

— *You could flee.* Thomas scrambled for a solution, thinking like an American: all problems could be solved if only one could imagine the solution.

— *To where? To my homeland? They will find me. I cannot leave the country. They will confiscate my passport at the airport. And besides, my friend, if I go, they will arrest my wife and son and threaten to kill them if I do not return. This is standard.*

On a Friday noon, near the end of term, Thomas had lingered in the classroom while Ndegwa had read — and edited — his last bit of work for the class. Then Ndegwa had glanced at his watch and had said he needed to catch a bus to Limuru. His wife had given birth to their firstborn son just the month previous, and he wanted to travel to the family shamba to be with them for the weekend. Thomas, wishing to postpone as long as possible the thin haze of tension that would obscure the landscape of his weekend with Regina, had volunteered to drive him — an offer Ndegwa happily accepted. Thomas and Ndegwa made their way into the Highlands, past the tea plantations and along a route that paralleled a dirt path. Men in pin-striped suits and old women bent under loads of firewood watched the passing car as if Thomas and Ndegwa were envoys on a diplomatic mission. Along the way, they discovered they were age mates, born on the same day in the same year. Had Thomas been a Kikuyu, Ndegwa explained, they'd have been circumcised together when they were twelve, would have been isolated from their families and community for a period of several weeks while they became men, and then would have been welcomed back into the fold with a great deal of ceremony. Thomas liked the concept: becoming a man in his own culture was a vague and unspecific thing, unmarked by ceremony or even awareness of the event, defined as it was, if at all, individually and idiosyncratically. When you took your first drink? Had sex? Got your license? Got drafted?

Thomas and Ndegwa parked when the road ran out. They wound their way down a

179

long murram path to a rectangular mud building with a rippled blue tin roof. Except for a small patch of hard-baked dirt in front of the house, all the other soil had been cultivated. The house stood on a rise in sun so bright Thomas had to squint his eyes nearly shut. An elderly woman emerged from the house wearing a kitenge cloth tied around her body and another cloth wound around her head. Ndegwa introduced Thomas to his mother. A wide gap in the bottom row of her teeth, Ndegwa had later explained, was the result of six teeth that had been deliberately pulled in adolescence to enhance her beauty. The woman came forward and shook hands and squinted as she listened to Thomas's name. Behind her, Ndegwa's several sisters shyly filed out, greeting Thomas just as their mother had done. A fire burned to one side of the front door, and a young goat lay on its back with its throat cut. Ndegwa began the skinning in his role as host. He hadn't even taken off his suit coat. Thomas felt narcoleptic from the altitude, queasy about the goat. He watched Ndegwa's knife make the first cut into the skin of the leg and peel back a bloody flap, and then turned to study the banana trees. One of the women, in a blue pantsuit and red platform shoes, stepped forward and introduced herself as Mary, Ndegwa's wife. She was wearing a large rhinestone ring. Thomas wasn't sure he'd ever seen such swollen breasts. Her platforms sank into the mud with her weight, but together, they negotiated the thin strip of grass that separated the banana trees from the maize fields.

The house was surrounded by a garden of moonflowers and frangipani, the scent so intoxicating Thomas wanted to lie down right there on the ground. The mildly hilly landscape was divided into intricate patterns of cultivation: just the shades of green alone made him dizzy. On the hills were other mud-and-tin huts, and overhead the sky was the deep cobalt he'd come to expect in the country. An ordinary day in Kenya, he reflected, would be cause for celebration in Hull.

Mary ordered a child to boil water on a charcoal burner, then invited Thomas to step inside the hut.

A red vinyl sofa and two matching chairs decorated the central room. In its center was a small plastic table, so that to sit down, Thomas had to climb over the table. The floor was dirt, and Thomas wondered what would happen to it in a heavy rain. Outside, through the doorway, the sun lit up a landscape of colors so garish they hurt the eye.

He knew he'd never be able to describe them: it had something to do with the equatorial light and the quality of the air — very fine. If you couldn't describe a country's colors, what did you have?

On the walls were framed Coca-Cola ads and severely posed photographs of family groupings. From a battery-operated record player crooned, improbably, an American twang: *Put your sweet lips a little closer to the phone.* Thomas was offered a glass of warm beer that he drank straight down. Mary laughed and poured him another. He tried not to look too surprised when she told him that she, too, was a poet, and that she had a degree in forensic medicine from the university at Kampala. She'd retreated to the family shamba, she explained, for the birth of her first child, who was then a month old. She asked him why he was in the country. He was in the country, he said, because Regina was, and Regina was in the country because she had a grant to study the psychological effects of sub-Saharan diseases on Kenyan children under ten years old. The grant was with UNICEF. From time to time, Thomas noticed, Ndegwa retreated to the back of the house to speak with men who had come especially to see him, and Thomas vaguely understood it had something to do with politics.

— *My husband says you are a wonderful poet.*

— *Your husband is very kind.*

— *In your country, writing poems is not dangerous work?*

— *In my country, writing poems isn't considered work.*

— *In my country, such a thing is sometimes very dangerous. But you are not writing of my country?*

— *No. I don't know it well enough.*

— *Ah,* said Mary enigmatically, patting him on the knee. *And you will not.*

Two sisters brought in a sufuria filled with pieces of burnt goat. A leg bone was sticking out. Ndegwa sliced the crispy black meat on a wooden table with a machete and passed bowls of the glistening goat around the room. Thomas held his plate in his lap until he watched Mary use her fingers. The grease on the rhinestone was fantastic.

The eating was painful. Ndegwa presented Thomas with a bowl of choice morsels reserved for the guest of honor. He explained that these were the goat's organs — the heart, lungs, liver and brain — and that they were sweet. To encourage Thomas, Ndegwa drank the raw blood which had been drained from the goat when it was slaughtered. Refusing the delicacies was not, Thomas already knew from having been in the country half a year, an option — not without embarrassment to himself and insult to Ndegwa. Thomas didn't care whether he himself was embarrassed, but he guessed he didn't want to insult his teacher. His gorge rose. He stuck his fingers into the pot, closed his eyes, and ate.

Another African experience, he knew at once, that could never be described.

After a time, Mary rose and said they must all excuse her because she was uncomfortable and needed to nurse her baby. Ndegwa laughed and added, *Her breasts are so big, she is now a bent tree.*

The good-byes, Thomas remembered, had taken an hour.

— *Now you know where to find us, you will come again,* Ndegwa said to Thomas when he was leaving.

— *Yes, thank you.*

— *Don't get scarce.*

— *No. I won't.*

— *We will have two goats next time.*

— *Perfect,* Thomas said.

— *When will the arrest be?* Thomas asked Ndegwa at the café.

— *In a week? Two weeks? In five days? I do*

not know. Ndegwa flipped his hand back and forth.

— *Is a poem worth dying for?*

Ndegwa licked his lips. *I am a symbol to many who are like me. I am a better symbol arrested, where my people can hear of me and read of me, than if I flee.*

Thomas nodded, trying to comprehend the political act. Trying to understand the reasoning of a man who would put himself and his family at risk for an idea. All through history men had died in droves for ideas. Whereas he couldn't think of a single idea worth dying for.

He wanted to tell Ndegwa that his work was too good, that it shouldn't be sacrificed for politics. But who was he to say? In this country of so much suffering, who could afford the luxury of art?

— *Stay with Regina and me,* Thomas said. *They'll never look for you in Karen.*

— *We shall see,* Ndegwa said. Noncommittal, having committed himself elsewhere. As good as arrested already.

The big man stood. Thomas, shaken, rose with him. A feeling of helplessness overtook him. *Tell me what I can do,* Thomas said.

Ndegwa looked away and then back again. *You will go to visit my wife.*

— *Yes,* Thomas said. *Of course.*

— *This you will promise me.*

— *Yes.* And did he see then, on Ndegwa's face, the tiniest flicker of fear?

Thomas paid for the beers and left the Thorn Tree. He felt dizzy and disoriented. It was the beer on an empty stomach. Or Ndegwa's news. A man approached him, naked but for a paper bag. The bag was slit up the sides to allow for legs, and the man was holding the two openings closed with his fists. He looked as though he were wearing diapers. His hair was dirty with bits of different-colored lint. He stopped in front of Thomas — the American, the easy mark. Thomas emptied his pockets into a pouch the man had slung around his neck.

He needed to find Regina.

He passed the street that led to the Hotel Gloria, where he and Regina had spent their first night in the country, not realizing it was a brothel. The sink had been stopped up with a brown matter he hadn't wanted to investigate, and when they'd woken, they'd been covered with fleas. A woman was passing him now, carrying a child on her back, the baby's eyes clouded with flies. Thomas needed a drink of water. Colors seemed louder now, more garish; sounds bolder and brighter than they'd been an hour ago. He remembered the first time he'd seen a long red trail of shiny ants and how he'd realized too late they were crawling up his leg. At Gil Gil, a naked woman had lain motionless on the asphalt paving of the courtyard. Naked men had hung from barred windows. They had spit at his feet. Why were so many without clothing in this country? The vision in his right eye was replacing itself with hundreds of bright moving dots. Not a migraine, please, he thought — not now. SCHOOL-GIRL DIES AFTER CIRCUMCISION. He re-membered the night express to Mombasa, the rhythm of the rails sexually intoxicating. He and Regina had shared a narrow bunk, and it had been a tender night between them, a kind of truce. He'd been reading *Maurice*, by E. M. Forster. Where had he left the book? He'd like to read it again. Kenyans hated homosexuals, never men-tioned them, as though they simply didn't exist. Rich was coming, and maybe Thomas would let him chew the twigs. What had his mother written? The gas lines were terrible. THREE AMERICANS BEHEADED. Would the car still be there? Or had he not paid enough? Pots and clothing were for sale in the street. A storefront window advertised a Cuisinart. Regina would be seriously worried now. He'd had Welsh rarebit yesterday at the Norfolk, and in his imagination he could still taste it. In reality, he could taste the Tusker. Words. They haunted him in the night. Once twenty lions had walked past him. He had stood frozen, at the side of the car, unable even to open the door to get in. Regina screaming silently from within. They'd gone up to Keekorok with a low battery and four bald tires. The gearshift had come off in his hand. Another time, on a safari, when everyone had left camp, he'd stayed behind to write. He'd been attacked by baboons, and had had to fend them off with a wooden spoon and a metal pot. WITCH DOCTOR HELD IN RUGBY FIX. MAN CAUGHT IN ZEBRA TRAP. At a party at the embassy, a woman in a white suit had taken him for a spy. The air in Karen tasted like champagne. It was even better in the Ngong Hills. He longed for their coolness, for the green of them. He leaned his head against the wall of a building, the cement hot and rough, not soothing. Regina would have the medicine in her purse. If only he could get to a quiet room. He remembered a cave with thousands of bats overhead, Regina falling to her knees, terrified. He'd pleaded with her to move, and in the end, he'd had to drag her out bodily. *I am just all right. I have no bad luck.* A pleasantry, not meant to be taken as truth. Ndegwa was having spectacularly bad luck. Or was he simply creating it? RAINS CAUSE HAVOC. POOR WATCH HOMES BULLDOZED. AMBULANCE FOUND FULL OF IVORY. Regina would be furious at first, angry to have been kept waiting. But she'd relent when she saw the migraine.

In the market, he let his eyes adjust to the gloom. The stench was even worse now, and he was trying to breathe through his mouth. The people and stalls in the market took shape, photographs emerging from a bath. He saw a woman in a kanga, the cloth wrapped tightly around her hips. She had a lovely, muscular ass. Ndegwa had looked at African women, whereas he, Thomas, was noticing the long, narrow waist of a white woman, the way her cotton blouse billowed over the kanga. And then his chest was so tight, he had to suck the fetid air to breathe.

It was not possible, he thought. Even as he knew it was.

The pain stayed, but his head cleared. The disturbance in his vision subsided. She had her back to him, her long slender back. A basket over her arm. She was bent slightly toward a display of pineapples, examining them for ripeness. A long row of silver

189

bracelets on her right wrist jingled as she moved her hand. Her legs were bare from mid-calf to foot. He looked at the slim, tanned legs, the dusty heels, the leather sandals, well worn. Was it possible he was mistaken? Never. About this he could not be mistaken. The hair a miracle, blonder than he remembered. Tied in a loose knot at the back of her neck.

Now the woman was paying for her pineapple. She turned and moved in his direction. For a moment, she looked quizzical, straw basket in one hand, the wallet in the other. Her face was leaner, not as rounded as he remembered. Even in the gloom of the market, he could see the gold cross. He heard the gasp.

— *Thomas,* the woman said.

She took a step forward.

— *Is it really you?*

He put his hands in his pockets, afraid that he might inadvertently touch her. Her presence a grenade, detonating.

— *Linda.*

His mouth already dry.

She smiled tentatively and cocked her head.

— *What are you doing here?*

What was he doing in Africa? It seemed a valid question.

190

— *I've been here. A year.*

— *Really? So have I. Nearly, anyway.*

Her eyes slid off his own for just a second, and the smile flickered. She wouldn't have seen the scar before.

— *This is very strange,* he said.

An elderly man in a royal-blue jacket approached him and tugged at his sleeve. Thomas was rigid, unable to move, as though he might shatter something important. He watched as Linda reached into her wallet and took out shillings. The beggar, appeased, moved away.

She put the backs of her fingers to her nose, assaulted by one of the smells that wafted through the building. He thought her fingers might be trembling. Regina would be somewhere, waiting for him now. *Regina.* He struggled to say something sane.

— *My wife is with UNICEF.*

The words *my wife* not possible, he thought. Not here. Not now.

— *Oh,* she said. *I see.*

Thomas glanced at her fingers for a wedding band. Something that might have been a ring on her left hand. *You're in Nairobi?*

— *No. I'm in the Peace Corps. In Njia.*

— *Oh,* he said. *I'm surprised.*

— *Why?*

— *I never figured you for the Peace Corps.*

— *Well. People change.*

— *I suppose they do.*

— *Have you changed?*

He thought. *I don't think so.*

His lips were dry, and he had to lick them. His breathing was too shallow, and he needed air. The pain in his temple was excruciating. Regina would have the medicine in her purse. He put a hand to his head, almost before he realized he'd done so.

— *You have a migraine.*

He looked at her, astounded.

— *It's a pinching you get around your eyes.*

She who had seen dozens.

— *I don't get them as often as I used to. The doctor tells me that by the time I'm fifty, they'll have disappeared.* He took in a great suck of air, hoping to disguise it as a sigh.

— *It's hard to imagine living that long,* she said lightly.

— *I used to think I'd be dead by thirty.*

— *We all did.*

She had water-blue eyes and long, blond lashes. Shallow wrinkles already spoking out from the eyes. Her face tanned, an Indian red. After the accident, it had not been possible to be together. Her aunt and her uncles had forbidden it. He had besieged her house for days. Until, finally, they had sent her away. He still didn't know

192

where she had gone.

He had sent four letters, none of which had been answered. And then it was fall, and he had enrolled at Harvard. She had chosen Middlebury. He'd made himself give it up then, accept her silence as his punishment.

A decade had changed her. She looked a woman now. Her breasts were loose inside her blouse, and he struggled not to look at them.

— *We live in Karen,* he said.

She nodded slowly.

— *It's west of here.* He waved his hand in a direction that might be west.

— *I know the place.*

— *I never got the chance to tell you how sorry I was,* he said. *I tried to write you.*

She looked away. Her chest was red in the deep V of her blouse.

— *For the accident,* he said. *It was inexcusable. If I hadn't been driving so fast. If I hadn't been drinking.*

She glanced quickly back at him. *I was there. I was as much a part of what happened as you.*

— *No, you weren't. I was the one who was driving.*

She put a hand out and touched his wrist. The touch so electric that he flinched.

Thomas, let's not do this. That was years ago. Everything is different now.

Her kanga was only a single piece of cloth she had wrapped at her waist like the African women did. A slight tug, and it would slide to her sandals. He couldn't think about that now.

— *I just want to know where they sent you,* he said. *I've always wondered.*

She withdrew her hand. *I went to stay with Eileen in New York.*

He nodded slowly.

— *Then I went to Middlebury.*

He took a long breath.

— *There's so much to catch up on,* she said. As any woman might. Trying, he knew, to make it normal.

— *How's your aunt?* he asked. For the moment, acquiescing.

She pressed her lips together. She shrugged. Her relationship with her aunt would always be complex. *The same, I guess.*

— *Why didn't you answer my letters?* he asked too quickly — unable, after all, to keep it normal.

She put a hand to the side of her head and tucked a stray strand of hair behind her ear. *I didn't get any letters.*

— *You didn't get my letters?*

She shook her head.

His chest felt squeezed.

— *So,* she said. A small frown disappearing. *You're shopping?*

— *Oh,* he said. Confused. *I did the shopping. Well, my part. Although I should get some cashews.* Hoping she wouldn't notice the Tusker on his breath. It wasn't even noon.

From the corner of his eye, he could see Regina approaching. Carrying a straw basket filled with food in her arms. Panic swelled inside of him. It seemed important that he speak to Linda before Regina got there.

— *Linda,* he said, but then he stopped. Words, heartless and fickle, failed him.

Her eyes flicked up at his, and he held them.

Regina stood beside them, and there seemed a terrible pause. Linda smiled in Regina's direction. *Hello. I'm Linda Fallon.*

Thomas struggled toward the surface. He glanced at Regina and wondered if Linda's name would register. He hoped it wouldn't. *Linda, this is my wife, Regina.*

Regina set down her straw basket and shook Linda's hand. Regina's pink sleeveless blouse stained beneath her arms, her hair wild and sticky about her face. She looked at Thomas, at his empty hands. She had worn shorts, and, disloyally, he felt

195

embarrassed for her.

— *Didn't you get the fruit?* Regina asked. Even now, a slight whine.

— *It's in the car.*

She studied him. *You have a migraine?*

Linda looked away.

Thomas sought and failed to find a normal voice. *Linda's an old friend. From Hull.*

Regina turned to the stranger. *Really? Are you on safari?*

— *No. I'm in the Peace Corps.*

— *In Nairobi?*

— *In Njia.*

— *Oh, really. What do you do?*

— *I teach.*

— *Oh, wow.* The *wow* automatic, without emotion. Behind Linda, the shopkeeper was packing up his leftover fruit.

— *They're closing up,* Thomas said. Racked between wanting the two women to separate as soon as possible and wishing to make his conversation with Linda last forever. He had so many questions he wanted to ask her, questions he'd been asking her for years.

Linda let them see that she was checking her watch. *I've got to run. Peter's waiting for me to go to lunch.*

The name a slug to the center of his chest.

That there was a Peter might have been expected, but the name shocked him even so.

Linda turned to Regina. *It was so nice to meet you.* She glanced at Thomas. There was nothing she could say. She smiled instead.

Thomas watched her walk away, all the blood in his veins following her.

He bent to pick up Regina's basket. Giving himself something to do to cover the hole inside him. Regina was silent as they made their way through the stalls and into the noonday sun.

— *Roland and Elaine want us for dinner,* she said.

Roland, Regina's supervisor, was an asshole, but Thomas was relieved there would be a party. He didn't think he could bear a long night in the cottage with Regina. Not this night.

— *Wasn't that the gal you used to go out with in high school?*

Willing himself to sound casual, even bored. *For a couple of months.*

— *And didn't you have some sort of car accident with her?*

— *She was in the car.*

Regina nodding. *I remember now. You told me that.*

Thomas put the basket in the trunk. He

opened the driver's-side door and slipped inside, the seat so hot it burned his thighs. The parking boy was watching him, waiting for a tip. Thomas rolled down his window, and the boy was on him in a flash.

Regina settled in beside him. *Blondes shouldn't let themselves get that much sun,* she said. *Did you notice how she's ruining her skin?*

He stood on Roland's verandah, a Pimm's in his hand, his chest suffused with a sensation he thought, from no recent recognizable experience, must be joy. A feeling that went all the way to his thighs. At the start of the evening, arriving amid a welter of cool but paradoxically welcoming asides — *Roland, aren't Americans funny the way they walk to everything? Now this dress I like* — he'd felt his attention sparingly lent, plucked from him unwillingly. And so had sought refuge on the verandah, where no one else had yet gone.

And knew himself to be in love. If, indeed, he'd ever not been. Not since a day in 1966 when a girl in a gray skirt and a white blouse had crossed the threshold of a schoolroom. It was as if he'd merely been distracted all these years, or had grown weary of loving only memories. And had, against all the odds, been returned to a rightful state. Not reminded, but restored. As a sightless man who once had sight will learn to live with his condition, adjust to his darkened universe, and then, years later, when astonishingly he can see again, will know how glorious his world once was. And all this on nothing but an unlikely meeting and the exchange of a dozen sentences — small miracles in themselves.

The verandah overlooked a garden of hibiscus and moonflowers, the latter giving off a spectral glow from the lit lanterns hanging in the trees. On the equator, the sun set at six every night of the year, a light that extinguished itself without apology or dimming, a fact Thomas found disconcerting. He missed the slow leaching of summer evenings, and even the dawns he had hardly ever seen. He also, to his vast surprise, missed snow, and occasionally he had snow dreams in the night. Eye-level now with an avocado tree ponderous with fruit — so close he could have leaned over and picked one of the scaly green pears — he remembered he'd never eaten one until he'd gone to college, the fruit far too exotic for his mother's Calvinist table.

Roland had insisted he have a Pimm's, a sweetish gin drink, though Thomas had wanted a simple beer. Roland was as executive at home as he was on the job, a man who made insistent pronouncements with a certitude that was baffling. Mark his words, there would be tribal anarchy when Kenyatta died. He'd tell you right now, if an African bought a European house it could be counted on to go to ruin. It was axiomatic that you could never trust an Asian. Thomas, having no opinions on these subjects, found the acknowledged — no, *brandished* racism — appalling. In turn, Roland thought Thomas hopelessly naive and said so. Amusingly naive, actually. An earnest American was an entertainment. *You'll see,* Roland was fond of adding.

The night air floated around Thomas's arms, bare to the elbows. In the distance, he could hear music and the fading away of a woman's laughter. Smoke rose from the cement garage where the servants lived, raising, as it always did, the question of degree: Was the confinement of servants in a cement garage any different from slavery? Beneath this thought, also wanting to know: Where was Linda right now? What was she doing this very minute? He imagined her in a hut in the bush — why, he couldn't have said. It was the idea of the Peace Corps, he supposed, with its suggestion of good works and mild suffering. How easily they might have missed each other in the market, might never have known the other was even in the country. It made him weak in the knees just to think of it. He saw again the shallow curve of her waist and hips, the way her breasts swayed inside her blouse. A longing he hadn't felt since adolescence made his bones ache.

Her fingers had trembled when she'd brought them to her face; he was certain he had seen that. And yet she had seemed so calm, so preternaturally composed. Had the chance meeting meant something to her, or would she have regarded it merely as a wistful moment, something to be put aside so that one could get on with life? It seemed impossible that either should have forgotten the other. And yet he had married another woman, and she was with a man named Peter. He pictured an anemic academic for no more reason than he wished it so. He wondered if they lived together, guessed that they did. Didn't everyone these days, especially in this country of lawlessness and illicit love?

He turned slightly, leaned his hip against the railing, and looked through the set of casement windows into a room that Elaine repeatedly referred to as the drawing room, another British export that seemed anachronistic in a country where nearly everyone lived in huts. Just at this party alone, he could count three affairs he knew about, and who could say how many others lay beneath this modest number? Roland, himself, was sleeping with Elaine's best friend, Jane, and the odd thing was, Regina had said, Elaine knew about it and didn't care. Which raised the question: with whom was Elaine sleeping? Regal Elaine, who would not have gone without. Lanky Elaine, with her hard, nut-brown face and her hair bleached nearly platinum by a lifetime on the equator. Imperious Elaine, who had been born in Kenya and had once told Thomas huffily that she was a Kenyan citizen (though it didn't seem to have made her like Africans any better, he had noticed). She kept horses and had the thighs of a rider. She had a unique sort of beauty, but her personality was as weather-beaten as her face. Worse than Roland at hiding her contempt for Americans. She glanced up at that moment and saw that Thomas was staring at her. He quickly slid his eyes away. She might misinterpret the examination, might even flirt with him later.

Jesus, he thought, turning back to the railing. That was all he needed.

He'd had the migraine for hours and had

been glad for the darkened room. Regina had been puttering in the kitchen and then had been reading on the verandah. In the privacy of the bedroom, he'd felt the joy even then, even through the nauseating haze of the pain. And when the unbearable had subsided, he'd been nearly euphoric with happiness. He'd played the conversation he'd had with Linda in the market over and over, the repetition of the phrases like a poem he was trying to memorize.

Is it really you?

This is very strange.

Have you changed?

That was years ago. Everything is different now.

He heard the soft click of the door to the verandah behind him. He sent up a quick prayer that it wasn't Elaine.

— *Our resident rhyming fool.*

Roland, generous golden drink in hand, sidled up to Thomas and leaned his elbows on the wrought-iron railing, a position that looked, but couldn't be, at ease. His arms were swathed in some synthetic shirt material Roland let you know had specially been sent from London.

— *I don't rhyme,* Thomas said.

— *Really not? I didn't realize.*

Roland took a sip of his drink and

brushed a greasy forelock from his forehead. His smell was rank with an overlay of cologne. Not to mention his lethal breath, evident at a yard. The British didn't bathe but once or twice a week; well, no one did out here.

— *Where can one get your books, anyway?*

— *There aren't any books.*

Thomas was certain they'd already had this conversation, months ago.

— *Oh. How disappointing.*

Roland's trousers, also of some synthetic material, were tight against his thighs and belled over his shoes. He wore a heavy silver watch with an expansion band too big for him.

— *Broadsides? Pamphlets?* Roland asked, with seeming insouciance.

— *Literary magazines,* Thomas said, immediately regretting the note of pride.

— *I suppose there's a market for that sort of thing in the States?*

Thomas wondered where Roland's lover was tonight. Jane, whose husband led safaris and was often conveniently away from home. Whose husband complained loudly at parties about not being allowed to shoot the game anymore.

— *None.*

— *Oh, dear,* Roland said with faint

dismay. *Regina must do well?* He meant financially.

Thomas thought about, and then decided against, revealing that he was putting Regina through school.

— *There's a Ugandan fellow here runs a magazine might be of use to you*, Roland said, making a sour face and leaning conspiratorially toward Thomas. *Of course, it's a grotty little magazine, mind you, and the fellow is a bit of a slime, but, still, I suppose any publication is better than none?*

Roland put his back to the railing and surveyed his own party.

— *And what were we being so reclusive about all alone on the verandah, if one may ask?* Roland asked, giving himself permission. He smiled and took a sip of his drink. The man's condescension was insufferable. The *we* put Thomas over the edge.

— *Actually, I was thinking about Jane,* Thomas said.

Arab furniture from the coast mixed with English antiques to produce a fussiness that needed editing; though there was a magnificent secretary Thomas had admired once before and did again tonight. He examined the books that lay behind the leaded glass cabinets. Nothing surprising, just the usual:

206

Dickens and Hardy, T. E. Lawrence and Richard Burton. He might ask Roland tonight if he could borrow the Burton. An African in a white uniform took his glass and asked, in melodic Kikuyu accent, if he'd like another Pimm's. Thomas shook his head, the medication for the migraine mixing with the alcohol, making him both high and groggy. Desperate for sleep.

In the corner, Regina was talking to a boy. She had worn her hair in a twist, a style she knew Thomas liked. Her sleeveless red dress revealed arms tanned from long afternoons spent at outdoor clinics. Her neck was damp from the heat, tiny dots of moisture on her skin. Once he had craved to make love to his wife. When they'd met in a hardware store in Boston — she wearing a yellow T-shirt and overalls, looking for a hoe; he standing at the checkout line with a plunger in his hand — he'd noticed her porcelain-fine skin and her astonishing breasts outlined beneath the bib of the overall and had felt compelled to capture her attention. He'd followed her to her car, feigning an interest in gardening that hadn't survived the evening. In bed that night at her apartment (*wallowing* in bed, he thought now), he'd confessed he'd known nothing about gardening, and she'd laughed and told him he'd been as transparent as glass. She'd been flattered, however, she added, which he hadn't understood until months later when he'd learned how much she hated her large body. And by then, it was too late. He thought the words, *too late*. A fatal construction he'd never really put together until now. Already the chance meeting with Linda was rearranging his thinking.

Regina bent to the boy, hair whipped blond by constant wind and sun, who had come out to say hello to the guests. Looking shy and miserable, though Regina was good at coaxing a smile and might manage one soon. He seemed a sweet kid, only ten years old. In another year, Roland would send him to England to boarding school. It struck Thomas as an extreme measure to take to give a child an education, Roland's culture sometimes as foreign to him as the African. Regina beckoned to Thomas to join them.

— *You remember Richard,* Regina said in a bright voice used by adults in the presence of children.

Thomas put out his hand, and the boy shook it, the delicate bones nearly lost in Thomas's grip.

— *How do you do?* the boy asked politely, eyes everywhere but on Thomas.

— *Very well. And yourself?* Thomas bent slightly to the boy, who shrugged. Manners could take him only so far.

— *Richard said he's racing tomorrow in Karen. He's invited us to come and watch.*

Thomas could scarcely imagine the boy controlling a horse, never mind racing. Though, as Elaine's son, he'd have grown up with horses. Once, Thomas and Regina had been invited to the Karen Hunt, an anachronism if ever Thomas had seen one: sherry on silver trays, scarlet coats, the immense underbellies of the beasts brushing the tops of the hedges. The hedges of Karen, he thought. They told a story all their own.

— *I think we might just have to do that*, Thomas said to the boy, thinking, again, even as he spoke: And where is Linda now? Right this very minute?

— *You're kind of quiet tonight.* This from Regina when the boy had left, summoned by his mother.

— *Am I?*

— *You're being almost rude.*

— *To whom?*

— *To Roland and Elaine, to start.*

— *Considering the fact that Roland just expressed deep sympathy over the fact that I'm a failed poet who needs to be supported by his wife, I don't suppose I give a fuck.*

— *Thomas.*

Beyond Regina, Elaine watched them intently.

— *It's the migraine,* he said, searching for an explanation his wife might find acceptable. *It's made the day seem not normal.*

Regina slipped a finger between the buttons of his shirt. *All your days are abnormal.*

Thomas understood the finger for what it was. Regina would want to make love when they got home.

— *I know you've had the migraine,* Regina said, whispering. *But tonight's the night.*

Thomas felt a sinking in his chest.

— *I've done the charts,* she said, perhaps defensively.

He hesitated just a second too long, then tried to put his arm around her. But distance or mild panic had already conveyed itself to Regina, who moved inches to one side of him. Too often, it seemed to Thomas, he unintentionally hurt his wife.

— *I assume you've heard the news.* Her voice cool now, the barometer lowered, looking away from him and taking a sip of her drink, a rosy wine.

— *What news?* Thomas, in cautious ignorance, asked.

— *They've arrested Ndegwa.*

Thomas simply stared.

— *This afternoon. Around five o'clock. Norman what's-his-name, the one from the London paper, just told me.*

She gestured in Norman what's-his-name's direction. Noting Thomas's surprise. It would not be fair to say that Regina was enjoying Thomas's distress.

— *Impossible,* Thomas said. For the second time that day, daunted by the impossible. *I just saw the man at lunch. I had a drink with him at the Thorn Tree.*

Regina, who had not known he'd had a drink at the Thorn Tree, looked sharply up at him. *They arrested him at the university,* she said. *There are demonstrations even now.*

Thomas, saturated, couldn't absorb the news.

— *He must have a tremendous following,* Regina said, now as watchful as Elaine.

— *Jesus,* Thomas said, shaken by possibility become reality. He thought of the casual way Ndegwa had looked at African women. Of his joke about the worm.

— *Big enough to be news in London anyway,* Regina said.

He waited in the bedroom of the villa, the room lit only by the moon, the bluish light outlining the odd feminine bits of furniture

211

that had been lent to them after the robbery: the dressing table with its chintz skirt; the camelbacked settee that had some age; the heavy mahogany wardrobe with the door that didn't quite fit and in which both he and Regina kept ridiculously few clothes. He imagined the ornate wardrobe traveling from London by ship to Mombasa, brought up by horse and cart from the coast. A woman's treasure, a piece of furniture she'd said she wouldn't go to Africa without. And what had happened to the woman? Thomas wondered. Had she died in childbirth? Been afraid during the long nights when her husband had been on safari? Danced at the Muthaiga Club while her husband made love to her best friend in the backseat of his Bentley? Been sick with chronic malaria in this very bed? Or had she become browned and hardened like Elaine, the boredom and dust sharpening her tongue? The house was a perk from Regina's research grant, its unexpected luxury surprising them both when they'd arrived in the country. Regina had at first balked at staying in Karen, but the bougainvillea and the Dutch door in the kitchen had seduced her before they'd even had their gin and tonics on the verandah. Now his wife adored the house, couldn't imagine returning to the States. Couldn't imagine living without the servants now, for that matter: the cook, the gardener, and the ayah they would hire if only Regina could bear a child.

Behind the bathroom door, he could hear the swishing of limbs in the water of the clawfooted bathtub. He knew that Regina would soon put on the black silk-and-lace nightgown he'd bought her on a homesick whim during a stopover in Paris on their way to Africa. A nightgown she'd worn every night she thought herself fertile; a nightgown that now gave off a whiff of failure, its intended allure long since worn away, like a woman's scent fading. He wished he could somehow signal to Regina not to wear the thing — had even, oddly, thought of hiding it — but she would almost certainly misinterpret the comment, would take it personally to mean that he thought her too fat. A word he'd never used, never even suggested, her own distaste for her body so pervasive she assumed everyone shared her own distorted image. It had, he knew now, ruined her life, in the way a cleft lip or a misshapen limb might twist a future. Nothing he could say or do could erase the picture she had of herself, and he thought the damage must have been done early in her life, though he thought it pointless to blame a parent.

He got out of the bed and stood naked at the window. He could just make out, in the eerie light, the jacarandas and the euphorbia trees, and on the air was the smell of jasmine. Returning from the party, slightly drunk, he'd been assaulted by a rush of memories, a neap tide he hadn't been able to hold back, even when Regina had said, rusty note, *Thomas, are you listening?* He'd pleaded preoccupation with Ndegwa's detainment, true enough, though it had not been the source of the nostalgic flood. In the car, he'd seen a young girl — and yes, she had been only a girl then — walking late into a classroom already filled with students and a teacher, her swagger an announcement, a surprise. Her charcoal skirt had come only to the middle of her thighs, a shocking length in school. Every boy and even the teacher had gawped at the long legs (legs as long as birches, he thought now) and at the white cotton shirt, fastened one button too short, that opened to a deep V above her breasts. (And even now a cotton blouse on a woman could arouse Thomas, a mildly disconcerting cue in a country where short skirts and white cotton blouses were *de rigueur* on schoolgirls.) The girl had stood in the doorway, books in hand and chewing gum, and he was certain Mr. K. would bark at her to spit it out. But even Mr. K. had been rendered speechless, able to do little more than ask her name and check it against his roll, fingers trembling as he did so. And somehow Thomas had known, even then, that the skirt and the blouse and the gum were wrong for her, a costume she was trying on. And had wondered immediately how it was that he had not seen this girl before, for he knew that she was someone he'd have followed for days until he'd made her speak to him. Her expression had not been brash, but rather cautious, and he'd realized then that under the mask she might be afraid; that she was someone who might easily be taken advantage of. He'd willed her to choose the seat next to him, one of the six or seven empty seats in the room (actually *prayed* for it: *Dear Jesus, please let her sit next to me*), and, miraculously, as if will or desire were enough, or God Himself had intervened, she had moved forward, hesitated, and then taken the seat behind Thomas. And the relief he'd felt had been so profound that he'd been, for the first time in his life, frightened of himself.

From the bathroom, he could hear the tub draining. Regina would be pink from the hot water. He imagined her naked and tried to work up a kind of desire, touching himself without enthusiasm as he did so. Once, lust for Regina had been thoughtless and automatic, but now he had to forget the frown between her eyebrows, the whining tone in the market, the fact that she despised her body. In attempting to forget, however, he succeeded only in remembering — one set of images replaced by another, a slide show he couldn't control. A girl jumping off a pier in the October night. A duffel bag flung high and wide into the sea. A dark warren of tiny rooms, smelling of onions and Johnson's baby oil. Sliding a blouse over the soft bony knob of a shoulder, an image that had retained its erotic hold over him for years. A small girl carrying a tricycle.

Regina opened the bathroom door, and the light flooded the bedroom. She wasn't wearing the nightgown, but instead had wrapped a kitenge cloth around her hips. He would never know whether the gesture was deliberate or merely unconscious, but his heart ratcheted within his chest. She switched off the bathroom light and stood provocatively in the doorway, her breasts white globes in the moonlight. He had only seconds, if that, before she would see his hesitation and cover herself. And then the rest of the night would be tears and apologies, words that both of them would regret. In the distance, as he sometimes did during the night, he heard the sound of drums, of people singing. Kikuyu Catholics, he knew, returning from a midnight service. An awakened ibis cawed in the night, and a donkey, disturbed, made its raw and awful cry. Thomas walked toward his wife and prepared to tell her she was beautiful.

— *I don't understand. It's a Sunday.*
— *I promised Ndegwa.*
— *Promised him what?*
— *That I'd visit his wife.*
— *What good will that do?*
— *None, probably. It's just a promise, Regina.*
— *Why didn't you tell me you'd had a drink with the man?*

He walked to the car, always surprised that it was still in the driveway. Inside the house, Regina was fuming and might be still when he returned later in the evening. He'd invited her to come along, but, either truly stubborn or simply needing to study, she had refused his half-hearted offer. Yet not before she'd told him (arms crossed, her mouth aggrieved) that she had planned a picnic in the Ngong Hills for later in the day, a picnic that would now obviously have to be scrapped. He had winced for her lie, though he'd been relieved when she'd said finally that the trip would simply take too long. He had wanted desperately to be alone.

He left the jacaranda-shaded driveway and made his way along Windy Ridge Road toward the center of town, marveling, as he often did, at the hedges of Karen — thick, impenetrable walls that hid estates from less-privileged eyes. Karen, named for its most famous citizen, Karen Blixen (*I had a farm in Africa. . . .*), had once been an almost exclusively white enclave, a kind of mini-Cotswolds with rolling farms and white-fenced stables and an Anglo-expatriate fondness for racing horses and excessive drinking. Now, scattered amongst the signs at the ends of driveways were African names as well — Mwangi and Kariuki and Njonjo — wealthy Luo or Kikuyu or Kalinjin, an African elite, the money often made mysteriously through politics. And always, at the ends of these driveways, the ubiquitous signs: *Mbwa Kali.* Fierce Dog.

The Escort lurched along the Ngong Road into Nairobi, its tattered muffler announcing itself rudely to anyone at the racecourse or in the Ngong Forest. He negotiated the streets of the city, quiet now on a Sunday morning, and left Nairobi for Limuru, the scenery a kind of diary of time spent in the country: the Impala Club, where he played tennis with the Kenyan executive for Olivetti; the Arboretum, where he and Regina had once fallen asleep after making love; and the house of a UNICEF administrator, where he had gotten drunk nostalgically on scotch. He had been out to the Ndegwa shamba only the once, and he hoped he would remember the way to the outskirts of the central Highlands, once called "the Happy Valley" for the sexual license and alcoholic excess of the Anglo-Kenyan expatriates who had owned the large wheat and pyrethrum plantations. The Mau Mau rebellion and Independence had put an end to the party, the vast farms broken into smaller plots, on which bananas, cassavas, beans, potatoes, and tea now grew. The green of the tea plantations was a color that awed Thomas every time he saw it: a seemingly iridescent emerald that contained within it the essence of both light and water.

In Limuru, he bought a packet of Players at a duka and asked directions to the Ndegwa shamba, noting the practiced manner in which the shopkeeper gave them, as if repeating the well-traveled way to a tourist shrine. Thomas remembered the road when he saw it, little more than a twisting curb on a terraced hill. He parked amidst an array of vehicles: black bicycles with rusty fenders and wicker baskets, a Peugeot 504 with sheepskin seats, a white van that looked like a bakery truck. Beyond the vehicles was a circle of men, sitting casually on benches, like brothers or uncles sent out after a meal by the women in the kitchen. They moved aside for Thomas, his presence not remarkable, and continued their conversations without interruption, mostly in Kikuyu with bits of Swahili Thomas recognized and even phrases in English when only English would do. *Methyl bromide. Irrigation systems. Sophia Loren.* Most were mzees, old men, with dusty sports jackets plucked from Anglican jumble sales, though one tall African had on large gold-rimmed sunglasses and a beautifully cut suit with a Nehru collar. He hardly moved a muscle, his poise impressive. The scene reminded Thomas of a wake. From time to time, women brought out matoke and irio and sukimu wiki from the kitchen. Thomas declined the food but accepted a gourd of pombe, a beer of bananas and sugar he'd had before. Cool drafts of air drifted over the terraces, and in the dis-

221

tance, on another precipice, a waterfall fell silently. He was awed by the strangeness and the beauty of the scene, the colors rich and saturated. A man, appearing in the doorway of Ndegwa's house, was escorted out by another of Ndegwa's sisters. The woman looked at Thomas, but then ignored him in favor of the African with the exceptional poise. Thomas understood then that the men, like himself, were waiting for an audience with Ndegwa's wife.

He was made to wait an hour and a half, but, curiously, he did not feel impatient. He thought of Linda, endless occupation, exhausting every detail of their short meeting in the market: the surprise on her face when she'd seen him, the manner in which she'd looked away when Regina had said the word *migraine,* the way her fingers had trembled. He drank several gourds of the pombe, and knew himself to be distinctly drunk, which felt inappropriate to the occasion. From time to time, one of the African mzees blew his nose onto the ground, a custom Thomas could not get used to, even after a year in the country. He tried to make a poem as he sat there, but could form only disembodied and alien images that he knew would never coalesce into a single entity. He needed very badly to piss, and asked, *Wapi choo,* of the mzee beside him. The man laughed at his Swahili and pointed to a small shack a hundred feet from the house. Thomas was not surprised to find a hole in a cement floor, the smell so foul he had to hold his breath. Glad for Regina's sake that she hadn't come with him.

When he returned to the bench that had numbed his butt, Ndegwa's sister was waiting for him. His walk was surprisingly steady as he followed her into the darkened hut, and he was all but blinded by the sudden darkness after the sunlight. Ndegwa's sister took the blinded man by the hand and led him to his seat. Thomas remembered the feel of the red vinyl before he could even see it.

He would not have recognized Ndegwa's wife. A tall headdress of purple-and-gold kitenge cloth hid the contours of her hair and head. Her body was sheathed in a caftan of similar colors. Thomas was, however, reassured to see the red platforms poking beneath the dress, the rhinestone ring on her finger. She sat — he thought, *regally* — with a glass of water on a table in front of her, and as she spoke, she took small sips. She did not seem the distraught wife of a political martyr or even a forensic scientist who'd had to excuse herself because her breasts were too big. Rather, she held herself as one who had inherited too soon a mantle of power, like the teenage son of a dead king.

Thomas crossed his legs and folded his hands before him. He struggled to find appropriate words for the occasion. *I'm sorry that your husband has been detained,* he said. *I'm hopeful that this will sort itself out quickly. If there's anything I can do.*

— *Yes.*

The *yes* matter-of-fact, as if she had expected the offer.

— *I saw your husband yesterday,* Thomas continued. *At the Thorn Tree Café. He told me he might be arrested. I had no idea it would happen so soon.*

Mary Ndegwa was silent and very still. Thomas tried to imagine her life on her mother-in-law's shamba: would there be a hierarchy, a chain of command? Both women reduced to lesser status when Ndegwa came home on weekends?

— *He told me that if he was arrested, I should visit you,* Thomas said.

— *I know this,* she said.

Thomas, disoriented, nodded slowly. *You've been expecting me, then?*

— *Oh, yes.*

And yet he himself hadn't known until

224

this morning that he would come. A lizard slithered on the wall. Mary Ndegwa adjusted her bulk on the settee.

— *How is your son?* Thomas asked, the breasts reminding him of the child.

— *Baby Ndegwa is just all right.*

The pombe was already giving him a kind of hangover. Incredibly, he needed to piss again.

— *My husband said that you tell the truth in your verses,* Mary Ndegwa said.

Thomas was momentarily buoyed by the compliment, rare enough these days. *Your husband is very generous in his criticism, but I can invent the truth when it suits me.*

— *The truth may be seen from many doorways, Mr. Thomas.*

The pronouncement had the ring of having been rehearsed. He imagined a hillside of huts, all with open doorways, mzees standing at the thresholds and looking at a single light on a distant hill.

His eyes adjusting, he could now make out dark circles around Mary Ndegwa's eyes that spoke of fatigue. He half expected the record player to begin at any minute with another country-and-western tune.

— *Have they told you where Ndegwa is?* Thomas asked.

— *They are keeping him at Thika.*

225

— Will you be allowed to visit him?

She made a face as if to say, Of course not. *Our government will not release my husband. They will not tell us the charges or set a date for trial.*

Thomas nodded slowly.

— This is a fact that should be spoken of in many places, is it not?

A tiny hitch inside his chest, a moment of enlightenment. Understanding now, as he had not before, why he had been granted an audience, why Ndegwa had sat with him yesterday at the Thorn Tree. Had the man been trolling for journalists? For Americans? Had Ndegwa choreographed his own detention?

— This is a violation of human rights, Mary Ndegwa said.

Thomas was hot beneath his blue sports coat, misshapen now from having been washed by mistake in the bathtub. He, the least political of men, even when there had been marches against the Vietnam War. He had gone simply to be there, to watch the people around him. That the marches might be a means to an end, he hadn't much credited.

— My government can detain my husband for years. This is not right.

— No, of course not, Thomas said. *I am*

226

happy to help in any way I can.

— You and my husband spoke of these things?

— Yesterday we talked briefly about the fact that he might be detained. Normally, we spoke of literature. And poetry. Words.

Mary Ndegwa sat forward on the sofa. *They have arrested demonstrators at the university. There are now fifty being detained along with my husband. Why have they been arrested? I will tell you, Mr. Thomas. To silence them. To keep them from uttering words.*

Thomas ran his fingers back and forth over his forehead.

— Dissidence is only words, she added.

It was a kind of catechism, he thought. *I must confess I'm not much of a political man,* he said.

— What is a political man? she asked sharply, a sudden spark, noticeably absent before, in her voice. *Do you recognize suffering?*

— I hope I do.

— Injustice?

— Again, I hope I would.

— Then you are a political man.

There seemed no point in saying otherwise. For her purposes, then, he would be political and would do whatever it was she wished: dispatch himself to embassy officials? Write eloquent letters? Call the press?

Mary Ndegwa struggled to her feet. *Come with me,* she said.

Thomas, having no wish to disobey, followed her. They left the house through a back entrance. Ndegwa's mother, whom he had not seen that day, sat on a bench under a baobab tree. She held her head in her hands and shook it back and forth, crooning, or possibly keening, as she did so, and did not speak to them, or even appear to notice them. Old woman's breasts and missing teeth. Fear for her firstborn son.

They walked along a steep terrace through a mango orchard and bushes laden with red coffee beans. Mary Ndegwa held the skirts of her caftan, planting her red platform shoes firmly along the murram path. He noticed that they had been freshly polished. She stopped on a knoll.

— *Mr. Thomas, you have heard of the Mau Mau rebellion?*

— *Yes, of course.*

— *This is the place where Ndegwa's father was executed,* she said. *He was shot in the back of the head by British soldiers.*

Thomas studied the ground, and reflected that once it had been soaked with blood.

— *He was made to dig his own grave before*

228

he was shot. His wife and children were brought out and forced to watch. Ndegwa was ten years old when he saw this.

Thomas looked at the cross and its inscription: *Njuguna Ndegwa. Freedom Fighter. Husband. Father. Go with God.*

Ndegwa, his friend, had watched a soldier shoot his father when he was only ten years old. Age mates. What, in his own childhood, Thomas wondered, had been remotely comparable?

Mary Ndegwa put a hand on Thomas's arm. He knew her words before she spoke. Yes, he wanted to say, he was a poet, standing in a doorway.

A dozen children, in shorts made gray with use and age, swarmed over the Escort — peering inside, turning the steering wheel, touching the radio. He patted the pockets of his sports coat and was relieved to discover that he hadn't left the keys in the car. He'd have liked to give the children a ride but knew himself too drunk or dazed to do so.

He pulled away from the shamba slowly, terrified he would hit a child, and drove along the steep terraces, distracted by too many thoughts, not sequential, that were crowding his mind for attention — so that he had only bits of sentences, half-told stories, pictures skittering behind themselves. Regina with her arms crossed; Mary Ndegwa with her fly whisk; Linda bent to pineapples.

He arrived at the crossroads at Ruiru, not entirely sure how he had gotten there. A wrong turn? A left fork taken when he ought to have taken a right? He hadn't been paying attention. The sign said Njia to the north, Nairobi to the south. It would not be truthful, he knew, to say that the wrong turns had been accidental. Njia: 80 kilometers. With any luck, it would take him an hour. He pulled to the side of the road and sat with the motor running, watching a matatu, loaded past possibility with people and luggage and chickens and goats, lurch recklessly past him. They were death traps, they told you in the training sessions. If you had to use one, sit in the back and wear sunglasses to protect you from shattering glass when the vehicle tipped over.

Sunday afternoon, and Linda might be with the man she called Peter. They could be sitting on a verandah, or (he hoped not) lying in bed. He preferred to imagine her sitting alone in the doorway of a mud-and-wattle hut, reading. He didn't try to tell himself that he was in the general neighborhood, or that it was perfectly acceptable to go an hour out of his way to see an old friend from home. He understood, even as he put the Escort in gear and turned north, exactly what he was doing.

He traveled through dark forests of eucalyptus, between thickets of bamboo, and along moors trailing mists like veils, emerging to a landscape of soft green hills and broad valleys, watched over by snow-capped Mount Kenya in the distance. A buffalo stood in the middle of the road, and Thomas stopped the car just feet before he would have hit the massive beast. He rolled the windows up and sat unmoving. Of all the animals in Africa, they told you in the training sessions, the buffalo was the most deadly. It could kill a man in seconds, goring him with deadly accuracy, stomping him to death if the goring only wounded. You were supposed to lob stones at it, and theoretically it would run away; but Thomas thought the only strategy simply to walk slowly backward. In the Escort, he didn't move. Cars piled up behind him, but no one honked a horn. After a time — fifteen minutes? twenty? — the buffalo, at its own stately pace, moved on. Thomas put the car in gear. He was covered with sweat now.

The town of Njia was larger than he had thought it would be. He drove along a street called Kanisa, past a clock tower and a bar called the Purple Heart Pub. He stopped at the Wananchi Café and asked the proprietor, an old woman with scattered teeth and one bad eye, if she spoke English. She did not, but agreed to speak in Swahili, which reduced Thomas to words and phrases that could not be put into sentences. He said *mzungu* and Peace Corps and *manjano* (yellow) for the color of her hair and *zuri* for beautiful. The old woman shook her head but beckoned for him to follow her next door to another duka, where he bought a bottle of Fanta, his mouth parched, from nerves or from the drive. The woman and the man spoke in their own tribal tongue and seemed to argue extensively about the matter. As they gestured, Thomas listened to a group of street musicians with soda bottles and bottle caps. The air was cool and moist, like an early June day at home. Finally, the woman turned to Thomas and said, in Swahili, that there was a *mzungu* just off the Nyeri Road who was a teacher. Thomas thanked the pair, finished the Fanta, and left them.

At a small church on the Nyeri Road, he needed only to say the words *mzungu* and

Peace Corps to a sexton who was sweeping the steps. The man himself supplied the word *beautiful*.

The way was not so simple, after all. The road diverged twice, and Thomas had to guess at the correct fork, not having been given any clues at the church. As he drove, he ascended into a landscape washed clean by a recent shower. Water droplets from macadamia trees overhead sometimes stormed across his windshield. The air was so crisp he stopped the car to get out and breathe, just to taste it. And to slow his racing heart. He practiced the beginnings of conversations, preparing for all contingencies. The man named Peter would be there. Or Linda might be leaving to go elsewhere. Or she'd be frosty, not welcoming his visit. I was in the area, he rehearsed. I thought I'd just stop by. I forgot to ask you. Regina and I would like.

In his electrified state, it seemed to him that the very road itself hummed and vibrated. Beyond his destination, a purple backdrop advanced, signaling a cataclysmic rain. He had seen these deluges before, the rain pouring straight down, as though someone had simply pulled a plug and let down a lake of water. The sun, behind him,

lit up fields of chrysanthemums, vast im-
probable plains of yellow and mauve, and
then, at the end of the road, the white stucco
of a cottage, bright geometry against the
blackened sky. A beacon, if he had chosen
to see it that way. Rusty-red tiles made a
pattern on the roof, and around the door
and windows frangipani and jasmine
climbed. An old Peugeot was parked in a
driveway, and he left his own car behind it.
Announcing himself to anyone inside the
cottage, as isolated as a hermitage on an
Irish cliff.

She opened the door as he reached the
steps, having had ten, maybe twenty, seconds to prepare herself, which was as good
as no preparation at all. She had bathed or
had been swimming, her hair in long ropes
down her back. She wore a halter top and a
kanga, a different-colored one than before.
She did not dissemble, made no pretense
that this was normal. She merely watched
him. Standing face-to-face on a doorstep
somewhere at the end of the world.

Thomas said hello.

Her face unreadable, her eyes searching
his. *Hello, Thomas,* she said.

In the light of the doorstep, he saw her
more clearly than he had yesterday in the
gloom of the market. Her face was washed

clean, without artifice, a spray of freckles across her nose. She had sun wrinkles at her eyes, tiny commas at the sides of her mouth. Her lips were full and pale, with hardly any bow at all.

— *My desire to talk to you won out,* he said, abandoning *in the area* and *just stopping by.* Recklessly, for he did not yet know if a man named Peter was within. *Though it wasn't much of a debate.*

She moved aside so that he could enter. It was a small room with two paned windows, casements rolled open to the air. A table with two chairs had been snugged up against one window. Armchairs, relics from the 1940s (Thomas imagined war-torn Britain, a Bakelite radio between) faced the other window. There was a low bookcase along one wall. A carpet, old and Persian, underfoot. A single lamp.

There were flowers on a table, a kitenge cloth neatly folded over a chair. Behind the small dining area, a kitchen and an open door in the back. There was a sisal basket on a hook, a Makonde sculpture on the floor against the wall.

The water fell from her hair, hit her shoulder blades and the parquet floor. She wore an elephant-hair bracelet on her wrist. She had amber earrings in her palm, which she hooked into her ears as she stood there.

— *You've come from Nairobi,* she said.

— *I was in Limuru.*

She was silent.

— *I needed to see you.*

No man in evidence, despite the two of everything.

— *Your presence in the market was a shock,* he said. *I felt as if I were seeing a ghost.*

— *You don't believe in ghosts.*

— *Having been in this country a year, I think I'd believe in almost anything.*

They stood facing each other, not a foot apart. He could smell her soap or her shampoo.

— *Your hands shook,* he said boldly, and he could see that she was taken aback by this assertion. She moved a step away from him.

— *Simple shock doesn't mean much in itself,* she said, not willing to credit the trembling hands. *Our time together ended so abruptly, there will always be a certain amount of shock associated with you, no matter what the circumstances.*

An adequate defense. They moved further into the room. On the bookcase was a photograph, and he squinted in its direction. He recognized the cousins with whom Linda had grown up: Eileen and Michael and Tommy and Jack and the rest. A family grouping. There was another photograph, of Linda and a man. Who would be Peter, he thought. Not academic and anemic after all, but rather tall and dark and boyishly handsome. Smiling. A proprietary arm snaking around Linda's slender waist. Her smile slightly less exuberant. Insanely, he took heart from this.

— *Can I get you something to drink?*

— *Water would be good,* he said.

The birds outside were a frantic wind ensemble on a Sunday afternoon. They, too, signaled the approaching storm that blackened the kitchen window, even as sun poured in at the front of the house. A cool breeze, gusty, snapped blue-checked curtains. He watched her take a pitcher of water from the half fridge and pour him a glass.

— *It's been purified,* she said, handing it to him.

He drank the ice-cold water and realized only then the terrible thirst his nerves had produced. *How are you?* he asked.

— *How am I?*

Having come — having, against all the odds, found her again — he could not now speak. He sought desperately for a reference point.

— *Do you remember anything from the accident?* he asked.

She was silent, perhaps surprised by the question so soon.

— *I have a blank,* he said. *It begins with seeing the little girl on the tricycle and ends with my nose filling with water. When I couldn't see you, I felt a sense of panic so terrifying that even now it can make me sweat.*

She smiled and shook her head. *You were never any good at small talk.*

She sat at the table, an invitation to join her. He shed his jacket, the sweat drenching him.

— *What happened to your jacket?* she asked.

— *It got washed by mistake in the bathtub.*

She gave a small laugh. And for a moment, lit the room with sound. But then the light went out as abruptly as it had come. *Is the scar from then?* she asked.

He nodded.

— *It must have been bad,* she said.

— *I hardly noticed at the time. I didn't feel a thing. Didn't even realize the extent of it until my mother started screaming.*

— *I remember the car tumbling,* she said, offering him a memory after all. *And I thought, This can't be happening. The window brace, or whatever that piece between the windows is, buckled, and we rolled. I never lost consciousness. I swam out the other side and started shouting. Some boys were ice-fishing nearby.*

Well, you must know that. They got you out. It can't have been a minute that you were unconscious. Though you were groggy, and the police put you on a stretcher.

— *I was calling your name.*

— *They wrapped me in a blanket and took me away. I had burns on my side. They had to cut my clothes off me at the hospital.*

— *Burns?*

— *Scrapes. From what, I don't know. The embankment, I guess.*

— *I'm so sorry.*

She took a sip of water, reached back and squeezed her hair, then brought it forward of her shoulder. *We did this already,* she said.

— *Do you live alone?* he asked.

She hesitated. She wiped her hands on her kanga. Her feet were bare. Callused on the heels. *More or less. Peter commutes.*

— *Peter is?*

— *My husband. He lives in Nairobi.*

Thomas tried to deflect the blow. *Is that Peter?* he asked. He pointed to the picture.

— *Yes.*

— *What's he do?*

— *He's with the World Bank. He's here working on a pesticide scheme.*

— *You knew him before?*

— *I met him here.*

Thomas stood, the better able to process

these unwelcome bits of information. He clenched and unclenched his hands. Restless, feeling jumpy.

— *Why the Peace Corps?* he asked.

She took another drink of water. She looked out the window at the incipient storm. *I had a friend,* she said ambiguously.

A great waft of scent blew in with a gust, like an announcement of a woman standing in a doorway.

— *It's not so unusual, is it?* she added. *It seemed like the right thing to do.*

Her shoulders brown and polished, her arms muscled. He wondered from what.

— *You're reading Rilke,* he said, surveying the low bookcase. He examined the titles and the authors. Jerzy Kosinski. Dan Wakefield. Margaret Drabble. Sylvia Plath. *Looking for Mr. Goodbar.*

— *I read anything I can get my hands on.*

— *I guess so,* he said, fingering a copy of *Marathon Man.*

— *I beg people to send me books. There's a pitiful library in Njia. In Nairobi, I go to the McMillan Library at the British Council. I've been on a Margaret Drabble kick.*

— *You teach.*

She nodded.

— *What?*

He picked up a copy of Anne Sexton and

flipped through it. He distrusted confessional poetry.

— A little bit of everything. The curriculum is based on the English system. There are exams the children have to pass. A levels and O levels and so forth. They have to memorize the counties of England. What good that will do them I've no idea.

Thomas laughed.

— I teach thirty children in a cement room the size of a garage. I use books published in 1954 — giveaways from some village in Britain. They have peculiar English graffiti in them. "Arthur is a wanker," and so on. What does your wife do?

Thomas leaned against the wall and rolled his shirtsleeves. The humidity had saturated the room. A crack of thunder startled both of them, though they might have expected it.

— The storm, she said.

She stood up and cranked the windows closed, even as the deluge began. The rain came straight down, at no angle, and created a dull roar on the tile roof so that they had to raise their voices. From somewhere outside the house, there was a wild riot of wind chimes.

— My wife's father was a missionary in Kenya shortly after World War II, Thomas

explained. *An Episcopal minister. He's reverent about the time he spent here, says they were the best years of his life, et cetera, et cetera. Privately, I suspect there's a woman somewhere in the story.*

— *It's a challenge any daughter might have to take on,* Linda said.

— *Regina has a fellowship to study the psychological effects of sub-Saharan diseases on children. What she sees is pretty grim,* he said.

— *Your wife must be very brave.*

He felt cautious, discussing Regina. He wished they didn't have to. *About this, very.*

Linda turned her head away and gazed out at the storm. Nothing to see but sheets of rain. When it was over, he knew, white and cream petals would blanket the ground. There was a smell of ozone in the air that he particularly liked: it reminded him of summer afternoons as a boy.

— *You still wear the cross,* he said.

Her fingers automatically touched it. *I don't know why.*

Thomas was momentarily stung. He had, after all, given it to her.

— *God is everywhere in this country,* she said. *And yet, I hate Him passionately.*

The comment was so startling, Thomas immediately forgot his hurt. The anger with which she'd spoken shocked him. He waited for her to explain.

— *You can't even look at the rain, at its excess, and not think of God,* she said. *He's everywhere you turn. And viciously cruel.*

Even Thomas, whose own belief amounted to nothing, worried for her blasphemy.

— *So much poverty,* she said. *So much death and disease and heartache. You can blame colonialism, which is what everyone does. Or tribalism, as good a cause as any. But in the end, it's God who allows it.*

Thomas was impressed with the strength of her belief. *To hate so passionately is to value immensely,* he said.

Her cheeks were pinkened with her sudden passion, a frown between her brows. She wasn't actually beautiful, though he and others had called her so. It was more that she was *pretty*. Which meant, he supposed, *accessible* in some undefined way.

— *You see a lot of poverty?* he asked.

She turned to him. *They have no shoes, Thomas.*

— *The Kenyan elite. They, too, allow it,* he said.

— *You mean the Wabenzis?* she asked with evident distaste, using the common nickname for Kenyans who owned Mercedes-Benzes. *You mean the Africans who come in on foot and leave by jet?*

She fingered her hair. It was drying, even in the humidity. She rose and went into a room he imagined to be the bedroom. She returned with a brush. She sat in an armchair and began to untangle her hair.

— *It's not our struggle,* he said.

— *We borrow it while we're here.*

— *I didn't want to come to Africa,* he said. *It was my wife's idea. I'd just, believe it or not, learned the value of routine.* He paused, embarrassed. *I write,* he said.

She smiled. Not surprised. *What do you write?*

He turned away. *Poetry,* he said, trying to make it a throw-away line. As if his entire life did not depend on it. *I don't feel I belong here,* he said.

— *It can be a weird, dissonant life,* she said.

— *We live in Karen, in relative luxury, when all around us. . . . Well, you know as well as I do what's all around us.*

She nodded.

— *It's not what I imagined,* he said. *All these paradoxes.*

The neckline of her blouse revealed her collarbone. He was reminded of the sweater she had worn on the last day he had seen her. A pale blue sweater with an open collar. Her wool skirt had lain in soft folds around her shins in the car.

— *What did you do after Middlebury?* he asked.

— *I went to graduate school in Boston. In between, I taught high school in Newburyport.*

— *You were in Boston and Newburyport? All that time?* Thomas, incredulous, calculated the distance between Newburyport and Cambridge. An hour at best. Two from Hull.

He tried to sound casual. *You lived alone? You had a roommate?*

— *I had a boyfriend for a time.*

He willed himself not to ask about the boyfriend. *I used to try to talk to your aunt when I'd see her around. For about six months, I was in Hull after I graduated. She wouldn't speak to me. Wouldn't even acknowledge I was standing there.*

— *She's very good at that.*

— *I went to grad school trying to evade the draft. Then my number came up and it was a good one, so I dropped out. If you add it all together, there are probably a couple of years I can't account for very well. I spent a lot of it drifting. I went to Canada for a while. Then to San Francisco. I was pretty heavily into drugs.*

— *Which?*

— *Dope. LSD. I still smoke dope from time to time.*

She set her hairbrush on an end table. *I've always been grateful to you,* she said. *I'm glad you've come, because I've always wanted to tell you that. I don't know what would have happened to me . . .*

He let her thought trail off. He did not deny the gratitude. He'd always had a keen sense of how easy it might be to lose oneself.

— *Would you like some food?* she asked. *Something to eat?*

— *Something,* he said. *Not a meal.*

She went into the kitchen. He spoke to her back as she moved from counter to fridge to counter. *You have electricity?* he asked.

— *Sometimes.*

The cottage was so dark inside they might have turned a light on.

— *Have you ever eaten giraffe?* he asked.

— *No, but I've had antelope. And crocodile.*

— *Crocodile isn't so bad. It tastes like chicken.*

She put bread and cheese on a plate. Something that looked like jelly. He had a sudden craving for sugar.

— *I sometimes feel like the wrong person in the right place,* he said. His unease was so great, he was grasping at ways to explain. *Or vice versa.*

— *You've always been that way.*

The kanga a second skin knotted at her hip. The cloth moved easily about her calves as she worked.

— *Living here is like watching an endless documentary,* he said.

She laughed.

— *Tell me about Peter,* he said.

She thought a minute. *No.*

Thomas was daunted by her refusal, though he admired the loyalty. A loyalty he hadn't quite been able to manage himself.

— *It's exhilarating,* he said. *Talking to you. It must be a form of blood-letting, this desire to pour the soul into another person.*

— *You don't believe in the soul.*

She brought food to the table, gestured for him to sit. He put a generous amount of cheese and jelly on a piece of bread.

— *We have no good word for it, do we?*

— *Spirit?* she suggested.

He shook his head. *Too religious.*

— *Ghost?*

— *Too supernatural.*

— *Personality?*

— *God, no.*

— *The word* life *is too broad, I suppose.*

— *I need another fucking thesaurus,* Thomas said. *Mine was stolen while I was having a beer at the Thorn Tree.*

She laughed. *What a funny thing to steal,* she said.

She had made tea. The mention of beer

made him want one. *I have an overwhelming urge to spill myself messily at your feet*, he said.

Her hands froze as she poured the tea.

— *Sorry*, he said. *You should ignore the sexual implications of that remark.*

She shrugged.

— *You look wonderful*, he added. *I should have said that sooner.*

— *Thank you.*

— *Do men follow you in the streets?* he asked.

She put the teapot down. *Kenyan men are normally very respectful of women that way*, she said. She paused. The rains had suddenly ceased, as if someone had turned off the faucet. Their voices were now too loud. *Wouldn't your wife have told you this?*

— *My wife might want me to think they did*, he said without hesitation when he should have hesitated. Linda turned her face to the window. It was the most disloyal thing he'd said about Regina. Doubly disloyal, implying not only that his wife would lie to her advantage, but might also want to make him jealous.

— *I'm sorry*, he said. To whom or about what, he wasn't sure.

— *Do you have children?* she asked.

— *No.* He paused. *Regina was pregnant*

248

once, but she miscarried when she was five months along.

— I'm sorry.

— It was a hideous miscarriage that ended in the delivery room. It was a week before our wedding.

He didn't add that backing out of the marriage would have been unthinkable, though, miserably, the thought had crossed his mind. Since then — fit punishment — Regina had not been able to conceive, a fact that sometimes made her sad and paradoxically maternal. The way she carried on with Kenyan children — any child — was heartbreaking to watch. It had been three years, and it was time to take the tests, but she, who would know, had little faith in Kenyan medicine. She wanted to wait until they got home. Which was fine with him.

— You don't have children? he asked.

— Oh, no.

No more than he had expected, but he felt relief all the same. *I feel like someone just hacked open my chest with a machete,* he said.

— Another scar, she said lightly.

There was a long silence between them.

— Rich is coming, he said after a time.

— Rich? she asked, brightening. *How old is he now?*

— Sixteen.

— *Imagine!* She shook her head slowly back and forth. *What's he like?*

— *He's a good kid. He likes boats. He works at the yacht club during the summer, ferrying the launch.*

— *He was seven when I knew him. Such a sweet boy.*

— *Well, maybe if you're in Nairobi, you'll come to dinner and meet him.*

The insanity of the dinner invitation was like a boy's voice breaking in mid-speech.

— *I'm sure he remembers you,* Thomas added. *Well, I know he does. He still talks about what a good ice-skater you were.*

— *It seems like so long ago,* she said wistfully.

— *It seems like only yesterday.*

He studied her arm on the table. The hair there was nearly white as well. She seemed to notice his scrutiny, for she withdrew her arm. Perhaps she was still self-conscious about her hands.

— *Tell me about your work,* she said.

He thought a moment. *No.*

She looked up and smiled. *Touché.*

He knew the work was good. It was a simple fact that never left him. And he knew that one day someone else would see this if only he could be patient. He sometimes marveled at his confidence and wondered where it had come from. And though he seldom talked about it, he never mistrusted it.

She rose. *Would you like to go for a walk? I could show you the school.*

He felt he could have sat in her cottage forever.

His legs were weak as she led him through the back door. He had expected her to put on sandals, but she didn't, and he noted the toughness of her feet. The path through the bush was narrow, causing them to have to walk single file, making conversation all but impossible. The low grasses, wet from the recent rain, soaked his trouser cuffs, and he stopped for a moment to roll them. They walked through a pale yellow chrysanthemum field and past what appeared to be a small cluster of huts. True huts, with grass roofs, not the sophisticated version with the tin roof and the red vinyl furniture of the Ndegwa shamba. He watched her back, her drying hair. It was chilly after the storm, though the sun was strong, and as they walked through shady patches, they passed from cool to warm to cool again. Occasionally, Linda waved at a woman or a child. He might have noticed the scenery, but he could hardly take his eyes off her. Her walk strong, the cloth of the kanga swaying languidly as she moved. Her hair growing lighter by the minute. They edged a dense forest, and he grew momentarily nervous about encountering another buffalo or an elephant, but she moved without concern, and he chose simply to follow her lead. The forest opened to a village with a dusty duka, a bar, a school — all made of cement. It might have been the Wild West, for its lack of adornment and its isolation.

He meant to catch up to her as soon as they had left the path, but on the road she was immediately surrounded by children, calling to her, reaching out to touch her. *Jambo. Miss Linda. Habari yako? Mzuri sana.* She scratched the tops of their heads, bent down to hug them. They spoke to Linda in a rapid patois of Swahili and English, and wanted to know, shyly, the identity of the man with her, pointing at him with one hand and hiding their mouths with the other. She introduced Thomas as a friend, and he shook hands all around, their happiness infectious. But then a boy asked Linda where Peter was, and Thomas felt the happiness drain from his body. They began to walk on, the children like grasshoppers beside them. Thomas wanted to take Linda's hand, ached to do so. She told him that once the village had been a thriving community, but that most of the men had gone into the city, looking for work. Some came back to their women and children on the weekends; others would never come back at all. Women with babies wrapped in slings at their chests waved at Linda from doorways, the ebullience of the children not in evidence there, the waves friendly but somber: the women knew too much, or their men had left them.

Heat radiated from the road. Thomas took off his jacket, threw it over his shoulder. His clothes were now as dusty as the dirt and gravel. Linda opened the door to the school, and the children squeezed past them. It was unexpectedly cool inside the building, the walls solid until shoulder height, where, just below the tin roof, there were open windows with no glass.

— *When it rains, the sound on the roof is so loud, we have to stop the class.*

— *The kids must love that.*

— *They don't, actually. The children want to go to school. It's not just this school. It's the same everywhere.*

Some attempt had been made at cheer. Colorful drawings hung from the walls, one or two of them bold and very good. The children tugged at Thomas, and he happily went where they led him. He wished he had treats for them inside his jacket — lollipops or cookies or small toys. Something. There were no desks, except for Linda's.

— *What do they write on?* he asked her. She sat with a spindly boy on her lap. Disease appeared to have made bare patches on his scalp.

— *Their books.*

Behind her desk was a charcoal grill. She noticed him looking at it.

— *I feed them when I get here in the mornings. I make them eggs and give them milk. I get deliveries once a week from a farm, and I bring the food down to the school each morning. There's no way to keep it refrigerated here.*

Which explained the muscles, he thought.

The boy on her lap coughed, spit onto the floor. Linda thumped his back. *The women sometimes besiege me for medical treatment,* she said. *They bring me their babies, and they cry, and, of course, I can't do anything. I sometimes think this is a test from God. That I'm supposed to go to medical school and come back here and practice.*

— *Would you consider it?*

— *I don't have what it takes.*

— *I'm sure you're doing a world of good as a teacher.*

— *I'm hardly doing any good at all.*

She put the child down and took him by the hand to a taller girl against a wall. Linda and the girl spoke for a moment, and when Linda had returned to Thomas, she explained that the boy's sister would take him home. Together Linda and Thomas left the classroom and walked along a short path up a hill to a church.

— *It's a Catholic church,* she said, opening the door for him. *One of few in the area.*

The church was a revelation after the barren schoolroom — the cool interior lit with five stained-glass windows; the colors primary and rich with thick lines of lead between the glass, as if a Picasso or a Cézanne had painted them. A fresh smell, as of reeds or wheat, permeated the small building. It might have sat a hundred in a pinch.

He watched her cross herself with holy water from a font adjacent to the front door, genuflect at a pew, and kneel for a moment before she sat. His chest felt seared, as though a hot wind had blown through it, the memories so keen he needed to put a hand to the back of a pew to steady himself. He stood at the rear of the church and waited until she had been sitting alone for a few moments before he joined her. Giving her time to offer prayers to the God she passionately hated.

They sat in silence, her head and feet astonishingly bare. He remembered, years ago, the mantilla hastily put atop the hair for Saturday afternoon Confession, when she believed she could not enter a church without a hat. He wanted to take her hand, but some residual sense of propriety stopped him.

— *Do you recognize the woman in that one?* she asked, slightly squinting and pointing to one of the colorful windows at the side of the church. It was a depiction of a woman who looked both sensuous and adoring, her eyes cast upward, as if to Heaven. She wore a garment of bright yellow, and her African hair was wild about her face. She, unlike the rest of the figures in the depiction, was black.

— *Magdalene.*

— *You remembered.*

— *Of course I remembered. It's a wonderful painting. Very similar in concept to one by Titian I saw last year in Florence. In fact, I think it must be modeled after the Titian. The hair was amazing. Very, well, Titian-like. Magdalene is often depicted partially nude with long, flowing reddish-blond hair. Very beautiful.*

— *You went last year?*

— *On my way here. I saw two others in Italy. The Bernini in Siena. It's a sculpture. Her breasts are exposed, and her hair flows over them. The Donatello is very different. Gaunt.*

Ascetic. More the penitent.

— *Interesting that she's African. Yes,* he said.

— *You're squinting.*

— *I think I need glasses.*

— *She's thought to be the embodiment of eros and femininity in Christianity,* he said.

— *You've made a study of this,* she said.

— *I have. For something that I'm working on. Have you read* The Last Temptation of Christ *by Nikos Kazantzakis?*

— *How amazing. I'm reading* Report to Greco.

— *Kazantzakis presents Magdalene as a local whore, someone Jesus had yearnings for since childhood. Someone with whom he had a lifelong sexual relationship. Some think she bore him children.*

— *All the institutions for unwed mothers are called Magdalene.*

— *I remember,* he said.

— *Did you see* Jesus Christ Superstar?

— *"I don't know how to love Him."*

— *I've never stopped loving you,* she said.

His breath caught, and he closed his eyes. Behind them, the pure pain of time lost was a star exploding. He put his hands on his thighs, as if bracing himself against some great hurt.

— *I'd come to think of it like childhood,* she

257

said. *Something I once had that I shouldn't expect to have again.*

He looked up toward the ceiling, as a man does when he doesn't want to admit to tears. *Why didn't you let me know?* he asked, his voice husky.

She crossed her legs and then had to bend them sideways in the narrow pew. *For all the reasons I told you. I assumed you'd moved on, forgotten me.*

— *Never.*

— *I knew that you had married. My aunt couldn't wait to tell me. I think she actually called me on the phone as soon as she heard.*

— *Oh, Linda.*

— *And that was that.*

He couldn't touch her in the church. No matter how passionately she hated her God, he knew she would mind such an overture. Nor, when they left the church, could he touch her then, the children having waited for them patiently and followed them along the path. Not until they had left the village behind and were out of sight did he reach ahead and stop her. She turned — so willingly, he might have thanked God — and folded herself into him. The first kiss was not familiar, and yet he felt himself arrived, come home, safe to shore. And might have told her this, had she not stopped his mouth with a second kiss, her taste reminding him now of a thousand others. She laced strong fingers around the nape of his neck and bent his head helplessly toward hers. He stumbled and then knelt, not intentionally, his balance gone. She pulled him toward her so that he was drawn up against her bare midriff. The pleasure so great, he groaned with gratitude. She bent her head to his.

— *Linda,* he said, relief lowering his voice.

He tried to take in the room and make it his, even as she lay upon the coverlet. The kanga unknotted now, the halter top untied, her breasts a white shock against the color of her skin. He could not then remember anything of how they had been before, and yet they moved together as if they hadn't ever been apart. He had never felt himself so thoroughly at home in time. It was a revelation that this could be his, that she might give him this again and again and again, that discontent might ease. She rose above him and said his name, her hair a damp curtain at the sides of her face. She lowered her shoulders and offered her breasts, which he took into his hands and mouth, wanting all of her.

Sweet recompense for all the days and nights unlived.

November 27

Dear Thomas,

Today we had a visit from the MP for Nyeri. Unexpected, because he had come from Nairobi to negotiate a bride-price for a second wife, whom no one is supposed to know about; the first wife, to her grave misfortune, is infertile. He arrived in a Mercedes, and came in with such pomp, I expected to be blessed. He sat on a bench at the back of the room and listened to a lesson on multiplication, nodding from time to time, as if there were points about which one might agree or disagree, all the while picking his teeth with a twig. The children were cowed and kept sneaking surreptitious looks at the big man who had come from the city. He wore a gold watch, and I don't know much about men's clothing, but the fabric of his suit looked expensive. He had a retinue of eight. He travels with a car in front of him and a car in back as a security measure against thieves and political opponents. Should he be stopped by a panga gang on the A104, his underlings are supposed to take the blows. I'm told he has a heated swimming pool in Lavington, a fleet of Mercedes, and a fat Swiss account. What did he make, I wonder, of the children's bare feet?

I am sitting at the back of the cottage under a thorn tree, which gives a twig-like illusion of shade. The wind rustles in from the chrysanthemum plains, and the fever trees are creaking. There is an enormous vulture in a branch above me, sitting patiently, so I know there must be a fresh kill nearby. I don't want to think about what animal it might be, or about its specific killer. Superb starlings of iridescent turquoise twitter in the branches, but the vulture refuses to be annoyed. It seems scarcely credible that today is Thanksgiving. Very strange to celebrate a holiday when everyone else is at work.

I feel stunned, as I do sometimes when I emerge from a darkened schoolroom or my cottage and am hit with the light of Africa at noon: blinded by it, made dizzy, as though I'd taken a blow to the side of my head. Disoriented, slightly nauseous even, unable to eat. I walk around the cottage, touching things because you touched them. A book of Rilke. A plate that once had jelly on it. A hairbrush from which I have not yet removed the chestnut hairs. It's a kind of sickness, isn't it? An illness that has invaded me. Or rather the return of a chronic illness. This bout fatal, as I know it must be.

I think that words corrupt and oxidize love. That it is better not to write of it. Even memory, I think, is full of rust and decay.

I have always been faithful to you. If faithful means the experience against which everything else has been measured.

Yours always,
Linda

December 1

Dear Linda,

When I left you and arranged that we would write each other, I thought that you would not, that your overdeveloped sense of guilt would make you silent. Worse, I feared that if I got in the car and drove to Njia, you'd have vanished without a trace, like the veils of mist over the moors near your cottage. So that when I saw your letter in the box — lavender paper, delicate backward hand — I wept. There, in front of the mzees chewing twigs and the schoolboys throwing pebbles at a hyrax. No shame, none at all. Only joy and considerable relief.

Magdalene. Beautiful Magdalene. Lost and then found again. I don't think I ever before knew the meaning of happiness.

About Regina. Should I write to you of the quiet fury with which I was greeted when I returned on Sunday night, all the more daunting for being so justly deserved? Or the equanimity — absent elsewhere in her life — with which she regards the most harrowing cases of childhood disease (Kenyan children being, despite their lot, the best-behaved in the world — some mysterious parenting secret I haven't yet been able to discover); or her desire to bear a child of her own — all-consuming, constant, and crippling? No, I will not. I do love Regina. It is irrelevant, however. I assume you love your Peter as well — about whom you were justifiably silent on Sunday.

I remember your body on the bed. For

long moments at a time, that is all there is.

You are so beautiful to me. (Do you have a mirror? I forgot to notice. We don't. Regina does her makeup in the tea kettle.)

Proof of my own constancy: All of my poems are about you, even when they appear not to be. More to the point, they are all about the accident, in case you doubted the sincerity of my own guilt. I assume these are not available in any form at the British Council library.

I felt disloyal writing to you in my house — disloyal to you or Regina? both, I think — so I have driven in my battered and twice-stolen Escort to Nairobi, have taken a table at the Thorn Tree and have ordered a Tusker without the worm (long story). There is a strange white smoke emerging from what must be the kitchen, which I suppose I should ignore since everyone else is (though it looks as though it will poison us all). I have never had a message left for me at the message board, but, insanely, I checked it today on the off chance that you had written to me in code. (Leave one for me next time you are in Nairobi, just to humor me; though if you come to the city and don't tell me, I will surely die of heartbreak.)

Just last Saturday, I sat at this very café with Ndegwa. (Not knowing you were in the country. How was that possible? Why were there no signs or portents in the sky, no audible vibrations I'd have recognized as your footsteps?) Today, I went to the American embassy on Ndegwa's behalf and was rewarded with an appointment with an embassy official — officially *what* was never made clear. He looked — I hesitate to say it, because it is such a cliché — like an aging Marine, his crew cut so short, there was more scalp than hair. He was bluff and hearty, actually glad to see me, though he had no idea initially why I had come. I distrust an egalitarian welcome. He said — I kid you not — "Where you from, Tom?" I said, "Boston." He said, "Heeey, Red Sox!" So we discussed the Red Sox, about which I knew less than I should have, and I felt it was a kind of test I didn't pass. My official grew suspicious, and seemed only then to notice my excessively long hair ("Hippie," I could hear him thinking), and said, finally, "So what can I do you for?" and "What's on your mind, Tom?" Truthfully, it was you, as it always is now, but I told him of my mission, which was vague enough when I left my house, even more vague in the telling of it. I wanted to help Ndegwa get released, I said. Failing that, I wanted to put pressure on the Kenyan government to state the charges and to set a trial date. It seemed an absurd request and hopelessly naive, which is how he took it. He smiled and was indulgent. "Well, Tom," he said, pushing his chair back from the desk and lacing his fingers in his lap, "this is a sensitive area," and, "You know, Tom, the U.S. has a strategic base in Kenya," and, "I'd like to help as much as you, Tom, but these things take time." I felt like a kid who'd gone to his father for money.

Having cheerfully put me in my place, he asked me what I was doing in the country. I dissembled, mentioned Regina, and finally confessed to being a writer. "For whom?" he asked. Reasonable question. "For no one," I said, and I could tell he didn't believe me. After all, who would write for no one? Name-dropping, he mentioned that Ted Kennedy would be coming soon to the country and that he (my official) was in charge of putting together a party in the senator's honor. Uttering the first political statement of my life — indeed having the first political *thought* of my life — I

266

blurted, "I know Ted Kennedy." And finally snagged the man's attention. "Actually," I said, "my father knows him. He was once at our house for dinner."

Really, said my embassy official.

And so the "Ndegwa matter," as he put it, may be looked into after all.

Write me. For God's sake, keep writing. A day without you seems a day unlived, bearable only because I summon memory, mine subject to the merest oxidation, a faint rust blowing in the breezes.

Love me as you did on Sunday. Is that so much to ask?

Thomas

P.S. Today's headline: WOMAN GRABBED IN BUSH BY HYENA

December 15

Dear Thomas,

I am writing to you from a hospital named Mary Magdalene (no, I am not making this up) where I have had to bring David, the boy who collapsed in a fit of coughing in my classroom. Brave boy. He refuses to be excluded. He has a mysterious disease the doctors cannot name — it gives him pneumonia and makes him so gaunt, I'm afraid he won't be able to stand up. They have taken him in to be examined, and I am waiting for him, since his mother is ill as well and cannot leave her hut. A daughter cares for the smallest children. Oh, Thomas, we never knew the first thing about misery, did we?

The hospital, a small one, was built in the 1930s to house wayward girls of European extraction whose parents were too poor to send them back to Europe to have their babies. (Or who would not spend the money on such hopeless causes. Where did the babies go, I wonder?) Now, of course, no one cares about that anymore, and so the hospital is a sort of emergency clinic for the region. There is a Belgian doctor here who is very good. He is young and funny and all the women fall in love with him. I don't believe he sleeps at all; he is always here when I come. He is baffled by David's case and has sent blood samples back to Brussels to be analyzed. How can a doctor treat an illness he can't even identify?

Sister Marie Francis, formidable and large, keeps passing by and regarding me with disapproval. As well she might, though I think it is only my kanga. Or perhaps she sees the wayward Catholic girl in me as I study the lurid cross on the wall opposite. The girl who used to ponder the subjects of joy and guilt and punishment. The nun walks silently by, and our eyes lock — I cannot help myself; possibly I am looking for a sign, a message from her? — and I feel exposed, more naked than even my casual dress implies.

I didn't tell you that Peter came unexpectedly after you had left. I was startled by this second apparition of the day, and I backed away from the door. He took my alarm for normal surprise, which he had intended. You still on my skin. I had to plead illness, exhaustion, anything. Ashamed not of you, nor of us, but of my fear of discovery.

Oh, Thomas, despite all this, I am so happy.

Yesterday, I arranged to take the children into Nyeri for a parade in Jomo Kenyatta's honor. Thirty children crowded into two VW vans and one Peugeot 504 (you don't want to think about it too much). We stood on a hillside and watched the parade marchers, who were in tribal dress and sneakers and wearing Coca-Cola sunshades, all the while eating

Popsicles. We listened to Jomo Kenyatta deliver a speech on *harambee* and the future of Kenya. Of course, in the presence of the children, one had to be respectful and ignore the irony of the use of the word *freedom* when men like Ndegwa languish in prison. (Have you heard anything further from your Marine?) Though it must be said that amongst the spectators and marchers alike, tensions were high: Kenyatta, as you know, is not as beloved as he once was. The point of my story is that, quite suddenly and without warning, panic broke out on the hill, and a stampede began. Hundreds of people started running, not realizing they were headed for a barbed-wire fence. The hysteria was infectious. We herded the children into a tight circle and made them crouch down, and essentially we lay on top of them. I thought, Kenyatta has been shot. And then, This is a coup. Peter took a knee to his spine. Soldiers with bayonets kneeled beside us and aimed at the crowd. No one was killed, but dozens were injured as they were crushed into the barbed wire. Later we learned that the panic had been caused by a swarm of bees. Overhead, oblivious to the melee, six fighter planes roared by in a salute to

Kenyatta. As we watched, one of them rolled out of formation and crashed on a nearby golf course.

I write of these events as I once wrote of movies or of trips to the beach. I will not say I have gotten used to them, but they don't shock me anymore.

What shocks me is my love for you.

I would like to think that what we have could exist outside of real time, that it could be a thing apart and not invade. Foolish and dangerous thinking. It has already invaded every part of my life.

Yours,
L.

December 21

Dear Linda,

You write of panic and hysteria, but all I can think about is Peter with you on that hillside, Peter surprising you in your cottage (while I was returning to a fuming Regina). Jealous already. Intense, consuming jealousy that reduces me to a petty, twisted, unlovable creature. Did you sleep with him? That night? So soon after we had been together? That I have no right to be jealous is irrelevant. It is a human passion: the sick, white underbelly

271

of love. Worse, I am jealous of your doctor with whom all the women fall in love. Do you include yourself?

Don't answer my questions.

Last night, Regina and I attended the launch of a book called *Silence Will Speak* by Errol Trzebinski. Essentially a biography of Denys Finch Hatton, Blixen's lover when she was living on her coffee farm, the book is also about Blixen's own life and writings about Africa. (Perhaps you know the book already? In any event, I am sending it with this since you said you'd already read all the books in Njia.) The party was at the Karen Country Club — unremarkable anachronism. Virtually everyone at the gathering was white, with one notable exception. An old man wearing a dark suit and an ill-pressed overcoat, with his cane resting on his chair, sat in a corner and sipped tea as he chatted with two "little old ladies" (how women must hate to graduate to that distinction) in plum-colored suits and hats. At first glance, the tableau reminded me of maiden aunts gossiping with a bachelor uncle at a family reunion. But then I was informed that the old man was actually *Out of Africa*'s Kamante, Blixen's faithful cook, the man whose story forms a large segment of her book. He'd been only a small boy when she discovered him fifty years ago, alienated and diseased, tending goats on her land; and now he was an old man who had, I assumed, personally witnessed the astonishing transformation of his country. He'd been hauled out for the occasion, I suspect, to lend a certain cachet to the proceedings, and he was something of a guest of honor. Though he seemed, I must say, largely indifferent to the fate that had contrived to position him there in that corner, reminiscing over tea about an Africa that no longer existed with women who, in Blixen's day, would not have allowed him at their table.

I write to you from home now, having lost my scruples (jealousy having set them adrift). Our house sits amidst manicured gardens and acacias and eucalyptus trees that rise above the stone cottages of Karen, smoke curling from their chimneys, the four green humps of the Ngong Hills in the background. Imagining I am in England is not hard to do. The hedges create mini-fortresses, reaching twelve feet high, and are impenetrable, connected by gates with guards to watch them. Children play by appointment only. It is an odd thing, all this beauty, all this ordered loveliness, all this soft prettiness of landscape — for it is hard not to think of it as a malignant tumor that will one day have to be excised.

No, I don't believe in your hospital and will have to come to see for myself. Write me and tell me I may come. Or meet me somewhere. I can't stand not seeing you. When are you coming to Nairobi?

The U.S. has lodged a formal complaint about the Kenyan government's detention of Ndegwa. I flatter myself if I think I had anything to do with it. And delude myself if I think it will help. I have written to Amnesty International, but will not receive a reply for several weeks. How agonizingly slow the mail is! Do you have a telephone? I forgot to ask. We do not. I resisted having one installed after the robbery (another long story), but Regina has been lobbying for one for some time. And I, faithless husband, would do it in an instant if I thought it would connect me to you.

I make light of this, but our situation is a painful one. We do not discuss the future. Do we have one?

There are rumors of a mass grave with fifty students in it. I find it hard to credit, but it may be true.

Christmas approaches. Weird in the

heat, don't you think? How I wish I could spend it with you.

Yours,
Thomas

P.S. Today's headline: LEOPARD ATTACK IN KAREN.

January 4

Dear Thomas,

Peter and I have just returned from Turkana, where we went for Christmas week. We drove through rivers and were nearly defeated by the 100-degree temperatures. We passed through a landscape of such desolation one cannot imagine how the Turkana, walking from one deserted area to another, manage to survive. The lake, to our astonishment, resembled the seashore, with palm trees and miles of sandy beach lining it. We ignored the threat of parasites and crocodiles and body-surfed in the 80-degree water. In the morning, we woke to a blood-red sunrise — a swath, hundreds of miles long that, despite its awful beauty, promised blistering heat for the rest of the day. The landscape is beautiful, violent and menacing — like stepping onto another planet where one breathes poisonous gases in splendid colors.

Thomas, we are linked together, however much we might not wish it. As to the future, I cannot say.

So much has been left unsaid.

I could hear you calling my name when they took me away. I was in shock and couldn't speak, or I'd have answered you. My aunt arrived at the hospital shortly after I did. To her credit, she cried once and then spent the rest of the time telling me she'd told me so. Her distrust of you has always puzzled me. Perhaps she hates all men. I'd have thought she'd have welcomed someone to take me off her hands.

I was in the hospital for five days. The uncles and cousins were vigilant, and I was never left alone. Strange treasure they were protecting, one that had already been stolen.

I went home for a day and then was sent by car to New York, Uncle Brendan driving (we hit three bars in Connecticut alone). The drive was an agony as I recall, since one whole side of me was raw. (All of me raw inside.) The days passed. They took the dressings off sometime in March. Eileen was working as a massage therapist and was gone all day. I walked the streets when I was able to. I thought of you. I used to sit for hours looking out the window, thinking of you. For several days after I was able to get out of bed, I called you repeatedly. But there was never any answer. Later my aunt wrote that you and your family had gone to Europe for a trip. Was this true? I forgot to ask you on Sunday. Then my aunt wrote that you were going out with Marissa Markham (and good riddance and so forth). Her motives were entirely transparent, but I couldn't know for sure that it wasn't true. People change, don't they? You might have been angry I'd gone away without telling you where. My aunt might have lied to you as well.

I thought: He's forgotten me so soon.

I never got the letters you sent. Not hard to imagine what was done with them. Read and then disposed of, I imagine. How dearly I would love to have those letters back. I feel we are the blood and bone of one person. I love you with your hair grown long. I love you.

Please send me your poems. I hope it is absolutely true that only you collect the mail.

Lovingly,
Linda

P.S. Thank you for the Trzebinski. I read it in a day. Wish I were a slower reader so that books would last longer.

Dear Linda,

I am in agony thinking that you imagined I had forgotten you.

Never.

If only I had ignored your aunt and kept trying. If only I had called Eileen. If only I had gotten in the car and driven up to Middlebury. I can't think about this anymore. It is making me ill, literally.

And it is making it hard to enjoy my news, however wonderful it seemed only an hour ago. I received a letter yesterday (it took seven weeks to get here) from an editor at the *New Yorker* who wants to publish two of my poems. I was in a panic that the editor might have thought I wasn't interested because it had taken me so long to reply, so I drove into Nairobi and found a telephone and called him straightaway. He was a bit taken aback that I should call all the way from Africa (clearly this was not as important to him as it was to me), but I explained the mail situation. In any event, the poems will be published, and I will actually be paid for them (astonishing in itself). Regina is quite happy about this. I believe she thinks this justifies my existence. So do I, for that matter.

I have other news as well. My embassy official has dropped me a note saying that he plans to put together a party at which several influential people will be (including Mr. Kennedy), and he wonders if I might persuade Mary Ndegwa to come as well. He thinks this is my best chance of promoting her cause, and I was actually cheered to see that the "Ndegwa matter" was still on his mind. (Kennedy will, of course, not remember me, and it will doubtless be embarrassing; but I can't care about that now.) I don't have a precise date yet for this event, but when I do, I will let you know. Perhaps you and Peter could attend? (Is it insane to imagine we could be in the same room and not touch each other? Surely, we'd have more self-control? Perhaps not.)

Rich is coming on Tuesday, and we will be going on safari for a couple of weeks. I was looking forward to this (and I suppose I still am), though I am distraught at the thought of not being able to receive a letter from you. (You should perhaps not write to me for two weeks. No, do write, just don't send them until I'm back. I hate this fucking subterfuge. It demeans us as well as Peter and Regina. But I don't see how it can be avoided, do you?)

I followed a tip from a friend (acquaintance) and went to visit a man in Nairobi who runs a magazine to see if he would want to publish any of my poetry. It was a long shot, but I was in Nairobi anyway (making my twelve-dollars-a-minute phone call to the *New Yorker* — probably spent all of forthcoming check), and I thought I'd give it a try. It's a strange hybrid of a magazine, something between *McCall's* and *Time* (interviews with high-ranking politicians next to recipes), but I liked the editor. He was educated in the States — in Indiana, as it happens — and he invited me to lunch. He will publish several of the poems. (Actually getting paid there, too. An embarrassment of riches.) An offshoot of this visit, however, was that he said he was desperate for reporters, and he asked if I would do one or two pieces for him. I told him I'd never been a journalist, but that didn't seem to bother him — my qualifications chiefly, I gather, that I am available and can write in English. I thought, Why not? and so said yes. As a result, I am to leave to-

280

morrow to cover a *siku kuu* (literal translation: big day) at the Masai bomas in the Rift. Accompanied by a photographer. I don't see how it can't be interesting on some level.

Linda, I am dying. I must see you soon. Is there any chance you could get away for a few days? I am thinking (probably hopelessly) about meeting somewhere on the coast. Regina, who will be with us on safari, will go back early after we get to Mombasa (she can't tolerate humidity). I could persuade Rich to go back with her (he'll have had more than enough of his big brother by then and will probably be desperate to be alone). To be with you in Lamu would be heaven. Have you ever been there? Alternatively, forget the coast and just come to Nairobi. Or tell me that I can come to Njia. Could we meet in Limuru? My body is aching.

Love always,
Thomas

P.S. I hate the way letters close — either too tepid or too sappy for the occasion.

P.P.S. Today's headline: RAMPAGING ELEPHANTS DESTROY CROPS.

Dear Thomas,

I am very sad today. David died this morning at Mary Magdalene. Dr. Benoît did everything he could, but the pneumonia had invaded both lungs, and David hadn't the strength to fight it. I have just come from telling his mother, who herself is gravely ill; she seemed hardly to hear my news. What is this terrible disease, Thomas? Dr. Benoît is furious with himself and with Brussels; they took too long to send back the results of the culture. They, too, are baffled, however, and have sent the samples to the CDC in America. Dr. Benoît says he has seen other, similar, cases and is concerned about the disease spreading before he can discover what it is.

David was a brave boy. There will be a funeral tomorrow.

Yes, it may be possible to meet you on the coast. I would have to arrange either to go with Peter or return with him, but it might be possible to find two days to be with you. I, too, am aching, though I am fearful of seeing you again. Perhaps it is my disheartened mood today, but I see no good outcome to our being together. None. Someone — and I believe we have to hope it will be us — will be desperately hurt.

I am glad for your news from the *New Yorker*. You must send me the poems they are going to publish.

Thomas, I love you beyond anything I thought possible. It makes me sad for Peter, for what he never had from me.

I will omit the tepid closing. No words are adequate.

Linda

P.S. I took the chance of writing you the one letter before you leave for the coast. I pray it is you who retrieves it.

January 26

Dear Linda,

I am so sorry about David. I hope he didn't suffer. In a strange way, I am glad the mother is not completely aware of what happened. That has always seemed the worst part of any child's death: that the mother should suffer the intolerable loss. I wish you did not hate your God so passionately, since you might take comfort in the thought that David is with Him now.

Such extraordinary emotions in the

space of paragraphs. I was delirious with the news that you might be able to meet me at the coast. Would Lamu be possible? I will send you the dates tomorrow, and I will find a place for us to meet. My God, Linda, this has to happen. Another man might be able to put scruples above want and need, but not I. Sometimes I tell myself we owe this to ourselves for all the days and nights that were lost to us, even though I know that makes no moral sense whatever. Another person (your nun perhaps) would simply say *too bad,* that we have made commitments to others and will have to honor them. But I wonder: did you and I not make a stronger commitment nine years ago in front of a blue cottage by the ocean? Am I to pay for the rest of my life for a careless moment on a slippery curve? Would I understand this if it were happening to Regina? God, I hope I would.

I have just finished writing my first article for the magazine I told you about. The siku kuu was an extraordinary event after all — a ceremony during which a thousand Masai men gathered to anoint their women with honey beer to ensure the continued fertility of the tribe, a spectacle that takes place every twenty years

— and I hope I have done justice to it. I would rather have written a poem, but that's hardly what the editor wants right now. I won't bore you with a travelogue, but I'll give you the highlights: Dawn coming up faintly as we reached the Magadi Road. Sleepy conversation with my photographer companion. Two hundred and fifty manyattas, two thousand Masai all in one place. The red-and-brown cloth of the women, their Maridadi, their earrings with perpendicular appendages, the film canisters in the ear holes. Hundreds of children — curious, touching, friendly, laughing. A biblical-looking man named Zachariah, who patiently explained the ceremony to us. The women, some resigned, some solemn, some half-crazy in catatonic states and epileptic-like fits. Deep, agonized groans. Wearing a kid's hat to keep out the sun since I'd forgotten my own. Passing out cigarettes. Going off to take a leak and wondering if I was pissing on sacred ground. Handing out plums. The cruel faces of some of the younger men, like decadent Romans. The long negotiations for the women, who seemed frighteningly passive, considering their fate.

I can't imagine what part love plays in

this. It was impossible, from the outside, to tell.

It would be best if we could meet some time between the 28th and the 3rd. Perhaps the 1st? I am, literally, counting the hours until then.

Thomas

P.S. Today's headline: BABOON SNATCHES BABY.

January 27

Dear Linda,

We delude ourselves. We delude ourselves. Meet me anyway. Please. In front of Petley's Hotel, Lamu, twelve noon, the 1st. We will go for a walk.

T.

Below them lay plains of scrub trees that were already casting precise shadows on the barren ground. Grasses undulated like a familiar crop in an unfamiliar heartland, and vast papyrus swamps threatened to devour entire countries. The pilot — ultimate cool: feet on the console, smoking a cigarette (wasn't that illegal?) — flew so low to the ground that Thomas could see individual elephants and wildebeests, a lone giraffe, its neck craning to the stuttering sound above it. A sky blue-cloaked moran with a spear walked from one seemingly empty place to another, and a woman in a red shawl carried an urn atop her head. Thomas saw all this — watched the rosy light turn the lakes turquoise, watched the light of dawn come up as theater — and thought, In six hours, I will see her.

If Thomas had understood the pilot correctly, they were flying without a generator, which Thomas had been assured could be done, provided they didn't stall, necessitating a restart of the engine. The pilot, who had longish hair and a short-sleeved suit jacket that narrowed at the waist (like something the Beatles might have worn years ago), had seemed supremely indifferent to the trip and had given Thomas the choice of deciding whether or not to turn back when he'd discovered the errant generator. Thomas, thinking of Linda standing in front of Petley's Hotel at twelve noon, had seen no alternative, and somewhere over Voi, he'd decided that the plane would not plummet from the sky as punishment for his intended infidelity. As if he'd not been unfaithful every moment since he'd first seen Linda in the market. Still, he could not stop himself from imagining a fiery death in a desolate place where no one would ever find him.

In the distance, he saw a village of huts with grass rooftops and nearby a pen of animals. Cattle, he imagined. And he thought, as he had often thought before — although this time with a finality that brought a kind of resolution — that Africa was, after all, impenetrable. It was ancient and it was dignified in a way no other continent could equal, its soul unblemished, even with all the Wabenzis and the Swiss accounts and the parking boys. And being unmarred was unknowable. He'd seen it on the faces of the women and their preternaturally calm eyes in the face of disaster, and in the shy smiles of the children, constantly tickled by some joke understood only by them. And he accepted — as Regina with her academic mission could not; or as Roland, who made pronouncements, could not — that he, Thomas, was no more significant in this country than a single member of the herd of wildebeests migrating west beneath him (less significant, actually). He was merely a visitor, destined to move on. So that Ndegwa could never be entirely known to him, nor Mary Ndegwa, nor even the woman who washed his shirts in the bathtub (particularly not the woman who washed his shirts in the bathtub). Although — and this was odd — he had a distinct sense that they knew him, that he was, as Regina had once said of him, as transparent as glass; his own soul, for all its current turmoil, as easy to read as a bowl of water.

— *You'll want that strap pulled tight,* the pilot beside him said.

In preparation for landing, the pilot sat up and put both hands on the wheel, which was reassuring to Thomas. He himself could not be a pilot — he hadn't the math — though the job seemed pleasant enough, even thrilling. The pilot pointed to the coast, a pale peach scallop against the liquid blue of the Indian Ocean, and as Thomas's heart began to beat slightly faster with proximity to the place where he would see Linda once again, he thought how unlikely the entire venture was, how very nearly it had not happened at all. Rich, unhappily, had contracted a wild bout of malaria on safari and had had to return with Thomas and Regina to Nairobi. Causing Thomas, after Rich had been admitted to the hospital and then sent home with a battery of drugs, to have to invent a reason to fly to the coast, which they'd only just left, using the barely credible excuse that his new employer had mandated it. It would be a quick trip, he'd told Regina; he'd be back before Thursday. And she, weary from the dirt and boredom of safari, had not seemed to mind, or even, to be truthful, to notice.

The plane left the continent below, circled the Swahili archipelago of Lamu, and landed on a runway in a mangrove swamp on nearby Manda. Thomas thanked the pilot and said he hoped the generator got fixed soon. The pilot (Thomas was sure the liquor breath was from the night before) merely shrugged. Thomas made his way to the place where sailing dhows with wide lateen sails waited to ferry the passengers across to Lamu village. He placed his gear in an overcrowded boat that reminded him of refugees from Vietnam and gave its captain eighty shillings. He found a seat next to a woman dressed head-to-toe in bui-bui, so that only her eyes — dark and kohl-rimmed — were visible.

The muezzins were chanting already from the minarets as Thomas stepped ashore — a haunting and melodic string of vocal sounds in a minor key that, for Thomas, would forever be associated with love and the foreknowledge of loss (so much so that in future years just the sound of a muezzin chanting in the background of a news broadcast about Palestine or Iraq could make his throat catch). He hoisted his backpack onto his shoulder. The heat was immediate — paradoxically enervating and seductive. To walk was to swim through water up the hill, past Harambee Avenue, toward the museum where the editor of the magazine (Thomas, to turn a lie into a truth, had asked for and received an assignment) had told him he might be able to secure lodgings. Thomas followed a map, losing himself in a warren of narrow streets with shops and cafés and stone houses sealed with intricately carved wooden doors. Along the cobbled streets that ran up the hill from the harbor (streets on which no cars ever drove), there was a hint of coolness that tempted him away from his route. Men in kanzus and kofias eyed him speculatively, while women in black bui-bui with babies cradled in their arms glided silently past. Donkeys brayed constantly, and underfoot cats athletically avoided his feet. In the gutters, open sewers ran, giving off a sickly, sweet stench.

He asked directions and was shown the way to the museum by a boy who ran ahead of him with a stick. Thomas had to hustle to catch up to the boy, who waited for him patiently at each corner, just as he waited silently for his tip when he'd delivered Thomas to the museum door. Thomas stepped inside and barely had time to notice the replicas of ancient sailing vessels and heavy plates of silver before a woman who looked vaguely official asked if she could help. He said he was looking for a man named Sheik. Ah, said the woman, Bwana Sheik was away. Thomas offered his own name. A smile and an envelope were produced. On the envelope were written directions, and inside was a key, surprising Thomas, who had not known that phone calls had been made and arrangements negotiated in advance of his arrival. There was no mention of payment, and Thomas guessed it would be impolite to suggest one, having no idea what favors might have changed hands on his behalf.

The boy with the stick who had led him to the museum was waiting for him when he emerged, and Thomas was only too happy to hand over the envelope with the address. The boy led him through a maze in which cooking smells competed with the sewer stench, to a narrow building with an unprepossessing door. Thomas had expected a room or at best an apartment, and so was surprised when the boy unlocked the door and led him into an inner courtyard of what appeared to be a house. Thomas was confused and would have queried the boy had the key not fit so easily in the lock.

A bald, Arab-looking man in an apron — presumably a servant — emerged from the shadows, dismissed the errand boy with a bark, and introduced himself as Mr. Salim. Would Thomas care to look around before Mr. Salim brought him cold tea? Thomas checked his watch as he'd done just ten minutes earlier, vaguely afraid, on this exotic island, that time might spool ahead of itself with its own set of rules. Yes, said Thomas, he would look around, and he would be grateful for a glass of tea.

The servant disappeared into the shadows. Thomas stood for a moment in the courtyard, open to the sky, its narrowness casting cool shadows on the stone floor. A low well was at its center, surrounded by yellow flowers, and in the corner was a pawpaw tree. There seemed to be a kitchen on the first level, though Thomas did not venture inside, unwilling to disturb Mr. Salim at his preparations. Instead, he went up a flight of stairs with sculptures in recessed niches, a sense of water flowing over stones. The stairway led to a second level, meant as a kind of sitting room, with low carved furniture and bleached-cotton bolsters. Engraved copper and silver plates and large ceramic urns decorated the walls and niches. Still the stairs went up, and on the third level, open to the sky, Thomas discovered bedrooms with canopied beds and mosquito netting. There was a jasmine tree near one of the beds, and frangipani on a coral terrace. The perfume of the flowers filled the rooms and erased the smells of the streets. He looked at the roofless bedroom and thought to himself that it must never rain in Lamu, and he wondered how that could possibly be true. Exploring further, he found a bedroom with a basin of fresh water and washed his face and hands. Above the marble-topped dresser on which the basin rested, a hibiscus tree rose, bright blooms against the navy of the sky. As he left the room, he saw that someone (Mr. Salim?) had placed jasmine blossoms on the pillows.

The servant had prepared a meal of eggs and yogurt and cold tea, which Thomas accepted gratefully at a table in the courtyard. He wished the Arab man would linger, for he had questions — Who owned the house? Did people like himself often stay there? — but Mr. Salim had vanished into the kitchen. Thomas ate the eggs and yogurt and felt as though a benign spirit (or at least a mildly sympathetic one) had arranged his astonishing good luck; and it was hard not to take it for a sign that what he was about to do was, in a world that might run parallel to his own, accepted — perhaps even encouraged. But then, in the next instant, thinking of Regina at home nursing Rich back to health, Thomas put his hands over his eyes. It was pure delusion, he knew, to imagine that this trip was acceptable in any universe.

★ ★ ★

He saw her walking toward him, and he ground out his cigarette with his shoe. She wore a sundress of white linen that fell to midcalf, and she held a scarf around her shoulders to cover them. She had dressed respectfully, as women on Lamu were advised to do, and yet Thomas saw, as she approached, that every man raised his eyes to stare at the blond mzungu. She'd worn her hair up in a knot at the back of her head, but still the gold, in that village of dark skin and bui-bui, turned heads. Another bit of gold, the cross at her neck, seemed wildly out of place in the Muslim town, but he was glad she hadn't thought — or hadn't chosen — to hide it. A Swahili man, beside her, carried her suitcase and seemed particularly short next to the tall, willowy woman walking toward Thomas, who stood at the front of the hotel. For a moment, neither spoke nor moved, each supremely conscious of the porter beside them, of the men in the streets who watched her still.

— *Linda,* Thomas said.

They embraced. Chastely, as a couple might in public, with no kiss or prolonged touch. The skin of her arms cool under his fingers. Wordlessly, he turned and tipped the boy who waited with the suitcase.

296

Thomas picked up her bag. *I have a house,* he said.

She only nodded, which he took as permission to lead her there. They walked in silence, Thomas having memorized the way, neither of them willing to break the spell that had enveloped them in front of Petley's — one of anticipation within a framework of restraint. He watched her sandaled feet emerge from the hem of her dress, felt her elbow brush his arm from time to time. Above them, the muezzins again began their chanting from the minarets, and the world seemed suffused with both the religious and the sensual, qualities he'd always associated with the woman beside him. They weren't precisely shy with each other, though Thomas was certain they shared a sense of moment; that each was, beneath the calm exterior of a couple moving slowly forward in the heat, supremely aware of bargains being made, lifelong contracts that might have to be honored.

He found the one door out of hundreds that would open to him, and he wondered, as he put the key into the lock, how precisely to deal with the matter of Mr. Salim, who would surely emerge and want to be introduced to the mzungu woman and would ask her if she would like a glass of cold tea. But, in the end, Mr. Salim did not appear, and it was Thomas who had to ask Linda if she wanted a cool drink. She shook her head slightly, her eyes never leaving his, despite her exotic surroundings. He stood still a long moment, watching her as well, and then took her hand and led her up the stairs to the third floor where the beds were. The muezzins had stopped their chanting, and birds, strange creatures with mournful cries, picked up where the holy men had left off, as mockingbirds will do. He shut the heavy wooden door of a bedroom.

She touched his scar. Ran the tips of her fingers lightly along its edges.

If there were words now, they were just names, exclamations possibly. Whispers of astonishment that they should be together at all. He held her face close to his and wouldn't let her go, though she made no effort to release herself. Either he was crying or she was — it was to be expected — and he was astounded at how profound was his sense of relief. He thought the words *drinking her in* even as he was, his mouth so thirsty, so greedy, he could not even take the time to speak to her. There would be hours later when they could talk, he thought, but for now it was simply skin and breasts and long limbs and the awkwardness of needing to pull back to lift a dress overhead or to unbuckle a belt. And it was as though they were again teenagers inside a Buick Skylark convertible. Not needing to be anywhere else. Unable even to conceive of being elsewhere.

The sheets were rough but clean, a thick, textured cotton. He felt lust, but distantly — not as with Regina, when lust was essential to accomplish the act, when lust was necessary to blot out resentment or even fondness. In the canopied bed, there wasn't room for anything but an exultant sense of love regained and of a finite amount of time reserved to them. And that sense of time increased sensation, increased meaning, so that for an hour, possibly two, the bed, with its rough sheets, was all there was of the known universe.

He woke with the sun in his eyes. It was hot inside the room, and the sheets, so newly crisp just an hour earlier, were limp and damp. He moved, causing the top sheet to slide off the bed. He and Linda lay naked, covered only by the thin canopy above them that billowed in the slight breeze. He shifted his face from the direct sun and woke her as he did so. The jasmine petals had been ground into the pillows, and her hair and their perfume mingled with the musk of their bodies. They lay, as he had dreamed them, with her head on his shoulder, his arms around her, a leg curled up and over another. It was a simple posture, accomplished thousands — no, millions — of times a day, and yet so serious he could hardly breathe. He wondered how much time was left to them: an hour, a day, a year? And so he asked her. Determined not to leave before she did, no matter when that was. His body incapable of abandoning her, of walking away.

— *I have a day,* she said.

— *One day.*

— *A day and a night, actually.*

The sense of time so stupefying that he had to repeat the allotment aloud. The sun moved overhead; they hardly moved at all. As if, not moving, time might forget about them altogether. Until thirst compelled her to ask for a glass of water. He pulled on his trousers, reluctant to leave her, and went in search of a water source, encountering Mr. Salim reading at a kitchen table. Thomas explained, in Swahili, what he wanted, and instantly Mr. Salim produced from an icebox that looked to be from the 1930s a pitcher of cold water. The servant, seemingly pleased to have been consulted, added delicate confections of honey and nuts that he didn't name. Thomas took the tray up-

300

stairs, noting the two glasses instead of one.

She might never have drunk before. She sat upright, entirely naked, and he admired her breasts and the shallow curve of her stomach as she tilted her throat. In similar fashion, she devoured her portion of the sweets, which made him laugh, so that he offered her his, which she took with little hesitation.

— *Sex makes you ravenous,* he said, and immediately hated himself for it. Reducing what they'd had moments earlier to an experience she might have shared with any man, might daily share with the man named Peter.

She understood the slip and lightly corrected him. *That wasn't sex,* she said.

He sat beside her on the bed and wanted to make love again. Wanted to touch her shoulders and feel between her legs. Would a honeymoon be like this? he wondered. He didn't know, not ever having had a true one of his own, Regina weeping almost constantly for the loss of the baby just the week before the wedding. A kind of wake it was. The grieving, however necessary, badly timed. Though truth to tell, he'd been relieved, too aware of pretense.

— *You promised me a walk,* she said, touching him.

301

They walked through the town hand in hand, looking at the Islamic carvings and the Swahili silver jewelry, seeing neither the carvings nor the jewelry, but only the past, the recent past, the wife or the husband of the other, imagined marriages, houses and apartments never lived in, and once, poignantly, a future with a child, though the future was a blank to them, unknowable and unimaginable. He could not stop himself from thinking *only one day* and *only one night,* and was on the verge, once or twice, of crossing the line between what was likely and what was possible. But did not, for fear that any plan that involved the hurt of others would frighten Linda off. It was a calculus problem he couldn't solve — how to be together without catastrophe — and as with calculus, which had been his nadir, he felt his brain go hard and empty with resistance.

They had lunch at Petley's, neither of them hungry, ordering too much food — pweza; supa ya saladi; kuku na kupaka (lobster cocktail; watercress soup; chicken in coconut sauce) — lingering after most of the other diners had left, staying long after a confused waiter had taken away their barely touched plates. They sat with too many drinks (she surprisingly overtaking him), until he looked up and saw that the help were waiting to leave for their breaks. He stood, slightly woozy from the alcohol (really four scotches?), and suggested they walk to Shela, an insane idea in the middle of the day after the drinking, with no shelter to speak of along the way. When what he really wanted to do was go back to the bed-room with the jasmine blossoms ground into the pillows and sleep with her body pressed close to him.

They followed hand-lettered signs for Shela and caught a ride on a military truck that made its way through sand-clogged roads. They sat on benches at the back of the truck, and briefly she fell asleep with her head in his lap. One of her shoulders was burned by the time they had arrived at the beach, the scarf having lost itself at a jew-eler's counter or at Petley's. They sat on the verandah of Peponi's, the only beach hotel, and drank water and ate grapefruit — hungry after all — the sense of fog in the brain dissipating in the shade.

— *How did you get here?* he asked, having been too preoccupied to have imagined her arrangements.

— *I came up from Malindi.*

— *That must have been an adventure.*

She looked away, perhaps knowing the question that would come next even before he did.

— *Why Malindi?*

She hesitated. *Peter is there,* she said.

That she had been with Peter on the coast should not have been remarkable at all — no more remarkable, say, than the fact that he had left Regina only that morning — but it disturbed him nevertheless.

Linda did not elaborate. She took a sip of water. It was bottled, but the water at the museum house hadn't been. In her thirst, he remembered, she'd drunk nearly a pitcherful.

— *That's why you have to go back tomorrow?* he asked, knowing better than to ask. The answers would hurt no matter what they were, the only acceptable answer being that she would never leave him.

But she, perhaps wiser in this regard than he, or seeing the future more clearly, said nothing. And asked no questions of her own. Her hair, which had come loose when they had made love, had been put into a twist again, and he saw, from the inexpertness of the hastily made knot, how painstakingly she must have prepared for their reunion.

— *It couldn't be helped,* she said.

304

Jealousy squeezed his chest. *Did you sleep with him last night?* he asked, shocking himself with the question. She crossed her arms over her white linen dress. A defensive posture.

— *Thomas, don't.*

— *No, seriously,* he said, unable to give up what even a fool could see should be given up. *Did you sleep with him last night? I just want to know.*

— *Why?*

— *So I know where I stand,* he said. He pulled a pack of cigarettes from his shirt pocket, the shirt having been soaked through on the walk. Across from him, a couple were drinking Pimm's. He envied them their easy boredom. *So I can know the parameters,* he said.

She looked away. *There are no parameters.*

— *So you* did *sleep with him,* Thomas said sullenly, gazing into his water glass. Ashamed or afraid of the truth, he wasn't sure. Distracted, as he'd been all afternoon, by her body. The way, now, her breasts rested on her forearms.

— *It was the only way I could arrange it,* she said. He noticed that there was a sheen of sweat on her brow. *Don't let's do this, Thomas,* she added. *We have so little time.*

She uncrossed her arms and sat back in her chair. She put her fingers to her forehead.

— *You have a headache?* he asked.

— *A bit.*

— *Do you love him?*

The question, having waited in the wings, wanting the limelight now.

— *Of course I love him,* she said impatiently, and then paused. *Not in the way I love you.*

— *How do you love me?* he asked, needing endless reassurance.

She thought for a moment, picked a piece of lint off her dress. Choosing her words carefully.

— *I think of you constantly. I imagine a world in which we can be together. I regret not writing to you after the accident. I lie awake at night feeling you touch me. I believe we were meant to be together.*

He drew in a long breath.

— *Is that enough?* she asked.

— *Oh, Jesus.* He put his head into his hands. Looking at their table, the slightly bored couple with the Pimm's might have thought it was he who had the headache.

She reached across and touched his arm. In one fluid motion, he seized her hand. *What will happen to us?* he asked.

She shook her head back and forth. *I don't*

know, she said. Perhaps he was hurting her. *It's so much easier not to think about it.*

He let go of her hand. *We could have found each other if we'd really tried,* he said, challenging her. *It wasn't totally impossible. So why didn't we?*

She massaged her temple with her fingers. *Maybe we didn't want to spoil what we had,* she said.

He sat back and ground the cigarette, barely smoked, under his foot. Yes, he thought. That might have been it. But, then again, how would they have known, at seventeen, that it was possible to spoil love? He remembered them together — in front of the cottage, at the diner, walking the empty streets of Boston.

— *What?* she asked, noticing his incongruous smile.

— *I was remembering when I used to make you tell me what you'd said in Confession.*

— *That was awful,* she said.

— *This is awful,* he said.

He watched her take a sip of water — the movements of her delicate jaw, the contractions of her long throat. Beyond her was the white beach, an ocean so bright he could barely look at it. Palm trees rose high above them, and from open windows, gauze curtains billowed outward with a snap and then were sucked in again as if by a giant lurking in the shadows. It was a striking hotel, the only one in Shela. The only one in all of Lamu, his editor had said, with a decent bathroom.

He slipped another cigarette from its pack and lit it. He was smoking too much, eating too little. *We take life too seriously, you and I,* he said.

She pulled the pins from her hair and, in a perfectly ordinary but at that moment extraordinary gesture, let her hair fall the length of her back. He watched it sway as it settled. The surprising abundance of all that hair springing from a knot no bigger than a peach hurtled him back through the years.

— *It's what I've always loved about you,* she said.

— *Other people might just fuck and be done with it. Enjoy the fuck.*

— *We enjoyed the fuck.*

He smiled. *So we did.*

He let his gaze shift slightly toward the beach. Something had caught his attention, something he hadn't noticed before: at either end of the bathing area, the beachgoers were nude. A man with saggy buttocks had his back to him and was speaking to a woman lying on a blanket. He could see her hair, but not her body.

— *Was it ever easy?* he asked.

— *You mean light?*

— *I mean not serious.*

— *No.*

He rubbed his face. Sunburn had tightened his skin. He leaned forward, his elbows on his knees. They were wasting precious moments together. He wanted to return to the house, where they could make love again, but he knew they might have to wait until it was cooler. Perhaps there was a military truck returning to the village.

— *The one thing I miss,* he said, *is music.*

— *You don't have any tapes?* she asked.

— *I had tapes. But they were stolen. The tape recorder, too. I wonder what's popular right now.*

They sat in easy silence. A dhow skimmed the horizon. Ancient. Unchanged for centuries.

— *What was Rich's visit like?*

— *Oh, it was wonderful, apart from the fact that he got sick with malaria. We'd told him to take the pills in advance, but, I don't know, he's only sixteen.*

— *Is he OK?*

— *Yes. He's recovering in Nairobi.*

— *Are you making any progress with Ndegwa?* she asked.

— *Well, there's the embassy party at the In-*

tercontinental. Will you come?

— *I don't know.*

— *You'd come with Peter?* he asked.

She glanced away. She seemed exhausted. The bus from Malindi would have been grueling. He remembered a long trip to Eldoret that he and Regina had once taken on a bus, and how the driver had stopped so that all the passengers could get out to piss. The women, including Regina, had squatted, letting their long skirts cover themselves.

— *You never had a problem with the letters?* she asked.

— *No,* he said. *I loved them.*

— *I find them frustrating,* she said. *Inadequate.*

He sat up, a sudden anger straightening his spine. *How could you?* he asked, tossing his cigarette onto the cement floor.

She flinched, startled by the non sequitur, the sudden change of tone. *How could I what?*

— *Sleep with Peter.*

— *Sleep with Peter?*

Thomas refused to retract the question. He thought it a reasonable one: how could she, after that Sunday in Njia, be with another man?

He combed his hair with his fingers. He

310

needed a bath. Jesus, he must stink. An ugliness that had no place at that table, a stench more sickly sweet than the open sewers of Lamu, was suffocating him. He made an effort to breathe in the ocean air.

— *You expected on the strength of one meeting after nine years apart that I would tell Peter our marriage was over?* she asked, her voice conveying her incredulity.

— *Yes,* he said. *Basically.*

— *I can't believe you're saying this.*

— *Why not?* he asked. *Would you walk away from this now? Just tell me you could go back to a life with Peter and never see me again.*

She was silent a long time.

— *So,* he said. *Then.*

She put her fingers to her forehead. He saw that she had gone deathly pale.

— *Are you all right?* he asked.

— *I need to lie down.*

It was the water or the lobster or the drinking or the walk in the heat or the ridiculously painful questions he'd been asking her. She'd grown so pale so quickly that he thought she might faint. She said, *Please,* and he didn't know if she meant please stop talking or please help me. He did both. She leaned her weight on him and let him help her inside. But once inside, she lurched away, spoke rapidly to a middle-aged blonde behind a desk, and then disappeared around a corner. Thomas stood in the middle of the small, trim lobby wondering what had just happened.

— *Has she been ill?* the woman asked. British accent. Polka-dot dress.

Thomas shook his head.

— *Pregnant?*

The question rattled him. It was a moment before he could respond. *I don't know,* he had to say, admitting that he might not know her that well.

— *What did she eat?*

— *Here? Grapefruit and water.*

— *Well, it's unlikely to have been the grape-fruit. The water is bottled. Anything earlier today?*

Thomas thought about their lunch at Petley's. *Chicken,* he said. And then he remembered. *Lobster. She had lobster cocktail.*

— *Where?*

— *Petley's.*

— *Oh,* the woman said, as if that settled it.

But had Linda actually eaten the lobster? He tried to remember. And how could either she or he have been so foolish as to have ordered lobster in the first place? Never eat shellfish that you didn't know positively was fresh, they told you in the training sessions.

— *Let me see to her,* the woman said.

He waited on a camelbacked couch and watched bathers come and go in varying states of undress. One woman had tied a kanga at her breasts and was clearly naked underneath, the cloth barely covering her. An elderly gentleman in a pale blue seersucker suit sat beside him and said, by way of a pleasantry, *Lovely day.*

— *Yes, it is,* Thomas said, though he didn't believe it. Many words might apply to the day — *momentous; heart-breaking; wrenching* — but *lovely* was not among them.

The man's eyes watered some. He had high color and white hair, and Thomas thought the words *Old gentleman.* A peculiar smell of age, masked by cologne or hair tonic, seemed to emanate from deep inside his body. His cheeks, blotchy pink and red-veined, might have to be described as rosy. An elderly woman entered the lobby, and the old gentleman stood, waiting for her. She walked with slow steps, her back slightly stooped. Her white hair had been carefully combed and pinned, and she wore long ropes of pearls over a peach-colored silk blouse. She had the high waist of middle-age, but still there was a waist. Her mulberry pumps moved slowly forward in short steps.

She took the old gentleman's arm, and Thomas noticed that he put his hand over hers. Together they walked out to the verandah. Were they widowed? Were they married?

Christ, he thought, turning.

Another man, nearer his own age, dark-haired and good-looking, took a step backward into the lobby from the verandah. He seemed to be trying to take a picture of the ocean. For a moment, he fiddled with his camera, pressing buttons and trying levers; but then the camera, with a life of its own, popped open, surprising him. The man extracted the film from the camera and tossed the now useless canister into the wastebasket.

The blond proprietress returned from the bathroom and went directly to her desk. She unlocked a cupboard.

— *How is she?* Thomas asked, standing.

— *A bit peaky,* the woman said. Thomas wondering if this might be an example of British understatement. She poured a brown liquid into a tiny paper cup.

— *What's that?* Thomas asked.

— *Oh,* said the woman, turning. *Best not to think about it.*

Pure opium, Thomas thought, deciding to think about it.

— Is there a doctor we could call?

— No, I shouldn't think so, the woman said. *You'll want to get her home, though. Not tonight, but first thing in the morning. We have a provisions lorry that goes into the village at six forty-five a.m. Get you there in time for the seven-thirty to Nairobi.*

But she's not going to Nairobi, Thomas thought.

— In any event, the woman continued, still holding the spoon in her hand, *you're in luck.* (No, I'm not, Thomas thought.) *A man and a woman who came separately have decided to share a room.*

— Optimistic, Thomas said.

— Yes. Quite. But it leaves a room free.

— Thank you. Is it ready now?

— Take the key, the woman said over her shoulder as she walked to the rest room. *It's in the box there. Number twenty-seven. I'll bring her in.*

Implicit in the instructions: She wouldn't want you to see her now.

The room was surprisingly simple and appealing. Done almost entirely in white. White walls, white bedding, white curtains, a khaki-colored sisal rug. A dressing table with an ivory skirt. The lack of color drew the eye through the windows to the ocean, to the turquoise and navy of the water. A good room to be sick in, he reflected. Easy on the eye. Though it was impossible not to think of how it might have been: a night in that room with Linda feeling well. Feeling happy.

He walked to the window and examined the view. Could they ever be happy? he wondered. All their meetings — assuming that there would be any meetings at all — would have to be furtive, a framework in which neither of them could be truly happy. And if they allowed the catastrophic to happen, could either of them live with the consequences? What chance for happiness then?

At a table not far from his window, the elderly man in the seersucker suit gazed with rheumy eyes at the woman across from him. No one would doubt that he loved her. Thomas might have drawn the drapes, but he was reluctant to shut out the tableau of the older couple, who might be secret lovers themselves. They seemed reassuring, a good omen.

It would be easy to say how unfair it had all been. Yet it was he who hadn't driven to Middlebury; she who hadn't written to him that summer. Why hadn't he broken down doors to get to her?

— *I'm so sorry,* Linda said behind him.

— *Don't,* Thomas said, going to her.

She averted her face, unwilling to be kissed, even on the cheek. She sat on the bed. The British woman, who had helped her in, set open bottles of mineral water and Coca-Cola on the dressing table.

— *Give her sips of the Coca-Cola,* the woman said. *It will help to settle her stomach. Though I'd be very surprised if she didn't sleep now.*

When she left, Thomas removed Linda's sandals. Her feet were hard and dirty, lined at the heels. Her legs, the color of toast, contrasted sharply with the milk-white of her face; the legs and the face seemed to belong to two different people. Already, he could see, her lips had gone dry and were cracked and split at the center.

— *You need water,* he said. He brought her a glass of water and held her head, but she was almost too tired to swallow. Some trickled onto her neck, and he wiped it away with the sheet. He didn't try to remove her dress, but laid her under the sheet. She drifted in and out of consciousness, seemed lucid when she came to, saying his name and *I'm sorry,* which he let her do. He propped pillows against the headboard and sat with his hand on her head — sometimes stroking

317

her hair, sometimes just touching her. Whatever storm had blown through her earlier appeared to have passed, though Thomas knew it would come again, and it might be days before she could eat. He hoped it wasn't shellfish poisoning. (And she must have had a cholera shot, he thought.) Despite the crisis, he felt content just to sit there with her, nearly as content as he'd felt at the museum house. And thinking of the house, he remembered Mr. Salim, who might worry when Thomas did not return for the night. He thought of calling, but then realized he knew neither the phone number nor the name of the owner of the house. Checking his watch, he saw that it was too late for any museum to be open.

The sickness woke her. She bolted up, as if startled, and then catapulted herself into the bathroom. Thomas didn't follow, knowing she wouldn't want him to, that she might mind the loss of her privacy the most. He hoped one day they would talk about this: (*Remember that day on Lamu? When I got sick? It's one of the five or six most important days of my life. The others being? Today, for one*). Possibly they would even laugh about it. Though that implied a future. Each moment in time presupposing a future, just as it contained the past.

The proprietress brought him a meal (practiced innkeeper: she brought food that had no smell) which he left under a tea towel until Linda had fallen asleep again. He had a headache of his own, nothing more than a hangover. She woke sometime after midnight, while he himself was dozing. When he came alert, he could hear the water in the bathtub running. He would not go in, though he dearly wanted to see her. He'd never seen her in the bath, he reflected, and then he thought of all the other things they'd never done together as well — cooked a meal, gone to the theater, read the Sunday paper. Why this overwhelming desire to share the dull agenda of daily life?

She came out in a robe the hotel had given her and lay down beside him. Her face was gaunt and etched. He was embarrassed for his body, which was not clean. *I need a bath,* he said.

— *Not now,* she said. *Just hold me.*

He slid down, curling himself behind her.

— *It was stupid,* she said. *The lobster.*

— *You think it was that?*

— *I know it was that.*

The room lit only by the light from the bathroom.

— *You'll take a plane in the morning,* he said.

— *Peter's meeting the bus.*

— *You can't take the bus. It's out of the question.*

She didn't argue.

— *I'll have the hotel call him.*

He could feel a slight tension leave her body. She was drifting off.

— *Do you know where Peter is staying?* he asked quickly.

— *The Ocean House,* she said, closing her eyes.

He lay with her until daybreak, occasionally dozing off himself. Extricating himself as gently as he could, he picked up the key and left the room and walked out to the lobby, which was empty and still. He searched for a phone book, but couldn't find one. Not surprising. He picked up the phone — a black, old-fashioned phone — and asked for Malindi information. When he had the number, he rang it and asked a sleepy desk clerk if he would put him through to Peter Shackland's room. He waited, tapping a pen nervously on the wooden desk.

— *Hello?* A British accent apparent, even in the hello. She hadn't told him that.

— *Is this Peter Shackland?*

— *Yes. It is.* British and boyishly handsome. An unbeatable combination.

— *I'm calling from the Peponi Hotel on Lamu.*

— *Really? Peponi's?*

— *Linda's had a bout of food poisoning,* Thomas said. *From lobster she ate, she thinks. She's asked us to call to say she'll be flying back to Malindi early in the morning. The plane leaves at seven forty-five. I'm sorry I don't know when it gets in.*

— *Not much after eight-thirty, I shouldn't think.* There was a pause. *Oh Lord. Poor thing. Of course I'll be there. Has she had the doctor?*

— *You might have better luck in Malindi.*

— *Yes, I see. Well. Is she asleep?*

— *I believe so.*

— *Right, then. Well, thank you. I'm sorry, I didn't catch your name?*

Thomas was ambushed by the question. *John Wilson,* he said quickly, borrowing the name of the airport.

— *American.*

— *Yes.*

— *You work for Marguerite?*

Thomas hadn't even asked the woman her name. *Yes.*

— *Lovely woman. You don't by any chance*

321

know how Linda got there, do you? She was meant to be staying at Petley's. The hotel must have been full?

— I think so.

— No matter. I'll ask her tomorrow. Thanks for looking after her, the man named Peter said.

— Not at all, Thomas said.

Thomas put the telephone back in its cradle. He walked through the lobby onto the verandah. The air was mild, the sea nearly flat. Peter, who was British, knew Marguerite. Peter, who knew Peponi's, had quite possibly taken Linda there on a vacation.

He took his shoes off. At the horizon, the sky was pink. He began to walk in the sand, cool and damp on the soles of his feet. He would not ask Linda why she hadn't told him Peter was British; nor would he ask if she and he had made love in one of the rooms in the hotel behind him. A fishing dhow skirted the shore, and a man aboard it leaned gracefully over the side, letting go of a net.

He would not walk out very far or for very long. In an hour and a half — less now — he would put the woman he had lost and then found again on a plane.

February 15

Dear Thomas,

I want to say *thank you* and *I'm sorry,* knowing perfectly well you don't want either my gratitude or an apology.

I feel as though I have left all of me in Lamu, that nothing remains. I am hollowed out, empty without you.

The several days after I flew to Malindi are barely worth mentioning. I stayed in a hotel until I had recovered enough to make the trip to Nairobi and then to Njia. In Malindi, Peter had a doctor come — a drunken quack who kept wanting to talk about the good old days — and apart from a packet of pills we never quite caught the name of, but which worked extremely well, he seemed to be pretty useless, unable even to identify what was wrong with me. Though I'm sure it was the lobster. (I think I can promise you I will never eat another lobster again as long as I live.)

Oh, Thomas, I am dying for you. You asked me questions that made perfect sense in the context of the world only you and I inhabit, and I answered you curtly, because I didn't want to think how all this will end. Our situation seems all the more unfair to me, since we have had so little time together. Or do I delude myself in thinking we are entitled to even a minute outside of our marriages? I wish sometimes I didn't hate God so much; if I were obedient, life would be so much simpler.

I hardly remember the night we spent together, but I remember very well our brief time in that lovely house you managed to get hold of. (I realize now I never asked you how.) What an extraordinary room! Open to the sky, as if we had nothing to hide. Jasmine petals on the pillow, which I cannot help but think of as a token someone might have left on a wedding night. How I would like to go back there, to spend days without end in that house, which surely must be the most unique residence in all of Lamu. Or are they all so beautiful and sensuous?

I wake in the mornings. I go to my job. I

think of you. I come home in the evenings, and I drink too much. I try to drown sensation. I try to numb agitation. Peter comes and goes and waits for me to recover, though I haven't the heart to tell him I will not recover. We haven't slept together since Lamu, which he attributes to my illness. There, I have given you this. You needn't tell me about you and Regina. I don't want to know. If you haven't slept together, I will feel guilty and sorry for her. If you have, I'm not sure I could bear the images.

We are really not so different, you and I.

But our problems seem petty in the face of what we see daily, don't they? Just yesterday, I met a woman named Dymphina, who is twenty-four and has three children that until a week ago she hadn't seen in over a year. She lives in a one-room shack attached to a long wooden building in Nairobi. She leaves her children with her mother in Njia so that she can find money with which to pay her children's school fees, or as she puts it, to seek her fortune. That fortune amounts to $40 a month she makes as a servant in a European household. She labors from six in the morning until seven at night, six days a week, to make that $1.50 a day. Of the $40, she sends $20 back to her children, and pays $10 for the single room that has neither electricity nor running water. She often worries at night because drunken men from nearby bars try to force her locked but flimsy door. I met the woman when her mother brought her to my schoolroom; the mother wanted me to help her daughter because she was ill. "My titties hurt," Dymphina said.

To mind that I cannot see you should be nothing in the face of this. Why, then, am I able to think of little else?

I am sending with this letter a box I bought in Malindi. It is not alabaster, though I am pretending it is.

Love,
L.

February 20

Dear Linda,

I have waited and waited for some news of you, sick with worry that you were still ill, that you were not recovering. Convinced that I would never hear from you again. That you would take the debacle on Lamu for what it seemed, but was not: punishment for loving each other.

326

I must see you again. Will you let me come to Njia? Is there a time that you know Peter will not be there?

I am hardly a sane man. I smoke too much and drink too much as well. It seems the only antidote. Regina notices my distraction, but takes it for ordinary dissatisfaction with life, which she has seen before and assumes is more or less the norm. I can hardly speak to her or to anyone else. I'm too impatient; all I want to think about is you.

I work. I write about you. Oddly, not about you here in Africa, but in Hull. I do not understand Africa. I see this thing or that thing (a lobelia in bloom; a tourist berating an Asian shopkeeper; a hyena lurking at the edge of the forest), and it is as though I watch an exotic, imagistic movie. It does not include me. I am not a principal player. I am in the audience. I suppose that allows me to critique the movie, but I don't feel capable of even that.

Thank you for the Kisii stone box. I will treasure it always. I assume this is a reference to the box in which Magdalene was thought to have carried precious ointments? (I see you've done your own research.) I know you too well to think you glorify men, or one man, with this gesture, so I will accept it as a token of love, which I know it is. God is in all of us anyway. Isn't that what you said?

The plans for Ndegwa are "hotting up," as they say here. Will you be in Nairobi on the 5th? I will arrange an invitation all the same. There will be a cast of characters in attendance I would like you to meet, principally Mary Ndegwa, who has just published her first book of poems — trenchant and harsh and deeply rhythmic, which I like. It would not be fair to say she has benefited from all the publicity, but there it is. She seems a calm ship in a tempest, weathering the controversy magnificently. There is always the danger, when one makes a fuss over something the government has done, of poking at a nest of vipers with a stick. At this point, she risks her own freedom. I risk possible expulsion from the country (which before I met you, I wouldn't have minded so much; now it would be a torture, and I would have to insist that you go home, too; but of course you couldn't, could you? — not until your tour of duty is up; how strict are they about that?). Regina hates my involvement. She calls it insincere, which, though I have great admiration for

Ndegwa and loathe what has happened to him, of course is true. I have no idea what I'm doing in this arena. I feel I've taken on this cause as one would the latest fashion, the fact that progress can only be made with gala parties enhancing this queasy realization. More to the point, Regina is afraid my involvement will get her kicked out of the country as well, or that someone in authority will take away her grant. (In a country without many precedents and subject to a certain lawlessness, one has to believe anything is possible.) Ndegwa, who languishes in an underground prison for having written Marxist poems in the Kikuyu vernacular (political prisoners are not treated well; and even being treated "well" in a Kenyan prison would be an experience from which you and I would not emerge intact), risks his life. I hope we know what we are doing.

My Marine at the embassy, of course, risks nothing.

Kennedy is due to arrive on the 5th. My Marine is all atwitter. There will be a special reception that afternoon, and that night the gala, after which Kennedy will go on safari (the point of his journey, I suspect). The next morning, he'll have an audience with Mary Ndegwa (or is it the other way around?). I will be standing in the wings, trying to remain alert and useful, but all the while thinking only of you.

Amnesty International has written me. They have, as I suspected, already lodged a formal protest.

I would like someday to write of Ndegwa's courage. Did I tell you that we were born on the same day in the same year, eight thousand miles apart from each other? Astonishing to think that while I was delivered to the sterile hands of my mother's physician, Ndegwa was born on a sisal mat in a mud hut, delivered to the hands of his father's first wife. I remember that when I met Ndegwa, I used to think of us as two parallel lines that had arrived by design in Nairobi. He grew up during Mau Mau and didn't start school until he was ten because of the chaos of that era. When he was a child, he witnessed the execution of his father over a self-dug grave. By the time we'd met, he'd caught up to me in terms of schooling: indeed, he'd far surpassed me. At the university, I learned a great deal from him of a purely classical nature, which I hadn't expected to do. I'd like to create a portrait of him, highlighting the contrasts between his past as a sheepherder and his current status at the university; his legal battles to avoid paying a dowry of sheep and goats to his father-in-law for his wife; his practice, though secretive, of polygamous marriages; his revelation to me that wife-swapping is a time-honored Kikuyu custom; and his pervasive malaise regarding the risks and losses entailed in traveling too fast through history.

Yet I know I am not the one to write this portrait. Always, there was a barrier between us, a kind of inability to cross the border between our cultures, a demarcation that seemed studded with the barbed wire of misread symbols, separated by a wide gulf of differing experiences. Again and again we would lose our way. We would seem to make it to the very point of entry, when suddenly the ground would lurch beneath us, leaving us on separate sides of a fault, slipping past each other.

Write immediately. Tell me you will come, or that I may go to you.

I love you.
T.

P.S. Today's headline: FOOD AND FUEL RUNNING OUT.

Dear Thomas,

I received your letter and the invitation to the embassy party in the same mail. And have thought of little else since. I know that I should not go anywhere near Nairobi on that weekend, that I should flee to Turkana or Tsavo instead, that I should try to be as far away as possible. But, as luck or fate would have it, Peter wants me in town then because an old friend from school is coming to the country, and he would like me to meet him. If I decided to go to the party, I would have to bring Peter with me; I couldn't really go without him. Perhaps even his friend as well, depending on the circumstances. I assume that would not be a problem? I really would like to meet Mary Ndegwa and lend my support to the cause, though it will be you I come to see.

I can't promise anything.

I write to you from Lake Baringo. Peter has long wanted to visit this godforsaken place, and I agreed to go with him for the weekend. We have been at each other's throats lately — entirely my fault, and due to my distraction — and I hoped that this might ease tensions. (It does not: nothing seems to help, except the one thing I cannot do, which is to sleep with him. I would, I think, do it purely out of kindness at this point, though I'm afraid it would make me too sad. Why must love reduce one to sordid confessions?)

There is more to be frightened of at Lake Baringo than anywhere I have ever been. The land is unloving and unwelcoming. The dirt is hard and gray-brown with only thorn trees for vegetation. What little green exists is dust-colored as are the very black bodies of the tiny children, which makes them look ancient. The lake, with its island in the center, is brown and ripe with crocodiles. Last night, Peter swam while the sun sank, and this morning, I heard the sound of something large splashing in the water. A hippo, I suspect. Yet everywhere, even on this landscape where nothing young should flourish, there is life — noisy, cacophonous, teeming and quick. Just now, I am watching a lizard slither across the screen, eating mosquitoes. Cormorants, like old jesters, tread cumbersomely along the branches of the thorn trees outside our "cottage," which more closely resembles a wooden tent with a screened-in porch than a true building, the mesh of the screens just large enough to let in all manner of flying insects. My table is piled with beer bottles and mosquito coils, my writing paper and my pens. Across the road, four women in faded red cloth are brushing knots from their hair. It is almost unbearably hot. Only the faintest swish of air moves dryly over the hairs on my skin. There seems enough air to breathe, but barely more than that. The heat enervates, the light stuns, the mosquitoes carry malaria. There is little relief.

A few minutes ago, a meat truck rumbled down the road and sent from its wheels an enormous cloud of dust. In this cloud, there seemed to be a small creature hopping, like a large bird in preflight. When the dust cleared, however, I saw that it was just a boy chasing the truck with his basket. The truck stopped, and the boy held out his basket and waited for it to be filled with scraps not good enough for the market, the quality of which doesn't bear thinking about. I could have gone out onto the road to watch this scene more closely, but couldn't summon the energy to do so. I'd rather catch a scene midflight, imagining other realities. Is this what it means to be a writer? And on what level of life is this a valid enterprise? What can such an exercise offer to anyone, except easy distortions? To give a reader something of substance, I would have to chronicle the scene with precise detail as a historian would do, or reconstruct it so that it presented some truth about the nature of women and small boys and meat vendors. Which I cannot do.

I thought it was you who loved me more. But it is not true. It's me who loves you more.

I cry all the time now. I'm just as glad you're far away and can't see this. Peter is baffled, as well he might be. I have let him think it's an overlong bout of hormones. He doesn't deserve any of this.

I will leave a message for you on the message board. You will be called Roger, myself Gabrielle. I have always wanted a more exotic name.

L.

He was dozing fully clothed in the bed when the ibises woke him. Dozing because he had willed himself to sleep, unable to tolerate all the hours of the afternoon, which seemed to stretch interminably, leading up to the time when he and Regina could get into the Escort and drive to the Intercontinental Hotel for the party. He had tried, unsuccessfully, to write, his thoughts preoccupied, his nerves frayed. This after returning to Karen from town, where he had searched for and found a note to Roger from Gabrielle on the message board at the Thorn Tree. *My darling,* she had written, and he had felt the thrill of the endearment even as he had known it was a pose she would be trying on, in keeping with the Gabrielle, having a bit of fun, if fun could be had in such a desperate situation. Thin fun. Meager fun. Were there people, he wondered, who had genuine, more-or-less continuous fun when they fell in love? It didn't seem possible, the enterprise too fraught to sustain the lightheartedness fun required. *My darling,* she had written, *I am counting the hours until I see you tonight. Folly even to contemplate. But I shall be there. Your Gabrielle.*

And he had written back: *My darling Gabrielle, No man ever loved a woman more. Roger.*

The dogs from next door, Gypsy and Torca, were asleep in the kitchen as they often were. Regina cooked bones for them and let them in and had made beds for them in the corner, maternal instinct gone awry; though Thomas liked the dogs and had to admit that their owners seemed largely indifferent to their pets, who enjoyed the pampering, just as people do. Through the window, Thomas could see Michael sitting on a rock, unemployed, eating cooked meat he had just unwrapped from a paper packet. The grass was brown, the trees had dropped their leaves, there was nothing for a gardener to do. The entire country was waiting for rain.

Thomas turned on the tap in the kitchen (thinking of a cup of tea) and a dozen ants slid out, drowning themselves in the waterfall. In the dry season, there were always too many ants. They irritated the dogs when they tried to sleep under the trees, and sometimes when he entered the bathroom, he would see a trail of ants that Regina had squished with her thumb. Where was Regina, anyway? It was unlike her to be so late. She who had been known to spend an hour and a half getting ready for a dinner party.

But Regina was generally baffling these days. Not normally a baffling or complicated person, she seemed lighter, as if she'd lost weight or had learned how to levitate. Her voice a near lilt, even as she had said, during an argument regarding the wisdom of so publicly supporting Ndegwa's cause, *Do what you want. You always have.* Causing

Thomas to wonder, genuinely, had he? The question suddenly interesting, as if he'd discovered that someone had taken a film of his life and had invited him to watch it. For it seemed to Thomas that he'd been mostly thwarted from doing as he pleased, even though he couldn't have said with any accuracy exactly what it was that would have pleased him.

He laid his clothes out on the bed. He would dress with care tonight. He'd bought a suit for the occasion — a gray suit with a new white shirt — having realized that his laundered and line-dried blazer wouldn't do for a gala cocktail party. He had no idea what he would say to Kennedy, that defrocked priest. A man all the more engaging, Thomas thought, for his trials and tribulations, far more interesting than he'd have been without them, even with that prodigious legacy. Kennedy wouldn't remember him; Thomas had been only eighteen or nineteen when he'd met the man. It was after Jack had died — Robert, too, for that matter — power distilled and concentrated in the one remaining brother. Thomas's father — closet Catholic within the household tyranny of his mother's aggressive Calvinism — did penance by way of politics, raising large sums of money from unlikely

338

Democrats, wealthy bankers and entrepreneurs from the South Shore of Boston. Sums large enough to warrant gratitude and a royal visit. Thomas, summoned by his father, had come home from school — Cambridge no great distance from Hull — and had watched the senator at dinner and been rendered nearly mute by the obvious lack of any political fiber of his own.

On his writing desk, anchoring a corner of the bedroom, the Kisii stone box sat brazenly, as if naked. He'd picked it up on safari, he'd told Regina. When Rich bought that figure of a woman, remember? Yes, Regina thought she might remember. The box had arrived with a tiny chip in it, which made it all the more dear to Thomas — why, he couldn't have said; the imperfection, he supposed, causing it to seem like something Linda had used. He'd thought, briefly, of hiding the box and putting her letters in it, a foolish idea he'd abandoned in the next instant, knowing a hidden box would almost certainly invite inspection. He'd put the letters in the one place Regina would never look for them — amongst the hundreds of pages of the drafts to his poems, his poetry being just about the last thing Regina would want to poke through. It wasn't that she didn't appreciate

Thomas's gifts; she did, in her way. It was just that poetry bored her, the repetitious drafts of the poems tedious beyond endurance.

They were waiting for the rains. The country so dry now it seemed to crackle. They said that cattle were dying and that soon the reservoirs would be empty. Already, there were headlines: WATER CRISIS SHUTS HOTELS. He'd begun, like everyone else, to dream of rain, to lift his face to it in his sleep. Unifying the country in a way nothing else quite could do (or couldn't do at all); the mzungus and the Asians and the warring tribes all searching for a stray cloud, ready to celebrate with cocktails or dancing in the bush the minute the skies opened up. It was atavistic the way the longing got under the skin and into the bones, so that nothing seemed quite so luxurious as water falling from the heavens. The dust was everywhere — on his shoes, on the dogs (red with murram sometimes), in his nostrils, in his hair. Water was rationed to one bathtub a day. Thomas had taken to sponge baths to give Regina a half-tub of it at least. Though sometimes he'd ask her not to drain the tub so that he could get a good wash (washing in the leavings of someone else's water just about the height of intimacy, he thought).

He'd planned in fact to do that today, in preparation for the party, but Regina was so late — it was already half past five — he wondered if he oughtn't to just draw a bath for himself, give Regina the leavings, which seemed, on second thought, in that dry season, unchivalrous in the extreme.

Would they be giving baths at the Norfolk? He thought of Linda in a hotel room with boyishly handsome Peter, getting ready for the party. He couldn't see her as calm, though he wanted to; instead, he saw her on the verge of tears. Her letters had an odd, desperate quality that worried him; she seemed to be unraveling faster than he was, if such a thing were possible. Their situation was intolerable — more than intolerable, it seemed dishonorable, as though by staying with Regina, and she with Peter, they lacked honor or courage. But that soon would have to change. Though he dreaded the chaos, confessions were inevitable: one day he would tell Regina (he couldn't even imagine the horror of that), and Linda would tell Peter, who seemed like someone who might take the news with dignity, might even shrug it off in his boyishly handsome way (self-serving fantasy). What was Thomas waiting for? For a moment when Regina seemed sturdy enough to survive without disintegrating, without spiraling off into shrieking hysteria? A moment that might not ever come, even with her new levitating lilt. Though people, he knew, did not actually disintegrate, did not actually come apart into bits. They survived. They told themselves they were better off, didn't they?

He was buttoning his shirt when he heard Regina's car on the brick-like dirt beside the cottage. So unlike Regina to be so late, she who would have wanted an hour anyway to put herself together. He braced himself for panic, or at least for a whine about being stuck in a terrible traffic jam. The roads had simply crumbled, she would say; there'd been a dust storm on the AI.

But that was not her news.

— *I'm pregnant,* his wife said from the doorway. Flushed and radiant, as if, even in the car, she'd been running toward him with her blessed announcement. She looked beautiful, the burst secret giving her a color and a gaiety he hadn't seen in, literally, years. *We won't have absolute results until Friday, but Dr. Wagmari thinks I'm three months along.*

Thomas stood, unmoving.

The tide, responding to a crack in the universe, drained from the pool that he had, until that moment, thought of as his life, his

342

essence, his soul, though he hadn't been absolutely certain of the existence of the latter until this moment. The loss, the physical sensation of loss, was devastating and utterly complete. And oddly comforting, like a truly sad thought. He couldn't move or speak, even knowing that not speaking was unforgivable, would never be forgiven. And in the silence, he felt the cry beginning, a silent wail tearing through him, obliterating in an instant the odd comforting sensation, replacing it with a soundless scream. His life was over. It was that simple. Even as a new life was beginning.

— *What's wrong with you?* Regina asked, perhaps hearing a faint and distant echo of the silent scream. *You're just standing there.*

— *I'm* . . . Words deserted him. His system, trying to save itself, was shutting down bit by bit.

— *You're stunned,* she said.

Still he couldn't move. To move was to go on with the other life, the one he would have after this one. How hideous that it should be such joyous news that hurt so much. *Yes,* he managed.

It was, apparently, enough. Regina moved to embrace him, petrified statue, and his arms, involuntary appendages, responded with something like an embrace on his part.

— Oh, I'm stunned, too! she cried. *I never thought. Oh, God, isn't it fabulous?*

His hand, without signal from his brain, gently patted her back.

— It's what we've always wanted, she said, burying her face into his shoulder and beginning to sob.

Tears popped to the lower lids of his own eyes as well, horrifying him, and he tried to blink them back. They seemed treacherous, beside the point now. Though they, too, would be misread, might be taken for joy.

She pulled away from him, remembering the hour, ordinary things, already having crossed over into the new life.

— I'm so late, she crowed happily.

He sat on the bed in his underwear and socks, his shirt half buttoned, left unfinished by the natural disaster, as women holding cooking pots had been found at Pompeii. Thinking half-sentences from time to time, not often, the rest a misty white blank. *I need to warn* and *If only I hadn't.* Thinking, in particularly lucid moments, and as all men will inevitably try to calculate, *The night of Roland's party.* Having obeyed the biological clock, he and Regina were being rewarded with a child. But then the mist furled, and the fog

344

swamped him, and he wanted never to have to move again. Bitter irony. Had he not just said he would do the honorable and courageous thing? Unthinkable now. Not possible. Honor and courage flipped head over heels.

Regina emerged from the bathroom, more awed than annoyed by his immobility, the half-buttoned shirt. *My God,* she said. *You really are stunned.*

She was radiant. In a simple black dress with thin straps. Her breasts pushed somehow out and up so that their smooth white crests were exposed. Voluptuous Regina, who would become more voluptuous now. With his child.

— *How do I look?* she asked, spinning happily.

They were late. He might have said *embarrassingly late,* though embarrassment belonged to his other life. They ascended stairs and emerged into a crowd, voices already risen past a decent decibel. The party seemed to be held in a series of rooms, like chambers in a museum — the drinks in here, the food in there. White-coated waiters, diplomatically not African, moved from room to room with silver trays. Regina, beside him, turned heads, as she did not normally do, her glow like plutonium, the radiation high. His own radar tuned elsewhere, a personal early warning system deploying. Needing to find Linda before Regina crowed. He searched for blond hair and a cross, found blond hair more often than it occurred in nature, but not a cross. As disastrous as the circumstances were, he wanted nothing more than to see Linda — if only a glimpse — though that would simply fuel desire. And he was surprised by how much it hurt, this returning to life. Numbed limbs remembering pain.

Thomas, not discovering Linda, found his Marine instead. The man looking uncharacteristically deflated, a defeated Marine a sorry sight. Introductions were offered and received, Regina towering over the Marine's wife, a diminutive dun-colored woman in a royal-blue suit.

— *Your boy's not here,* the embassy official said.

Thomas, at first not understanding the reference to "your boy," thought the man had the wrong person. And then, suddenly, he comprehended. *Kennedy?* he asked.

— *Not coming.* The Marine took a large swallow of what looked to be straight scotch. No ice. His face was white and hollow-cheeked.

— *What happened?*

— *Scheduling conflict. So they say.* The Marine spoke through tight lips. Bearing up. Though the wife looked as though she had been crushed long ago.

— *He's in the country?* Thomas asked.

— *No,* the man said, aggrieved. *That's the point.*

There seemed nothing to say but I'm sorry. *I'm sorry,* Thomas said.

— *It's your gig,* the unhappy official said.

Thomas, out of politeness — manners instilled from long ago, seemingly irrelevant now — lingered with the Marine as one would with a man who'd just been fired or lost a valuable contract. All the while scanning the crowd, unable to help himself, breaching irrelevant manners with his sporadic inattention. Regina, contrary to expectation, kept her secret to herself, though to be fair, she didn't know the embassy wife at all. Still, Thomas had expected a joyous blurting out. Had braced himself for an announcement that couldn't fail to reach unwilling ears. Perhaps Regina was simply being prudent, waiting for confirmation. She had, after all, already lost one child late into the game. Or possibly his wife was superstitious, a trait he'd failed to notice before.

When it was feasible, Thomas excused

himself from the crestfallen embassy official (Regina remaining, the wife and she apparently having found something in common) and made a more determined search for Linda. Though the event was not black-tie, everyone was attired just a notch down from that, so that there were many long dresses and dark suits. He saw his editor across the floor and might have tried to part the crowd to get to him, the editor being nearly the most interesting person Thomas knew. But Thomas, a man with a mission, merely waved instead. He spotted Roland, who did not, mercifully, see him, as well as a journalist he knew from somewhere — the university or the Thorn Tree. Men and women seemed locked in conversations that required shouting. Thomas took a glass of champagne from a silver tray and guessed the waiters were Marines. Was that possible? He entertained for a moment the notion they were spies — an idea abandoned in the next minute with the realization there'd be little of value to spy *on*. Still he could not find Linda. From the center of the room, Mary Ndegwa waved to him. Thomas gravitated to her, as a subject will be drawn toward a royal personage. She was holding court in a gold headdress with a caftan of a similar color that made him think of frankincense and myrrh. Thomas could not suppress the thought that Ndegwa's imprisonment had freed the wife and mother. Freed her to become what had perhaps all along been her nature: a leader with a following. Which raised the question: What would happen if and when Ndegwa were ever released?

— *Mr. Thomas,* she said. *You are looking very handsome tonight.*

Power had made her flirtatious. *No more handsome than you,* he said as expected.

— *I was hoping I would meet your wife.*

— *She's here somewhere,* Thomas said, making an effort to search the gathering, growing like a culture in a petri dish, crowding other cells. *I'll find her in a minute and bring her over.*

— *I have thanked you already for arranging this,* she said. *But may I be permitted to thank you again?*

— *It's not necessary,* Thomas said, waving his hand. *Actually, I had very little to do with it.*

— *Mr. Kennedy did not come.*

— *No. I'm surprised.*

— *It is no matter.*

And Thomas thought, no, it wasn't. That now Mary Ndegwa was the personage without peer, though there were supposed to be one or two MP's at the party as well. The guest list had been composed largely of people the embassy wished to reward with attendance at a party at which Kennedy would be (and now wasn't) present.

— *And how is Ndegwa?* Thomas asked.

— *I fear for him,* she said, though Thomas noted she did not look distraught.

— *Your book is doing well,* he said.

— *Yes. Very well. It, too, will be repressed one day.*

— *You seem certain.*

— *Oh, but I am,* she said, amused that he should doubt this perfectly obvious truth.

— *I'm sorry to hear that.*

— *Mr. Thomas, you must not desert us,* she said, touching him on the shoulder.

He was slightly taken aback by the imperative. He hadn't been thinking of deserting, though, truthfully, he hadn't been thinking of Ndegwa at all. He sought a suitable reply, but already Mary Ndegwa had lost interest in him, was looking over his shoulder at a woman Thomas vaguely recognized as an Italian journalist. It was an abrupt and total dismissal, not intended to dismiss so much as to discard and move along.

He wandered to the edges of the gathering, trying to get outside of the building so that he could have a cigarette, though the rooms were filled with smoke already and he needn't have bothered. He wanted to watch for Linda, anxious now lest she not come at all. And then what would happen? Would he have to go to the Norfolk tomorrow only to tell her his wife was pregnant? It was inconceivable, like the earth shifting in its orbit.

He leaned upon a wall at the top of the steps and smoked. There were stragglers and fashionably late arrivals. It was nearly eight o'clock and soon, he thought, people would begin to leave to go to their dinners. Marines stood at attention at the bottom of the steps and made a kind of honor guard through which the guests, in uncomfortable shoes, paraded. He saw her before she had even crossed the street, her companion looking to his right for traffic, his hand at her back, nudging her forward when he thought it was safe. She wore a shawl around her shoulders, holding it closed with her hands just above her waist, and it was such a precise repetition of the image of her walking toward him at Petley's that his breath caught. For a moment, before she saw him, he endured the sweet mix of pleasure and pain that observing her cross the street caused, running a step at the end (a rude driver) and then lifting the skirt of her dress, white linen, as she stepped onto the curb (she had worn her best dress in Lamu to meet him, he realized now). And watching her, he understood why she was late: she'd been drinking already. How did he know this? It was in the slight loss of balance as she stepped up onto the sidewalk, the ready hand of the man she was with, as if he knew her condition. Peter, it had to be, though the man looked older than in the photograph.

She negotiated the stairs with her head bowed, studying her feet, so that she passed by without noticing him. Or if she'd seen him, it was an expert performance. He had to step from the shadows and call her name. Her very common name.

— *Linda.*

No, she hadn't known he was there. He could see that at once — her emotions, less carefully guarded now, twitching across her face. The shock. The joy. Then remembering her circumstances. She took a step toward him. Not unsteadily. Perhaps he had been wrong about the drinking. It was all he could do not to touch her arms, which seemed to beg to be touched.

The man with her, momentarily disconcerted, turned as well.

— *Thomas,* she said. And then repeated herself. *Thomas.*

It was he who had to put out his hand and introduce himself to the man with her. Who was Peter after all. Perhaps it was simply that she hadn't been able to say the word *husband*.

— *Peter,* she said, recovering. *Thomas and I knew each other in high school.*

— *Really,* Peter said, unwittingly parroting Regina in similar circumstances.

— *We met each other in the market one day a few months ago,* she said. *We've already been amazed.*

It was an astonishing sentence. Perfectly acceptable in its context, even ordinary and without real interest, yet utterly true. They had been amazed by each other, by the chance meeting. So thoroughly amazed.

— *You're still in Njia?* Thomas asked, plucking dialogue from the air. Would being a playwright instead of a poet make one a better conversationalist?

— *Well, Peter's in Nairobi,* she said, explaining what had already been explained once before.

— *The pesticide scheme,* Thomas said, as if he'd just remembered.

The man had slightly thicker jowls than as photographed and was narrow-shouldered in the way that Englishmen often are. Still, he was undeniably handsome, and his gestures — brushing back a forelock, his hands draped casually half in and half out of his pockets — suggested he might be charming as well. But then Thomas saw the puzzlement on Peter's face, as though the man had just perceived an odd, even alarming, sound. He'd be working out where he'd heard the voice before, Thomas thought, and he wondered how long it would be before Peter guessed. As if in anticipation of that discovery, Peter put his arm around Linda, cupping her bare shoulder.

The tide abruptly went out again, beaching Thomas like a stranded seal.

— *And how is it you're in Nairobi?* Peter asked.

— *My wife has a grant with UNICEF,* Thomas said. And thought, hopelessly, And is pregnant.

He wanted to glance at Linda and yet was afraid to. It became a kind of adolescent struggle.

— *There's champagne and food,* he said, releasing husband and wife. He gestured to the door. Even as he was foundering inside. Flopping on a beach.

She went — slight reluctance in her turn — with Peter, her Englishman. Thomas followed them in, not wanting to lose sight of her, so recently found. Peter seemed to know people. Thomas watched Linda take a glass of champagne from a tray (holding the shawl closed with one hand) and sip from it immediately, as if she were thirsty. Thomas observed Peter in conversation and hated the man for his charm, for the way he bent his head, face turned slightly away as he listened to a man who had just hailed him. Thomas followed at a barely decent distance, as close as he dared, yet altogether too far from her. She had wonderful posture, he realized, the back of her dress as low as he remembered (complicated bra, he recalled), and thought, She doesn't know. She doesn't know.

Roland, who seemed to thread through the crowd like a python (no, that was unfair; Roland wasn't that bad), was making his way, Thomas realized, toward him. He cast around for a plausible exit, saw none, and knew he ought to be pleasant to Regina's boss, however much he found the man distasteful.

— *Who's your friend?* Roland asked, stupefying Thomas.

— *What friend?* Thomas asked, pretending to be oblivious.

— *The woman you spoke to on the steps? The one you've been following and staring at.*

Thomas said nothing.

— *Pretty,* said Roland, looking at Linda. She stood sideways to Thomas, and, shattering pretense altogether, glanced over at him and smiled. As one might smile at a friend. Nothing in it under normal circumstances; everything in it now.

Roland, old sage, nodded to himself. *So,* he said, wanting a story.

— *She's just someone I went to school with,* Thomas said. *We just ran into each other one day.* (The repetition of the word *just* giving him away, he thought.)

— *Indeed,* Roland said, making it clear he didn't believe a word of it. *So you say.*

— *Jane here?* Thomas asked, needled, and wanting, foolishly, to needle back.

Canny Roland smiled even as he narrowed his eyes.

— *Elaine?* Thomas asked.

— *Of course,* Roland said smoothly. *Where's Regina, by the way?*

Thomas saw his wife, a tall woman in heels, making her way toward Thomas from across the room. *She's just coming,* Thomas said.

— *No Kennedy then?* Roland asked.

— *Afraid not.*

— *Not a bodge on your part, I hope.*

— *Amazingly not,* Thomas said, snagging another glass of champagne.

— *Ah, the beautiful Regina,* Roland said. And what ought to have been pure compliment sounded oily on his tongue.

Regina kissed Roland just off the mouth, as people who are something more than acquaintances will do. She looked at Thomas and beamed — shared secret, it would appear, still intact.

— *It's a shame about Kennedy,* Regina said sympathetically to Thomas. Her flush had lowered itself to a place just above her bosom, hard not to stare at. Indeed, Thomas saw, Roland was staring.

— *Did you get something to eat?* Regina, normally not solicitous, asked solicitously. She could well afford it now.

— *I'm fine,* Thomas said. Outrageous lie. He was frantic. Out of the corner of his eye, he could see that, by some principle of crowd physics unknown to him, the throng between himself and Linda was thinning and that she and Peter were being inevitably nudged in Thomas's direction. Linda, he saw, was now drinking a scotch. Neat, no ice. A half dozen reasons why Linda's meeting Regina and Roland would be disastrous hurtled through his mind.

— *Let's find Elaine,* Thomas suggested, Regina and Roland looking at him oddly, as, indeed, the suggestion warranted. But it was already too late. Linda, detached from Peter, stood beside him.

— *Hello,* Regina said, surprised. *You're Linda, right?*

— *Yes. Hello.* Linda's bare arm not an inch from Thomas's elbow.

— *Linda, this is Roland Bowles. Regina's supervisor.*

Linda put out her hand. *How do you do?*

— *Thomas and Linda went to high school together,* Regina said.

Roland giving Linda the once-over and not bothering to hide it, either. Jesus, the man was insufferable.

— *In fact,* Regina said, *Thomas and Linda were once in a car accident together. Isn't that right, Thomas?*

The mention of the accident stopping, for a moment, Thomas's heart. He was certain it had done the same to Linda.

— *It's how he got the scar,* Regina said in a necessarily loud voice, shouting as everyone had to do.

— *I'd wondered about that,* Roland said.

— *It must have been terrible,* Regina added, examining first Thomas, and then Linda, her eyes darting from one to the other as they stood side by side. But then, remembering her good news, her slight scowl vanished. Her face lit with recollection — so much so that Thomas was sure she would say something.

— *I hardly remember it now*, Linda said. The scotch nearly gone.

And as if a kind of critical mass had been reached in the room, raising the temperature six or seven degrees, Thomas suddenly felt uncomfortable and began to sweat beneath his white shirt and gray suit. Linda, too, he could see, had sweat beads on her upper lip, a delicate moustache he wanted to lick off. And with the perceived rise in temperature, so also did his emotional temperature rise — seemingly making *more* of everything. So that, looking at Regina, he felt a sense of claustrophobia so profound he began to think he couldn't breathe. And he wondered, as he had never wondered before, if he didn't actually hate Regina, and if he didn't hate smug Roland as well. Roland, who made pronouncements and who was now saying something about Kingsley Amis and did Thomas know him, he was a neighbor of a cousin, and so on. And Thomas wondered as well if he didn't hate boyishly handsome Peter, too, for sleeping with the woman he loved, the woman he was meant to be with. And so foul was the air from this sudden temperature rise that he almost felt as though he hated Linda for having walked into his life too late, stirring up old emotions better left dormant. (Though, strictly speaking, he supposed he had walked into her life.)

He spun away from the group and threaded a path through backless dresses and thickened necks, faintly aware of his name being called, ignoring the summons, walking past an Asian woman wrapped in silken saris and a slender Frenchman (he could only be French with that mouth), hearing as he walked — or did he only imagine it? — a voice raised in argument, a snarl from somewhere deep inside the crowd. It was the weather, he knew — parched and gritty and oppressive — that chafed skin and tightened jaws and loosed snarls where before snarls had been unthinkable. He reached a table and stood against it, not knowing where else to go, and smoked a cigarette, his back to the crowd, not wanting to see them.

He heard his name and turned.

— *Keep moving,* Linda said, putting a hand out to touch him.

He walked, not blindly, for he was aware of searching for an empty corner, of moving at the edges of the party, of not being able to find the exit and so wandering into a hallway, into an anteroom and through a door into a darkened office. She was behind him, in full sight, he supposed, of anyone wishing to notice, but he was so glad she was there he thought his lungs would burst.

She slid inside the door and turned the lock.

He understood that she was drunk, but he couldn't help himself. This might be the last time — *would* be the last time — they'd ever be together. The moment doubly stolen, like borrowing from an overdraft, the original capital depleted. And far from thinking it dishonest, he considered it a mercy she herself didn't know. His own grief enough for both of them.

In the darkness, he found her mouth and her hair, kissed the one, held the other, then kissed them both. He could barely see her face, the only light a streetlamp outside the window. She was wiry against him, more passionate than he had known her before — more *expert* — and it was her lust as much as his own that made them impatient to be undressed. They strained at fabric, stepped on it, had no time for buttons. She took her shoes off and suddenly was smaller, more fluid against him, and for a time they were up against a wall, then leaning on a leather chair. They slid or knelt to the carpet between the chair and a table, a corner of the table catching him in a kidney, and he thought there must be some anger of her own fueling her, for she was unlike herself — more abandoned in the way that anger can produce abandon, as, indeed, it had just done in him when he'd spun away from the grouping. He didn't stop to ask himself longer than a second what Regina and Peter and Roland might be thinking, because they were not important now. Not right now. This would be all that mattered if it had to last a lifetime. And, fuck it, it *would* have to last a lifetime. And he said, or she said, *I love you,* as lovers will, though he knew the words — devalued (had he not said them to Regina? she to Peter?) — didn't explain what it was they had, for which he knew only one word, a word both blank and precise, now repeating itself endlessly in his head: *This,* he thought. *This.*

And then again, *This.*

They lay in the squalid dark of the office. He was aware of bunched clothing at his head, the heel of a shoe poking into his thigh. Their naked hips wedged between a table leg and a chair. Maybe they would not be able to get out, would have to stay until they were found. She felt for his hand and laced her fingers through his, and there was something in that gesture, in the slow lacing of fingers and in the way she lowered their clasped hands to the floor, that told him that she knew. Knew it would be the last time. Nothing needed to be said, the gesture seemed to imply. Or perhaps it was just that he was too exhausted to summon words.

She stood and gathered her clothes. He watched her put on her complicated bra, zip her much-wrinkled linen dress, step into heels — the reverse of love, the reverse of expectation. And, in a moment he would remember for the rest of his life, she knelt and bent over his face, her hair hanging in sheets that gave them ultimate privacy and whispered into his mouth the unforgivable thing she had just done.

It might have been Confession.

Roland had his arm around Regina. In a corner, a baffled Peter was speaking to the back of Linda's head. Guests were leaving — casually, normally, unaware of catastrophe — or if they were aware, giving it a sidelong glance, a quizzical stare. It would entertain, this story, become part of the pantheon of stories of illicit love in Kenya, a footnote to the Happy Valley days. Or not even that. Forgotten before the nightcap, the principal players not prominent enough to warrant sustained attention.

He had missed the central drama.

In the end — strangely, but perhaps to be expected — it came down to his soul. He who thought he did not have one. A concept he could not even name. It was elegantly simple: he couldn't let Regina lose the child.

Regina's wail rose on the street; and in the car, she threw herself from side to side, battering herself against the door, asking, demanding to know: Did you sleep with her? And, How often? Screaming at the answers and the silences alike. Wanting dates and details, horrendous details he would not give her. In the cottage, she hurled herself against a wall. He tried to calm her, to touch her, but she was wild, having had, despite her news, her own goodly amount to drink. She vomited in the bathroom and wanted him to help her just as much as she wanted him to die. And all the time he was thinking: I cannot let her lose the baby.

He shook his wife to stop the hysteria. Telling her, as one would tell a child, to go to bed. She whimpered and begged for him to hold her and he did, dozing for seconds only, waking to fresh wails. Waking to fury and accusations and threats. She would kill herself, she said, and he would have two lives on his conscience. She kept this up for hours, seemingly beyond endurance — his or hers — astounding him with the depth of her anger. Till finally she fell asleep, and for a time — blessed hours — there was silence.

In the morning Thomas dressed, thinking that he had to go in person, that this could not be done by letter. His only theatrical gesture was to take the letters and put them in his pocket.

It was the saddest drive of his life. She was sitting at a table when he arrived. She might have been there for hours. Just waiting. Just smoking. A chaste cup of tea in front of her. Her skin was blotchy, her hair and face unwashed. Doubtless fresh from personal horrors of her own.

— *Why?* he asked in the nearly empty café.

She couldn't answer him.

— *It has to end,* he said. *I have no choice.*

No need to mention that Regina was pregnant, for that had been revealed to Linda, out of his hearing, the night before. No need for Linda to say she loved him, for that, too, had been said to Regina the night before. Out of his hearing. Though he'd heard the words repeated often enough in Regina's shrill voice as she'd hurtled around the room.

— *I'll always* . . . Thomas began. But he couldn't finish the sentence.

There was a great clap of thunder then — the clap of a jester at a royal performance (pay attention now!) — and the rains began, a sudden deluge that released a thousand — no, a hundred thousand — knots of tension in an instant. The rain was warm, nearly hot, the café umbrella furled and not giving them any protection. Linda was crying with no shame. He put the letters on the table, tucked them under her hand.

He made himself walk away, thinking as he walked: this would be the worst he'd ever know; nothing would ever hurt this much again.

Part Three

Seventeen

She stands at the edge of the pier in the October cold. The moon is high and so bright that she could read a book. The boys are silent behind her, not believing their luck. One of them says, "Don't," but she knows that he wants her to, that he can't help himself. The water twitches in a cone of light, and, briefly, she has an image of swimming to the horizon. She steps to the edge, and in the next instant, she is out over the water in a perfect dive.

The ocean closes over her head, the water like silk along her body, a phrase she will later give to the boy who said *Don't*. The sea is briny in her sinuses and eyes. She swims out and away from the pier before surfacing, enjoying the perfect clean of the water, though she knows that at the bottom there might be old shoes and broken bottles and used tires and saggy bits of underwear.

In a moment, she will have to break the surface, and she will hear, as though distantly, the hoots and awed cries of the boys who will be calling to her. But for now there is just the clean and the dark, a perfect combination.

She is sent away for years. The word *slut* flung across a room and hitting her like a thrust stone. An aunt returning too soon and shrieking at the girl and the man, who scuttles away like a beetle. The aunt approaching, arms flailing, all fury and righteousness, shouting *whore* and then *slut* again, and then *ungrateful* and then *bitch*. Words that ring in the air like notes from a bell.

The place that she is sent to is beautiful and harsh. A house stands above the ocean. The surf is constant and comforting, a whisper-rumble of indifference. The house is cavernous and is filled with other girls who have been called *whore* and *slut* as well. They live in small bedrooms and go to a Catholic girls' school around the corner, but the center of their lives is the laundry. In the basement of the house are a hundred tubs and washing machines and whenever the girls aren't otherwise engaged — with school or with studying or with sleeping or with eating or, on rare occasions, watching television — they do the laundry. Girls, like herself, with hot faces and reddened hands from the water and the bleach, wash the laundry of the rich and the merely harried: linen sheets and oblong tablecloths; Oxford shirts and belted dresses; babies' sleepers and soiled diapers. It gets so that Linda can guess the story of any family who has left their laundry. Men's and boys' overalls and corduroy shirts speak of a household without a woman. Sheets stained from a birth speak for themselves. Boxer shorts with stiffened crotches suggest furtive pleasures, and women's underpants with blood on them tell them no more than they already know. A household that quite abruptly ceases to send the baby sleepers suggests a tragedy that requires silence.

The hands of the girls will always be red, the damage too deep to be salved with ointments. They will remain chapped for years, the nuns repeatedly tell them, a reminder of their lot, as if it had been planned. The hands will be, for years, a badge of shame.

Good drying weather. The phrase is a clarion call. The damp laundry that never dries properly inside the basement is pinned to ropes with wooden clothespins, then left to furl in the breezes, smelling of the sun when the wash is brought inside in wicker baskets.

Coming back from her classes, rounding a corner, Linda sees the wash on the line: acres of white and colored shapes moving in the wind. It takes the breath away, the sight of all that wash, and seems like fields of crisp flowers, a strange, enchanting crop. The bloodied sheets are clean, the labor pains forgotten, the stains of all that lust rinsed away. Shirts fill with air and move, so that she can believe that they are occupied. Overalls kick out sturdy legs, and night-gowns drift fetchingly in the air. Sheets billow and snap and seem to have a life of their own, defying their owners and the girls alike.

The house is called Magdalene, as are all the establishments that take in wayward girls for sins committed or imagined. There seems to be little difference: the parents wish them there and pay. Insurance money that cannot be used elsewhere is sent by a bank to settle Linda Fallon's bills.

Occasionally one of the nuns refers to the Home as a boarding school for young Catholic women. But nobody is ever fooled.

Sometimes a girl runs away, and who can say where she has gone? Other girls give birth, and the babies are taken from them. Sometimes — rarely — a family whose wash has been laundered and delivered repeatedly by a certain girl asks if she can come to live with them.

None of this happens to Linda.

And, actually, she has no desire to run away. She cannot see the point. She endures the school, but likes the sight of the wash on the line. She has learned to count on the white noise of the surf and the front porch and a nun who is kind and befriends her.

In the beginning, there are letters from the aunt. Blunt missives with bulletins of news, mere notes of discreet pretending that nothing serious has ever happened. A month before Linda turns seventeen, however, a different sort of letter arrives at the house for wayward girls. Linda is to return home. Linda Fallon is going home. She protests to the nuns that she has no home, that she will be a stranger there, that she has less than a year to go before she graduates from the Catholic girls' school. The sisters merely look at her.

You have to go, they say, consulting their bookkeeping. The money has run out.

Linda has only indistinct memories of her mother and no real ones of her father. Her mother, she is certain, had long brunette hair folded into waves. When she laughed, she held her hand in front of her mouth. She wore slender woolen dresses with jewel necks, or she was a woman in a fur coat clutching the hand of a small child as they walked along the street. She had perfectly shaped brown pumps and tiny feet.

In the photographs, her father is tall and despite his crooked teeth, resembles, in an anemic sort of way, a movie star. Leslie Howard, say. In the photographs, her father always wears a fedora and is smiling.

In the upstairs bedrooms of the home for wayward girls, Linda cries with the other girls who live in the house. Hysterically, as teenage girls will do in the face of calamity. She promises to write and smiles bravely through her tears, as she has learned to do from the occasional uplifting movie they have been allowed to see.

When Linda arrives home, she discovers that the aunt's boyfriend has gone off with another woman, abandoning the aunt with six children of her own from a failed marriage and a niece in a school for wayward girls. As a result of this defection, the aunt and her cousins have had to move to a succession of smaller and smaller apartments, settling like a tumble of blocks down a flight of stairs. So that when Linda returns to the fold, the aunt and the cousins are living on the top floor of a triple-decker in an undesirable neighborhood in a working-class town.

The apartment into which Linda moves is a warren of tiny rooms smelling of Johnson's baby oil and onions. She shares a room with two of her cousins, Patty and Erin, girls whom she hasn't seen in over three years and who hardly know her now. Linda will wear Eileen's clothes, the aunt decrees; there will be no money for new ones. The clothes that once fit Eileen, who has gone to New York to seek her fortune, are, however, just slightly too small on Linda, since she is taller than Eileen. The clothes are skirts as short as the public school will allow and tight sweaters with low V-necks. For years, Linda has worn a uniform, and so the clothes are strange to her and oddly exciting, as if they were a costume she were trying on. She can theoretically become a different person.

Faint echoes of the word *slut* still ping against the walls. Linda wears bright shades of lipstick that Patty lends her, and she learns to tease her hair. Linda's aunt remains tight-lipped in the face of Linda's youth and presence.

The cousins, variously, resent Linda or are solicitous. It is understood that she is damaged, though they do not know, and will never know, the specific crime that caused her to be banished. It is a secret between the aunt and Linda.

The aunt is now the unimaginable age of fifty. She has papery skin with fan wrinkles, eyebrows dotted with bits of gray. Her mouth has puckered, creasing her upper lip. To make herself look younger, the aunt has dyed her hair blond, the result a strange alloy of brassy gold with dark silver roots. Despite the difference in age, however, it does not escape Linda's notice that, in certain lights, she resembles her aunt. In fact, she looks more like her aunt than some of the cousins do — an intimate connection that makes none of them very happy.

Every day, the aunt goes to Mass. Her missal sits like a bomb on the arm of the sofa in the den — a bomb about to explode with liturgy and dire predictions of the aftermath of sin.

Linda begins her senior year at the public high school during the first week of October. She dresses in a charcoal skirt and a white blouse of Eileen's, but she refuses Patty's offer to paint her nails, being self-conscious about her hands.

The school is located at the end of a long peninsula. It appears, at first glance, to be a prison. The low brick building is flat-roofed and is bordered by chain-link fencing to keep the students away from the water. There are no trees and only an asphalt parking lot. It is the sort of building that suggests guards in towers.

The high school seems to have little to do with its surroundings, as though it purposefully ignored them. On that particular October morning, the ocean dazzles, and the sky is an unblemished blue. In the distance, Linda can see Boston. The school is, like the town itself, anomalous: as if a working-class community had been transplanted onto what might have been, had things turned out differently, the most expensive real estate south of Boston.

Inside the high school, the windows are

opaque with sea salt and wire netting, protection from the gulls that periodically try to batter the glass to get in. They want the students' lunches. High on the list of school rules is this one: Never feed the gulls.

The cousins have not been discreet, and rumors have flown before Linda has even arrived. The vice principal regards her warily, making note already of infringements. "Get rid of the skirt," he says.

Putting Linda in her place. Just in case she has ideas.

Linda follows corridors and stands before an orange door with a narrow slit of glass. Through the slit, she can see a teacher and a group of students — the boys in colored sport shirts, the girls with curled hair. When she opens the door, the teacher stops talking. The faces of the students are a blur. There is a long silence, longer than it should be — seeming to stretch beyond endurance, though it cannot be more than ten or twelve seconds at the most. The teacher, who wears black-framed glasses, asks her her name.

"Linda," she has to say, wishing she were a Gabrielle or a Jacqueline. Anything but a Linda.

The teacher gestures with his hand to take

a seat. In Eileen's stacked heels, she walks to a desk behind a boy.

"We're doing Keats," he tells her under his breath.

Linda studies the boy's profile. Arrogant and aristocratic are words that come to mind. He has brown hair, slightly dirty and worn as long as is acceptable, and when he turns, the jawline of a man. There is a boil on his neck she tries to ignore. He must be very tall, she thinks, because even slouching he is taller than she is in her seat.

He hovers in a half-turn, as if bringing her within his sphere, and from time to time he gives her, *sotto voce*, bits of information: "Keats died when he was twenty-five"; "Mr. K. is a good guy"; "You have to pick a poet for your paper."

But Linda knows all about Keats and the Romantic poets. Apart from having learned how to use a washing machine, she had a solid education with the nuns.

Before he has curled out of his desk, the boy introduces himself as Thomas. His books are folded under his arm, and a scent of something like warm toast wafts from his body. He has navy eyes, and like most boys his age, a moderate case of acne. Her shoes pinch as she walks out of the classroom. She has not worn stockings and is supremely conscious of her bare legs.

After school, Linda takes the bus to Allerton Hill and sits on a rock overlooking the ocean. The activity is familiar to her and reminds her of the home for wayward girls, about which she is now vaguely nostalgic. She chooses a place to sit that is not precisely in one yard or in another, but in a sort of no-man's-land in between. From there, she can see most of the town as well: the hill itself, which winds around in concentric circles, each house grander than the next, though most are boarded up for the winter and the grounds look unkempt; the village, set apart from the rest of town, a community of quaint homes and historic landmarks; the beach, where cottages built in the 1930s and 1940s are occasionally washed into the sea during the hurricanes; Bayside, a neighborhood of bungalows and cottages neatly divided into alphabet streets that run from A to Y (what happened to the Z?); her own neighborhood of two- and three-family houses with rickety fire escapes and breathtaking views; and along Nantasket Beach, the amusement park and its honky-tonk arcade. The centerpiece of the amusement park is its roller coaster.

When Linda arrives home, she walks into the den to talk to her aunt about clothes. Her aunt, however, is not there. Linda sees, instead, the missal on the arm of the sofa and picks it up. It is a small, leather-bound book with gilt-edged paper, demarcated by ribbons in yellow and black and red and green. On the cover are the words SAINT ANN DAILY MISSAL, and in the lower right-hand corner, a name: *Nora F. Sullivan.* The book is laced with Mass cards and with lurid depictions of the Five Joyful Mysteries, the Five Sorrowful Mysteries and the Five Glorious Mysteries. Looking at these illustrated medallions, the name of *Thomas* catches her eye. She studies the picture in the circle: it is of a clearly penitent and disastrously ill-looking Thomas being crowned with thorns. Under the picture is written: *Crowned with Thorns: For Moral Courage.*

She flips to the page marked by the red ribbon, and reads the prayer written there: "O God, Who by the humility of Your Son have raised up a fallen world, grant everlasting joy to Your faithful people; that those whom You have rescued from the perils of endless death, You may cause to enjoy endless happiness. Through the same, etc. Amen."

With a snap that echoes through the apartment, Linda closes the missal so as not to let any of the words escape into the air.

The aunt works in the coat department of a store in Quincy. The cousins more or less fend for themselves. The dinner hour is an unknown event in the triple-decker, and consequently there is no dining table, only a table covered with oilcloth in the kitchen. One of the cousins is assigned each week to prepare the meals, but since Jack and Tommy are too young, and Michael is usually too busy, the work almost always falls to Linda and Patty and Erin. By common agreement, each of the cousins eats when he or she is hungry in front of the television in the den.

The noise in the apartment is constant. Jack and Tommy are always underfoot. Michael plays his radio loudly. Patty and Erin fight like cats.

The bedroom that Linda shares with Patty and Erin has green wallpaper and two twin beds. A mattress has been set between them to make a bed for Linda. In the morning, it is almost impossible to tuck in the sheets and covers, which is, under normal circumstances, something Linda can do well (the nuns insisted). When Patty and Erin get out of bed, they sometimes inadvertently step on her. To read, Linda has to lean against the nightstand.

A feature of the room that appeals to Linda is a small window set beneath a gable. If she sits on Patty's bed, she can see the harbor, and beyond the beach, the open water of the ocean. She can also see the roller coaster.

It is in that room that Linda reads Keats and Wordsworth, studies advanced algebra, memorizes French verbs, lists the causes of the Great Depression, and, on the sly, looks at Eileen's high school yearbook in which there is a picture of a boy who was a junior the year before: "Thomas Janes, *Nantasket* 2, 3; Varsity Hockey 2, 3; Varsity Tennis 2, 3."

On Saturday afternoon, Linda walks to Confession. She wears a navy blue skirt and a red sweater, a peacoat and a mantilla on her head. She tells the priest that she has had impure thoughts. She never mentions the aunt's boyfriend.

That night Linda announces that she is going to visit a new friend she has made at school (a lie she will have to confess the following Saturday). There is a bit of a flurry amongst the cousins, because Linda has not been told any of the rules and doesn't have a curfew as they do. Though no one ever follows it anyway. She leaves the house in the same blue skirt and red sweater and peacoat she wore to Confession. She has on as well a silk head scarf that Patty has lent her because the wind from the water is blowing the flags straight out.

Linda walks down the hill, passing other apartment houses like her own with asbestos shingles and tiers of balconies with charcoal grills and bicycles on them. She walks along the boulevard and crosses Nantasket Avenue. She keeps her hands in her pockets and wishes it were cold enough to wear gloves. At night, Patty rubs Oil of Olay into all the cracks and creases.

The lights of the amusement park are dazzling. Tens of thousands of bulbs illuminate the park by the beach on this last weekend of the season. Nearly all of the lights are moving — on the Giant Coaster, on the Ferris Wheel, on the Carousel, on the Caterpillar, on the Lindy Loop and on the Flying Scooters. The entrance is surprisingly ugly, though: only a chain-link fence and a sign. Flags whip at the tops of tall poles, and Linda's scarf snaps at the back of her neck. She pays for her ticket and steps inside.

She knows that Michael would have taken her to the park if she had asked. He, of all of the cousins, even Patty, who has been nothing but sisterly, seems the most distraught by what has happened to Linda and is, consequently, the most eager to please. To make Linda feel welcome, he has given her his John Lennon poster, his denim pillow, and his royal-blue Schwinn. In the mornings, he always asks her if she has a ride to school. Perhaps it is too soon to tell, but Tommy and Erin do not seem as generous, possibly having inherited their mother's temperament or simply resenting another mouth to feed.

Jack, the youngest, is smitten with his new cousin. Anyone who is willing to pay attention to a four-year-old in that family of seven children is, in his opinion, a goddess.

Linda plays Shooting Waters, Hoopla, and Ball Toss and buys penuche at the candy concession at the arcade. When she has finished the fudge, she walks directly to the Giant Coaster and stands in a short line with people who have their collars up. She has never been on a roller coaster before, but logic tells her she will probably survive the experience.

The sense of terror on the steep incline is

deeply thrilling. She knows the drop is coming, and there is nothing she can do about it.

She rides the Giant Coaster seven times, using the money she has saved at the home for wayward girls (thirty-five cents an hour for ironing; twenty-five an hour for delivering). The ride lasts only a minute, but she thinks the Giant Coaster has probably provided her with the best seven minutes of her life.

While she is on the Ferris Wheel, from which she can see Boston, the wind blows the cars sideways, and people scream. In fact, people are squealing and screaming all through the park. Which is, after all, she thinks, the point.

To one side of the park is a pier of thick planking that runs out over the water. Above it, a lone streetlamp shines. She is slightly nauseous from the cotton candy and hot chocolate back-to-back, not to mention the penuche and the Lindy Loop, and so she is drawn to the pier for fresh air. She treads over the damp planks and listens to the shouts and squeals of the people on the rides, muffled now by the white noise of the mild surf. She is nearly to the end of the pier before she notices the group of boys, in sweaters and parkas, smoking. They hold their cigarettes down by their thighs, pinched between thumbs and forefingers, and take deep drags like Jimmy Dean. They shove each other's shoulders with the heels of their hands for emphasis, and occasionally a high giggle rises like a thin tendril of smoke into the air. She has walked too close to them for anonymity, and now she finds herself in the awkward position of having to continue forward or having to turn and retreat, which she isn't willing to do, not wishing to give the message that she is afraid of the boys, and not liking the image that she has of a dog retreating with a tail between its legs.

She moves sideways to the northern edge of the pier and glances down. The tide is in, lapping high on the posts. The boys have noticed her and are quieter now, though they still continue to whack each other on the shoulders. She watches as one boy throws his cigarette into the surf and sticks his hands into his pockets. His posture is unmistakable. She decides she will remain where she is for a good minute anyway, and then, having held her ground, will stroll casually away, just as she would have done had they not been there.

But the boy with his hands in his jacket pockets detaches himself from the others and walks to where she stands.

"Hello," he says.

"Hi," she answers.

"You're Linda."

"Yes."

He nods, as if needing to ponder this important fact. Beyond him is their audience.

"Did you go on the rides?" he asks.

"Yes."

"The Coaster?"

"I did."

"How many times?"

"Seven."

"Really?" He seems genuinely surprised. She imagines a raised eyebrow, though they are standing side by side and she can't see his face.

"Do you want a cigarette?"

"Sure."

He has to bend away from the wind to light it. He takes it from his mouth and hands it to her. She sucks a long drag and suppresses a cough. At the home for wayward girls, she smoked often. The breezes from the ocean blew the smoke away almost immediately. It was the one sin the girls could easily commit.

"Did you pick a poet yet?"

"Wordsworth," she says.

"Do you like him?"

"Some of his stuff."

"Did you like 'The Prelude'?"

"I like 'Tintern Abbey.' "

The boy sniffs. His nose is running in the cold. Beneath his navy parka, he has on a dark sweater with a crew neck. The sweater looks black in the streetlamp, but it might well be green. A sliver of white collar shows itself.

"Who are you doing?" she asks.

"Keats."

She nods, taking another drag.

"The park is going to close in half an hour," he says. "Do you want to go on the Coaster one more time?"

It is unclear whether this is an invitation or a reminder.

"No, that's OK," she says.

"Do you want to meet them?" Thomas asks, gesturing toward the boys.

She doesn't know. Or, rather, she supposes that she doesn't. She shrugs.

But the boys, wanting to meet her, are moving slowly closer, drifting on a tide of curiosity.

"They're jerks, anyway," Thomas says, but not without a certain kind of grudging affection.

A raised voice punctuates the air. "It is so, warmer than the air," one of them is saying.

"Fuck that," another says.

"No, seriously, the water's warmer in October than it is in August."

"Where'd you get that shit?"

"All you have to do is feel it."

"You go feel it, dickhead."

The boys start pushing the boy who said the water was warmer. But he, small and wiry, bobs and weaves and deftly outmaneuvers them so that he is standing in the middle of the pier and they are now on the edge.

"So what do you say, dickhead, you want to go test it out now?" The boys laugh. "I'll bet you twenty-five you won't go in."

Thomas turns to Linda and snorts, as if to say, I told you they were jerks.

Linda glances down at her feet and over toward the boardwalk. Lovers are walking arm in arm, and some are descending to the beach. Overcoats will become blankets. In the wind, the streetlamp, on a wire, swings wildly, making the shadows lurch.

"He's right," Linda says quietly to Thomas.

He looks at her, a quizzical expression on his face.

"The water's warmer in October. It'll feel like a bath on a night like tonight," she says.

At the home for wayward girls, Linda sometimes slipped out of her room when the nuns were asleep and walked out onto the rocks. There was one rock from which it was safe to dive. She would take off her robe and pajamas and plunge into the surf. She liked being naked, the sense of being free of the nuns.

Beside them, the argument continues. The boy who is sure the water is warm, whose name is Eddie Garrity, gets down on his belly, rolls his sleeves, and extends his arm to the water to test it. He can't reach. It is, of course, too much trouble to leave the pier, take off his socks and shoes, roll his cuffs, and test it at the shore, as any sensible person would.

"Hey, Eddie, I'll lower you down you want to test it," a boy named Donny T. says and laughs hysterically. He means, I'll lower you down and then let you fall in.

"Screw you," says Eddie, scrambling to his feet.

"I told you twenty-five," says Donny T.

Linda listens to the argument. She leaves Thomas's side and walks to the far end of the pier. With her back to the boys, she takes off her peacoat and head scarf, her sweater and skirt, her shoes and socks. In her slip, she dives into the water.

★ ★ ★

When Linda comes up for air, she can see Thomas kneeling on the pier. He has an overcoat in his hands. Behind Thomas, within the pod of boys, Eddie has his arms wrapped around his chest. He is silent. The girl has gone in for him.

She hitches herself onto the pier, does a quick turn mid-air and sits with her back to Thomas. She is hunched in the cold. Thomas wraps her in the wool overcoat.

"Donny, give me your shirt," he demands.

There is no sound of protest from Donny T. Within a minute, Linda feels a cotton shirt grazing her shoulder.

She uses the shirt to dry her face and hair. She puts on her sweater and her skirt as best she can with her back to the boys. She lays a hand on Thomas's shoulder to balance herself as she steps into her shoes. Thomas holds her peacoat open for her, and she slips her arms into it. The boys are absolutely silent.

"The water's warmer than the air," Thomas says to them as he and Linda leave the pier.

Linda and Thomas have to walk quickly because she is shivering.

"I have a car," he says. "I'll give you a ride."

"No," she says. "I just live across the way."

She has an image, which she doesn't like, of leaving a wet spot on the seat of Thomas's car. More important, she doesn't want the cousins asking questions.

He walks her across Nantasket Avenue and up Park. Her sweater is scratchy on her arms, and as she walks sea water drips from her slip onto her calves and runs down into her socks.

"Why did you do it?" Thomas asks.

Her teeth are chattering beyond her control. Thomas puts an arm tightly around her to stop the shaking. Watching them, one might think the girl was sick, had perhaps drunk too much, and that the boy was walking her home.

Why has she done it? It's a valid question. For the theatrics? To prove a point? To overcome the commonness of her name? To cleanse herself?

"I don't know," she says truthfully.

Her hair is plastered to her head, all the fuss with the rollers forgotten. She looks her worst, her nose running from the sea water.

Her hair is, and always has been, her one

vanity. Normally, it is thick and long, the color running to warm pine. At the home for wayward girls, she sometimes grew it to her waist, though the nuns always made her wear it in braids.

"Well, it was great," he says, rubbing her arms to keep the circulation going. And then he laughs and shakes his head. "Jesus," he says, "they'll be talking about this for weeks."

Linda leaves Thomas at the bottom of her street.

"I'm all right now," she says and detaches herself from his arm.

"Can I call you tomorrow?" he asks.

She thinks a moment. No one has yet called her at the apartment.

"It would be better if I met you," she says.

"Here?" he asks. "At noon?"

"I'll try."

She runs up the street, though her limbs are shivering and stiff, and she knows she looks ungainly. As she turns the corner, she cannot resist glancing back. He is standing where she left him. He raises a hand and waves.

Her aunt is in the hallway when she enters

the apartment. The aunt's hair is rolled in pin curls and is secured with a hairnet: little coils of gold on silver stems behind a wire fence. Normally, her hair is frizzy, and sometimes Linda can see her scalp. The aunt has a pronounced widow's peak that she tries to hide with bangs.

The aunt has on a pink seersucker bathrobe and flannel pajamas with teapots on them. The slippers, once pink, are worn beige. The aunt's eyebrows are unkempt, but she has traces of maroon lipstick on her mouth, as though she were ambivalent about her vanity.

They stand on separate sides of a fault, each wanting something from the other.

"Where have you been?" the aunt asks.

"I fell in," Linda says, walking past her.

Thomas picks Linda up the next day in a white Buick Skylark convertible with leather trim the color of her aunt's lipstick. Linda is wearing dungarees in defiance of the Sunday, even though she has dutifully gone to church with the cousins. Thomas has on the same jacket he wore the night before, but good trousers, like a boy would wear to school.

"I didn't bring a scarf," she says. "I didn't know it would be a convertible."

"Do you want to go back and get one?"

"No," she says.

They sit in the car for a moment before he starts the engine. There seems to be something each wants to say, though for a time neither of them speaks.

"Did you get yelled at?" Thomas asks finally.

"I got looked askance at," she says, and he smiles.

"Do you want to go for a drive?"

"Where?"

"Anywhere. Just a drive."

"Sure," she says.

In the car, there is an ocean of space between Thomas and Linda. She studies the chrome dashboard, the plugs that say *Light* and *Wiper* and *Lighter* and *Accessory*. What exactly will the Accessory be? she wonders. Thomas turns on the radio, and an energetic patter issues forth. It is all wrong for them, as though Ricky Nelson had wandered into a chamber orchestra. Thomas switches it off at once.

"Sometimes when I drive," he says, "I don't play the radio. I need time to think."

"So do I," she says. "Need time to think, I mean."

She sits with her hands in the pockets of her peacoat. If she hadn't worn a coat, she would sit on her hands.

She likes the open air of the convertible, even though her hair whips into her eyes, and she knows it will be snarled and stringy when he stops the car. When the aunt's boy-friend was around and there was actually a car, she and her cousins were routinely packed into a backseat meant for three. On rainy days, the windows were shut tight, and her aunt smoked. Just thinking about it now gives Linda a headache.

Linda notes, as Thomas is driving, that the color of the water and the sky have intensified since the day before; the sun glints painfully from the sea. It is a fabulous piece of jewelry with a million diamonds.

Diplomatically, Thomas moves away from the neighborhood where Linda lives. Diplomatically, he does not point out his own house on Allerton Hill.

"Did you go away?" he asks as they make a turn onto Samoset.

"Yes."

"Did you have a baby?"

She is stunned by the boy's boldness, but exhilarated nonetheless. She might have spent the entire year without a single direct question, learned to live with sniggered looks and aspersions.

"No," she says.

"I don't care about that," he says. He amends himself. "Well, I care, because it happened to you, but it wouldn't have made me like you any less. I don't care about reputation."

"Why do you like me?" she asks.

"I liked the way you walked into the classroom," he says. "That first day. You were trying for something — trying to be cool — but I could see that you weren't. That you might be someone others could take advantage of." He thinks a minute. "Now, I'm not so sure about that."

"What made you change your mind?"

"You. Last night. When you jumped into the water."

"Dove."

"Dove into the water. You did that for yourself, didn't you?"

She is silent. Even with the ocean between them, she can smell the boy — that warm toast scent, and something else. Of course, a laundered shirt.

"I'm a fallen woman," Linda says, only partly joking.

"Magdalene," he says, half turned toward her and steering with one hand.

"That was the name of the home," she says.

"Really?"

"They're always called Magdalene."

"You're a Catholic."

"Yes. You're not?"

"No."

"How do you know about Magdalene?"

"Everybody knows about Magdalene," he says.

"Do they? I always thought she was an especially Catholic idea."

"Do you go to church regularly?"

"That's a personal question."

"I'm sorry."

"Yes, I do."

"And Confession?"

"Yes."

"What do you confess?"

She is unnerved by his questions. No one has ever probed her quite like this. Not even the nuns. Their questions were predictable and rote. A catechism.

"I'm just asking," he says, somewhat apologetic. "What a girl like you would possibly have to confess."

"Oh, there's always something," she says. "Impure thoughts, mostly."

"Impure meaning what?"

"Impure," she says.

Thomas takes her to a diner on the beach and leads her to a booth near the entrance with seats as red as those they've just left. She is embarrassed about her hair, which she tries to finger-comb in the sun visor. Thomas looks away while she does this. Her hair is hopeless, and she gives it up.

"Next time, I'll bring a scarf," he says. "I'll keep it in the glove compartment."

She is elated by his assumption that there will be a next time.

She might not have eaten in years. She eats her hamburger and fries, his cheese-burger, drinks both milkshakes, and witnesses the first of dozens of meals that Thomas will hardly touch.

"You're not hungry?" she asks.

"Not really," he says. "You eat it."

She does, gratefully. It seems there is never enough food at home.

"I know Michael. We play hockey together," Thomas says.

Varsity Hockey 2, 3.

"You're playing already?" she asks.

"Not yet," he says. "We'll start soon. I see Michael around."

"Do you have cousins?" she asks flippantly.

"Hardly. Only two."

"Let me guess. You're Episcopal."

"Nothing, really. Why don't you live with

your parents? Did something happen to them?"

"My mother died," she says, mopping up the ketchup with her bun. "In a bus accident. My father just sort of disappeared after that."

"Broken heart?"

"Not really."

"I'm sorry."

"It was a long time ago."

He asks her if she wants anything else to eat.

"No," she says. "I'm stuffed. Where do you live?"

"Allerton Hill," he says.

"I thought so."

He looks away.

"Did we go by your house?" she asks.

"Yes."

"Why didn't you point it out?"

"I don't know," he says.

Later, he says, "I want to be a writer."

This is the first of a hundred times someone will tell Linda Fallon that he or she wants to be a writer. And because it is the first, she believes him.

"A playwright, I think," he says. "Have you read O'Neill?"

She has, in fact, read Eugene O'Neill. A

Jesuit priest at the Catholic girls' school made the class read *Long Day's Journey into Night* on the theory that some of the girls might recognize their families. "Sure," she says.

"Denial and irresponsibility," he says.

She nods.

"The fog. The obliteration of the fog."

"Erasing the past," she says.

"Right," he says, excited now. "Exactly."

He sits sideways in the booth, one long leg extended.

"Did you write your paper yet?"

"God, no," she says.

"Can I read Keats to you later?"

"Keats?"

From time to time, boys who know Thomas come by the booth and kick Thomas's foot or rap their knuckles on the Formica tabletop. No words are ever exchanged, but the boys study Linda. It is a pantomime of sorts.

In a booth across the room, Linda recognizes Donny T. from the night before. Sipping a Coke, eyeing her carefully. Will he hate her for having proven him wrong? Yes, she thinks, he will.

A table of girls, in the center of the room, also watch her. Then they turn and make comments to their companions that are clearly about Linda. She notes their perfect curls, their skirts, the nylons running into the loafers.

When they leave the diner, Donny T. is sitting in the back of a powder-blue Bonneville counting money.

"That's your friend," Linda says to Thomas.

"Yeah," Thomas says. "I guess."

"Why is he counting money?"

"You don't want to know."

Thomas drives to the beach and parks behind a deserted cottage. He reaches into the backseat for a book that says, simply, *Keats*. Linda decides she won't pretend to like the specific poems if in fact she doesn't. Thomas reads to her in a voice oddly rich and gravelly.

> *"When I have fears that I may cease to be*
> *Before my pen has gleaned my teeming*
> *brain . . ."*

As he reads, she gazes at the dirt drive that leads through the dune grass to the back of a shingled gray-blue cottage. It is small, two stories tall, and has a wraparound porch of white trim. There is a hammock and a screen door, and all the shades are drawn. The cottage has a kind of poverty-stricken charm and makes her think of the Great Depression, about which they are reading in history. Clay pots with withered geraniums stand by the back door, and roses have turned to beach plums beneath a window.

She can see, if she tries, a dark-haired woman in a dress and an apron. A small girl with blond hair playing on the porch. A man in a white shirt with suspenders. A boater on his head. Is she confusing her father with Eugene O'Neill?

"Thou still unravished bride of quietness,
Thou foster-child of silence and slow
*   time . . ."*

To one side of the house, two posts have been hammered into the ground. Between the posts runs a length of clothesline with wooden pins on it that someone has forgotten to put away.

"Now more than ever seems it rich to die
To cease upon the midnight with no
*   pain . . ."*

"She was a whore, a prostitute," Linda is saying.

"She repented her past," Thomas argues. "She's Christ's symbol of penance."

"How do you know all this?"

"I've been reading."

"I hardly know anything about her," Linda says, which isn't strictly true.

"She was present at the Crucifixion," he says. "She was the first to bring word of the Resurrection to the Disciples."

Linda shrugs. "If you say so."

The papers about Keats and Wordsworth have been written. The amusement park has closed. A hurricane has blown in and out, washing cottages on the beach into the sea. Thomas has read Prufrock and passages from *Death of a Salesman* to Linda in the Skylark. The aunt has relented and bought

405

Linda an outfit on discount at the store where she works. Linda, in response to a vague reference to someone else's hair by Thomas, has stopped teasing her own. They are sitting on a hill overlooking the Atlantic.

"We've known each other exactly a month," Thomas says.

"Really?" she asks, though she has had precisely the same thought earlier in the day.

"I feel like I've known you all my life," he says.

She is silent. The light on the water is extraordinary — as good as any of the poets Thomas often reads to her: Robert Lowell, Theodore Roethke, John Berryman, Randall Jarrell.

"Do you sometimes think that, too?" he asks.

The straining toward the light on the water feels instinctive. It encompasses the specific moving of the waves, the boy beside her in his parka and loafers, the steep slope of mown grass down to the rocks, and the expanse, the endless view, Boston crisply to the north, a lone fisherman, late to his pots, to the east.

"Yes," she says.

She wants to be able to paint the light on the water, or to put it into words at the very least. Capture it, hold it in her hands. Bottle it.

"You're crying," Thomas says.

She wants to deny that she is crying, but cannot. She sobs once quickly, like a child. It would be delicious to let go, she thinks, but disastrous: once started, she might not be able to stop.

"What's wrong?"

She can't answer him. How can she explain? No one cries because of the light. It's absurd.

She sniffs, trying to hold back the snot that wants to run out of her nose. She has no handkerchief or tissue. Thomas searches his pockets, producing a stick of gum, a pack of cigarettes, and a ditto sheet from school. None of which will do. "Use your sleeve," he says.

Obediently, she does. She takes a long breath through her nose.

"You're . . . ," he begins.

But she shakes her head back and forth, as though to warn him not to say another word. Reluctantly, she has to let the light go. She has to think about what might be on the ditto sheet, about how she'll have to sit on the mattress to do her homework later, about her aunt — thoughts guaranteed to stop the tears.

"Linda," Thomas says, taking her hand.

She squeezes his, digging in her finger-
nails as if she were about to fall. He moves
to kiss her, but she turns her head away. His
lips graze the side of her mouth.

"I can't," she says.

He lets go of her hand. He moves an inch
or two away from her. He shakes a cigarette
from the pack and lights it.

"I like you, Thomas," Linda says, sorry to
have hurt him.

He twists his mouth and nods, as if to say
he doesn't believe a word of it. "You don't
seem to want any part of me," he says.

"It's just . . ." she begins.

"It's just what?" he asks tonelessly.

"There are things you don't know about
me," she says.

"So tell me," he says.

"I can't."

"Why?"

"I can't."

"There isn't anything I wouldn't tell
you," Thomas says, and she can hear that
he's aggrieved.

"I know," she says, wondering if that's altogether true. Everyone has things, private
things, embarrassing things, one keeps to
oneself.

She shudders as she takes a breath. "Let's
not do this, OK?"

It is much the same in a dark car parked later that week at the beach. They can hear, but cannot see, the surf. The windows are steamed from the talking. In addition to the steam, she notices, the windshield has a film of smoke on it in which she could write her name. She is staring at the line of rust where the top of the convertible meets the body of the car.

"So where will you apply?" Thomas asks.

"Apply?"

"To college. You're smart. You must know you could get in anywhere."

He has a plaid scarf wound around his neck. It isn't that late, only seven o'clock. She is supposed to be at the library. He's supposed to be at hockey practice.

"I don't know," she says. "I was thinking about secretarial school."

"Jesus Christ, Linda."

"I'll have to get a job."

"So go to college and get a better job."

"Money might be a problem."

"There are scholarships."

She doesn't want to talk about it. She is wearing a rose heather cardigan and a matching wool skirt. She has on one of Eileen's white blouses. She's begun parting her hair in the middle and letting it curl down on either side. She likes the way it obscures her face when she bends forward.

Thomas is looking out the driver's-side window, annoyed with her. "You have to get over this . . . inferiority thing," he says.

She scratches a bit of crust from the knee of her skirt. She has nylons on, but her feet are freezing. The Skylark has any number of holes through which the cold seeps.

"Thomas, if I told you, you wouldn't ever be able to think about me in the same way again," she says.

"Fuck that."

She has never heard him use the word.

She is silent for so long, and he is breathing so shallowly, that the windshield begins to clear of fog. She can make out the cottage fifty feet in front of them. It looks lonely and cold, she thinks. She would like to be able to open the door, turn on the lights, make a fire, and shake out the bedclothes. Make a pot of soup. Have a place of her own.

If only she could have a place of her own, she thinks.

She is sweating under her sweater.

"My aunt had a boyfriend," she begins just at the very moment Thomas leans forward to kiss her. She digs her fists into the red leather seats.

His mouth is tentative against her own. She can feel his straight upper lip, the fullness of the lower. He puts his hand to the side of her face.

She is embarrassed and looks down. He follows her eyes and sees her balled fists.

"Don't be afraid of me," he says.

Slowly, she opens her hands. She can smell his breath and the sweat on his skin, as unique and as identifiable as a fingerprint.

He is twisted in his seat, the parka jammed against the steering wheel. He presses his mouth against hers, and she feels his fingers on her collarbone. Despite herself, she flinches.

He withdraws his hand.

"I'm sorry," she says.

He pulls her head to his shoulder.

"What about the boyfriend?" Thomas asks.

"He went away," she says.

This goes on in increments, the way a timid swimmer might have to enter a frigid ocean, inch by inch, getting used to the brutal cold. Linda has had no way, before, to know how hard it might be; it has not been necessary to imagine physical love with a boy. Her mind does not flinch, but her body does, as if it had different memories, memories of its own. Another boy might have laughed at her, or given her up for hopeless, not worth the effort. Or might have insisted, so that she would have had to grit her teeth and think of something else, ruining pleasure forever. But Thomas doesn't push.

One morning in November, the aunt says to Linda, "You have to get a job. Eileen works. Tommy and Michael work. Patty works. You want clothes, you've got to get a job."

In her travels through the town, Linda has seen several possibilities for employment: a discount jewelry store; a Laundromat; a bowling alley; a photographic studio. In the end, she takes a job at the diner, waiting tables. She wears a gray uniform of synthetic material that crackles when she sits down. The dress has cap sleeves and a white collar and deep pockets for tips.

On a good night, she will go home with fifteen dollars in coins. It seems a fortune. She likes to walk out of the diner with her hands in her pockets, feeling the money.

Linda is a good waitress, lightning-fast and efficient. The owner, a man who drinks shots from a juice glass when he thinks no one is looking and who tries once to pin her

412

up against the refrigerator and kiss her, tells her, in a rare sober moment, that she is the best waitress he's ever had.

The diner is a popular spot. Some of the students are regulars. Donny T. sits in the same booth every day and holds what seems to be a kind of court. He also has what appears to be a long memory.

"Our Olympic hopeful," he says as Linda takes her pad out. He has bedroom eyes and a canny grin and might be attractive were it not for his yellow teeth.

"A cherry Coke and fries," says Eddie Garrity, skinny and blond and nearly lost inside his leather jacket, a precise imitation, she notices, of Donny T.'s.

"How many laps you do today?" Donny T. asks Linda, a snigger just below the surface.

"Leave her alone," Eddie says under his breath.

Donny T. turns in his seat. "Hey, cockroach, I want your advice, I'll ask for it."

"Do you want anything to eat?" Linda asks evenly.

"Just you," Donny T. says. He puts his hands up, mock-defending himself. "Only Kidding. Only Kidding." He laughs, the snigger unleashed. "Two cheeseburgers. Fries. Chocolate milkshake. And don't make me one of those thin jobbies, either. I like a lot of ice cream."

Linda glances beyond Donny T. to the next table, where a man is having trouble with his briefcase: one of the latches keeps popping open every time he tries to shut the case. Linda watches him fiddle with the latch a half-dozen times and then, in seeming defeat, set the briefcase on a chair. He looks familiar, and she thinks that she might know him. He is twenty-two, twenty-three, she guesses, good-looking in a jacket and a tie. She wonders what he does for a living. Will he be a salesman? A teacher?

Linda takes the orders of the other boys in the booth. Donny T. travels with a retinue. She snaps her order book shut, slips it into her pocket, and bends to clear the booth of the previous party's trash.

"You settling in OK?" Donny T. asks an inch from her waist.

"Just fine," she says, reaching for a glass of Coke that is nearly full.

"Don't you miss that place where you came from? What was it, a Home or something?" Donny T.'s voice has risen a notch, just enough to carry to the next table. The man with the errant briefcase looks up at her.

"I'm fine," she repeats, letting the Coke

tip so that it spills onto the Formica in front of Donny T.

"Watchit!" he cries. He tries to press himself into the back of the vinyl booth as the Coke drips over the edge of the table and onto his jeans. "That's my leather coat there."

"Oh," says Linda. "Sorry."

"What does Donny T. do in the backseat of Eddie Garrity's Bonneville?"

This to Thomas later that night as they are driving home in the Skylark.

"You don't know?"

"No, why?"

"He deals."

She has an image of a deck of cards. And then she realizes. "Drugs, you mean?"

"Yes."

"Marijuana?"

"That," he says. "And then some."

"Why do you hang around with him?" Linda asks.

"We've been friends since first grade." He pauses. "Do you think it's immoral to deal drugs?" A slight challenge in his voice.

"I don't know," she says. She hasn't thought about this much.

"He doesn't deal to kids," Thomas says.

"Aren't we kids?" she asks.

In increments, Thomas kisses her mouth and her face and her neck. He opens the top two buttons of her blouse. He gives her a back rub, lifting up her blouse from the waistband of her skirt. Once, his hand lightly brushes her breast. This takes two and a half months.

They are in the car in back of the cottage at the beach. It seems a good place to park: the beach is deserted, and the car is mostly hidden by the dunes. Though it is just before Christmas, the windows are steamed. The top four buttons of Linda's blouse are opened. Thomas has his hand on the smooth skin of her collarbone, inching his way down. She feels nervous, breathless, the way she did on the roller coaster. A sense that once she reaches the top, she will have no choice but to go down the other side. That there will be nothing she can do about it.

He brings her hand to himself. She is surprised and not surprised — boys betrayed so visibly by their bodies. She wants to touch him and to please him, but something putrid hovers at the edges of her consciousness.

He feels her resistance and lets her go.

"I'm so sorry," she says.

A light swings wildly through the car. It bounces off the rearview mirror and blinds Thomas, who looks up quickly.

"Oh, Jesus," he says, as the other light, the flashing light, reveals itself.

Linda and Thomas are frantic in the front seat, a kind of comedy routine. Thomas gets his shirt buttoned and his trousers zipped, and Linda pulls her peacoat around herself. Impossible not to be reminded of the aunt shouting *whore* and then *slut*. Flailing her arms.

The cop bangs hard on the window. Thomas rolls it down.

A flashlight explodes in Linda's face, and for a moment, she thinks: it isn't the police; it's someone who will kill us. So that when the cop swings the flashlight away and asks to see Thomas's license, she is nearly relieved.

"You folks know this is private property?" the policeman asks.

"No, I didn't, Officer," Thomas says in a voice she's never heard before — exaggeratedly polite, verging on parody. Of course Thomas knew it was private property.

The policeman studies the license, and it seems to take an age.

"You Peter Janes's boy?" the cop asks finally.

Thomas has to nod.

The cop bends down and peers in at Linda, as though trying to place her. "You all right, Miss?" he asks.

"Yes," she answers, mortified.

The policeman straightens. "Move along," he says brusquely to Thomas. "You need to be getting on home."

Parental now, which she knows will annoy Thomas no end. She wills him to hold his tongue. Thomas rolls the window as the cop walks to his car.

In the Skylark, Thomas and Linda are silent, waiting for the cruiser to drive away. When it has, Thomas leans his head back against the seat and puts his hands over his face. "Shit," he says, but she can see that he is smiling.

"It was bound to happen," she offers.

"I can't believe he knows my father!" Thomas says, a high hysterical giggle beginning.

"You were awfully polite," Linda says.

Passing by her aunt on the way to the bathroom, Linda thinks of Thomas. Sitting in the classroom or handing a menu to a customer, Linda thinks of Thomas. Between classes, they exchange notes or turn corners and kiss. He is waiting for her every morning when she walks down her street, and when she gets into the Skylark, she sits as close to Thomas as she can, the ocean of space on the other side now. They shave minutes from the rest of life and are always late.

Linda,
Can you meet me after school?

Thomas,
I was reading O'Neill again. There's this passage: "None of us can help the things life has done to us. They're done before you realize it, and once they're done they make you do other things until at last everything comes between you and what you'd like to be, and you've lost your true self forever."

Linda,
I like O'Neill, but that's crap. Of course we can help the things life has done to us. I prefer this passage: "I became drunk with the beauty and singing rhythm of it, and for a moment I lost myself — actually lost my life. I was set free! I dissolved in the sea, became white sails and flying spray, became beauty and rhythm, became moon-

light and the ship and the high dim-starred sky! I belonged, without past or future, within peace and unity and a wild joy, within something greater than my own life, or the life of Man, to Life itself!"

Better, no?

Jesus, this class is boring.

Linda,

I really like the sweater you have on today. You were driving me crazy in fourth period.

Thomas,

Thank you. It's Eileen's.

Linda,

What are you doing this weekend? I have to go skiing at Killington. I don't want to go because it will mean four days away from you. What's happening to me anyway?

Thomas,

I have to work all weekend. I've never been on skis.

Linda,

There's a hockey game tonight. Will you come?

★ ★ ★

Linda thinks the hockey game is brutal. The rink reeks of sweat and beer. There is slush underfoot. She sits on the bleachers in her peacoat with a sweater underneath, her hands in her pockets, shivering all the same.

The din is deafening. The shouts and calls, the drunken patter, the thwack of the puck, and the blades shushing on the ice echo through the cavernous hockey rink. The imagination provides sound effects for the bits they cannot hear: a stick thrust against the back of a leg; the thud of a hip-bone as a player's skates go out from under him; the crack of a helmet snapping to the ice with the force of a whip. She flinches and then flinches again. The crowd eats it up.

She doesn't recognize Thomas when he comes out onto the ice. His shoulders and legs are gargantuan in the pads. His teeth are blotted out by the mouth guard. The contours of his head have been erased by the helmet. This is a side of Thomas she has never seen before and couldn't have imagined: bent forward, stick outstretched, thighs pumping, his movements as fluid as a ballerina's, as deft as a tap dancer's. Thomas plays aggressively. She has trouble following the game, doesn't know the rules. Sometimes she doesn't even know a goal has been scored until she hears the crowd roar.

That night, inevitably, there is a brawl. This one over an intentional tripping that sends Thomas sprawling, spinning belly down on the ice. He is up in a flash, gathering himself like a spider, digging the tips of his skates into the ice, and then he is all over the player who has done this to him. Linda, who has gone to school with girls and nuns, has never seen a physical fight before, never seen the blows that land, the ricocheting of the limbs, the tugging at the jerseys, the vicious kicks. The fight takes only seconds, but the scene evokes centuries and seems more like gladiatorial combat than anything she has ever witnessed. Thomas shrugs off the referee and heads for the box to serve out his penalty, his helmet in his arm, his hair stiffened upward. He executes a neat stop just before the wire fencing, takes his punishment as his due.

Not contrite. Not contrite at all.

On the morning of Christmas Eve, Linda fails to meet Thomas at the bottom of her street as planned. Eileen has just walked in the door, back from New York for the holiday, and Linda cannot bring herself to leave, particularly since it seems to be Linda

422

whom Eileen most wants to see. Though, in truth, they are strangers. Linda has been careful that day not to wear anything that once belonged to Eileen (not wishing to seem a diminished model of the older cousin) and has dressed in clothes bought from her tips: a slim gray woolen skirt and a black cardigan, the sleeves rolled. She is saving up to buy a pair of leather boots.

Linda needn't have worried. Eileen comes home in tie-dye, fresh from Greenwich Village, where she now lives. She doesn't wear a bra and has on long leather boots like the ones Linda wants. There are beads around her neck and not a trace of makeup on her face. Linda, with her hair curled for the holiday, looks her cousin over carefully after they embrace.

In the privacy of the girls' room, Eileen speaks of head shops and sensual massage. Of a band called "The Mamas and the Papas." Of hash brownies and a job with a project called Upward Bound. She has a boyfriend who plays harmonica for a blues band, and she likes the music of Sonny and Cher. She talks about why women shouldn't use mascara and why hair is a political statement. Why Linda and Patty and Erin also shouldn't wear a bra.

"Don't be ashamed of your past," Eileen

says privately to Linda when the others have left the room. "It was just your body acting, and you should never be ashamed of your body."

Linda appreciates the kindness inherent in the advice but is more than a little worried about what Eileen thinks she knows.

During Christmas Eve dinner, Jack bounces back from the door to the apartment to say that Linda has a visitor. She freezes in her chair at the kitchen table, knowing who it is.

"You'd better see to it," the aunt says after a time.

Thomas stands outside in the hallway, a small package in his hand. The box is inexpertly wrapped with a noose of Scotch tape. He has his overcoat on, the collar up, his ears reddened from the cold.

She is embarrassed at the thought that she has nothing for him.

"I couldn't get away," she says. "Eileen had just come."

He looks hurt all the same. She has hardly ever seen him look hurt, and the knowledge that she has caused this squeezes her chest.

He holds the box out. "This is for you," he says.

Embarrassment and remorse make her

forget manners. She opens the package in the hallway while he stands awkwardly, his hands in his pockets. It takes an age to excavate the package through the noose of tape. Inside the box is a gold cross with a tiny diamond in its center. A gold cross on a chain. A note reads, "For Magdalene."

She shuts her eyes.

"Turn around," he says. "I'll put it on for you."

At the nape of her neck, she feels his fingers — too large for the delicate clasp. "I'll do it," she says, when Jack, whose curiosity can't contain itself, opens the door to get another look at the mysterious stranger. Linda has no choice then but to invite Thomas in.

She sees it all from Thomas's eyes: the wallpaper, water-stained in the corner. The Christmas Eve dinner table next to the sink full of dishes. The counter littered with pie crust and potato skins, crusted fish in a frying pan. The lamp hanging over the center of the table, knocked so often the shade has split.

They walk into the den with the plaid sofa. The smell of cigarette smoke is a pall in the air. The TV is on, a Christmas special.

Linda introduces Thomas to the cousins

and the aunt, the cross like a beacon at her throat. The aunt is reserved and wary, taking in the good overcoat and the Brooks Brothers shirt, the leather gloves and the best shoes. Jack is levitating from excitement: here is an older boy who talks to him, winks at him. Thomas nods to Michael, then sits, still in his overcoat, on the plaid sofa answering questions put to him by intrepid Eileen. The aunt, in red lipstick and tight curls, watches all the while. Giving no quarter.

Linda, in a white noise of mortification, watches as from a distance. Watches Thomas shed his coat and bend over from the sofa to race tiny metal cars with Jack. Watches an eerily knowing glance pass between the aunt and Thomas. Watches as Patty and Erin, saddled with dish duty in the kitchen, peek in from time to time, clearly intrigued by the handsome boy.

In an hour, Thomas has Jack on his knee, and they are listening to Bing Crosby.

Thomas stays until the aunt begins ordering the cousins to dress for the cold. They will take the bus to church for midnight Mass, she says, Thomas pointedly uninvited.

Before they all leave, Thomas and Linda kiss behind the kitchen door. "Merry

Christmas," Thomas whispers, a sentimental boy after all. Even for all the Lowell and the O'Neill.

"Thank you for the cross," she says. "I'll always wear it."

"I like your cousins," he says. "Jack especially."

She nods. "He's a good boy."

"Your aunt doesn't like me," he says.

"It has nothing to do with you," she says.

"Can you get away tomorrow?" he asks.

She thinks. "In the afternoon, maybe."

"I'll pick you up at one o'clock," he says. "We'll go to Boston."

"Boston?"

"I love the city when it's shut down," he says.

In the hallway, after Thomas has left, the aunt slips on her coat and says so that only Linda can hear, "He's the type that'll break your heart."

They walk empty streets, the rest of the world trapped inside by the cold that whistles in from the harbor and snakes through the narrow lanes of the North End. Christmas trees are lit in windows, even in the middle of the day. Linda imagines mountains of torn wrapping paper, toys hidden underfoot, a scene she's just come from herself. Eileen gave her a tie-dye shirt; Michael a Beatles album; Erin a hat she knit herself. The aunt gave her sensible cotton underwear bought on discount at the department store and a missal with her name printed in gold letters in the lower right-hand corner. *Linda M. Fallon.* The *M.* for Marie, a confirmation name she never uses.

Linda shivers, the peacoat hopelessly inadequate in the chill. She has on Erin's hat, but her hair flies in the wind all the same. She has deliberately not worn a scarf so that the cross will show, but now she has to hold her coat closed with her hand. With her other hand, she holds Thomas's. Glove to glove.

The emptiness is strange and magnificent. Snow falls and sticks to eyelashes. The entire city is ensconced within a bubble of intense quiet, with only the odd, slow rolling of chains on the tires of the intermittent cabs. It's not hard to imagine the city as a stage set, with all the shops shuttered, the cafés closed. People existing only in the imagination. All the bustle and the smell of coffee needing to be guessed at.

"This is perfect," Linda says to Thomas. "Absolutely perfect." She means the sense of endless time, the promise of possibility, the clarity of the air.

They walk up the back end of Beacon Hill and then down Beacon Street itself. They stroll along the tree belt on Commonwealth Avenue and imagine what it would be like to have an apartment in one of the town-houses. They have vivid imaginations and describe to each other the mantels, the covers on the bed, the books in the book-case. They agree they will always be friends, no matter what happens to them. They walk along Boylston Street and up Tremont along the Common and stop in at the only place that is open, a Bickford's across from the Park Street subway station.

Stragglers and winos sit in chairs set apart from each other, their watch caps still on, the tips missing from their mittens. They have come in to get out of the cold, and one of them is drinking milk. The smell in the restaurant is of unwashed bodies, old bacon, and sadness. The bacon, doubtless cooked earlier in the day, lingers like a layer of air they might have to breathe. The sad-ness is thick in the atmosphere and cannot be ignored. The café feels to Linda oddly like church, with the men sitting in their separate pews.

Linda and Thomas take a table near the entrance, as far into the restaurant as

Thomas is willing to go, an innate claustrophobia making him more comfortable near exits. They order hot chocolate and sit in the quiet, for the moment not speaking, the only sounds the clinking of silverware against china, the register drawer popping open. She watches Thomas watch the bums, and she has a clear sense that he knows more about what has happened to the men than she does, that he instinctively understands, that his skin might be more permeable than hers. There is something in the shape of his mouth that suggests that he contains within himself some great corruption, not related necessarily to sex or to alcohol, but to chaos and subversion.

Beloved, she wants to say aloud, not knowing how or why the word has sprung to her lips.

There is a duffel bag in the backseat of the Skylark, a tan bag with a zipper and a handle. It might be a sports bag, though it is made of such heavy and thick canvas, it reminds Linda of the army.

"What's in the bag?" she asks.

Thomas has come back on the team bus, Linda on the spectator bus, hers skidding into the parking lot like a skier. Thomas's hair, still wet from his shower, freezes before he can get the heat going in the Skylark. The storm came in fast from the ocean in the afternoon, and the roads are treacherous and slick. Thomas drives hunched against the steering wheel, peering through a small patch in the windshield that hasn't yet iced over. The leather top of the convertible muffles the ping of the sleet.

"It's just something for Donny T.,"

Thomas says absently, concentrating on his driving.

"What for Donny T.?" Linda asks.

"Just some stuff he wants me to hold for him."

The hockey game was at Norwell, and their team lost two-zip. "Were you hurt?" Linda asks.

"What?"

Thomas inches slowly along Main to Spring, following a truck. On Fitzpatrick, the truck speeds up and Thomas does as well, thinking the roads must be better, though the visibility is still poor. Thomas takes the turn at Nantasket Avenue too fast, and the car makes a one-eighty. Linda puts her hands out to the dashboard to brace herself.

"This is insane," Thomas says.

He tries to turn the car around, but the street is so slippery that the Skylark slides across the road, and, as if in slow motion, comes to rest against a telephone pole. Thomas guns the engine, attempting to pull away, but the tires merely spin on the ice. Above them, heavily coated wires sway in the wind.

"We're going to have to walk," Thomas says. "We'll leave the car here and come back for it when they've salted the roads."

"Walk where?" Linda asks. It's miles still to the apartment.

"My house is just up the hill," he says.

All week, the newspapers have been reporting that it has been the worst January in fifty-four years. At the beach, sleet freezes a house so thoroughly that when the sun rises the next morning, it seems a castle encased in ice. The harbor freezes as well, pushing the boats trapped there higher and higher until the ice cracks the hulls. Power goes out for days, and school is canceled four times: the buses can't get through. There is a thaw, and the entire town thinks the worst is over. But then the storm comes and surprises everyone, even the weathermen, who have predicted mild temperatures.

Thomas and Linda have to side-step up the hill, holding on to tree branches. Linda has worn her new knee-high leather boots that she bought with her tip money; they have slippery soles and are useless now. Thomas, who has more traction, grips her hand so that she won't slide down the hill. Periodically, they stop for breath by a tree and kiss. Sleet runs down their necks. Snot has frozen on Thomas's upper lip, and he looks like a bum with his watch cap pulled down low over his eyebrows and ears. His mouth and tongue are warm.

Though it is a miserable month for school and transportation, it has been a good one for ice-skating. In his basement, Thomas has unearthed a pair of children's ice-skates with runners, and periodically he has come by the apartment for Jack. He's taken the boy to the marshes, where he's taught him to skate. He holds Jack's hand while the boy falls on his knees, and he skates with Jack between his legs, holding him up under the arms. The boy grows giddy with accomplishment. Thomas makes Jack a small hockey stick and arranges "games" between Michael and Jack on one side and himself and Rich, his seven-year-old brother, on the other. Linda sometimes puts on Eileen's skates and hovers near Thomas and the boys, but mostly she stays on the sidelines, wrapping her arms around herself and stomping her boots to keep warm. She watches Thomas with Jack and Rich the way a wife might watch a husband with her cherished sons. Proud and happy and feeling a sort of completion that cannot be gotten elsewhere.

The journey to Thomas's house takes nearly forty-five minutes. In decent weather, it can be done in five. Thomas's father meets them at the door, worry creasing his long face. Thomas's mouth has frozen, and he can't even make the introductions. Thomas's mother, a tall, angular woman with navy eyes that slice through Linda, brings them towels and helps them out of their coats. When Thomas can speak, he introduces Linda, whose hands are stiff and red. She hopes the red will be taken for a reaction to the cold.

"The storm came on fast," the father says.

"We worried about you in the car," Thomas's mother says.

Linda removes her boots and stands in her stocking feet in Thomas's living room, her arms crossed, tucking her hands into her armpits. She has never seen such a room, has lacked even the imagination to picture it. It is long and elegant, with banks of leaded-glass windows that face the sea. Two fires are burning in separate hearths, and at least a half-dozen chairs and two sofas in matching stripes and chintzes are arranged in groupings. Linda wonders how one decides, on any given night, where to sit. She thinks then of the den in the triple-decker, the TV flickering, the single sofa threadbare at the arms, Michael and Erin and Patty and Jack using the couch as a backrest while they watch *The Wonderful World of Disney*. She hopes none of them is out in the storm.

Thomas leads Linda to a sofa, and they sit together with the mother opposite. It feels to Linda like an examination. The father comes in with hot chocolate and seems festive with the occasion, as a small boy might be who's just been told that school has been canceled. Thomas's mother, in her periwinkle cardigan and matching skirt, scrutinizes Thomas's girlfriend, taking in the lipstick and the denim skirt and the sweater under which Linda isn't wearing a bra.

"You're new to town," the mother says, sipping her hot chocolate. Linda holds her mug with both hands, trying to warm them.

"Sort of," Linda says, glancing down. Not only has she worn a sweater through which her nipples, erect now from the cold that has penetrated her bones, are plainly visible (stupid Eileen), but the sweater has a low V-neck, showcasing the cross.

"And you live in what part of town?" the mother asks, hardly bothering with pleasantries.

"Park Street," Linda says, putting the mug down and crossing her arms over her breasts. Beside her, Thomas is flexing his fingers, trying to get the circulation back. He hasn't touched the hot chocolate. The denim skirt is too short and too tight on her thighs. Linda resists the urge to tug at it.

"That would be in . . . ?" the mother asks.

"Rockaway," Linda says.

"Really," the mother says, not even bothering to hide her incredulity.

"Great storm," Thomas's father says beside them.

"I'm going to give Linda a tour," Thomas says, standing. And Linda thinks how remarkable it is to have a house in which one can give a tour.

They climb the stairs to Thomas's room, step behind the door and kiss. Thomas lifts her sweater and puts his cold hands on her breasts. He raises the damp denim of her skirt to her hips. She is standing on her toes, up against the wall. She can hear one of the parents at the bottom of the stairs and is certain he or she will come up and enter the room. It's the risk, or the thrill, or her panic that brings the image, unbidden, to her mind: a man lifting the skirt of a dress.

"I can't," she whispers, pushing at Thomas.

Reluctantly, Thomas lets her go. She jigs her skirt and sweater down. They hear footsteps on the stairs, and Thomas kicks the door shut.

"What is it?" he asks.

She sits on the bed and, trying to erase the image, takes in the details of the room: the wooden desk, the piles of papers, the pens scattered on its surface. A dress shirt and a pair of trousers are crumpled in a corner. White curtains make a diamond of the window and seem too pretty for a boy's room. A bookcase is in the corner. "Oh God," she says quietly, and she covers her face with her hands.

"Linda, what is it?" Thomas asks, crouching in front of her, alarm in his voice.

She shakes her head back and forth.

"This?" he asks, clearly bewildered. "That?" he asks, pointing to the wall.

Footsteps pass once again by the door.

In the mirror over the dresser she can see the two of them: Thomas now sitting on the bed, his hair hastily finger-combed, his back slightly hunched. Herself, standing by the bookcase, arms crossed, her eyes pink-rimmed from the cold, her hair flattened from her hat.

On the desk next to the bookcase are pages of writing. She looks a bit closer. "Is that a poem you're working on?" she asks.

Thomas looks absently at the desk, and

then stands, realizing that he's left his work exposed. He moves to the desk and picks up the pages.

"Is it something you can read to me?" she asks.

"No," he says.

"Are you sure?"

He shuffles the papers in his hand. "I'm sure."

"Let me see."

He hands her the first page. "It's just a draft," he says.

She turns the page around and reads what he has written there. It's a poem about a dive off a pier, a girl in the water in her slip. About moving lights in the background and the taunts of boys.

She reads the poem through and then reads it again.

"Water's silk," she says. "It felt like silk."

There is hell to pay when they go downstairs: a mother who is frosty; a father who's had an earful from his wife. The father drifts into a room from which Linda can hear a television; the mother, a woman with a mission, calls a cab with chains. Linda puts her boots back on and stands, dismissed, with Thomas in the vestibule, waiting for the cab.

"In the duffel bag?" he says. "It's drugs."

The next day, in the car in back of the cottage, Thomas slides Linda's blouse and jacket off her shoulder and kisses the bony knob there.

"I love this part of you best of all," he says.

"Really? Why?" It seems, in light of all the parts he has recently got to know, sort of beside the point.

"It's you," he says. "It's all you."

"Isn't that a song title?" she asks.

They have on sunglasses. Beyond them, the world is all aglitter. On their way to the beach cottage, they passed the Giant Coaster, St. Ann's Church, and the diner, all of which were encased in ice. The sun made a sheen against walls that were too bright for the naked eye; it made the branches of the trees seem to have come from Paradise.

"A different kind of Heaven than we imagined," she says.

"What?"

"It's a wonderland," she says, admiring.

Thomas has retrieved his car. He has, along with most of the rest of the other holdouts in town, finally had chains put on his tires. There is still February to go, and

March, and who knows what freak storms April might bring?

"They cost me twenty bucks," he said earlier. "Worth it, though. Otherwise, I couldn't have picked you up."

He kisses her. Though they are parked — daringly — in their usual spot, Thomas argues that the cop isn't likely to start his rounds so early in the afternoon.

"Why are you doing it?" Linda asks.

He knows precisely what she is referring to. "Donny T. asked me to," he says.

"That's not a very good reason," she says, leaning forward and turning on the radio. There has been no school this day, but it's taken Thomas all morning to get the car towed. She inhales deeply. She can't get enough of his smell, that scent of toast. It seems to her the essence of human warmth.

"Last night at your house?" she says. "That was a disaster."

"It was OK," he says.

"No, it wasn't," Linda says. "She hated me."

"She's overprotective."

She puts her face in her hands. "I can't believe I wore that sweater without a bra," she says.

"I loved it," Thomas says. He touches her breast and stops, an animal waiting for the signal to approach.

"It's OK," she says.

"Whatever it is, you should tell someone."

"I would tell you if I could," she says. She thinks a moment. "I would tell God if I could."

"Isn't He supposed to be able to see and know everything anyway?"

"It's part of the contract. You have to be able to tell Him what you've done."

"It's illogical."

"Well, of course," she says.

"I don't want to be rude," Thomas says a few minutes later, "but do you really think God cares?"

The question doesn't shock or even surprise Linda. It's a query, phrased differently, that has gnawed at her for some time: the illogic of caring whether Darren sleeps with Donna before marriage when the Holocaust has happened. Logic demands common sense: God can't possibly care about premarital sex in the face of all that horror. Yet the thought that He might not care fills her with despair.

Thomas removes Linda's sunglasses, and she squints.

"Take yours off, too," she says, and he

does. They sit face to face.

"I have to ask you this," he says.

"OK," she says, ready for anything. Curiously buoyed up in fact.

"Please tell me what happened."

But her confidence is false. She opens her mouth to speak and can't.

Thomas puts his head back against the seat and shuts his eyes. She runs a finger down his chest. Beyond them the sun sets. The sparkle in the dunes goes out, and the temperature drops.

"Where did you live before here? Before the Home, I mean?" he asks.

"Marshfield," she says.

"Oh."

"Why? What's wrong?"

"Nothing. I guess there are quite a few things I don't know about you."

She is silent.

"Where did you go in the summers?"

"Thomas."

"Can't you just answer one lousy question?" A testy note in his voice she has never heard before stiffens her shoulders.

"What is this?" she asks.

"When you go to Confession," he asks, "do you confess letting me touch your breast?"

She pulls her blouse closed.

"Will you tell the priest about last night? About when I lifted your skirt?"

She is tight-lipped, staring straight ahead.

"Will you?" he asks.

She puts her sunglasses back on.

"How detailed do you have to get?"

"Thomas, stop."

The diamonds on the windshield are gone. She pulls her coat tightly around herself. "Take me home," she says.

"I just want to understand what you're all about," he says.

The wind from the ocean rattles the loose bits of the Skylark and waffles against the windows. There is frost inside the car as well, she realizes. She can see their angry puffs of breath.

"I guess I'm angry," he says.

"With who? With me?" she asks.

"I guess I'm angry at you."

"Good," she says, hugging the door now. She begins to button her blouse.

"I'm not angry at you," he says.

"You should be," she says.

"Why?"

"I've spoiled something for you, haven't I?"

"That's a myth."

"It's in your bones. It's not a myth."

"Linda. Look at me."

444

She refuses. "Speaking of not knowing everything about a person, why don't you tell me why you're carrying drugs for Donny T.?"

"So what if I do?"

"So what? So fucking what if you do? You could go to jail, that's what."

"Linda, look at me. Please."

She relents and turns.

"This is it," he says. "You're it. If I know anything in my bones, I know that."

She is silent.

"You're my family, for Christ's sake. You're my lover and my friend and my family." He pauses. "I assume I'm yours."

It might be true, she thinks. It might be possible. And what a relief that would be, she thinks. A different way to see the world: Thomas as her family. She crosses the ocean between them and touches his hand.

"You sound ridiculous when you say *fuck*," he says.

Thomas opens the door of the Skylark. He reaches into the backseat and takes out the duffel bag. Linda watches as he makes his way to the beach in front of the dune grass, slipping and sliding as he goes. She sits on her hands to get a better look. The tide is high, lapping at his feet. With the

445

strength of an athlete, he flings the bag high and wide into the sea. He watches it float for a minute until it sinks.

Her eye flickers between the vertical upright stalks of the dune grass, the horizontal clapboards of the cottage, the squares of the windowpanes. She hasn't noticed this before, but everything is a pattern. She has thought that her life until now was a random series of events. This thing happened and then that thing happened, and then that thing happened. When all along, there has been a pattern, a plan. A beautifully intricate plan.

Thomas slips into the car, shivering as he does so. Though his jacket is on, his shirt is still unbuttoned. He rubs his hands together.

"What will happen now?" she asks. "Won't Donny T. be mad? How much was in there?"

"A few kilos. He'll probably put a contract out on me."

"Thomas."

"I'm only kidding. I'll pay him. I'll think of something."

In the cafeteria the next day, Donny T. is making book on how many more days of school will be canceled before the winter ends. The high bet is six. The low is none. Linda thinks the low bet is closer to the truth. The minute changes in the light — the strength of it, the way it slants through the windows — suggests that spring is tantalizingly near.

There are pockets of slush on the tile floor beneath her table. She sits alone, with only five minutes left before class. She contemplates the iridescent sheen on the mystery meat in front of her, the congealed gravy that lies in lumps on the plate. She wishes she'd thought to bring an apple.

She watches Donny T. at his table: the deft way he takes the money from outstretched fingers; the sleight of hand as he slips it into a jacket pocket, the casual way he jots notations on a napkin, ready to ball it in his fist should an overcurious teacher wander his way. He is entrepreneurial and gifted.

She takes a bite of mystery meat and sends up a quick prayer to Mary to intercede on Thomas's behalf, to protect him and to guide him. They are nearly, but not quite, rote, these prayers. She says them for Jack and for Eileen, said them for Patty when she had the German measles, for Erin when she got a D in Latin. She thinks of the prayers as balloons and sees them squiggling up through the atmosphere, past the clouds, trailing string. Balloons of hope. A prayer is nothing if not a balloon of hope.

"Linda Fallon," a voice behind her says.

She turns and quickly swallows the lump of mystery meat. "Mr. K.," she says.

"May I join you?" he asks.

"Sure," she says, moving her tray aside.

"Don't let me keep you from your lunch."

"No, that's fine," she says. "It's disgusting anyway."

"Ain't that the truth."

Mr. K., a short, squat, barrel-chested man who tries without success to look professorial, swings his legs over the bench. He is nursing a cup of coffee, poking at it with a straw.

"You know," he says, "in addition to being an English teacher, I'm also the senior class adviser."

"I know," she says.

"And to make a long story short, I was going over the list of students applying to college, and I didn't see your name."

"No."

"You didn't apply."

Linda unclasps a barrette from her hair and then puts it back in. "No."

"May I ask why?"

She runs a finger along the edge of the

beige Formica. "I don't know," she says.

"You have tremendous potential," he says, still poking at his coffee. "You put sentences together in a very lucid way. Your writing has logic. Need I say, this is a rare enough commodity in student prose?"

She smiles.

"May I ask you a personal question?"

She nods.

"Is the reason financial?"

She has worked it out: even with all the tip money, she won't be able to make a tuition payment, and she hasn't saved all of her earnings. Tuition, room, and board run to $3,500. And that's just for the first year. "Pretty much," she says.

Not adding that the real reason she hasn't applied is that she can't imagine telling her aunt, who would, she knows, see it as only one more example of Linda getting the jump on her, trying to be better than the cousins.

"You know there are scholarships," Mr. K. says.

She nods.

"It's only the end of January," he says. "Admittedly, it's too late for a formal application, but I know some people and so does Mr. Hanson. We could make some calls. I could walk you through this."

Linda, embarrassed, looks over at Donny T. Will he be applying to college? Will he become a thief, a gambler, a banker? She doesn't even know where Thomas has applied. She has made the subject more or less taboo.

"Everything all right at home?" Mr. K. asks.

Everything is just ducky at home, she thinks.

"Do me a favor, OK?" he asks. "Promise me you'll come by my classroom and take a look at some college catalogues I have. You're familiar with Tufts? B.U.?"

She nods.

He catches sight of the cross. "B.C.?" he asks. The Catholic college.

She nods again, seeing little alternative but to agree.

"This afternoon? Are you free eighth period?"

"I am."

"Good. We'll do it then."

"All right."

He unfolds himself from the bench. "What do you have this semester? Twentieth century?"

"Yes."

"From my mother's sleep I fell into the State / And I hunched in its belly till my wet fur froze."

450

Linda smiles. "Randall Jarrell," she says.

She catches the bus that stops just beyond the student parking lot. The driver narrows his eyes at her as she gets on.

"I'm sick," she says. "I'm not skipping."

She rides along Main Street to Spring to Fitzpatrick to Nantasket Avenue, thinking it might just be possible to do this thing and get back in time for her appointment with Mr. K. She knows that if she dwells on what she is about to do, she'll lose her nerve, and so she doesn't. But her errand feels urgent nevertheless.

All around her, the world is melting. Sparkling and dripping and breaking and sending huge chunks of ice from rooftops, ropes of ice from telephone poles, fantastical icicles from gutters. The bus is overheated, and she opens her peacoat. She has two classes before eighth period and will have to come up with a plausible reason for her absence. Perhaps she can use Mr. K. as an excuse.

She gets off at the stop closest to St. Ann's. The rectory is beside the church. If it weren't for the sense of urgency, she would turn around and go back to the school. She forces herself to keep moving forward, even as she knows her request is likely to be met with derision. This is the boldest thing she's done since jumping into the ocean.

She walks up the stone steps and knocks at the heavy wooden door.

A young priest answers it. She has seen him before, from the pews at church, but now, up close, she notices that he looks like Eddie Garrity. His collar is askew, and he is holding a dinner napkin.

"Will you hear my confession?" she asks.

The priest is startled by her request. "Confessions are heard on Saturday afternoon," he says, not unkindly. Perhaps he is a cousin of Eddie's, with his pink-gold hair and skinny frame. The *good* cousin. "This isn't Saturday," he reminds her.

"I know," she says, "but I have to do this now."

"I'm having my lunch," he says.

"I'm sorry," she says and nearly leaves it at that. Maybe it's a sin to want more than she is entitled to, she thinks.

"I'll wait," she says.

The young priest slowly brings his napkin to his lips. "Come in," he says.

She steps into a dark paneled hall. Electric sconces provide the only light. It might not even be day outside. From a room beyond, she can hear the scrape of cutlery against dishes. A voice speaking.

"Shouldn't you be in school?" he asks.

"Yes," she says.

"Will they be worried?"

"No."

"What year are you?"

"A senior."

"If we do this, you'll go back to school?"

"I will."

"I won't ask your name."

"No. Thank you."

"Follow me," he says, leaving the napkin on a side table.

She follows the young priest to a small anteroom off the hall. But for the crosses, it might be a room in which a potentate would have an audience with a foreign dignitary. Two armchairs, side by side, face the entrance. Two matching sofas flank the wall. Apart from the furniture, there is nothing in the room.

She watches as the priest pulls the armchairs out into the center of the room and puts them back to back, so that the people sitting in them will not be visible to each other. He gestures to her to take one.

She sets her pocketbook on the floor beside the chair and slips her peacoat from her shoulders. Panic wells inside her. It seems inconceivable that she will actually announce her sins in this room with the two of them back-to-back — with no covering, no booth, nowhere to hide.

"Father, forgive me, for I have sinned," she begins, her voice barely a whisper.

There is, at first, a long silence.

"You have sins you wish to confess?" the priest prompts. He sounds, if not exactly bored, then perhaps tired.

"Years ago," Linda says, her heart thumping in her chest, "I had an improper relationship with my aunt's boyfriend. I was thirteen."

"How do you mean *improper?*"

"We . . ." She thinks about how to phrase this. Would *fornicate* be the right word? "We had sex," she says.

There is a slight pause. "You had sex with a man who was your aunt's boyfriend?"

"Yes."

"How old was this man?"

"I'm not sure. I think in his early forties."

"I see."

"He lived with my aunt. He lived with us."

"And how often did you fornicate with this man?"

"Five times," she answers.

"Did he force himself on you?"

"No. Not exactly."

"Have you ever confessed this before?"

"No."

"These are grave sins," the priest says. "Fornicating and withholding a sin from your confessor. No one knows about this?"

"My aunt. She found us. I was sent away for a long time."

"Ah," the priest says. Unmistakably, the "ah" of recognition. "Go on."

"The relationship ended. The man just kind of left the family."

"And you think this was because of you?"

"Possibly. I mean, it seems likely."

The priest is silent for a long time. His silence makes her nervous. This is not supposed to be how it happens. From outside the room, she can hear water running, voices in the hallway. Will the priest want more details?

"May I speak frankly to you?" the priest asks finally.

The question is unsettling, and she can't easily reply. The priest turns in his seat so that he is leaning over the arm of his chair in her direction. "This is unusual," he says, "but I feel I must talk to you about this."

Linda shifts slightly in her chair as well. From the corner of her eye, she can see the priest's sleeve, his pale hand. Freckled, like Eddie Garrity's.

"I know your name," he says. "You're Linda Fallon."

She sucks in her breath.

"I know something of your situation," he says. He sounds kinder, not quite as censorious. Definitely not as tired. "The individual you speak of was a despicable man. I knew him only slightly before he went away, but I saw enough and have since learned enough to convince me of this. What he did to you he did to other girls your age and even to younger girls. He did this repeatedly. Do you understand what I'm talking about?"

Linda nods, scarcely believing what she is hearing. Other girls? Younger?

"We can say that he was a sick man or an evil man," the priest explains. "Probably both. But what I'm trying to tell you is that you were not alone."

The information is so new to her, it sends the world as she has known it momentarily spinning out of kilter. She feels nauseated, as though she might be sick. She has a sudden memory of Eileen and her enigmatic comment: *It was just your body acting, and you shouldn't be afraid of your body.*

"I can't begin to imagine the heart of such a man," the priest says. "One must pray for his soul. But I can, I think, understand something of your heart."

The place where she can breathe seems to be rising higher and higher in her chest until, she is afraid, there won't be room at all for air.

"You feel responsible for what happened," the priest says.

She nods, but then realizes he might not be able to see the nod. She leans slightly more over the arm of the chair as the priest is doing, though she doesn't want to look directly at him. In the distance, she can hear what sounds like a farewell, a door shutting. "Yes," she says. "More or less."

"Though one might have wished for you to have been stronger and to have resisted this man, his is by far the graver sin. You were a child. You are a child still."

To Linda's horror, tears come unbidden into her eyes. They well up over the lower lids.

"It was wrong of your aunt to send you away. I can't imagine what it was like for you."

She shakes her head back and forth. The kindness, the kindness! It is almost more painful to her than a harsh word. No one has ever spoken to her like this before.

"This is not a sin you need to confess, because you did not commit a sin," the priest says. "Do you understand what I am saying?"

She doesn't. Not exactly. It contradicts all she has ever been told.

"Some might think so," the priest says. He sneezes once quickly and says, "Excuse me." He takes out a handkerchief and blows his nose. "I've got a cold coming on," he says, explaining. "Would you like to speak to someone about this? Someone who might be able to help you?"

She shakes her head quickly. "No," she says.

"I'm thinking of someone such as a doctor, who could talk to you about how you might be feeling about all of this."

"No," she says. "I don't think so."

"I could arrange, I think, for you to speak to a woman."

"Not really," she says.

"It's too hard to carry such a burden alone."

A great childish sob escapes her. A gulp, a hiccup of air. She turns away from the priest.

She hears the priest stand and then leave the room. She thinks that he has left her to cry alone without anyone to watch, but then he returns with a box of tissues. He stops in front of her, but she is unwilling to raise her eyes past his knees. She takes a tissue from the box and blows her nose. All these functions of the body, she thinks.

"Perhaps you would like some time to be alone," he says.

She shakes her head again. "I have to get back to class," she says, wanting more than anything to leave the rectory.

"I understand," he says. "Linda."

She looks up at him. She was wrong. He doesn't look a thing like Eddie Garrity. "Can you forgive the man?" he asks.

"I don't know," she says. "I try not to think about it."

"Can you forgive your aunt?"

She shakes her head. "She hates," Linda says. "Which seems worse."

"It is not for us to decide which is the worse sin."

"No," she says.

"You'll work on forgiving them. You'll try."

"Yes," she says, knowing this might not be true.

"Do you have friends?" he asks. "Anyone you can talk to?"

"I have a friend," she says.

"Someone you trust?" he asks.

"Yes. Very much."

"Is this person a boy or a girl?"

"A boy."

"Is he a Catholic?"

"No."

"Well, never mind."

"He is my life," Linda says.

"Now, now," the priest says gently. "God is your life. Your life is in God."

"Yes," she says.

"But now is perhaps not the time to get into that. I assume you have had quite a religious training."

She nods.

"More than you ever wanted."

She glances up at him and sees that he is smiling. No, he does not resemble Eddie Garrity at all, she thinks.

The priest holds out his hand. She takes it, and he helps her up.

"I'll see you to the door," he says. "If you ever want to talk, about this or about anything else, you have only to call."

"Thank you," she says. "I don't even know your name."

"Father Meaghan," he says. "Don't forget your pocketbook there."

Linda walks out to the sidewalk, knowing that the priest is watching her from behind a window. The light outside is so bright and so harsh she immediately has to take her sunglasses from her purse. She puts them on gratefully, makes the turn toward the bus stop, and when she knows she is out of sight of the rectory, she begins to cry.

She waits outside the *Nantasket* room, leaning against the wall. She marvels at the architect who can have created such a monstrosity as the school and have thought the building conducive to learning. Perhaps it *was* a prison after all. Yellow brick rises high over her head, allowing for only narrow transom windows. Years of student scratchings have turned the metal doors a muted blue or worn orange. Wire mesh is encased in the narrow slits of the glass in the doors, guarding, she supposes, against an errant fist. From time to time, she peers through the slit to see what Thomas is doing. He sits at the head of a long table with eight other students, and they seem to be deeply engaged in discussion. Stacks of the *Nantasket* have recently been delivered to the room from the printer and are in piles on student desks.

She shouldn't be here at all. She should, she knows, have taken the late bus home and closed the door to the bedroom and done her homework. She has a calculus test in the morning and a paper due on a book she hasn't yet read. With the job at the diner

461

and the hockey games (two a week) and her hours with Thomas (utterly necessary), she has less and less time for studying. Her discussion with Mr. K. in his classroom just now will be moot if she doesn't keep up her grades. Before, school always seemed effortless, but effortlessness is only possible, she is learning, if you give it time.

At the end of the corridor, the vice principal, who, months ago, was her introduction to the school, is berating a sullen student with long hair and a denim jacket. She can't hear what he is saying, but she can guess. *Get rid of the jacket. Cut the hair.*

She thinks about her meeting with the priest, an utterly astonishing event. So strange and so unreal, it might never have happened at all.

But it did, she thinks. It did.

The door opens, and Thomas emerges, carrying a copy of the *Nantasket.* He is reading as he walks.

"Hey," she calls.

"Linda," he says, turning. "Hi. I didn't expect to see you."

"What have you got there?"

"Look," he says.

He has the literary magazine opened to a page on which is printed a short poem by

Thomas Janes. She reads the poem. "It's very good, Thomas." And it is good. It really is. "Congratulations."

"Thank you. Thank you." He bows. "What are you doing here?"

"Well," she says. "I've been talking to Mr. K., and I think I'm going to apply to college."

"Yes?" Thomas asks, smiling. "Yes?" He backs her into the wall. "Where?"

"Middlebury, for one."

"Fucking Mr. K.," Thomas says.

"And Tufts and B.C., maybe."

"No kidding."

"I've passed the deadline, but he's made some calls and explained what he calls 'my situation' and they say they're willing to consider my application. Well, Middlebury has so far."

"He's a miracle," Thomas says and kisses her.

A voice calls to them from down the hall. "No fraternization between the sexes during school hours." Thomas, with his back to the vice principal, raises an eyebrow. The man stands with his hands on his hips. Any minute, Linda thinks, he will stamp his foot.

"Something funny going on down there?" he asks.

The parking lot is a sea of slush. The soles of Linda's boots are soaked.

"Now I've got the chains on," Thomas says, "we'll probably never have another day below freezing." He unlocks the door of the Skylark. The temperature is so freakishly warm that Linda takes off her coat at once. Thomas turns on the radio.

"It's the same with an umbrella," she says.

"What is?"

"If you remember it, it won't rain."

"Let's celebrate," he says.

"OK," she says. "Where?"

He drums his fingers on the steering wheel and thinks. "There's a nice seafood restaurant called the Lobster Pot not too far from here," he says. "We could go have dinner."

"Really? It's a Wednesday."

"So?"

"I have a test tomorrow."

"You can study later."

"I have to work."

"Not now you don't," he says, putting the car in reverse.

They drive along a twisting, narrow coastal route. Linda sits so close to Thomas that he has to borrow his arm back occasionally to steer. When he can, he puts his hand on her knee. Once, he hitches up her skirt so that he can see her thigh. Then he snakes his hand under the skirt. She doesn't push him away.

Thomas stops at a gas station so that she can call the diner. She holds her nose and pretends to have a cold, while Thomas stands outside the booth, banging on the glass and singing. *Help me, Rhonda. Help, help me, Rhonda.* When they get back in the car, Linda kisses him so hard and for so long, she leaves him gasping for breath.

As they drive, the setting sun lights up the trees and the old houses beside the road so that, for a time, the world seems happily on fire.

"This is the best day of my life," she says.

"Really?"

The water in the marshes turns a brilliant pink. Thomas reaches below his seat and pulls out a bottle of what looks to be scotch or whiskey. A shadow passes across the road.

"What's this about?" she asks.

"You want a drink? We're celebrating."

The bottle is only half full. Perhaps there are things about Thomas she doesn't know.

"You've never had a drink," he says.

"Thomas, can we stop somewhere? There's something I want to tell you."

"He used to have sex with me," she says, letting her breath out in a rush.

She waits for the car to buckle in, for the air to billow out. Thomas has parked the Skylark on a dirt lane in the marshes. They are partially hidden from the road by a grove of trees, glittering and melting in the setting sun.

"He raped you," Thomas says.

"It wasn't rape," she says.

This will be the moment, Linda thinks, when Thomas will have to open the door of the car and get out, letting in a cool gust of air. He will have to take a walk, get his bearings, and when he gets back in, she knows, everything will be different between them.

"Often?" Thomas asks.

"Five times," she says.

He lays his head back against the seat. Linda feels light-headed. She needs to eat.

"I knew it was something like that," Thomas says quietly.

"You did?" She is only a little surprised. And perhaps a bit deflated. One's terrible secret guessed after all.

"I didn't know for sure," Thomas says. "Actually, for a while, I thought it might have been your father."

"My father left when I was five," she says. "I told you that."

"I thought you might be lying about when he left," Thomas says. No judgment implied about the lying. It is understood she'd have had to do that.

"Was it awful?" he asks.

"It wasn't awful or not awful," she says carefully. And after a minute adds, "I don't think we should talk about this particular thing anymore."

He nods. What good can come of details? Of pictures that can never be erased?

"I love you," Thomas says.

She shakes her head. The words should not have been offered now. She might always have to think they had been said partly out of pity.

"I've loved you since the moment I saw you walk into that class," he says.

Yet words are momentous, she knows, and her heart lifts all the same.

"I sometimes think," he says, "that we were meant to be together."

"I agree," she says quickly. And it is true. She does very much agree.

Elation makes him turn to her.

"Are you sure?" he asks.

"I'm sure," she says.

He draws back and studies her. "This isn't something he made you do, is it?" he asks. "Take all your clothes off?"

She shakes her head and realizes that Thomas has images too — his worse for being the worst he can imagine. What's imagined always worse than what is.

She crosses her arms and removes her sweater, feeling more naked than she ever has before. She hitches her hips up so that she can take off her skirt. She hears Thomas's breath catch.

"Linda," he says.

Lightly, as you might touch a sculpture in a gallery, Thomas runs the tips of his fingers from her neck to her thighs. She sucks in her own breath as well.

"This is better," she says.

They move into the backseat to avoid the steering wheel. Outside, it is winter still, but inside it is all steam and hot breath. A kind of cocoon, the world opaque.

Linda has thought the ache of pleasure was all there was. It seemed to be enough: the kissing and the touching and the mysterious wetness she would take back with her to the triple-decker. But that afternoon, in the car, she understands finally what the ache is all about: how the body strains and bursts, showering itself.

They lie on the backseat, their legs twisted and bent to accommodate their length. She, with him on top of her, is warm, but he now feels the chill and reaches into the front seat and slips his overcoat over his back.

He smooths her hair from her face. "Are you all right?" he asks.

"Everything is new," she says. "Everything."

"We'll always be together," Thomas says.

"Yes."

"Nothing can separate us."

"No."

"Did you like that? Making love?"

"I loved it."

"You weren't afraid?"

"A little."

Thomas retrieves the bottle of scotch from the front seat and lifts his torso so that he can take a sip. "Do you want some now?" he asks.

If she hesitates, it is only for a second, two at best. "What is it?"

"Scotch."

The drink burns as it is going down, and she can feel almost immediately the heat in her stomach. She takes another drink and passes the bottle back to Thomas. After a time, she leans her head back down. The drink hits her, spins her out of the Skylark, and sets her afloat.

"Did it upset you?" she asks.

"What?"

"My not being . . . you know." She can't say the word.

"A virgin?"

"Yes," she says, relieved.

"No," he says.

"Something happens to you, it doesn't have to change your life for good," he says.

"This has changed my life for good," she says.

They dress awkwardly in the backseat. When they are done, they each leave the car to get into the front seat — another comedy routine. "We'll have children," he says, startling her.

"You think so?"

"I really like Jack," he says.

"OK," she agrees.

"How many do you think?" Thomas asks.

"I don't know. Three or four?"

"I was thinking seven or eight."

"Thomas."

He hunches over the steering wheel. "Run your nails down my back?" he asks.

"Like this?"

"All over."

"Like this?"

"Yeah," he says, sighing. "That's great."

"I feel so lucky," she says. "So fantastically lucky."

"To have met, you mean?"

"Yes."

"It's a goddamn miracle," he says.

"I have to ask you this," he says as they are once again driving on the coastal route. And perhaps he is driving a bit faster than before — a bit too fast, maybe.

"OK," she says.

"Why did you let it happen?"

She closes her eyes briefly and thinks. She knows that she must try to answer this. "I don't know," she begins. "I was always the odd one out . . ." She interrupts herself. "This isn't an excuse, you understand. It's just an explanation."

"I understand."

"With my aunt and cousins, even the ones who treated me well, I was always an outsider. I suppose you could say it was like being nice to a servant. But he was different.

It's pathetic to admit to this, but he made me feel special. He always had treats for me."

She stopped, hearing herself. It was *absolutely* pathetic. "I think in the beginning he felt sorry for me and was trying to compensate in his way. He'd take me to a movie or let me go with him when he did errands in town."

"Did he do it to Eileen?"

"I used to think not. But now I'm not so sure." She considers his original question. "The truest answer I can give you is that I did it for the attention. I craved attention then. I suppose I still do."

"Everybody does," he says.

Thomas turns the radio up, something he rarely does. He sings, badly and loudly, and she can't help but smile. She sits back against the seat. She can't believe her luck. She has Thomas and a future now — years of possibilities. The sun sets abruptly, rolling shadows up the sides of houses. The temperature drops, and she reaches for her coat.

"I love you," she says as they round a sharp corner.

And this is true. She knows that she will love him all her life.

A small child, a girl, perhaps five or six years old, sits on a tricycle in the middle of the road. She takes in the approaching Skylark, lifts the tricycle to her waist, and runs with its weight to the side of the road.

It is a fleeting scene, a tableau, and slightly comical. The O of surprise on the girl's face, the commonsensical decision to carry the tricycle, the run-waddle to safety. And if Linda and Thomas had continued on, they'd have been at first horrified and then tickled by the scene, the scotch turning laughter into giggles.

But they do not continue on.

Thomas brakes and swerves to avoid the girl. Linda screams as a telephone pole and a tree fill the windshield. Thomas jerks the wheel, the car skids across the narrow road, and a rear tire catches in a ditch.

It happens that fast.

In the seconds they are airborne — in these, the last seconds of Linda's life — she sees not the past, the life that supposedly flashes before one's eyes, but the future: not the life she has lived, but the life she might have had.

A cottage in a field of chrysanthemums in a country far away.

A small boy she holds on her lap whose scalp is patchy with disease.

A white room with lovely windows, a drafting table at its center.

A child named Marcus who is more fragile than his sister.

A spray of oranges on a kitchen floor.

A hotel room with a mirror, her aging face.

A plane rising from the clouds.

A party to celebrate a book.

A beach house with a man — long and elegant and beautiful — sitting on the porch.

The Skylark somersaults into the January afternoon and tumbles down an embankment. The windows shatter inward. Linda reaches a hand to Thomas and says his name.

Thomas. Her beloved Thomas. Who will go on to write a series of poems called *Magdalene* about a girl who died in a car crash when she was only seventeen. And who will one day win a prize, and then will lose his daughter and, shortly before four o'clock on a Saturday afternoon in Toronto, will take his own life — the weight of his losses finally too much to bear.

But not before he has known the unforgiving light of the equator, a love that exists only in his imagination, and the enduring struggle to capture in words the infinite possibilities of a life not lived.

We hope you have enjoyed this Large Print book. Other Thorndike Press or Chivers Press Large Print books are available at your library or directly from the publishers.

For more information about current and upcoming titles, please call or write, without obligation, to:

Thorndike Press
295 Kennedy Memorial Drive
Waterville, ME 04901 USA
Tel. (800) 223-1244
Tel. (800) 223-6121

OR

Chivers Press Limited
Windsor Bridge Road
Bath BA2 3AX
England
Tel. (0225) 335336

All our Large Print titles are designed for easy reading, and all our books are made to last.